The Prima
A Sequel to "Fai

F. Marion Crawford

Alpha Editions

This edition published in 2024

ISBN 9789362098788

Design and Setting By

Alpha Editions
www.alphaedis.com

Email - info@alphaedis.com

As per information held with us this book is in Public Domain.
This book is a reproduction of an important historical work.
Alpha Editions uses the best technology to reproduce historical work
in the same manner it was first published to preserve its original nature.
Any marks or number seen are left intentionally to preserve.

Contents

CHAPTER I .... - 1 -

CHAPTER II .... - 18 -

CHAPTER III .... - 31 -

CHAPTER IV .... - 51 -

CHAPTER V .... - 59 -

CHAPTER VI .... - 78 -

CHAPTER VII .... - 91 -

CHAPTER VIII .... - 109 -

CHAPTER IX .... - 124 -

CHAPTER X .... - 132 -

CHAPTER XI .... - 139 -

CHAPTER XII .... - 153 -

CHAPTER XIII .... - 171 -

CHAPTER XIV .... - 192 -

CHAPTER XV .... - 201 -

CHAPTER XVI .... - 206 -

CHAPTER XVII .... - 213 -

CHAPTER XVIII .... - 223 -

CHAPTER XIX .... - 236 -

CHAPTER I

When the accident happened, Cordova was singing the mad scene in *Lucia* for the last time in that season, and she had never sung it better. *The Bride of Lammermoor* is the greatest love-story ever written, and it was nothing short of desecration to make a libretto of it; but so far as the last act is concerned the opera certainly conveys the impression that the heroine is a raving lunatic. Only a crazy woman could express feeling in such an unusual way.

Cordova's face was nothing but a mask of powder, in which her handsome brown eyes would have looked like two holes if she had not kept them half shut under the heavily whitened lids; her hands were chalked too, and they were like plaster casts of hands, cleverly jointed at the wrists. She wore a garment which was supposed to be a nightdress, which resembled a very expensive modern shroud, and which was evidently put on over a good many other things. There was a deal of lace on it, which fluttered when she made her hands shake to accompany each trill, and all this really contributed to the general impression of insanity. Possibly it was overdone; but if any one in the audience had seen such a young person enter his or her room unexpectedly, and uttering such unaccountable sounds, he or she would most assuredly have rung for a doctor and a cab, and for a strait-jacket if such a thing were to be had in the neighbourhood.

An elderly man, with very marked features and iron-grey hair, sat in the fifth row of the stalls, on the right-hand aisle. He was a bony man, and the people behind him noticed him and thought he looked strong. He had heard Bonanni in her best days and many great lyric sopranos from Patti to Melba, and he was thinking that none of them had sung the mad scene better than Cordova, who had only been on the stage two years, and was now in New York for the first time. But he had already heard her in London and Paris, and he knew her. He had first met her at a breakfast on board Logotheti's yacht at Cap Martin. Logotheti was a young Greek financier who lived in Paris and wanted to marry her. He was rather mad, and had tried to carry her off on the night of the dress rehearsal before her *début*, but had somehow got himself locked up for somebody else. Since then he had grown calmer, but he still worshipped at the shrine of the Cordova. He was not the only one, however; there were several, including the very distinguished English man of letters, Edmund Lushington, who had known her before she had begun to sing on the stage.

But Lushington was in England and Logotheti was in Paris, and on the night of the accident Cordova had not many acquaintances in the house besides the bony man with grey hair; for though society had been anxious to feed her and get her to sing for nothing, and to play bridge with her, she had never been inclined to accept those attentions. Society in New York claimed her, on the ground that she was a lady and was an American on her mother's side. Yet she insisted on calling herself a professional, because singing was her profession, and society thought this so strange that it at once became suspicious and invented wild and unedifying stories about her; and the reporters haunted the lobby of her hotel, and gossiped with their friends the detectives, who also spent much time there in a professional way for the general good, and were generally what English workmen call wet smokers.

Cordova herself was altogether intent on what she was doing and was not thinking of her friends, of Lushington, or Logotheti, nor of the bony man in the stalls; certainly not of society, though it was richly represented by diamonds in the subscriber's tier. Indeed the jewellery was so plentiful and of such expensive quality that the whole row of boxes shone like a vast coronet set with thousands of precious stones. When the music did not amuse society, the diamonds and rubies twinkled and glittered uneasily, but when Cordova was trilling her wildest they were quite still and blazed with a steady light. Afterwards the audience would all say again what they had always said about every great lyric soprano, that it was just a wonderful instrument without a particle of feeling, that it was an over-grown canary, a human flute, and all the rest of it; but while the trills ran on the people listened in wonder and the diamonds were very quiet.

'A-a—A-a—A-a—A-a—' sang Cordova at an inconceivable pitch.

A terrific explosion shook the building to its foundations; the lights went out, and there was a long grinding crash of broken glass not far off.

In the momentary silence that followed before the inevitable panic the voice of Schreiermeyer, the manager, rang out through the darkness.

'Ladies and gentlemen! There's no danger! Keep your seats! The lights will be up directly.'

And indeed the little red lamps over each door that led out, being on another circuit, were all burning quietly, but in the first moment of fright no one noticed them, and the house seemed to be quite dark.

Then the whole mass of humanity began to writhe and swell, as a frightened crowd does in the dark, so that every one feels as if all the other people were growing hugely big, as big as elephants, to smother and crush him; and each man makes himself as broad as he can, and tries to swell out his chest, and squares his elbows to keep the weight off his sides; and with the steady strain and effort every one breathes hard, and few speak, and the hard-drawn breath of thousands together makes a sound of rushing wind like bellows as enormous as houses, blowing steadily in the darkness.

'Keep your seats!' yelled Schreiermeyer desperately.

He had been in many accidents, and understood the meaning of the noises he heard. There was death in them, death for the weak by squeezing, and smothering, and trampling underfoot. It was a grim moment, and no one who was there has forgotten it, the manager least of all.

'It's only a fuse gone!' he shouted. 'Only a plug burnt out!'

But the terrified throng did not believe, and the people pressed upon each other with the weight of hundreds of bodies, thronging from behind, towards the little red lights. There were groans now, besides the strained breathing and the soft shuffling of many feet on the thick carpets. Each time some one went down there was a groan, stifled as instantly and surely as though the lips from which it came were quickly thrust under water.

Schreiermeyer knew well enough that if nothing could be done within the next two minutes there would be an awful catastrophe; but he was helpless. No doubt the electricians were at work; in ten minutes the damage would be repaired and the lights would be up again; but the house would be empty then, except for the dead and the dying.

Another groan was heard, and another quickly after it. The wretched manager yelled, stormed, stamped, entreated, and promised, but with no effect. In the very faint red light from the doors he saw a moving sea of black and heard it surging to his very feet. He had an old professional's exact sense of passing time, and he knew that a full minute had already gone by since the explosion. No one could be dead yet, even in that press, but there were few seconds to spare, fewer and fewer.

Then another sound was heard, a very pure strong note, high above his own tones, a beautiful round note, that made one think of gold and silver bells, and that filled the house instantly, like light, and reached every ear, even through the terror that was driving the crowd mad in the dark.

A moment more, an instant's pause, and Cordova had begun Lucia's song again at the beginning, and her marvellous trills and staccato notes, and trills again, trills upon trills without end, filled the vast darkness and stopped those four thousand men and women, spellbound and silent, and ashamed too.

It was not great music, surely; but it was sung by the greatest living singer, singing alone in the dark, as calmly and as perfectly as if all the orchestra had been with her, singing as no one can who feels the least tremor of fear; and the awful tension of the dark throng relaxed, and the breath that came was a great sigh of relief, for it was not possible to be frightened when a fearless woman was singing so marvellously.

Then, still in the dark, some of the musicians struck in and supported her, and others followed, till the whole body of harmony was complete; and just as she was at the wildest trills, at the very passage during which the crash had come, the lights went up all at once; and there stood Cordova in white and lace, with her eyes half shut and shaking her outstretched hands as she always made them shake in the mad scene; and the stage was just as it had been before the accident, except that Schreiermeyer was standing near the singer in evening dress with a perfectly new and shiny high hat on the back of his head, and his mouth wide open.

The people were half hysterical from the past danger, and when they saw, and realised, they did not wait for the end of the air, but sent up such a shout of applause as had never been heard in the Opera before and may not be heard there again.

Instinctively the Primadonna sang the last bars, though no one heard her in the din, unless it was Schreiermeyer, who stood near her. When she had finished at last he ran up to her and threw both his arms round her in a paroxysm of gratitude, regardless of her powder and chalk, which came off upon his coat and yellow beard in patches of white as he kissed her on both cheeks, calling her by every endearing name that occurred to his polyglot memory, from Sweetheart in English to Little Cabbage in French, till Cordova laughed and pushed him away, and made a tremendous courtesy to the audience.

Just then a man in a blue jacket and gilt buttons entered from the left of the stage and whispered a few words into Schreiermeyer's ear. The manager looked grave at once, nodded and came forward to the prompter's box. The man had brought news of the accident, he said; a quantity of dynamite which was to have been used in subterranean blasting had exploded and had done great damage, no one yet knew how great. It was probable that many persons had been killed.

But for this news, Cordova would have had one of those ovations which rarely fall to the lot of any but famous singers, for there was not a man or woman in the theatre who had not felt that she had averted a catastrophe and saved scores of lives. As it was, several women had been slightly hurt and at least fifty had fainted. Every one was anxious to help them now, most of all the very people who had hurt them.

But the news of an accident in the city emptied the house in a few minutes; even now that the lights were up the anxiety to get out to the street and to know more of the truth was great enough to be dangerous, and the strong crowd heaved and surged again and pushed through the many doors with little thought for the weak or for any who had been injured in the first panic.

But in the meantime Cordova had reached her dressing-room, supported by the enthusiastic Schreiermeyer on one side, and by the equally enthusiastic tenor on the other, while the singular family party assembled in the last act of *Lucia di Lammermoor* brought up the rear with many expressions of admiration and sympathy.

As a matter of fact the Primadonna needed neither sympathy nor support, and that sort of admiration was not of the kind that most delighted her. She did not believe that she had done anything heroic, and did not feel at all inclined to cry.

'You saved the whole audience!' cried Signor Pompeo Stromboli, the great Italian tenor, who presented an amazing appearance in his Highland dress. 'Four thousand seven hundred and fifty-three people owe you their lives at this moment! Every one of them would have been dead but for your superb coolness! Ah, you are indeed a great woman!'

Schreiermeyer's business ear had caught the figures. As they walked, each with an arm through one of the Primadonna's, he leaned back and spoke to Stromboli behind her head.

'How the devil do you know what the house was?' he asked sharply.

'I always know,' answered the Italian in a perfectly matter-of-fact tone. 'My dresser finds out from the box-office. I never take the C sharp if there are less than three thousand.'

'I'll stop that!' growled Schreiermeyer.

'As you please!' Stromboli shrugged his massive shoulders. 'C sharp is not in the engagement!'

'It shall be in the next! I won't sign without it!'

'I won't sign at all!' retorted the tenor with a sneer of superiority. 'You need not talk of conditions, for I shall not come to America again!'

'Oh, do stop quarrelling!' laughed Cordova as they reached the door of her box, for she had heard similar amenities exchanged twenty times already, and she knew that they meant nothing at all on either side.

'Have you any beer?' inquired Stromboli of the Primadonna, as if nothing had happened.

'Bring some beer, Bob!' Schreiermeyer called out over his shoulder to some one in the distance.

'Yes, sir,' answered a rough voice, far off, and with a foreign accent.

The three entered the Primadonna's dressing-room together. It was a hideous place, as all dressing-rooms are which are never used two days in succession by the same actress or singer; very different from the pretty cells in the beehive of the Comédie Française where each pensioner or shareholder is lodged like a queen bee by herself, for years at a time.

The walls of Cordova's dressing-room were more or less white-washed where the plaster had not been damaged. There was a dingy full-length mirror, a shabby toilet-table; there were a few crazy chairs, the wretched furniture which is generally to be found in actresses' dressing-rooms, notwithstanding the marvellous descriptions invented by romancers. But there was light in abundance and to excess, dazzling, unshaded, intolerable to any but theatrical eyes. There were at least twenty strong electric lamps in the miserable place, which illuminated the coarsely painted faces of the Primadonna and the tenor with alarming distinctness, and gleamed on Schreiermeyer's smooth fair hair and beard, and impassive features.

'You'll have two columns and a portrait in every paper to-morrow,' he observed thoughtfully. 'It's worth while to engage such people. Oh yes, damn it, I tell you it's worth while!'

The last emphatic sentence was intended for Stromboli, as if he had contradicted the statement, or were himself not 'worth while.'

'There's beer there already,' said the tenor, seeing a bottle and glass on a deal table, and making for them at once.

He undid the patent fastening, stood upright with his sturdy stockinged legs wide apart, threw his head back, opened his huge painted mouth to the necessary extent, but not to the full, and without touching his lips poured the beer into the chasm in a gurgling stream, which he swallowed without the least apparent difficulty. When he had taken down half the contents of the small bottle he desisted and poured the rest into the glass, apparently for Cordova's benefit.

'I hope I have left you enough,' he said, as he prepared to go. 'My throat felt like a rusty gun-barrel.'

'Fright is very bad for the voice,' Schreiermeyer remarked, as the call-boy handed him another bottle of beer through the open door.

Stromboli took no notice of the direct imputation. He had taken a very small and fine handkerchief from his sporran and was carefully tucking it into his collar with some idea of protecting his throat. When this was done his admiration for his colleague broke out again without the slightest warning.

'You were superb, magnificent, surpassing!' he cried.

He seized Cordova's chalked hands, pressed them to his own whitened chin, by sheer force of stage habit, because the red on his lips would have come off on them, and turned away.

'Surpassing! Magnificent! What a woman!' he roared in tremendous tones as he strode away through the dim corridor towards the stage and his own dressing-room on the other side.

Meanwhile Schreiermeyer, who was quite as thirsty as the tenor, drank what the latter had left in the only glass there was, and set the full bottle beside the latter on the deal table.

'There is your beer,' he said, calling attention to what he had done.

Cordova nodded carelessly and sat down on one of the crazy chairs before the toilet-table. Her maid at once came forward and took off her wig, and her own beautiful brown hair appeared, pressed and matted close to her head in a rather disorderly coil.

'You must be tired,' said the manager, with more consideration than he often showed to any one whose next engagement was already signed. 'I'll find out how many were killed in the explosion and then I'll get hold of the reporters. You'll have two columns and a picture to-morrow.'

Schreiermeyer rarely took the trouble to say good-morning or good-night, and Cordova heard the door shut after him as he went out.

'Lock it,' she said to her maid. 'I'm sure that madman is about the theatre again.'

The maid obeyed with alacrity. She was very tall and dark, and when she had entered Cordova's service two years ago she had been positively cadaverous. She herself said that her appearance had been the result of living many years with the celebrated Madame Bonanni, who was a whirlwind, an earthquake, a phenomenon, a cosmic force. No one who had lived with her in her stage days had ever grown fat; it was as much as a very strong constitution could do not to grow thin.

Madame Bonanni had presented the cadaverous woman to the young Primadonna as one of the most precious of her possessions, and out of sheer affection. It was true that since the great singer had closed her long career and had retired to live in the country, in Provence, she dressed with such simplicity as made it possible for her to exist without the long-faithful, all-skilful, and iron-handed Alphonsine; and the maid, on her side, was so thoroughly a professional theatrical dresser that she must have died of inanition in what she would have called private life. Lastly, she had heard that Madame Bonanni had now given up the semblance, long far from empty, but certainly vain, of a waist, and dressed herself in a garment resembling a priest's cassock, buttoned in front from her throat to her toes.

Alphonsine locked the door, and the Primadonna leaned her elbows on the sordid toilet-table and stared at her chalked and painted face, vaguely trying to recognise the features of Margaret Donne, the daughter of the quiet Oxford scholar, her real self as she had been two years ago, and by no means very different from her everyday self now. But it was not easy. Margaret was there, no doubt, behind the paint and the 'liquid white,' but the reality was what the public saw beyond the footlights two or three times a week during the opera season, and applauded with might and main as the most successful lyric soprano of the day.

There were moments when she tried to get hold of herself and bring herself back. They came most often after some great emotion in the theatre, when the sight of the painted mask in the glass shocked and disgusted her as it did to-night; when the contrasts of life were almost more than she could bear, when her sensibilities awoke again, when the fastidiousness of the delicately nurtured girl revolted under the rough familiarity of such a comrade as Stromboli, and rebelled against the sordid cynicism of Schreiermeyer.

She shuddered at the mere idea that the manager should have thought she would drink out of the glass he had just used. Even the Italian peasant, who had been a goatherd in Calabria, and could hardly write his name, showed more delicacy, according to his lights, which were certainly not dazzling. A faint ray of Roman civilisation had reached him through generations of slaves and serfs and shepherds. But no such traditions of forgotten delicacy disturbed the manners of Schreiermeyer. The glass from which he had drunk was good enough for any primadonna in his company, and it was silly for any of them to give themselves airs. Were they not largely his creatures, fed from his hand, to work for him while they were young, and to be turned out as soon as they began to sing false? He was by no means the worst of his kind, as Margaret knew very well.

She thought of her childhood, of her mother and of her father, both dead long before she had gone on the stage; and of that excellent and kind Mrs. Rushmore, her American mother's American friend, who had taken her as her own daughter, and had loved her and cared for her, and had shed tears when Margaret insisted on becoming a singer; who had fought for her, too, and had recovered for her a small fortune of which her mother had been cheated. For Margaret would have been more than well off without her profession, even when she had made her *début*, and she had given up much to be a singer, believing that she knew what she was doing.

But now she was ready to undo it all and to go back; at least she thought she was, as she stared at herself in the glass while the pale maid drew her hair back and fastened it far above her forehead with a big curved comb, as a preliminary to getting rid of paint and powder. At this stage of the operation the Primadonna was neither Cordova nor Margaret Donne; there was something terrifying about the exaggeratedly painted mask when the wig was gone and her natural hair was drawn tightly back. She thought she was like a monstrous skinned rabbit with staring brown eyes.

At first, with the inexperience of youth, she used to plunge her painted face into soapsuds and scrub vigorously till her own complexion appeared, a good deal overheated and temporarily shiny; but before long she had yielded to Alphonsine's entreaties and representations and had adopted the butter method, long familiar to chimney-sweeps.

The butter lay ready; not in a lordly dish, but in a clean tin can with a cover, of the kind workmen use for fetching beer, and commonly called a 'growler' in New York, for some reason which escapes etymologists.

Having got rid of the upper strata of white lace and fine linen, artfully done up so as to tremble like aspen leaves with Lucia's mad trills, Margaret proceeded to butter her face thoroughly. It occurred to her just then that all the other artists who had appeared with her were presumably buttering their faces at the same moment, and that if the public could look in upon them it would be very much surprised indeed. At the thought she forgot what she had been thinking of and smiled.

The maid, who was holding her hair back where it escaped the comb, smiled too, and evidently considered that the relaxation of Margaret's buttered features was equivalent to a permission to speak.

'It was a great triumph for Madame,' she observed. 'All the papers will praise Madame to-morrow. Madame saved many lives.'

'Was Mr. Griggs in the house?' Margaret asked. 'I did not see him.'

Alphonsine did not answer at once, and when she spoke her tone had changed.

'Yes, Madame. Mr. Griggs was in the house.'

Margaret wondered whether she had saved his life too, in his own estimation or in that of her maid, and while she pondered the question she buttered her nose industriously.

Alphonsine took a commercial view of the case.

'If Madame would appear three times more in New York, before sailing, the manager would give ten thousand francs a night,' she observed.

Margaret said nothing to this, but she thought it would be amusing to show herself to an admiring public in her present condition.

'Madame is now a heroine,' continued Alphonsine, behind her. 'Madame can ask anything she pleases. Several milliardaires will now offer to marry Madame.'

'Alphonsine,' answered Margaret, 'you have no sense.'

The maid smiled, knowing that her mistress could not see even the reflection of the smile in the glass; but she said nothing.

'No sense,' Margaret repeated, with conviction. 'None at all'

The maid allowed a few seconds to pass before she spoke again.

'Or if Madame would accept to sing in one or two private houses in New York, we could ask a very great price, more than the manager would give.'

'I daresay.'

'It is certain,' said Alphonsine. 'At the French ball to which Madame kindly allowed me to go, the valet of Mr. Van Torp approached me.'

'Indeed!' exclaimed Cordova absently. 'How very disagreeable!'

'I see that Madame is not listening,' said Alphonsine, taking offence.

What she said was so true that Margaret did not answer at all. Besides, the buttering process was finished, and it was time for the hot water. She went to the ugly stationary washstand and bent over it, while the maid kept her hair from her face. Alphonsine spoke again when she was sure that her mistress could not possibly answer her.

'Mr. Van Torp's valet asked me whether I thought Madame would be willing to sing in church, at the wedding, the day after to-morrow,' she said, holding the Primadonna's back hair firmly.

The head moved energetically under her hands. Margaret would certainly not sing at Mr. Van Torp's wedding, and she even tried to say so, but her voice only bubbled and sputtered ineffectually through the soap and water.

'I was sure Madame would not,' continued the maid, 'though Mr. Van Torp's valet said that money was no object. He had heard Mr. Van Torp say that he would give five thousand dollars to have Madame sing at his wedding.'

Margaret did not shake her head this time, nor try to speak, but Alphonsine heard the little impatient tap of her slipper on the wooden floor. It was not often that the Primadonna showed so much annoyance at anything; and of late, when she did, the cause had been connected with this same Mr. Van

Torp. The mere mention of his name irritated her, and Alphonsine seemed to know it, and to take an inexplicable pleasure in talking about him—about Mr. Rufus Van Torp, formerly of Chicago, but now of New York. He was looked upon as the controlling intellect of the great Nickel Trust; in fact, he was the Nickel Trust himself, and the other men in it were mere dummies compared with him. He had sailed the uncertain waters of finance for twenty years or more, and had been nearly shipwrecked more than once, but at the time of this story he was on the top of the wave; and as his past was even more entirely a matter of conjecture than his future, it would be useless to inquire into the former or to speculate about the latter. Moreover, in these break-neck days no time counts but the present, so far as reputation goes; good fame itself now resembles righteousness chiefly because it clothes men as with a garment; and as we have the highest authority for assuming that charity covers a multitude of sins, we can hardly be surprised that it should be so generally used for that purpose. Rufus Van Torp's charities were notorious, aggressive, and profitable. The same sums of money could not have bought as much mingled advertisement and immunity in any other way.

'Of course,' observed Alphonsine, seeing that Margaret would soon be able to speak again, 'money is no object to Madame either!'

This subtle flattery was evidently meant to forestall reproof. But Margaret was now splashing vigorously, and as both taps were running the noise was as loud as that of a small waterfall; possibly she had not even heard the maid's last speech.

Some one knocked at the door, and knocked a second time almost directly. The Primadonna pushed Alphonsine with her elbow, speaking being still impossible, and the woman understood that she was to answer the summons.

She asked who was knocking, and some one answered.

'It is Mr. Griggs,' said Alphonsine.

'Ask him to wait,' Margaret succeeded in saying.

Alphonsine transmitted the message through the closed door, and listened for the answer.

'He says that there is a lady dying in the manager's room, who wants Madame,' said the maid, repeating what she heard.

Margaret stood upright, turned quickly, and crossed the room to the door, mopping her face with a towel.

'Who is it?' she asked in an anxious tone.

'I'm Griggs,' said a deep voice. 'Come at once, if you can, for the poor girl cannot last long.'

'One minute! Don't go away—I'm coming out.'

Alphonsine never lost her head. A theatrical dresser who does is of no use. She had already brought the wide fur coat Margaret always wore after singing. In ten seconds the singer was completely clothed in it, and as she laid her hand on the lock to let herself out, the maid placed a dark Russian hood on her head from behind her and took the long ends twice round her throat.

Mr. Griggs was a large bony man with iron-grey hair, who looked very strong. He had a sad face and deep-set grey eyes. He led the way without speaking, and Cordova walked quickly after him. Alphonsine did not follow, for she was responsible for the belongings that lay about in the dressing-room. The other doors on the women's side, which is on the stage left and the audience's right at the Opera, were all tightly closed. The stage itself was not dark yet, and the carpenters were putting away the scenery of the last act as methodically as if nothing had happened.

'Do you know her?' Margaret asked of her companion as they hurried along the passage that leads into the house.

'Barely. She is a Miss Bamberger, and she was to have been married the day after to-morrow, poor thing—to a millionaire. I always forget his name, though I've met him several times.'

'Van Torp?' asked Margaret as they hastened on.

'Yes. That's it—the Nickel Trust man, you know.'

'Yes,' Margaret answered in a low tone. 'I was asked to sing at the wedding.'

They reached the door of the manager's room. The clerks from the box-office and several other persons employed about the house were whispering together in the little lobby. They made way for Cordova and looked with curiosity at Griggs, who was a well-known man of letters.

Schreiermeyer stood at the half-closed inner door, evidently waiting.

'Come in,' he said to Margaret. 'The doctor is there.'

The room was flooded with electric light, and smelt of very strong Havana cigars and brandy. Margaret saw a slight figure in a red silk evening gown, lying at full length on an immense red leathern sofa. A young doctor was kneeling on the floor, bending down to press his ear against the girl's side; he moved his head continually, listening for the beating of her heart. Her face was of a type every one knows, and had a certain half-pathetic prettiness; the features were small, and the chin was degenerate but delicately modelled. The rather colourless fair hair was elaborately done; her thin cheeks were dreadfully white, and her thin neck shrank painfully each time she breathed out, though it grew smooth and full as she drew in her breath. A short string of very large pearls was round her throat, and gleamed in the light as her breathing moved them.

Schreiermeyer did not let Griggs come in, but went out to him, shut the door and stood with his back to it.

Margaret did not look behind her, but crossed directly to the sofa and leaned over the dying girl, who was conscious and looked at her with inquiring eyes, not recognising her.

'You sent for me,' said the singer gently.

'Are you really Madame Cordova?' asked the girl in a faint tone.

It was as much as she could do to speak at all, and the doctor looked up to Margaret and raised his hand in a warning gesture, meaning that his patient should not be allowed to talk. She saw his movement and smiled faintly, and shook her head.

'No one can save me,' she said to him, quite quietly and distinctly. 'Please leave us together, doctor.'

'I am altogether at a loss,' the doctor answered, speaking to Margaret as he rose. 'There are no signs of asphyxia, yet the heart does not respond to stimulants. I've tried nitro-glycerine—'

'Please, please go away!' begged the girl.

The doctor was a young surgeon from the nearest hospital, and hated to leave his case. He was going to argue the point, but Margaret stopped him.

'Go into the next room for a moment, please,' she said authoritatively.

He obeyed with a bad grace, and went into the empty office which adjoined the manager's room, but he left the door open. Margaret knelt down in his place and took the girl's cold white hand.

'Can he hear?' asked the faint voice.

'Speak low,' Margaret answered. 'What can I do?'

'It is a secret,' said the girl. 'The last I shall ever have, but I must tell some one before I die. I know about you. I know you are a lady, and very good and kind, and I have always admired you so much!'

'You can trust me,' said the singer. 'What is the secret I am to keep for you?'

'Do you believe in God? I do, but so many people don't nowadays, you know. Tell me.'

'Yes,' Margaret answered, wondering. 'Yes, I do.'

'Will you promise, by the God you believe in?'

'I promise to keep your secret, so help me God in Heaven,' said Margaret gravely.

The girl seemed relieved, and closed her eyes for a moment. She was so pale and still that Margaret thought the end had come, but presently she drew breath again and spoke, though it was clear that she had not much strength left.

'You must not keep the secret always,' she said. 'You may tell him you know it. Yes—let him know that you know—if you think it best—'

'Who is he?'

'Mr. Van Torp.'

'Yes?' Margaret bent her ear to the girl's lips and waited.

Again there was a pause of many seconds, and then the voice came once more, with a great effort that only produced very faint sounds, scarcely above a whisper.

'He did it.'

That was all. At long intervals the dying girl drew deep breaths, longer and longer, and then no more. Margaret looked anxiously at the still face for some time, and then straightened herself suddenly.

'Doctor! Doctor!' she cried.

The young man was beside her in an instant. For a full minute there was no sound in the room, and he bent over the motionless figure.

'I'm afraid I can't do anything,' he said gently, and he rose to his feet.

'Is she really dead?' Margaret asked, in an undertone.

'Yes. Failure of the heart, from shock.'

'Is that what you will call it?'

'That is what it is,' said the doctor with a little emphasis of offence, as if his science had been doubted. 'You knew her, I suppose?'

'No. I never saw her before. I will call Schreiermeyer.'

She stood still a moment longer, looking down at the dead face, and she wondered what it all meant, and why the poor girl had sent for her, and what it was that Mr. Van Torp had done. Then she turned very slowly and went out.

'Dead, I suppose,' said Schreiermeyer as soon as he saw the Primadonna's face. 'Her relations won't get here in time.'

Margaret nodded in silence and went on through the lobby.

'The rehearsal is at eleven,' the manager called out after her, in his wooden voice.

She nodded again, but did not look back. Griggs had waited in order to take her back to her dressing-room, and the two crossed the stage together. It was almost quite dark now, and the carpenters were gone away.

'Thank you,' Margaret said. 'If you don't care to go all the way back you can get out by the stage door.'

'Yes. I know the way in this theatre. Before I say good-night, do you mind telling me what the doctor said?'

'He said she died of failure of the heart, from shock. Those were his words. Why do you ask?'

'Mere curiosity. I helped to carry her—that is, I carried her myself to the manager's room, and she begged me to call you, so I came to your door.'

'It was kind of you. Perhaps it made a difference to her, poor girl. Good-night.'

'Good-night. When do you sail?'

'On Saturday. I sing "Juliet" on Friday night and sail the next morning.'

'On the *Leofric*?'

'Yes.'

'So do I. We shall cross together.'

'How delightful! I'm so glad! Good-night again.'

Alphonsine was standing at the open door of the dressing-room in the bright light, and Margaret nodded and went in. The maid looked after the elderly man till he finally disappeared, and then she went in too and locked the door after her.

Griggs walked home in the bitter March weather. When he was in New York, he lived in rooms on the second floor of an old business building not far from Fifth Avenue. He was quite alone in the house at night, and had to walk up the stairs by the help of a little electric pocket-lantern he carried. He let himself into his own door, turned up the light, slipped off his overcoat and gloves, and went to the writing-table to get his pipe. That is very often the first thing a man does when he gets home at night.

The old briar pipe he preferred to any other lay on the blotting-paper in the circle where the light was brightest. As he took it a stain on his right hand caught his eye, and he dropped the pipe to look at it. The blood was dark and was quite dry, and he could not find any scratch to account for it. It was on the inner side of his right hand, between the thumb and forefinger, and was no larger than an ordinary watch.

'How very odd!' exclaimed Mr. Griggs aloud; and he turned his hand this way and that under the electric lamp, looking for some small wound which he supposed must have bled. There was a little more inside his fingers, and between them, as if it had oozed through and then had spread over his knuckles.

But he could find nothing to account for it. He was an elderly man who had lived all over the world and had seen most things, and he was not easily surprised, but he was puzzled now. Not the least strange thing was that the stain should be as small as it was and yet so dark. He crossed the room again and examined the front of his overcoat with the most minute attention. It was made of a dark frieze, almost black, on which a red stain would have shown very little; but after a very careful search Griggs was convinced that the blood which had stained his hand had not touched the cloth.

He went into his dressing-room and looked at his face in his shaving-glass, but there was certainly no stain on the weather-beaten cheeks or the furrowed forehead.

'How very odd!' he exclaimed a second time.

He washed his hands slowly and carefully, examining them again and again, for he thought it barely possible that the skin might have been cracked somewhere by the cutting March wind, and might have bled a little, but he could not find the least sign of such a thing.

When he was finally convinced that he could not account for the stain he had now washed off, he filled his old pipe thoughtfully and sat down in a big shabby arm-chair beside the table to think over other questions more easy of solution. For he was a philosophical man, and when he could not understand a matter he was able to put it away in a safe place, to be kept until he got more information about it.

The next morning, amidst the flamboyant accounts of the subterranean explosion, and of the heroic conduct of Madame Margarita da Cordova, the famous Primadonna, in checking a dangerous panic at the Opera, all the papers found room for a long paragraph about Miss Ida H. Bamberger, who had died at the theatre in consequence of the shock her nerves had received, and who was to have married the celebrated capitalist and philanthropist, Mr. Van Torp, only two days later. There were various dramatic and heart-rending accounts of her death, and most of them agreed that she had breathed her last amidst her nearest and dearest, who had been with her all the evening.

But Mr. Griggs read these paragraphs thoughtfully, for he remembered that he had found her lying in a heap behind a red baize door which his memory could easily identify.

After all, the least misleading notice was the one in the column of deaths:—

BAMBERGER.—On Wednesday, of heart-failure from shock, IDA HAMILTON, only child of HANNAH MOON by her former marriage with ISIDORE BAMBERGER. California papers please copy.

CHAPTER II

In the lives of professionals, whatever their profession may be, the ordinary work of the day makes very little impression on the memory, whereas a very strong and lasting one is often made by circumstances which a man of leisure or a woman of the world might barely notice, and would soon forget. In Margaret's life there were but two sorts of days, those on which she was to sing and those on which she was at liberty. In the one case she had a cutlet at five o'clock, and supper when she came home; in the other, she dined like other people and went to bed early. At the end of a season in New York, the evenings on which she had sung all seemed to have been exactly alike; the people had always applauded at the same places, she had always been called out about the same number of times, she had always felt very much the same pleasure and satisfaction, and she had invariably eaten her supper with the same appetite. Actors lead far more emotional lives than singers, partly because they have the excitement of a new piece much more often, with the tremendous nervous strain of a first night, and largely because they are not obliged to keep themselves in such perfect training. To an actor a cold, an indigestion, or a headache is doubtless an annoyance; but to a leading singer such an accident almost always means the impossibility of appearing at all, with serious loss of money to the artist, and grave disappointment to the public. The result of all this is that singers, as a rule, are much more normal, healthy, and well-balanced people than other musicians, or than actors. Moreover they generally have very strong bodies and constitutions to begin with, and when they have not they break down young.

Paul Griggs had an old traveller's preference for having plenty of time, and he was on board the steamer on Saturday a full hour before she was to sail; his not very numerous belongings, which looked as weather-beaten as himself, were piled up unopened in his cabin, and he himself stood on the upper promenade deck watching the passengers as they came on board. He was an observant man, and it interested him to note the expression of each new face that appeared; for the fact of starting on a voyage across the ocean is apt to affect people inversely as their experience. Those who cross often look so unconcerned that a casual observer might think they were not to start at all, whereas those who are going for the first time are either visibly flurried, or are posing to look as if they were not, though they are intensely nervous about their belongings; or they try to appear as if they belonged to the ship, or else as if the ship belonged to them, making observations which are supposed to be nautical, but which instantly stamp them as unutterable land-lubbers in the shrewd estimation of the stewards; and the latter, as every old hand is aware, always know everything much better than the captain.

Margaret Donne had been the most sensible and simple of young girls, and when she appeared at the gangway very quietly dressed in brown, with a brown fur collar, a brown hat, a brown veil, and a brown parasol, there was really nothing striking to distinguish her from other female passengers, except her good looks and her well-set-up figure. Yet somehow it seems impossible for a successful primadonna ever to escape notice. Instead of one maid, for instance, Cordova had two, and they carried rather worn leathern boxes that were evidently heavy jewel-cases, which they clutched with both hands and refused to give up to the stewards. They also had about them the indescribable air of rather aggressive assurance which belongs especially to highly-paid servants, men and women. Their looks said to every one: 'We are the show and you are the public, so don't stand in the way, for if you do the performance cannot go on!' They gave their orders about their mistress's things to the chief steward as if he were nothing better than a railway porter or a call-boy at the theatre; and, strange to say, that exalted capitalist obeyed with a docility he would certainly not have shown to any other passenger less than royal. They knew their way everywhere, they knew exactly what the best of everything was, and they made it clear that the great singer would have nothing less than the very, very best. She had the best cabin already, and she was to have the best seat at table, the best steward and the best stewardess, and her deck-chair was to be always in the best place on the upper promenade deck; and there was to be no mistake about it; and if anybody questioned the right of Margarita da Cordova, the great lyric soprano, to absolute precedence during the whole voyage, from start to finish, her two maids would know the reason why, and make the captain and all the ship's company wish they were dead.

That was their attitude.

But this was not all. There were the colleagues who came to see Margaret off and wished that they were going too. In spite of the windy weather there was Signor Pompeo Stromboli, the tenor, as broad as any two ordinary men, in a fur coat of the most terribly expensive sort, bringing an enormous box of chocolates with his best wishes; and there was the great German dramatic barytone, Herr Tiefenbach, who sang 'Amfortas' better than any one, and was a true musician as well as a man of culture, and he brought Margaret a book which he insisted that she must read on the voyage, called *The Genesis of the Tone Epos*; and there was that excellent and useful little artist, Fräulein Ottilie Braun, who never had an enemy in her life, who was always ready to sing any part creditably at a moment's notice if one of the leading artists broke down, and who was altogether one of the best, kindest, and least conceited human beings that ever joined an opera company. She brought her great colleague a little bunch of violets.

Least expected of them all, there was Schreiermeyer, with a basket of grape fruit in his tightly-gloved podgy hands; and he was smiling cheerfully, which was an event in itself. They followed Margaret up to the promenade deck after her maids had gone below, and stood round her in a group, all talking at once in different languages.

Griggs chanced to be the only other passenger on that part of the deck and he joined the party, for he knew them all. Margaret gave him her hand quietly and nodded to him. Signor Stromboli was effusive in his greeting; Herr Tiefenbach gave him a solemn grip; little Fräulein Ottilie smiled pleasantly, and Schreiermeyer put into his hands the basket he carried, judging that as he could not get anything else out of the literary man he could at least make him carry a parcel.

'Grape fruit for Cordova,' he observed. 'You can give it to the steward, and tell him to keep the things in a cool place.'

Griggs took the basket with a slight smile, but Stromboli snatched it from him instantly, and managed at the same time to seize upon the book Herr Tiefenbach had brought without dropping his own big box of sweetmeats.

'I shall give everything to the waiter!' he cried with exuberant energy as he turned away. 'He shall take care of Cordova with his conscience! I tell you, I will frighten him!'

This was possible, and even probable. Margaret looked after the broad figure.

'Dear old Stromboli!' she laughed.

'He has the kindest heart in the world,' said little Fräulein Ottilie Braun.

'He is no a musician,' observed Herr Tiefenbach; 'but he does not sing out of tune.'

'He is a lunatic,' said Schreiermeyer gravely. 'All tenors are lunatics—except about money,' he added thoughtfully.

'I think Stromboli is very sensible,' said Margaret, turning to Griggs. 'He brings his little Calabrian wife and her baby out with him, and they take a small house for the winter and Italian servants, and live just as if they were in their own country and see only their Italian friends—instead of being utterly wretched in a horrible hotel.'

'For the modest consideration of a hundred dollars a day,' put in Griggs, who was a poor man.

'I wish my bills were never more than that!' Margaret laughed.

'Yes,' said Schreiermeyer, still thoughtful. 'Stromboli understands money. He is a man of business. He makes his wife cook for him.'

'I often cook for myself,' said Fräulein Ottilie quite simply. 'If I had a husband, I would cook for him too!' She laughed like a child, without the slightest sourness. 'It is easier to cook well than to marry at all, even badly!'

'I do not at all agree with you,' answered Herr Tiefenbach severely. 'Without flattering myself, I may say that my wife married well; but her potato dumplings are terrifying.'

'You were never married, were you?' Margaret asked, turning to Griggs with a smile.

'No,' he answered. 'Can you make potato dumplings, and are you in search of a husband?'

'It is the other way,' said Schreiermeyer, 'for the husbands are always after her. Talking of marriage, that girl who died the other night was to have been married to Mr. Van Torp yesterday, and they were to have sailed with you this morning.'

'I saw his name on the—' Schreiermeyer began, but he was interrupted by a tremendous blast from the ship's horn, the first warning for non-passengers to go ashore.

Before the noise stopped Stromboli appeared again, looking very much pleased with himself, and twisting up the short black moustache that was quite lost on his big face. When he was nearer he desisted from twirling, shook a fat forefinger at Margaret and laughed.

'Oh, well, then,' he cried, translating his Italian literally into English, 'I've been in your room, Miss Cordova! Who is this Tom, eh? Flowers from Tom, one! Sweets from Tom, two! A telegram from Tom, three! Tom, Tom, Tom; it is full of Tom, her room! In the end, what is this Tom? For me, I only know Tom the ruffian in the *Ballo in Maschera*. That is all the Tom I know!'

They all looked at Margaret and laughed. She blushed a little, more out of annoyance than from any other reason.

'The maids wished to put me out,' laughed Stromboli, 'but they could not, because I am big. So I read everything. If I tell you I read, what harm is there?'

'None whatever,' Margaret answered, 'except that it is bad manners to open other people's telegrams.'

'Oh, that! The maid had opened it with water, and was reading when I came. So I read too! You shall find it all well sealed again, have no fear! They all do so.'

'Pleasant journey,' said Schreiermeyer abruptly. 'I'm going ashore. I'll see you in Paris in three weeks.'

'Read the book,' said Herr Tiefenbach earnestly, as he shook hands. 'It is a deep book.'

'Do not forget me!' cried Stromboli sentimentally, and he kissed Margaret's gloves several times.

'Good-bye,' said Fräulein Ottilie. 'Every one is sorry when you go!'

Margaret was not a gushing person, but she stooped and kissed the cheerful little woman, and pressed her small hand affectionately.

'And everybody is glad when you come, my dear,' she said.

For Fräulein Ottilie was perhaps the only person in the company whom Cordova really liked, and who did not jar dreadfully on her at one time or another.

Another blast from the horn and they were all gone, leaving her and Griggs standing by the rail on the upper promenade deck. The little party gathered again on the pier when they had crossed the plank, and made farewell signals to the two, and then disappeared. Unconsciously Margaret gave a little sigh of relief, and Griggs noticed it, as he noticed most things, but said nothing.

There was silence for a while, and the gangplank was still in place when the horn blew a third time, longer than before.

'How very odd!' exclaimed Griggs, a moment after the sound had ceased.

'What is odd?' Margaret asked.

She saw that he was looking down, and her eyes followed his. A square-shouldered man in mourning was walking up the plank in a leisurely way, followed by a well-dressed English valet, who carried a despatch-box in a leathern case.

'It's not possible!' Margaret whispered in great surprise.

'Perfectly possible,' Griggs answered, in a low voice. 'That is Rufus Van Torp.'

Margaret drew back from the rail, though the new comer was already out of sight on the lower promenade deck, to which the plank was laid to suit the height of the tide. She moved away from the door of the first cabin companion.

Griggs went with her, supposing that she wished to walk up and down. Numbers of other passengers were strolling about on the side next to the pier, waiting to see the start. Margaret went on forward, turned the deckhouse and walked to the rail on the opposite side, where there was no one. Griggs glanced at her face and thought that she seemed disturbed. She looked straight before her at the closed iron doors of the next pier, at which no ship was lying.

'I wish I knew you better,' she said suddenly.

Griggs looked at her quietly. It did not occur to him to make a trivial and complimentary answer to this advance, such as most men of the world would have made, even at his age.

'I shall be very glad if we ever know each other better,' he said after a short pause.

'So shall I.'

She leaned upon the rail and looked down at the eddying water. The tide had turned and was beginning to go out. Griggs watched her handsome profile in silence for a time.

'You have not many intimate friends, have you?' she asked presently.

'No, only one or two.'

She smiled.

'I'm not trying to get confidences from you. But really, that is very vague. You must surely know whether you have only one, or whether there is another. I'm not suggesting myself as a third, either!'

'Perhaps I'm over-cautious,' Griggs said. 'It does not matter. You began by saying that you wished you knew me better. You meant that if you did, you would either tell me something which you don't tell everybody, or you would come to me for advice about something, or you would ask me to do something for you. Is that it?'

'I suppose so.'

'It was not very hard to guess. I'll answer the three cases. If you want to tell me a secret, don't. If you want advice without telling everything about the case, it will be worthless. But if there is anything I can do for you, I'll do it if I can, and I won't ask any questions.'

'That's kind and sensible,' Margaret answered. 'And I should not be in the least afraid to tell you anything. You would not repeat it.'

'No, certainly not. But some day, unless we became real friends, you would think that I might, and then you would be very sorry.'

A short pause followed.

'We are moving,' Margaret said, glancing at the iron doors again.

'Yes, we are off.'

There was another pause. Then Margaret stood upright and turned her face to her companion. She did not remember that she had ever looked steadily into his eyes since she had known him.

They were grey and rather deeply set under grizzled eyebrows that were growing thick and rough with advancing years, and they met hers quietly. She knew at once that she could bear their scrutiny for any length of time without blushing or feeling nervous, though there was something in them that was stronger than she.

'It's this,' she said at last, as if she had been talking and had reached a conclusion. 'I'm alone, and I'm a little frightened.'

'You?' Griggs smiled rather incredulously.

'Yes. Of course I'm used to travelling without any one and taking care of myself. Singers and actresses are just like men in that, and it did not occur to me this morning that this trip could be different from any other.'

'No. Why should it be so different? I don't understand.'

'You said you would do something for me without asking questions. Will you?'

'If I can.'

'Keep Mr. Van Torp away from me during the voyage. I mean, as much as you can without being openly rude. Have my chair put next to some other woman's and your own on my other side. Do you mind doing that?'

Griggs smiled.

'No,' he said, 'I don't mind.'

'And if I am walking on deck and he joins me, come and walk beside me too. Will you? Are you quite sure you don't mind?'

'Yes.' He was still smiling. 'I'm quite certain that I don't dislike the idea.'

'I wish I were sure of being seasick,' Margaret said thoughtfully. 'It's bad for the voice, but it would be a great resource.'

'As a resource, I shall try to be a good substitute for it,' said Griggs.

Margaret realised what she had said and laughed.

'But it is no laughing matter,' she answered, her face growing grave again after a moment.

Griggs had promised not to ask questions, and he expressed no curiosity.

'As soon as you go below I'll see about the chair,' he said.

'My cabin is on this deck,' Margaret answered. 'I believe I have a tiny little sitting-room, too. It's what they call a suite in their magnificent language, and the photographs in the advertisements make it look like a palatial apartment!'

She left the rail as she spoke, and found her own door on the same side of the ship, not very far away.

'Here it is,' she said. 'Thank you very much.'

She looked into his eyes again for an instant and went in.

She had forgotten Signor Stromboli and what he had said, for her thoughts had been busy with a graver matter, but she smiled when she saw the big bunch of dark red carnations in a water-jug on the table, and the little cylinder-shaped parcel which certainly contained a dozen little boxes of the chocolate 'oublies' she liked, and the telegram, with its impersonal-looking address, waiting to be opened by her after having been opened, read, and sealed again by her thoughtful maids. Such trifles as the latter circumstance did not disturb her in the least, for though she was only a young woman of four and twenty, a singer and a musician, she had a philosophical mind, and considered that if virtue has nothing to do with the greatness of princes, moral worth need not be a clever lady's-maid's strong point.

'Tom' was her old friend Edmund Lushington, one of the most distinguished of the younger writers of the day. He was the only son of the celebrated soprano, Madame Bonanni, now retired from the stage, by her marriage with an English gentleman of the name of Goodyear, and he had been christened Thomas. But his mother had got his name and surname legally changed when he was a child, thinking that it would be a disadvantage to him to be known as her son, as indeed it might have been at first; even now the world did not know the truth about his birth, but it would not have cared, since he had won his own way.

Margaret meant to marry him if she married at all, for he had been faithful in his devotion to her nearly three years; and his rivalry with Constantine Logotheti, her other serious adorer, had brought some complications into her life. But on mature reflection she was sure that she did not wish to marry any one for the present. So many of her fellow-singers had married young and married often, evidently following the advice of a great American humorist, and mostly with disastrous consequences, that Margaret preferred to be an exception, and to marry late if at all.

In the glaring light of the twentieth century it at last clearly appears that marriageable young women have always looked upon marriage as the chief means of escape from the abject slavery and humiliating dependence hitherto imposed upon virgins between fifteen and fifty years old. Shakespeare lacked the courage to write the 'Seven Ages of Woman,' a matter the more to be regretted as no other writer has ever possessed enough command of the English language to describe more than three out of the seven without giving offence: namely, youth, which lasts from sixteen to twenty; perfection, which begins at twenty and lasts till further notice; and old age, which women generally place beyond seventy, though some, whose strength is not all sorrow and weakness even then, do not reach it till much later. If Shakespeare had dared he would have described with poetic fire the age of the girl who never marries. But this is a digression. The point is that the truth about marriage is out, since the modern spinster has shown the sisterhood how to live, and an amazing number of women look upon wedlock as a foolish thing, vainly imagined, never necessary, and rarely amusing.

The state of perpetual unsanctified virginity, however, is not for poor girls, nor for operatic singers, nor for kings' daughters, none of whom, for various reasons, can live, or are allowed to live, without husbands. Unless she be a hunchback, an unmarried royal princess is almost as great an exception as a white raven or a cat without a tail; a primadonna without a husband alive, dead, or divorced, is hardly more common; and poor girls marry to live. But give a modern young woman a decent social position, with enough money for her wants and an average dose of assurance, and she becomes so fastidious in the choice of a mate that no man is good enough for her till she is too old to be good enough for any man. Even then the chances are that she will not deeply regret her lost opportunities, and though her married friends will tell her that she has made a mistake, half of them will envy her in secret, the other half will not pity her much, and all will ask her to their dinner-parties, because a woman without a husband is such a convenience.

In respect to her art Margarita da Cordova was in all ways a thorough artist, endowed with the gifts, animated by the feelings, and afflicted with the failings that usually make up an artistic nature. But Margaret Donne was a sound and healthy English girl who had been brought up in the right way by a very refined and cultivated father and mother who loved her devotedly. If they had lived she would not have gone upon the stage; for as her mother's friend Mrs. Rushmore had often told her, the mere thought of such a life for their daughter would have broken their hearts. She was a grown woman now, and high on the wave of increasing success and celebrity, but she still had a childish misgiving that she had disobeyed her parents and done something very wrong, just as when she had surreptitiously got into the jam cupboard at the age of five.

Yet there are old-fashioned people alive even now who might think that there was less harm in becoming a public singer than in keeping Edmund Lushington dangling on a string for two years and more. Those things are matters of opinion. Margaret would have answered that if he dangled it was his misfortune and not her fault, since she never, in her own opinion, had done anything to keep him, and would not have been broken-hearted if he had gone away, though she would have missed his friendship very much. Of the two, the man who had disturbed her maiden peace of mind was Logotheti, whom she feared and sometimes hated, but who had an inexplicable power over her when they met: the sort of fateful influence which honest Britons commonly ascribe to all foreigners with black hair, good teeth, diamond studs, and the other outward signs of wickedness. Twice, at least, Logotheti had behaved in a manner positively alarming, and on the second occasion he had very nearly succeeded in carrying her off bodily from the theatre to his yacht, a fate from which Lushington and his mother had been instrumental in saving her. Such doings were shockingly lawless, but they showed a degree of recklessly passionate admiration which was flattering from a young financier who was so popular with women that he found it infinitely easier to please than to be pleased.

Perhaps, if Logotheti could have put on a little Anglo-Saxon coolness, Margaret might have married him by this time. Perhaps she would have married Lushington, if he could have suddenly been animated by a little Greek fire. As things stood, she told herself that she did not care to take a man who meant to be not only her master but her tyrant, nor one who seemed more inclined to be her slave than her master.

Meanwhile, however, it was the Englishman who kept himself constantly in mind with her by an unbroken chain of small attentions that often made her smile but sometimes really touched her. Any one could cable 'Pleasant voyage,' and sign the telegram 'Tom,' which gave it a friendly and encouraging look, because somehow 'Tom' is a cheerful, plucky little name, very unlike 'Edmund.' But it was quite another matter, being in England, to take the trouble to have carnations of just the right shade fresh on her cabin table at the moment of her sailing from New York, and beside them the only sort of chocolates she liked. That was more than a message, it was a visit, a presence, a real reaching out of hand to hand.

Logotheti, on the contrary, behaved as if he had forgotten Margaret's existence as soon as he was out of her sight; and they now no longer met often, but when they did he had a way of taking up the thread as if there had been no interval, which was almost as effective as his rival's method; for it produced the impression that he had been thinking of her only, and of nothing else in the world since the last meeting, and could never again give a thought to any other woman. This also was flattering. He never wrote to her, he never telegraphed good wishes for a journey or a performance, he never sent her so much as a flower; he acted as if he were really trying to forget her, as perhaps he was. But when they met, he was no sooner in the same room with her than she felt the old disturbing influence she feared and yet somehow desired in spite of herself, and much as she preferred the companionship of Lushington and liked his loyal straightforward ways, and admired his great talent, she felt that he paled and seemed less interesting beside the vivid personality of the Greek financier.

He was vivid; no other word expresses what he was, and if that one cannot properly be applied to a man, so much the worse for our language. His colouring was too handsome, his clothes were too good, his shoes were too shiny, his ties too surprising, and he not only wore diamonds and rubies, but very valuable ones. Yet he was not vulgarly gorgeous; he was Oriental. No one would say that a Chinese idol covered with gold and precious stones was overdressed, but it would be out of place in a Scotch kirk; the minister would be thrown into the shade and the congregation would look at the idol. In society, which nowadays is far from a chiaroscuro, everybody looked at Logotheti. If he had come from any place nearer than Constantinople people would have smiled and perhaps laughed at him; as it was, he was an exotic, and besides, he had the reputation of being dangerous to women's peace, and extremely awkward to meddle with in a quarrel.

Margaret sat some time in her little sitting-room reflecting on these things, for she knew that before many days were past she must meet her two adorers; and when she had thought enough about both, she gave orders to her maids about arranging her belongings. By and by she went to luncheon and found herself alone at some distance from the other passengers, next to the captain's empty seat; but she was rather glad that her neighbours had not come to table, for she got what she wanted very quickly and had no reason for waiting after she had finished.

Then she took a book and went on deck again, and Alphonsine found her chair on the sunny side and installed her in it very comfortably and covered her up, and to her own surprise she felt that she was very sleepy; so that just as she was wondering why, she dozed off and began to dream that she was Isolde, on board of Tristan's ship, and that she was singing the part, though she had never sung it and probably never would.

When she opened her eyes again there was no land in sight, and the big steamer was going quietly with scarcely any roll. She looked aft and saw Paul Griggs leaning against the rail, smoking; and she turned her head the other way, and the chair next to her own on that side was occupied by a very pleasant-looking young woman who was sitting up straight and showing the pictures in a book to a beautiful little girl who stood beside her.

The lady had a very quiet healthy face and smooth brown hair, and was simply and sensibly dressed. Margaret at once decided that she was not the child's mother, nor an elder sister, but some one who had charge of her, though not exactly a governess. The child was about nine years old; she had a quantity of golden hair that waved naturally, and a spiritual face with deep violet eyes, a broad white forehead and a pathetic little mouth.

She examined each picture, and then looked up quickly at the lady, keeping her wide eyes fixed on the latter's face with an expression of watchful interest. The lady explained each picture to her, but in such a soft whisper that Margaret could not hear a sound. Yet the child evidently understood every word easily. It was natural to suppose that the lady spoke under her breath in order not to disturb Margaret while she was asleep.

'It is very kind of you to whisper,' said the Primadonna graciously, 'but I am awake now.'

The lady turned with a pleasant smile.

'Thank you,' she answered.

The child did not notice Margaret's little speech, but looked up from the book for the explanation of the next picture.

'It is the inside of the Colosseum in Rome, and you will see it before long,' said the lady very distinctly. 'I have told you how the gladiators fought there, and how Saint Ignatius was sent all the way from Antioch to be devoured by lions there, like many other martyrs.'

The little girl watched her face intently, nodded gravely, and looked down at the picture again, but said nothing. The lady turned to Margaret.

'She was born deaf and dumb,' she said quietly, 'but I have taught her to understand from the lips, and she can already speak quite well. She is very clever.'

'Poor little thing!' Margaret looked at the girl with increasing interest. 'Such a little beauty, too! What is her name?'

'Ida—'

The child had turned over the pages to another picture, and now looked up for the explanation of it. Griggs had finished his cigar and came and sat down on Margaret's other side.

CHAPTER III

The *Leofric* was three days out, and therefore half-way over the ocean, for she was a fast boat, but so far Griggs had not been called upon to hinder Mr. Van Torp from annoying Margaret. Mr. Van Torp had not been on deck; in fact, he had not been seen at all since he had disappeared into his cabin a quarter of an hour before the steamer had left the pier. There was a good deal of curiosity about him amongst the passengers, as there would have been about the famous Primadonna if she had not come punctually to every meal, and if she had not been equally regular in spending a certain number of hours on deck every day.

At first every one was anxious to have what people call a 'good look' at her, because all the usual legends were already repeated about her wherever she went. It was said that she was really an ugly woman of thirty-five who had been married to a Spanish count of twice that age, and that he had died leaving her penniless, so that she had been obliged to support herself by singing. Others were equally sure that she was a beautiful escaped nun, who had been forced to take the veil in a convent in Seville by cruel parents, but who had succeeded in getting herself carried off by a Polish nobleman disguised as a priest. Every one remembered the marvellous voice that used to sing so high above all the other nuns, behind the lattice on Sunday afternoons at the church of the Dominican Convent. That had been the voice of Margarita da Cordova, and she could never go back to Spain, for if she did the Inquisition would seize upon her, and she would be tortured and probably burnt alive to encourage the other nuns.

This was very romantic, but unfortunately there was a man who said he knew the plain truth about her, and that she was just a good-looking Irish girl whose father used to play the flute at a theatre in Dublin, and whose mother kept a sweetshop in Queen Street. The man who knew this had often seen the shop, which was conclusive.

Margaret showed herself daily and the myths lost value, for every one saw that she was neither an escaped Spanish nun nor the gifted offspring of a Dublin flute-player and a female retailer of bull's-eyes and butterscotch, but just a handsome, healthy, well-brought-up young Englishwoman, who called herself Miss Donne in private life.

But gossip, finding no hold upon her, turned and rent Mr. Van Torp, who dwelt within his tent like Achilles, but whether brooding or sea-sick no one was ever to know. The difference of opinion about him was amazing. Some said he had no heart, since he had not even waited for the funeral of the poor girl who was to have been his wife. Others, on the contrary, said that he was broken-hearted, and that his doctor had insisted upon his going abroad at once, doubtless considering, as the best practitioners often do, that it is wisest to send a patient who is in a dangerous condition to distant shores, where some other doctor will get the credit of having killed him or driven him mad. Some said that Mr. Van Torp was concerned in the affair of that Chinese loan, which of course explained why he was forced to go to Europe in spite of the dreadful misfortune that had happened to him. The man who knew everything hinted darkly that Mr. Van Torp was not really solvent, and that he had perhaps left the country just at the right moment.

'That is nonsense,' said Miss More to Margaret in an undertone, for they had both heard what had just been said.

Miss More was the lady in charge of the pretty deaf child, and the latter was curled up in the next chair with a little piece of crochet work. Margaret had soon found out that Miss More was a very nice woman, after her own taste, who was given neither to flattery nor to prying, the two faults from which celebrities are generally made to suffer most by fellow-travellers who make their acquaintance. Miss More was evidently delighted to find herself placed on deck next to the famous singer, and Margaret was so well satisfied that the deck steward had already received a preliminary tip, with instructions to keep the chairs together during the voyage.

'Yes,' said Margaret, in answer to Miss More's remark. 'I don't believe there is the least reason for thinking that Mr. Van Torp is not immensely rich. Do you know him?'

'Yes.'

Miss More did not seem inclined to enlarge upon the fact, and her face was thoughtful after she had said the one word; so was Margaret's tone when she answered:

'So do I.'

Each of the young women understood that the other did not care to talk of Mr. Van Torp. Margaret glanced sideways at her neighbour and wondered vaguely whether the latter's experience had been at all like her own, but she could not see anything to make her think so. Miss More had a singularly pleasant expression and a face that made one trust her at once, but she was far from beautiful, and would hardly pass for pretty beside such a good-looking woman as Margaret, who after all was not what people call an out-and-out beauty. It was odd that the quiet lady-like teacher should have answered monosyllabically in that tone. She felt Margaret's sidelong look of inquiry, and turned half round after glancing at little Ida, who was very busy with her crochet.

'I'm afraid you may have misunderstood me,' she said, smiling. 'If I did not say any more it is because he himself does not wish people to talk of what he does.'

'I assure you, I'm not curious,' Margaret answered, smiling too. 'I'm sorry if I looked as if I were.'

'No—you misunderstood me, and it was a little my fault. Mr. Van Torp is doing something very, very kind which it was impossible that I should not know of, and he has asked me not to tell any one.'

'I see,' Margaret answered. 'Thank you for telling me. I am glad to know that he—'

She checked herself. She detested and feared the man, for reasons of her own, and she found it hard to believe that he could do something 'very, very kind' and yet not wish it to be known. He did not strike her as being the kind of person who would go out of his way to hide his light under a bushel. Yet Miss More's tone had been quiet and earnest. Perhaps he had employed her to teach some poor deaf and dumb child, like little Ida. Her words seemed to imply this, for she had said that it had been impossible that she should not know; that is, he had been forced to ask her advice or help, and her help and advice could only be considered indispensable where her profession as a teacher of the deaf and dumb was concerned.

Miss More was too discreet to ask the question which Margaret's unfinished sentence suggested, but she would not let the speech pass quite unanswered.

'He is often misjudged,' she said. 'In business he may be what many people say he is. I don't understand business! But I have known him to help people who needed help badly and who never guessed that he even knew their names.'

'You must be right,' Margaret answered.

She remembered the last words of the girl who had died in the manager's room at the theatre. There had been a secret. The secret was that Mr. Van Torp had done the thing, whatever it was. She had probably not known what she was saying, but it had been on her mind to say that Mr. Van Torp had done it, the man she was to have married. Margaret's first impression had been that the thing done must have been something very bad, because she herself disliked the man so much; but Miss More knew him, and since he often did 'very, very kind things,' it was possible that the particular action of which the dying girl was thinking might have been a charitable one; possibly he had confided the secret to her. Margaret smiled rather cruelly at her own superior knowledge of the world—yes, he had told the girl about that 'secret' charity in order to make a good impression on her! Perhaps that was his favourite method of interesting women; if it was, he had not invented it. Margaret thought she could have told Miss More something which would have thrown another light on Mr. Van Torp's character.

Her reflections had led her back to the painful scene at the theatre, and she remembered the account of it the next day, and the fact that the girl's name had been Ida. To change the subject she asked her neighbour an idle question.

'What is the little girl's full name?' she inquired.

'Ida Moon,' answered Miss More.

'Moon?' Margaret turned her head sharply. 'May I ask if she is any relation of the California Senator who died last year?'

'She is his daughter,' said Miss More quietly.

Margaret laid one hand on the arm of her chair and leaned forward a little, so as to see the child better.

'Really!' she exclaimed, rather deliberately, as if she had chosen that particular word out of a number that suggested themselves. 'Really!' she repeated, still more slowly, and then leaned back again and looked at the grey waves.

She remembered the notice of Miss Bamberger's death. It had described the deceased as the only child of Hannah Moon by her former marriage with Isidore Bamberger. But Hannah Moon, as Margaret happened to know, was now the widow of Senator Alvah Moon. Therefore the little deaf child was the half-sister of the girl who had died at the theatre in Margaret's arms and had been christened by the same name. Therefore, also, she was related to Margaret, whose mother had been the California magnate's cousin.

'How small the world is!' Margaret said in a low voice as she looked at the grey waves.

She wondered whether little Ida had ever heard of her half-sister, and what Miss More knew about it all.

'How old is Mrs. Moon?' she asked.

'I fancy she must be forty, or near that. I know that she was nearly thirty years younger than the Senator, but I never saw her.'

'You never saw her?' Margaret was surprised.

'No,' Miss More answered. 'She is insane, you know. She went quite mad soon after the little girl was born. It was very painful for the Senator. Her delusion was that he was her divorced husband, Mr. Bamberger, and when the child came into the world she insisted that it should be called Ida, and that she had no other. Mr. Bamberger's daughter was Ida, you know. It was very strange. Mrs. Moon was convinced that she was forced to live her life over again, year by year, as an expiation for something she had done. The doctors say it is a hopeless case. I really think it shortened the Senator's life.'

Margaret did not think that the world had any cause to complain of Mrs. Moon on that account.

'So this child is quite alone in the world,' she said.

'Yes. Her father is dead and her mother is in an asylum.'

'Poor little thing!'

The two young women were leaning back in their chairs, their faces turned towards each other as they talked, and Ida was still busy with her crochet.

'Luckily she has a sunny nature,' said Miss More. 'She is interested in everything she sees and hears.' She laughed a little. 'I always speak of it as hearing,' she added, 'for it is quite as quick, when there is light enough. You know that, since you have talked with her.'

'Yes. But in the dark, how do you make her understand?'

'She can generally read what I say by laying her hand on my lips; but besides that, we have the deaf and dumb alphabet, and she can feel my fingers as I make the letters.'

'You have been with her a long time, I suppose,' Margaret said.

'Since she was three years old.'

'California is a beautiful country, isn't it?' asked Margaret after a pause.

She put the question idly, for she was thinking how hard it must be to teach deaf and dumb children. Miss More's answer surprised her.

'I have never been there.'

'But, surely, Senator Moon lived in San Francisco,' Margaret said.

'Yes. But the child was sent to New England when she was three, and never went back again. We have been living in the country near Boston.'

'And the Senator used to pay you a visit now and then, of course, when he was alive. He must have been immensely pleased by the success of your teaching.'

Though Margaret felt that she was growing more curious about little Ida than she often was about any one, it did not occur to her that the question she now suggested, rather than asked, was an indiscreet one, and she was surprised by her companion's silence. She had already discovered that Miss More was one of those literally truthful people who never let an inaccurate statement pass their lips, and who will be obstinately silent rather than answer a leading question, quite regardless of the fact that silence is sometimes the most direct answer that can be given. On the present occasion Miss More said nothing and turned her eyes to the sea, leaving Margaret to make any deduction she pleased; but only one suggested itself, namely, that the deceased Senator had taken very little interest in the child of his old age, and had felt no affection for her. Margaret wondered whether he had left her rich, but Miss More's silence told her that she had already asked too many questions.

She glanced down the long line of passengers beyond Miss More and Ida. Men, women, and children lay side by side in their chairs, wrapped and propped like a row of stuffed specimens in a museum. They were not interesting, Margaret thought; for those who were awake all looked discontented, and those who were asleep looked either ill or apoplectic. Perhaps half of them were crossing because they were obliged to go to Europe for one reason or another; the other half were going in an aimless way, because they had got into the habit while they were young, or had been told that it was the right thing to do, or because their doctors sent them abroad to get rid of them. The grey light from the waves was reflected on the immaculate and shiny white paint, and shed a cold glare on the commonplace faces and on the plaid rugs, and on the vivid magazines which many of the people were reading, or pretending to read; for most persons only look at the pictures nowadays, and read the advertisements. A steward in a very short jacket was serving perfectly unnecessary cups of weak broth on a big tray, and a great number of the passengers took some, with a vague idea that the Company's feelings might be hurt if they did not, or else that they would not be getting their money's worth.

Between the railing and the feet of the passengers, which stuck out over the foot-rests of their chairs to different lengths according to the height of the possessors, certain energetic people walked ceaselessly up and down the deck, sometimes flattening themselves against the railing to let others who met them pass by, and sometimes, when the ship rolled a little, stumbling against an outstretched foot or two without making any elaborate apology for doing so.

Margaret only glanced at the familiar sight, but she made a little movement of annoyance almost directly, and took up the book that lay open and face downwards on her knee; she became absorbed in it so suddenly as to convey the impression that she was not really reading at all.

She had seen Mr. Van Torp and Paul Griggs walking together and coming towards her.

The millionaire was shorter than his companion and more clumsily made, though not by any means a stout man. Though he did not look like a soldier he had about him the very combative air which belongs to so many modern financiers of the Christian breed. There was the bull-dog jaw, the iron mouth, and the aggressive blue eye of the man who takes and keeps by force rather than by astuteness. Though his face had lines in it and his complexion was far from brilliant he looked scarcely forty years of age, and his short, rough, sandy hair had not yet begun to turn grey.

He was not ugly, but Margaret had always seen something in his face that repelled her. It was some lack of proportion somewhere, which she could not precisely define; it was something that was out of the common type of faces, but that was disquieting rather than interesting. Instead of wondering what it meant, those who noticed it wished it were not there.

Margaret was sure she could distinguish his heavy step from Griggs's when he was near her, but she would not look up from her book till he stopped and spoke to her.

'Good-morning, Madame Cordova; how are you this morning?' he inquired, holding out his hand. 'You didn't expect to see me on board, did you?'

His tone was hard and business-like, but he lifted his yachting cap politely as he held out his hand. Margaret hesitated a moment before taking it, and when she moved her own he was already holding his out to Miss More.

'Good-morning, Miss More; how are you this morning?'

Miss More leaned forward and put down one foot as if she would have risen in the presence of the great man, but he pushed her back by her hand which he held, and proceeded to shake hands with the little girl.

'Good-morning, Miss Ida; how are you this morning?'

Margaret felt sure that if he had shaken hands with a hundred people he would have repeated the same words to each without any variation. She looked at Griggs imploringly, and glanced at his vacant chair on her right side. He did not answer by sitting down, because the action would have been too like deliberately telling Mr. Van Torp to go away, but he began to fold up the chair as if he were going to take it away, and then he seemed to find that there was something wrong with one of its joints, and altogether it gave him a good deal of trouble, and made it quite impossible for the great man to get any nearer to Margaret.

Little Ida had taken Mr. Van Torp's proffered hand, and had watched his hard lips when he spoke. She answered quite clearly and rather slowly, in the somewhat monotonous voice of those born deaf who have learned to speak.

'I'm very well, thank you, Mr. Van Torp. I hope you are quite well.'

Margaret heard, and saw the child's face, and at once decided that, if the little girl knew of her own relationship to Ida Bamberger, she was certainly ignorant of the fact that her half-sister had been engaged to Mr. Van Torp, when she had died so suddenly less than a week ago. Little Ida's manner strengthened the impression in Margaret's mind that the millionaire was having her educated by Miss More. Yet it seemed impossible that the rich old Senator should not have left her well provided.

'I see you've made friends with Madame Cordova,' said Mr. Van Torp. 'I'm very glad, for she's quite an old friend of mine too.'

Margaret made a slight movement, but said nothing. Miss More saw her annoyance and intervened by speaking to the financier.

'We began to fear that we might not see you at all on the voyage,' she said, in a tone of some concern. 'I hope you have not been suffering again.'

Margaret wondered whether she meant to ask if he had been sea-sick; what she said sounded like an inquiry about some more or less frequent indisposition, though Mr. Van Torp looked as strong as a ploughman.

In answer to the question he glanced sharply at Miss More, and shook his head.

'I've been too busy to come on deck,' he said, rather curtly, and he turned to Margaret again.

'Will you take a little walk with me, Madame Cordova?' he asked.

Not having any valid excuse for refusing, Margaret smiled, for the first time since she had seen him on deck.

'I'm so comfortable!' she answered. 'Don't make me get out of my rug!'

'If you'll take a little walk with me, I'll give you a pretty present,' said Mr. Van Torp playfully.

Margaret thought it best to laugh and shake her head at this singular offer. Little Ida had been watching them both.

'You'd better go with him,' said the child gravely. 'He makes lovely presents.'

'Does he?' Margaret laughed again.

'"A fortress that parleys, or a woman who listens, is lost,"' put in Griggs, quoting an old French proverb.

'Then I won't listen,' Margaret said.

Mr. Van Torp planted himself more firmly on his sturdy legs, for the ship was rolling a little.

'I'll give you a book, Madame Cordova,' he said.

His habit of constantly repeating the name of the person with whom he was talking irritated her extremely. She was not smiling when she answered.

'Thank you. I have more books than I can possibly read.'

'Yes. But you have not the one I will give you, and it happens to be the only one you want.'

'But I don't want any book at all! I don't want to read!'

'Yes, you do, Madame Cordova. You want to read this one, and it's the only copy on board, and if you'll take a little walk with me I'll give it to you.'

As he spoke he very slowly drew a new book from the depths of the wide pocket in his overcoat, but only far enough to show Margaret the first words of the title, and he kept his aggressive blue eyes fixed on her face. A faint blush came into her cheeks at once and he let the volume slip back. Griggs, being on his other side, had not seen it, and it meant nothing to Miss More. To the latter's surprise Margaret pushed her heavy rug from her knees and let her feet slip from the chair to the ground. Her eyes met Griggs's as she rose, and seeing that his look asked her whether he was to carry out her previous instructions and walk beside her, she shook her head.

'Nine times out of ten, proverbs are true,' he said in a tone of amusement.

Mr. Van Torp's hard face expressed no triumph when Margaret stood beside him, ready to walk. She had yielded, as he had been sure she would; he turned from the other passengers to go round to the weather side of the ship, and she went with him submissively. Just at the point where the wind and the fine spray would have met them if they had gone on, he stopped in the lee of a big ventilator. There was no one in sight of them now.

'Excuse me for making you get up,' he said. 'I wanted to see you alone for a moment.'

Margaret said nothing in answer to this apology, and she met his fixed eyes coldly.

'You were with Miss Bamberger when she died,' he said.

Margaret bent her head gravely in assent. His face was as expressionless as a stone.

'I thought she might have mentioned me before she died,' he said slowly.

'Yes,' Margaret answered after a moment's pause; 'she did.'

'What did she say?'

'She told me that it was a secret, but that I was to tell you what she said, if I thought it best.'

'Are you going to tell me?'

It was impossible to guess whether he was controlling any emotion or not; but if the men with whom he had done business where large sums were involved had seen him now and had heard his voice, they would have recognised the tone and the expression.

'She said, "he did it,"' Margaret answered slowly, after a moment's thought.

'Was that all she said?'

'That was all. A moment later she was dead. Before she said it, she told me it was a secret, and she made me promise solemnly never to tell any one but you.'

'It's not much of a secret, is it?' As he spoke, Mr. Van Torp turned his eyes from Margaret's at last and looked at the grey sea beyond the ventilator.

'Such as it is, I have told it to you because she wished me to,' answered Margaret. 'But I shall never tell any one else. It will be all the easier to be silent, as I have not the least idea what she meant.'

'She meant our engagement,' said Mr. Van Torp in a matter-of-fact tone. 'We had broken it off that afternoon. She meant that it was I who did it, and so it was. Perhaps she did not like to think that when she was dead people might call her heartless and say she had thrown me over; and no one would ever know the truth except me, unless I chose to tell—me and her father.'

'Then you were not to be married after all!' Margaret showed her surprise.

'No. I had broken it off. We were going to let it be known the next day.'

'On the very eve of the wedding!'

'Yes.' Mr. Van Torp fixed his eyes on Margaret's again. 'On the very eve of the wedding,' he said, repeating her words.

He spoke very slowly and without emphasis, but with the greatest possible distinctness. Margaret had once been taken to see a motor-car manufactory and she remembered a machine that clipped bits off the end of an iron bar, inch by inch, smoothly and deliberately. Mr. Van Torp's lips made her think of that; they seemed to cut the hard words one by one, in lengths.

'Poor girl!' she sighed, and looked away.

The man's face did not change, and if his next words echoed the sympathy she expressed his tone did not.

'I was a good deal cut up myself,' he observed coolly. 'Here's your book, Madame Cordova.'

'No,' Margaret answered with a little burst of indignation, 'I don't want it. I won't take it from you!'

'What's the matter now?' asked Mr. Van Torp without the least change of manner. 'It's your friend Mr. Lushington's latest, you know, and it won't be out for ten days. I thought you would like to see it, so I got an advance copy before it was published.'

He held the volume out to her, but she would not even look at it, nor answer him.

'How you hate me! Don't you, Madame Cordova?'

Margaret still said nothing. She was considering how she could best get rid of him. If she simply brushed past him and went back to her chair on the lee side, he would follow her and go on talking to her as if nothing had happened; and she knew that in that case she would lose control of herself before Griggs and Miss More.

'Oh, well,' he went on, 'if you don't want the book, I don't. I can't read novels myself, and I daresay it's trash anyhow.'

Thereupon, with a quick movement of his arm and hand, he sent Mr. Lushington's latest novel flying over the lee rail, fully thirty feet away, and it dropped out of sight into the grey waves. He had been a good baseball pitcher in his youth.

Margaret bit her lip and her eyes flashed.

'You are quite the most disgustingly brutal person I ever met,' she said, no longer able to keep down her anger.

'No,' he answered calmly. 'I'm not brutal; I'm only logical. I took a great deal of trouble to get that book for you because I thought it would give you pleasure, and it wasn't a particularly legal transaction by which I got it either. Since you didn't want it, I wasn't going to let anybody else have the satisfaction of reading it before it was published, so I just threw it away because it is safer in the sea than knocking about in my cabin. If you hadn't seen me throw it overboard you would never have believed that I had. You're not much given to believing me, anyway. I've noticed that. Are you, now?'

'Oh, it was not the book!'

Margaret turned from him and made a step forward so that she faced the sharp wind. It cut her face and she felt that the little pain was a relief. He came and stood beside her with his hands deep in the pockets of his overcoat.

'If you think I'm a brute on account of what I told you about Miss Bamberger,' he said, 'that's not quite fair. I broke off our engagement because I found out that we were going to make each other miserable and we should have had to divorce in six months; and if half the people who are just going to get married would do the same thing there would be a lot more happy women in the world, not to say men! That's all, and she knew it, poor girl, and was just as glad as I was when the thing was done. Now what is there so brutal in that, Madame Cordova?'

Margaret turned on him almost fiercely.

'Why do you tell me all this?' she asked. 'For heaven's sake let poor Miss Bamberger rest in her grave!'

'Since you ask me why,' answered Mr. Van Torp, unmoved, 'I tell you all this because I want you to know more about me than you do. If you did, you'd hate me less. That's the plain truth. You know very well that there's nobody like you, and that if I'd judged I had the slightest chance of getting you I would no more have thought of marrying Miss Bamberger than of throwing a million dollars into the sea after that book, or ten million, and that's a great deal of money.'

'I ought to be flattered,' said Margaret with scorn, still facing the wind.

'No. I'm not given to flattery, and money means something real to me, because I've fought for it, and got it. Your regular young lover will always call you his precious treasure, and I don't see much difference between a precious treasure and several million dollars. I'm logical, you see. I tell you I'm logical, that's all.'

'I daresay. I think we have been talking here long enough. Shall we go back?'

She had got her anger under again. She detested Mr. Van Torp, but she was honest enough to realise that for the present she had resented his saying that Lushington's book was probably trash, much more than what he had told her of his broken engagement. She turned and came back to the ventilator, meaning to go around to her chair, but he stopped her.

'Don't go yet, please!' he said, keeping beside her. 'Call me a disgusting brute if you like. I sha'n't mind it, and I daresay it's true in a kind of way. Business isn't very refining, you know, and it was the only education I got after I was sixteen. I'm sorry I called that book rubbish, for I'm sure it's not. I've met Mr. Lushington in England several times; he's very clever, and he's got a first-rate position. But you see I didn't like your refusing the book, after I'd taken so much trouble to get it for you. Perhaps if I hadn't thrown it overboard you'd take it, now that I've apologised. Would you?'

His tone had changed at last, as she had known it to change before in the course of an acquaintance that had lasted more than a year. He put the question almost humbly.

'I don't know,' Margaret answered, relenting a little in spite of herself. 'At all events I'm sorry I was so rude. I lost my temper.'

'It was very natural,' said Mr. Van Torp meekly, but not looking at her, 'and I know I deserved it. You really would let me give you the book now, if it were possible, wouldn't you?'

'Perhaps.' She thought that as there was no such possibility it was safe to say as much as that.

'I should feel so much better if you would,' he answered. 'I should feel as if you'd accepted my apology. Won't you say it, Madame Cordova?'

'Well—yes—since you wish it so much,' Margaret replied, feeling that she risked nothing.

'Here it is, then,' he said, to her amazement, producing the new novel from the pocket of his overcoat, and enjoying her surprise as he put it into her hand.

It looked like a trick of sleight of hand, and she took the book and stared at him, as a child stares at the conjuror who produces an apple out of its ear.

'But I saw you throw it away,' she said in a puzzled tone.

'I got two while I was about it,' said Mr. Van Torp, smiling without showing his teeth. 'It was just as easy and it didn't cost me any more.'

'I see! Thank you very much.'

She knew that she could not but keep the volume now, and in her heart she was glad to have it, for Lushington had written to her about it several times since she had been in America.

'Well, I'll leave you now,' said the millionaire, resuming his stony expression. 'I hope I've not kept you too long.'

Before Margaret had realised the idiotic conventionality of the last words her companion had disappeared and she was left alone. He had not gone back in the direction whence they had come, but had taken the deserted windward side of the ship, doubtless with the intention of avoiding the crowd.

Margaret stood still for some time in the lee of the ventilator, holding the novel in her hand and thinking. She wondered whether Mr. Van Torp had planned the whole scene, including the sacrifice of the novel. If he had not, it was certainly strange that he should have had the second copy ready in his pocket. Lushington had once told her that great politicians and great financiers were always great comedians, and now that she remembered the saying it occurred to her that Mr. Van Torp reminded her of a certain type of American actor, a type that has a heavy jaw and an aggressive eye, and strongly resembles the portraits of Daniel Webster. Now Daniel Webster had a wide reputation as a politician, but there is reason to believe that the numerous persons who lent him money and never got it back thought him a financier of undoubted ability, if not a comedian of talent. There were giants in those days.

The English girl, breathing the clean air of the ocean, felt as if something had left a bad taste in her mouth; and the famous young singer, who had seen in two years what a normal Englishwoman would neither see, nor guess at, nor wish to imagine in a lifetime, thought she understood tolerably well what the bad taste meant. Moreover, Margaret Donne was ashamed of what Margarita da Cordova knew, and Cordova had moments of sharp regret when she thought of the girl who had been herself, and had lived under good Mrs. Rushmore's protection, like a flower in a glass house.

She remembered, too, how Lushington and Mrs. Rushmore had warned her and entreated her not to become an opera-singer. She had taken her future into her own hands and had soon found out what it meant to be a celebrity on the stage; and she had seen only too clearly where she was classed by the women who would have been her companions and friends if she had kept out of the profession. She had learned by experience, too, how little real consideration she could expect from men of the world, and how very little she could really exact from such people as Mr. Van Torp; still less could she expect to get it from persons like Schreiermeyer, who looked upon the gifted men and women he engaged to sing as so many head of cattle, to be driven more or less hard according to their value, and to be turned out to starve the moment they were broken-winded. That fate is sure to overtake the best of them sooner or later. The career of a great opera-singer is rarely more than half as long as that of a great tragedian, and even when a primadonna or a tenor makes a fortune, the decline of their glory is far more sudden and sad than that of actors generally is. Lady Macbeth is as great a part as Juliet for an actress of genius, but there are no 'old parts' for singers; the soprano dare not turn into a contralto with advancing years, nor does the unapproachable Parsifal of eight-and-twenty turn into an incomparable Amfortas at fifty. For the actor, it often happens that the first sign of age is fatigue; in the singer's day, the first shadow is an eclipse, the first false note is disaster, the first breakdown is often a heart-rending failure that brings real tears to the eyes of younger comrades. The exquisite voice does not grow weak and pathetic and ethereal by degrees, so that we still love to hear it, even to the end; far more often it is suddenly flat or sharp by a quarter of a tone throughout whole acts, or it breaks on one note in a discordant shriek that is the end. Down goes the curtain then, in the middle of the great opera, and down goes the great singer for ever into tears and silence. Some of us have seen that happen, many have heard of it; few can think without real sympathy of such mortal suffering and distress.

Margaret realised all this, without any illusion, but there was another side to the question. There was success, glorious and far-reaching, and beyond her brightest dreams; there was the certainty that she was amongst the very first, for the deafening ring of universal applause was in her ears; and, above all, there was youth. Sometimes it seemed to her that she had almost too much, and that some dreadful thing must happen to her; yet if there were moments when she faintly regretted the calmer, sweeter life she might have led, she knew that she would have given that life up, over and over again, for the splendid joy of holding thousands spellbound while she sang. She had the real lyric artist's temperament, for that breathless silence of the many while her voice rang out alone, and trilled and died away to a delicate musical echo, was more to her than the roar of applause that could be heard through the walls and closed doors in the street outside. To such a moment as that Faustus himself would have cried 'Stay!' though the price of satisfied desire were his soul. And there had been many such moments in Cordova's life. They satisfied something much deeper than greedy vanity and stronger than hungry ambition. Call it what you will, according to the worth you set on such art, it is a longing which only artists feel, and to which only something in themselves can answer. To listen to perfect music is a feast for gods, but to be the living instrument beyond compare is to be a god oneself. Of our five senses, sight calls up visions, divine as well as earthly, but hearing alone can link body, mind, and soul with higher things, by the word and by the word made song. The mere memory of hearing when it is lost is still enough for the ends of genius; for the poet and the composer touch the blind most deeply, perhaps, when other senses do not count at all; but a painter who loses his sight is as helpless in the world of art as a dismasted ship in the middle of the ocean.

Some of these thoughts passed through Margaret's brain as she stood beside the ventilator with her friend's new book in her hand, and, although her reflections were not new to her, it was the first time she clearly understood that her life had made two natures out of her original self, and that the two did not always agree. She felt that she was not halved by the process, but doubled. She was two women instead of one, and each woman was complete in herself. She had not found this out by any elaborate self-study, for healthy people do not study themselves. She simply felt it, and she was sure it was true, because she knew that each of her two selves was able to do, suffer, and enjoy as much as any one woman could. The one might like what the other disliked and feared, but the contradiction was open and natural, not secret or morbid. The two women were called respectively Madame Cordova and Miss Donne. Miss Donne thought Madame Cordova very showy, and much too tolerant of vulgar things and people, if not a little touched with vulgarity herself. On the other hand, the brilliantly successful Cordova thought Margaret Donne a good girl, but rather silly. Miss Donne was very fond of Edmund Lushington, the writer, but the Primadonna had a distinct weakness for Constantine Logotheti, the Greek financier who lived in Paris, and who wore too many rubies and diamonds.

On two points, at least, the singer and the modest English girl agreed, for they both detested Rufus Van Torp, and each had positive proof that he was in love with her, if what he felt deserved the name.

For in very different ways she was really loved by Lushington and by Logotheti; and since she had been famous she had made the acquaintance of a good many very high and imposing personages, whose names are to be found in the first and second part of the *Almanack de Gotha*, in the Olympian circle of the reigning or the supernal regions of the Serene Mediatized, far above the common herd of dukes and princes; they had offered her a share in the overflowing abundance of their admirative protection; and then had seemed surprised, if not deeply moved, by the independence she showed in declining their intimacy. Some of them were frankly and contentedly cynical; some were of a brutality compared with which the tastes and manners of a bargee would have seemed ladylike; some were as refined and sensitive as English old maids, though less scrupulous and much less shy; the one was as generous as an Irish sailor, the next was as mean as a Normandy peasant; some had offered her rivers of rubies, and some had proposed to take her incognito for a drive in a cab, because it would be so amusing—and so inexpensive. Yet in their families and varieties they were all of the same species, all human and all subject to the ordinary laws of attraction and repulsion. Rufus Van Torp was not like them.

Neither of Margaret's selves could look upon him as a normal human being. At first sight there was nothing so very unusual in his face, certainly nothing that suggested a monster; and yet, whatever mood she chanced to be in, she could not be with him five minutes without being aware of something undefinable that always disturbed her profoundly, and sometimes became positively terrifying. She always felt the sensation coming upon her after a few moments, and when it had actually come she could hardly hide her repulsion till she felt, as to-day, that she must run from him, without the least consideration of pride or dignity. She might have fled like that before a fire or a flood, or from the scene of an earthquake, and more than once nothing had kept her in her place but her strong will and healthy nerves. She knew that it was like the panic that seizes people in the presence of an appalling disturbance of nature.

Doubtless, when she had talked with Mr. Van Torp just now, she had been disgusted by the indifferent way in which he spoke of poor Miss Bamberger's sudden death; it was still more certain that what he said about the book, and his very ungentlemanly behaviour in throwing it into the sea, had roused her justifiable anger. But she would have smiled at the thought that an exhibition of heartlessness, or the most utter lack of manners, could have made her wish to run away from any other man. Her life had accustomed her to people who had no more feeling than Schreiermeyer, and no better manners than Pompeo Stromboli. Van Torp might have been on his very best behaviour that morning, or at any of her previous chance meetings with him; sooner or later she would have felt that same absurd and unreasoning fear of him, and would have found it very hard not to turn and make her escape. His face was so stony and his eyes were so aggressive; he was always like something dreadful that was just going to happen.

Yet Margarita da Cordova was a brave woman, and had lately been called a heroine because she had gone on singing after that explosion till the people were quiet again; and Margaret Donne was a sensible girl, justly confident of being able to take care of herself where men were concerned. She stood still and wondered what there was about Mr. Van Torp that could frighten her so dreadfully.

After a little while she went quietly back to her chair, and sat down between Griggs and Miss More. The elderly man rose and packed her neatly in her plaid, and she thanked him. Miss More looked at her and smiled vaguely, as even the most intelligent people do sometimes. Then Griggs got into his own chair again and took up his book.

'Was that right of me?' he asked presently, so low that Miss More did not hear him speak.

'Yes,' Margaret answered, under her breath, 'but don't let me do it again, please.'

They both began to read, but after a time Margaret spoke to him again without turning her eyes.

'He wanted to ask me about that girl who died at the theatre,' she said, just audibly.

'Oh—yes!'

Griggs seemed so vague that Margaret glanced at him. He was looking at the inside of his right hand in a meditative way, as if it recalled something. If he had shown more interest in what she said she would have told him what she had just learned, about the breaking off of the engagement, but he was evidently absorbed in thought, while he slowly rubbed that particular spot on his hand, and looked at it again and again as if it recalled something.

Margaret did not resent his indifference, for he was much more than old enough to be her father; he was a man whom all younger writers looked upon as a veteran, he had always been most kind and courteous to her when she had met him, and she freely conceded him the right to be occupied with his own thoughts and not with hers. With him she was always Margaret Donne, and he seldom talked to her about music, or of her own work. Indeed, he so rarely mentioned music that she fancied he did not really care for it, and she wondered why he was so often in the house when she sang.

Mr. Van Torp did not show himself at luncheon, and Margaret began to hope that he would not appear on deck again till the next day. In the afternoon the wind dropped, the clouds broke, and the sun shone brightly. Little Ida, who was tired of doing crochet work, and had looked at all the books that had pictures, came and begged Margaret to walk round the ship with her. It would please her small child's vanity to show everybody that the great singer was willing to be seen walking up and down with her, although she was quite deaf, and could not hope ever to hear music. It was her greatest delight to be treated before every one as if she were just like other girls, and her cleverness in watching the lips of the person with her, without seeming too intent, was wonderful.

They went the whole length of the promenade deck, as if they were reviewing the passengers, bundled and packed in their chairs, and the passengers looked at them both with so much interest that the child made Margaret come all the way back again.

'The sea has a voice, too, hasn't it?' Ida asked, as they paused and looked over the rail.

She glanced up quickly for the answer, but Margaret did not find one at once.

'Because I've read poetry about the voices of the sea,' Ida explained. 'And in books they talk of the music of the waves, and then they say the sea roars, and thunders in a storm. I can hear thunder, you know. Did you know that I could hear thunder?'

Margaret smiled and looked interested.

'It bangs in the back of my head,' said the child gravely. 'But I should like to hear the sea thunder. I often watch the waves on the beach, as if they were lips moving, and I try to understand what they say. Of course, it's play, because one can't, can one? But I can only make out "Boom, ta-ta-ta-ta," getting quicker and weaker to the end, you know, as the ripples run up the sand.'

'It's very like what I hear,' Margaret answered.

'Is it really?' Little Ida was delighted. 'Perhaps it's a language after all, and I shall make it out some day. You see, until I know the language people are speaking, their lips look as if they were talking nonsense. But I'm sure the sea could not really talk nonsense all day for thousands of years.'

'No, I'm sure it couldn't!' Margaret was amused. 'But the sea is not alive,' she added.

'Everything that moves is alive,' the child said, 'and everything that is alive can make a noise, and the noise must mean something. If it didn't, it would be of no use, and everything is of some use. So there!'

Delighted with her own argument, the beautiful child laughed and showed her even teeth in the sun.

They were standing at the end of the promenade deck, which extended twenty feet abaft the smoking-room, and took the whole beam; above the latter, as in most modern ships, there was the boat deck, to the after-part of which passengers had access. Standing below, it was easy to see and talk with any one who looked over the upper rail.

Ida threw her head back and looked up as she laughed, and Margaret laughed good-naturedly with her, thinking how pretty she was. But suddenly the child's expression changed, her face grew grave, and her eyes fixed themselves intently on some point above. Margaret looked in the same direction, and saw that Mr. Van Torp was standing alone up there, leaning against the railing and evidently not seeing her, for he gazed fixedly into the distance; and as he stood there, his lips moved as if he were talking to himself.

Margaret gave a little start of surprise when she saw him, but the child watched him steadily, and a look of fear stole over her face. Suddenly she grasped Margaret's arm.

'Come away! Come away!' she cried in a low tone of terror.

CHAPTER IV

Margaret was sorry to say good-bye to Miss More and little Ida when the voyage was over, three days later. She was instinctively fond of children, as all healthy women are, and she saw very few of them in her wandering life. It is true that she did not understand them very well, for she had been an only child, brought up much alone, and children's ways are only to be learnt and understood by experience, since all children are experimentalists in life, and what often seems to us foolishness in them is practical wisdom of the explorative kind.

When Ida had pulled Margaret away from the railing after watching Mr. Van Torp while he was talking to himself, the singer had thought very little of it; and Ida never mentioned it afterwards. As for the millionaire, he was hardly seen again, and he made no attempt to persuade Margaret to take another walk with him on deck.

'Perhaps you would like to see my place,' he said, as he bade her good-bye on the tender at Liverpool. 'It used to be called Oxley Paddox, but I didn't like that, so I changed the name to Torp Towers. I'm Mr. Van Torp of Torp Towers. Sounds well, don't it?'

'Yes,' Margaret answered, biting her lip, for she wanted to laugh. 'It has a very lordly sound. If you bought a moor and a river in Scotland, you might call yourself the M'Torp of Glen Torp, in the same way.'

'I see you're laughing at me,' said the millionaire, with a quiet smile of a man either above or beyond ridicule. 'But it's all a game in a toy-shop anyway, this having a place in Europe. I buy a doll to play with when I have time, and I can call it what I please, and smash its head when I'm tired of it. It's my doll. It isn't any one's else's. The Towers is in Derbyshire if you want to come.'

Margaret did not 'want to come' to Torp Towers, even if the doll wasn't 'any one's else's.' She was sorry for any person or thing that had the misfortune to be Mr. Van Torp's doll, and she felt her inexplicable fear of him coming upon her while he was speaking. She broke off the conversation by saying good-bye rather abruptly.

'Then you won't come,' he said, in a tone of amusement.

'Really, you are very kind, but I have so many engagements.'

'Saturday to Monday in the season wouldn't interfere with your engagements. However, do as you like.'

'Thank you very much. Good-bye again.'

She escaped, and he looked after her, with an unsatisfied expression that was almost wistful, and that would certainly not have been in his face if she could have seen it.

Griggs was beside her when she went ashore.

'I had not much to do after all,' he said, glancing at Van Torp.

'No,' Margaret answered, 'but please don't think it was all imagination. I may tell you some day. No,' she said again, after a short pause, 'he did not make himself a nuisance, except that once, and now he has asked me to his place in Derbyshire.'

'Torp Towers,' Griggs observed, with a smile.

'Yes. I could hardly help laughing when he told me he had changed its name.'

'It's worth seeing,' said Griggs. 'A big old house, all full of other people's ghosts.'

'Ghosts?'

'I mean figuratively. It's full of things that remind one of the people who lived there. It has one of the oldest parks in England. Lots of pheasants, too—but that cannot last long.'

'Why not?'

'He won't let any one shoot them! They will all die of overcrowding in two or three years. His keepers are three men from the Society for the Prevention of Cruelty to Animals.'

'What a mad idea!' Margaret laughed. 'Is he a Buddhist?'

'No.' Paul Griggs knew something about Buddhism. 'Certainly not! He's eccentric. That's all.'

They were at the pier. Half-an-hour later they were in the train together, and there was no one else in the carriage. Miss More and little Ida had disappeared directly after landing, but Margaret had seen Mr. Van Torp get into a carriage on the window of which was pasted the label of the rich and great: 'Reserved.' She could have had the same privilege if she had chosen to ask for it or pay for it, but it irritated her that he should treat himself like a superior being. Everything he did either irritated her or frightened her, and she found herself constantly thinking of him and wishing that he would get out at the first station. Griggs was silent too, and Margaret thought he really might have taken some trouble to amuse her.

She had Lushington's book on her knee, for she had found it less interesting than she had expected, and was rather ashamed of not having finished it before meeting him, since it had been given to her. She thought he might come down as far as Rugby to meet her, and she was quite willing that he should find her with it in her hand. A literary man is always supposed to be flattered at finding a friend reading his last production, as if he did not know that the friend has probably grabbed the volume with undignified haste the instant he was on the horizon, with the intention of being discovered deep in it. Yet such little friendly frauds are sweet compared with the extremes of brutal frankness to which our dearest friends sometimes think it their duty to go with us, for our own good.

After a time Griggs spoke to her, and she was glad to hear his voice. She had grown to like him during the voyage, even more than she had ever thought probable. She had even gone so far as to wonder whether, if he had been twenty-five years younger, he might not have been the one man she had ever met whom she might care to marry, and she had laughed at the involved terms of the hypothesis as soon as she thought of it. Griggs had never been married, but elderly people remembered that there had been some romantic tale about his youth, when he had been an unknown young writer struggling for life as a newspaper correspondent.

'You saw the notice of Miss Bamberger's death, I suppose,' he said, turning his grey eyes to hers.

He had not alluded to the subject during the voyage.

'Yes,' Margaret answered, wondering why he broached it now.

'The notice said that she died of heart failure, from shock,' Griggs continued. 'I should like to know what you think about it, as you were with her when she died. Have you any idea that she may have died of anything else?'

'No.' Margaret was surprised. 'The doctor said it was that.'

'I know. I only wanted to have your own impression. I believe that when people die of heart failure in that way, they often make desperate efforts to explain what has happened, and go on trying to talk when they can only make inarticulate sounds. Do you remember if it was at all like that?'

'Not at all,' Margaret said. 'She whispered the last words she spoke, but they were quite distinct. Then she drew three or four deep breaths, and all at once I saw that she was dead, and I called the doctor from the next room.'

'I suppose that might be heart failure,' said Griggs thoughtfully. 'You are quite sure that you thought it was only that, are you not?'

'Only what?' Margaret asked with growing surprise.

'Only fright, or the result of having been half-suffocated in the crowd.'

'Yes, I think I am sure. What do you mean? Why do you insist so much?'

'It's of no use to tell other people,' said Griggs, 'but you may just as well know. I found her lying in a heap behind a door, where there could not have been much of a crowd.'

'Perhaps she had taken refuge there, to save herself,' Margaret suggested.

'Possibly. But there was another thing. When I got home I found that there was a little blood on the palm of my hand. It was the hand I had put under her waist when I lifted her.'

'Do you mean to say you think she was wounded?' Margaret asked, opening her eyes wide.

'There was blood on the inside of my hand,' Griggs answered, 'and I had no scratch to account for it. I know quite well that it was on the hand that I put under her waist—a little above the waist, just in the middle of her back.'

'But it would have been seen afterwards.'

'On the dark red silk she wore? Not if there was very little of it. The doctor never thought of looking for such a wound. Why should he? He had not the slightest reason for suspecting that the poor girl had been murdered.'

'Murdered?'

Margaret looked hard at Griggs, and then she suddenly shuddered from head to foot. She had never before had such a sensation; it was like a shock from an electric current at the instant when the contact is made, not strong enough to hurt, but yet very disagreeable. She felt it at the moment when her mind connected what Griggs was saying with the dying girl's last words, 'he did it'; and with little Ida's look of horror when she had watched Mr. Van Torp's lips while he was talking to himself on the boat-deck of the *Leofric*; and again, with the physical fear of the man that always came over her when she had been near him for a little while. When she spoke to Griggs again the tone of her voice had changed.

'Please tell me how it could have been done,' she said.

'Easily enough. A steel bodkin six or seven inches long, or even a strong hat-pin. It would be only a question of strength.'

Margaret remembered Mr. Van Torp's coarse hands, and shuddered again.

'How awful!' she exclaimed.

'One would bleed to death internally before long,' Griggs said.

'Are you sure?'

'Yes. That is the reason why the three-cornered blade for duelling swords was introduced in France thirty years ago. Before that, men often fought with ordinary foils filed to a point, and there were many deaths from internal hemorrhage.'

'What odd things you always know! That would be just like being run through with a bodkin, then?'

'Very much the same.'

'But it would have been found out afterwards,' Margaret said, 'and the papers would have been full of it.'

'That does not follow,' Griggs answered. 'The girl was an only child, and her mother had been divorced and married again. She lived alone with her father, and he probably was told the truth. But Isidore Bamberger is not the man to spread out his troubles before the public in the newspapers. On the contrary, if he found out that his daughter had been killed—supposing that she was—he probably made up his mind at once that the world should not know it till he had caught the murderer. So he sent for the best detective in America, put the matter in his hands, and inserted a notice of his daughter's death that agreed with what the doctor had said. That would be the detective's advice, I'm sure, and probably Van Torp approved of it.'

'Mr. Van Torp? Do you think he was told about it? Why?'

'First, because Bamberger is Van Torp's banker, broker, figure-head, and general representative on earth,' answered Griggs. 'Secondly, because Van Torp was engaged to marry the girl.'

'The engagement was broken off,' Margaret said.

'How do you know that?' asked Griggs quickly.

'Mr. Van Torp told me, on the steamer. They had broken it off that very day, and were going to let it be known the next morning. He told me so, that afternoon when I walked with him.'

'Really!'

Griggs was a little surprised, but as he did not connect Van Torp with the possibility that Miss Bamberger had been murdered, his thoughts did not dwell on the broken engagement.

'Why don't you try to find out the truth?' Margaret asked rather anxiously. 'You know so many people everywhere—you have so much experience.'

'I never had much taste for detective work,' answered the literary man, 'and besides, this is none of my business. But Bamberger and Van Torp are probably both of them aware by this time that I found the girl and carried her to the manager's room, and when they are ready to ask me what I know, or what I remember, the detective they are employing will suddenly appear to me in the shape of a new acquaintance in some out-of-the-way place, who will go to work scientifically to make me talk to him. He will very likely have a little theory of his own, to the effect that since it was I who brought Miss Bamberger to Schreiermeyer's room, it was probably I who killed her, for some mysterious reason!'

'Shall you tell him about the drop of blood on your hand?'

'Without the slightest hesitation. But not until I am asked, and I shall be very glad if you will not speak of it.'

'I won't,' Margaret said; 'but I wonder why you have told me if you mean to keep it a secret!'

The veteran man of letters turned his sad grey eyes to hers, while his lips smiled.

'The world is not all bad,' he said. 'All men are not liars, and all women do not betray confidence.'

'It's very good to hear a man like you say that,' Margaret answered. 'It means something.'

'Yes,' assented Griggs thoughtfully. 'It means a great deal to me to be sure of it, now that most of my life is lived.'

'Were you unhappy when you were young?'

She asked the question as a woman sometimes does who feels herself strongly drawn to a man much older than she. Griggs did not answer at once, and when he spoke his voice was unusually grave, and his eyes looked far away.

'A great misfortune happened to me,' he said. 'A great misfortune,' he repeated slowly, after a pause, and his tone and look told Margaret how great that calamity had been better than a score of big words.

'Forgive me,' Margaret said softly; 'I should have known.'

'No,' Griggs answered after a moment. 'You could not have known. It happened very long ago, perhaps ten years before you were born.'

Again he turned his sad grey eyes to hers, but no smile lingered now about the rather stern mouth. The two looked at each other quietly for five or six seconds, and that may seem a long time. When Margaret turned away from the elderly man's more enduring gaze, both felt that there was a bond of sympathy between them which neither had quite acknowledged till then. There was silence after that, and Margaret looked out of the window, while her hand unconsciously played with the book on her knee, lifting the cover a little and letting it fall again and again.

Suddenly she turned to Griggs once more and held the book out to him with a smile.

'I'm not an autograph-hunter,' she said, 'but will you write something on the fly-leaf? Just a word or two, without your name, if you like. Do you think I'm very sentimental?'

She smiled again, and he took the book from her and produced a pencil.

'It's a book I shall not throw away,' she went on, 'because the man who wrote it is a great friend of mine, and I have everything he has ever written. So, as I shall keep it, I want it to remind me that you and I grew to know each other better on this voyage.'

It occurred to the veteran that while this was complimentary to himself it was not altogether promising for Lushington, who was the old friend in question. A woman who loves a man does not usually ask another to write a line in that man's book. Griggs set the point of the pencil on the fly-leaf as if he were going to write; but then he hesitated, looked up, glanced at Margaret, and at last leaned back in the seat, as if in deep thought.

'I didn't mean to give you so much trouble,' Margaret said, still smiling. 'I thought it must be so easy for a famous author like you to write half-a-dozen words!'

'A "sentiment" you mean!' Griggs laughed rather contemptuously, and then was grave again.

'No!' Margaret said, a little disappointed. 'You did not understand me. Don't write anything at all. Give me back the book.'

She held out her hand for it; but as if he had just made up his mind, he put his pencil to the paper again, and wrote four words in a small clear hand. She leaned forwards a little to see what he was writing.

'You know enough Latin to read that,' he said, as he gave the book back to her.

She read the words aloud, with a puzzled expression.

'"Credo in resurrectionem mortuorum."' She looked at him for some explanation.

'Yes,' he said, answering her unspoken question. '"I believe in the resurrection of the dead."'

'It means something especial to you—is that it?'

'Yes.' His eyes were very sad again as they met hers.

'My voice?' she asked. 'Some one—who sang like me? Who died?'

'Long before you were born,' he answered gently.

There was another little pause before she spoke again, for she was touched.

'Thank you,' she said. 'Thank you for writing that.'

CHAPTER V

Mr. Van Torp arrived in London alone, with one small valise, for he had sent his man with his luggage to the place in Derbyshire. At Euston a porter got him a hansom, and he bargained with the cabman to take him and his valise to the Temple for eighteenpence, a sum which, he explained, allowed sixpence for the valise, as the distance could not by any means be made out to be more than two miles.

Such close economy was to be expected from a millionaire, travelling incognito; what was more surprising was that, when the cab stopped before a door in Hare Court and Mr. Van Torp received his valise from the roof of the vehicle, he gave the man half-a-crown, and said it was 'all right.'

'Now, my man,' he observed, 'you've not only got an extra shilling, to which you had no claim whatever, but you've had the pleasure of a surprise which you could not have bought for that money.'

The cabman grinned as he touched his hat and drove away, and Mr. Van Torp took his valise in one hand and his umbrella in the other and went up the dark stairs. He went up four flights without stopping to take breath, and without so much as glancing at any of the names painted in white letters on the small black boards beside the doors on the right and left of each landing.

The fourth floor was the last, and though the name on the left had evidently been there a number of years, for the white lettering was of the tint of a yellow fog, it was still quite clear and legible.

MR.I. BAMBERGER.

That was the name, but the millionaire did not look at it any more than he had looked at the others lower down. He knew them all by heart. He dropped his valise, took a small key from his pocket, opened the door, picked up his valise again, and, as neither hand was free, he shut the door with his heel as he passed in, and it slammed behind him, sending dismal echoes down the empty staircase.

The entry was almost quite dark, for it was past six o'clock in the afternoon, late in March, and the sky was overcast; but there was still light enough to see in the large room on the left into which Mr. Van Torp carried his things.

It was a dingy place, poorly furnished, but some one had dusted the table, the mantelpiece, and the small bookcase, and the fire was laid in the grate, while a bright copper kettle stood on a movable hob. Mr. Van Torp struck a match and lighted the kindling before he took off his overcoat, and in a few minutes a cheerful blaze dispelled the gathering gloom. He went to a small old-fashioned cupboard in a corner and brought from it a chipped cup and saucer, a brown teapot, and a cheap japanned tea-caddy, all of which he set on the table; and as soon as the fire burned brightly, he pushed the movable hob round with his foot till the kettle was over the flame of the coals. Then he took off his overcoat and sat down in the shabby easy-chair by the hearth, to wait till the water boiled.

His proceedings, his manner, and his expression would have surprised the people who had been his fellow-passengers on the *Leofric*, and who imagined Mr. Van Torp driving to an Olympian mansion, somewhere between Constitution Hill and Sloane Square, to be received at his own door by gravely obsequious footmen in plush, and to drink Imperial Chinese tea from cups of Old Saxe, or Bleu du Roi, or Capo di Monte.

Paul Griggs, having tea and a pipe in a quiet little hotel in Clarges Street, would have been much surprised if he could have seen Rufus Van Torp lighting a fire for himself in that dingy room in Hare Court. Madame Margarita da Cordova, waiting for an expected visitor in her own sitting-room, in her own pretty house in Norfolk Crescent, would have been very much surprised indeed. The sight would have plunged her into even greater uncertainty as to the man's real character, and it is not unlikely that she would have taken his mysterious retreat to be another link in the chain of evidence against him which already seemed so convincing. She might naturally have wondered, too, what he had felt when he had seen that board beside the door, and she could hardly have believed that he had gone in without so much as glancing at the yellowish letters that formed the name of Bamberger.

But he seemed quite at home where he was, and not at all uncomfortable as he sat before the fire, watching the spout of the kettle, his elbows on the arms of the easy-chair and his hands raised before him, with the finger-tips pressed against each other, in the attitude which, with most men, means that they are considering the two sides of a question that is interesting without being very important.

Perhaps a thoughtful observer would have noticed at once that there had been no letters waiting for him when he had arrived, and would have inferred either that he did not mean to stay at the rooms twenty-four hours, or that, if he did, he had not chosen to let any one know where he was.

Presently it occurred to him that there was no longer any light in the room except from the fire, and he rose and lit the gas. The incandescent light sent a raw glare into the farthest corners of the large room, and just then a tiny wreath of white steam issued from the spout of the kettle. This did not escape Mr. Van Torp's watchful eye, but instead of making tea at once he looked at his watch, after which he crossed the room to the window and stood thoughtfully gazing through the panes at the fast disappearing outlines of the roofs and chimney-pots which made up the view when there was daylight outside. He did not pull down the shade before he turned back to the fire, perhaps because no one could possibly look in.

But he poured a little hot water into the teapot, to scald it, and went to the cupboard and got another cup and saucer, and an old tobacco-tin of which the dingy label was half torn off, and which betrayed by a rattling noise that it contained lumps of sugar. The imaginary thoughtful observer already mentioned would have inferred from all this that Mr. Van Torp had resolved to put off making tea until some one came to share it with him, and that the some one might take sugar, though he himself did not; and further, as it was extremely improbable, on the face of it, that an afternoon visitor should look in by a mere chance, in the hope of finding some one in Mr. Isidore Bamberger's usually deserted rooms, on the fourth floor of a dark building in Hare Court, the observer would suppose that Mr. Van Torp was expecting some one to come and see him just at that hour, though he had only landed in Liverpool that day, and would have been still at sea if the weather had been rough or foggy.

All this might have still further interested Paul Griggs, and would certainly have seemed suspicious to Margaret, if she could have known about it.

Five minutes passed, and ten, and the kettle was boiling furiously, and sending out a long jet of steam over the not very shapely toes of Mr. Van Torp's boots, as he leaned back with his feet on the fender. He looked at his watch again and apparently gave up the idea of waiting any longer, for he rose and poured out the hot water from the teapot into one of the cups, as a preparatory measure, and took off the lid to put in the tea. But just as he had opened the caddy, he paused and listened. The door of the room leading to the entry was ajar, and as he stood by the table he had heard footsteps on the stairs, still far down, but mounting steadily.

He went to the outer door and listened. There was no doubt that somebody was coming up; any one not deaf could have heard the sound. It was more strange that Mr. Van Torp should recognise the step, for the rooms on the other side of the landing were occupied, and a stranger would have thought it quite possible that the person who was coming up should be going there. But Mr. Van Torp evidently knew better, for he opened his door noiselessly and stood waiting to receive the visitor. The staircase below was dimly lighted by gas, but there was none at the upper landing, and in a few seconds a dark form appeared, casting a tall shadow upwards against the dingy white paint of the wall. The figure mounted steadily and came directly to the open door—a lady in a long black cloak that quite hid her dress. She wore no hat, but her head was altogether covered by one of those things which are neither hoods nor mantillas nor veils, but which serve women for any of the three, according to weather and circumstances. The peculiarity of the one the lady wore was that it cast a deep shadow over her face.

'Come in,' said Mr. Van Torp, withdrawing into the entry to make way.

She entered and went on directly to the sitting-room, while he shut the outer door. Then he followed her, and shut the second door behind him. She was standing before the fire spreading her gloved hands to the blaze, as if she were cold. The gloves were white, and they fitted very perfectly. As he came near, she turned and held out one hand.

'All right?' he inquired, shaking it heartily, as if it had been a man's.

A sweet low voice answered him.

'Yes—all right,' it said, as if nothing could ever be wrong with its possessor. 'But you?' it asked directly afterwards, in a tone of sympathetic anxiety.

'I? Oh—well—' Mr. Van Torp's incomplete answer might have meant anything, except that he too was 'all right.'

'Yes,' said the lady gravely. 'I read the telegram the next day. Did you get my cable? I did not think you would sail.'

'Yes, I got your cable. Thank you. Well—I did sail, you see. Take off your things. The water's boiling and we'll have tea in a minute.'

The lady undid the fastening at her throat so that the fur-lined cloak opened and slipped a little on her white shoulders. She held it in place with one hand, and with the other she carefully turned back the lace hood from her face, so as not to disarrange her hair. Mr. Van Torp was making tea, and he looked up at her over the teapot.

'I dressed for dinner,' she said, explaining.

'Well,' said Mr. Van Torp, looking at her, 'I should think you did!'

There was real admiration in his tone, though it was distinctly reluctant.

'I thought it would save half an hour and give us more time together,' said the lady simply.

She sat down in the shabby easy-chair, and as she did so the cloak slipped and lay about her waist, and she gathered one side of it over her knees. Her gown was of black velvet, without so much as a bit of lace, except at the sleeves, and the only ornament she wore was a short string of very perfect pearls clasped round her handsome young throat.

She was handsome, to say the least. If tired ghosts of departed barristers were haunting the dingy room in Hare Court that night, they must have blinked and quivered for sheer pleasure at what they saw, for Mr. Van Torp's visitor was a very fine creature to look at; and if ghosts can hear, they heard that her voice was sweet and low, like an evening breeze and flowing water in a garden, even in the Garden of Eden.

She was handsome, and she was young; and above all she had the freshness, the uncontaminated bloom, the subdued brilliancy of nature's most perfect growing things. It was in the deep clear eyes, in the satin sheen of her bare shoulders under the sordid gaslight; it was in the strong smooth lips, delicately shaded from salmon colour to the faintest peach-blossom; it was in the firm oval of her face, in the well-modelled ear, the straight throat and the curving neck; it was in her graceful attitude; it was everywhere. 'No doubt,' the ghosts might have said, 'there are more beautiful women in England than this one, but surely there is none more like a thoroughbred and a Derby winner!'

'You take sugar, don't you?' asked Mr. Van Torp, having got the lid off the old tobacco-tin with some difficulty, for it had developed an inclination to rust since it had last been moved.

'One lump, please,' said the thoroughbred, looking at the fire.

'I thought I remembered,' observed the millionaire. 'The tea's good,' he added, 'and you'll have to excuse the cup. And there's no cream.'

'I'll excuse anything,' said the lady, 'I'm so glad to be here!'

'Well, I'm glad to see you too,' said Mr. Van Torp, giving her the cup. 'Crackers? I'll see if there're any in the cupboard. I forgot.'

He went to the corner again and found a small tin of biscuits, which he opened and examined under gaslight.

'Mouldy,' he observed. 'Weevils in them, too. Sorry. Does it matter much?'

'Nothing matters,' answered the lady, sweet and low. 'But why do you put them away if they are bad? It would be better to burn them and be done with it.'

He was taking the box back to the cupboard.

'I suppose you're right,' he said reluctantly. 'But it always seems wicked to burn bread, doesn't it?'

'Not when it's weevilly,' replied the thoroughbred, after sipping the hot tea.

He emptied the contents of the tin upon the coal fire, and the room presently began to smell of mouldy toast.

'Besides,' he said, 'it's cruel to burn weevils, I suppose. If I'd thought of that, I'd have left them alone. It's too late now. They're done for, poor beasts! I'm sorry. I don't like to kill things.'

He stared thoughtfully at the already charred remains of the holocaust, and shook his head a little. The lady sipped her tea and looked at him quietly, perhaps affectionately, but he did not see her.

'You think I'm rather silly sometimes, don't you?' he asked, still gazing at the fire.

'No,' she answered at once. 'It's never silly to be kind, even to weevils.'

'Thank you for thinking so,' said Mr. Van Torp, in an oddly humble tone, and he began to drink his own tea.

If Margaret Donne could have suddenly found herself perched among the chimney-pots on the opposite roof, and if she had then looked at his face through the window, she would have wondered why she had ever felt a perfectly irrational terror of him. It was quite plain that the lady in black velvet had no such impression.

'You need not be so meek,' she said, smiling.

She did not laugh often, but sometimes there was a ripple in her fresh voice that would turn a man's head. Mr. Van Torp looked at her in a rather dull way.

'I believe I feel meek when I'm with you. Especially just now.'

He swallowed the rest of his tea at a gulp, set the cup on the table, and folded his hands loosely together, his elbows resting on his knees; in this attitude he leaned forward and looked at the burning coals. Again his companion watched his hard face with affectionate interest.

'Tell me just how it happened,' she said. 'I mean, if it will help you at all to talk about it.'

'Yes. You always help me,' he answered, and then paused. 'I think I should like to tell you the whole thing,' he added after an instant. 'Somehow, I never tell anybody much about myself.'

'I know.'

She bent her handsome head in assent. Just then it would have been very hard to guess what the relations were between the oddly assorted pair, as they sat a little apart from each other before the grate. Mr. Van Torp was silent now, as if he were making up his mind how to begin.

In the pause, the lady quietly held out her hand towards him. He saw without turning further, and he stretched out his own. She took it gently, and then, without warning, she leaned very far forward, bent over it and touched it with her lips. He started and drew it back hastily. It was as if the leaf of a flower had settled upon it, and had hovered an instant, and fluttered away in a breath of soft air.

'Please don't!' he cried, almost roughly. 'There's nothing to thank me for. I've often told you so.'

But the lady was already leaning back in the old easy-chair again as if she had done nothing at all unusual.

'It wasn't for myself,' she said. 'It was for all the others, who will never know.'

'Well, I'd rather not,' he answered. 'It's not worth all that. Now, see here! I'm going to tell you as near as I can what happened, and when you know you can make up your mind. You never saw but one side of me anyhow, but you've got to see the other sooner or later. No, I know what you're going to say—all that about a dual nature, and Jekyll and Hyde, and all the rest of it. That may be true for nervous people, but I'm not nervous. Not at all. I never was. What I know is, there are two sides to everybody, and one's always the business side. The other may be anything. Sometimes it's good, sometimes it's bad. Sometimes it cares for a woman, sometimes it's a collector of art things, Babylonian glass, and Etruscan toys and prehistoric dolls. It may gamble, or drink, or teach a Sunday school, or read Dante, or shoot, or fish, or anything that's of no use. But one side's always the business side. That's certain.'

Mr. Van Torp paused, and looked at his companion's empty cup. Seeing that he was going to get up in order to give her more, she herself rose quickly and did it for herself. He sat still and watched her, probably because the business side of his nature judged that he could be of no use. The fur-lined cloak was now lying in the easy-chair, and there was nothing to break the sweeping lines of the black velvet from her dazzling shoulders to her waist, to her knee, to her feet. Mr. Van Torp watched her in silence, till she sat down again.

'You know me well enough to understand that,' he said, going on. 'My outside's my business side, and that's what matters most. Now the plain truth is this. My engagement to Miss Bamberger was just a business affair. Bamberger thought of it first, and suggested it to me, and he asked her if she'd mind being engaged to me for a few weeks; and she said she wouldn't provided she wasn't expected to marry me. That was fair and square, anyway, on both sides. Wasn't it?'

'It depends on why you did it,' said the lady, going to the point directly.

'That was the business side,' answered her companion. 'You see, a big thing like the Nickel Trust always has a lot of enemies, besides a heap of people who want to get some of it cheap. This time they put their heads together and got up one of the usual stories. You see, Isidore H. Bamberger is the president and I only appear as a director, though most of it's mine. So they got up a story that he was operating on his own account to get behind me, and that we were going to quarrel over it, and there was going to be a slump, and people began to believe it. It wasn't any use talking to the papers. We soon found that out. Sometimes the public won't believe anything it's told, and sometimes it swallows faster than you can feed to it. I don't know why, though I've had a pretty long experience, but I generally do know which state it's in. I feel it. That's what's called business ability. It's like fishing. Any old fisherman can judge in half an hour whether the fish are going to bite all day or not. If he's wrong once, he'll be right a hundred times. Well, I felt talking was no good, and so did Bamberger, and the shares began to go down before the storm. If the big slump had come there'd have been a heap of money lost. I don't say we didn't let the shares drop a couple of points further than they needed to, and Bamberger bought any of it that happened to be lying around, and the more he bought the quicker it wanted to go down, because people said there was going to be trouble and an investigation. But if we'd gone on, lots of people would have been ruined, and yet we didn't just see how to stop it sharp, till Bamberger started his scheme. Do you understand all that?'

The lady nodded gravely.

'You make it clear,' she said.

'Well, I thought it was a good scheme,' continued her companion, 'and as the girl said she didn't mind, we told we were engaged. That settled things pretty quick. The shares went up again in forty-eight hours, and as we'd bought for cash we made the points, and the other people were short and lost. But when everything was all right again we got tired of being engaged, Miss Bamberger and I; and besides, there was a young fellow she'd a fancy for, and he kept writing to her that he'd kill himself, and that made her nervous, you see, and she said if it went on another day she knew she'd have appendicitis or something. So we were going to announce that the engagement was broken. And the very night before—'

He paused. Not a muscle of the hard face moved, there was not a change in the expression of the tremendous mouth, there was not a tremor in the tone; but the man kept his eyes steadily on the fire.

'Oh, well, she's dead now, poor thing,' he said presently. 'And that's what I wanted to tell you. I suppose it's not a very pretty story, is it? But I'll tell you one thing. Though we made a little by the turn of the market, we saved a heap of small fry from losing all they'd put in. If we'd let the slump come and then bought we should have made a pile; but then we might have had difficulty in getting the stock up to anywhere near par again for some time.'

'Besides,' said the lady quietly, 'you would not have ruined all those little people if you could help it.'

'You think I wouldn't?' He turned his eyes to her now.

'I'm sure you would not,' said the lady with perfect confidence.

'I don't know, I'm sure,' answered Mr. Van Torp in a doubtful tone. 'Perhaps I wouldn't. But it would only have been business if I had. It's not as if Bamberger and I had started a story on purpose about our quarrelling in order to make things go down. I draw the line there. That's downright dishonest, I call it. But if we'd just let things slide and taken advantage of what happened, it would only have been business after all. Except for that doubt about getting back to par,' he added, as an afterthought. 'But then I should have felt whether it was safe or not.'

'Then why did you not let things slide, as you call it?'

'I don't know, I'm sure. Maybe I was soft-hearted. We don't always know why we do things in business. There's a great deal more in the weather where big money is moving than you might think. For instance, there was never a great revolution in winter. But as for making people lose their money, those who can't keep it ought not to have it. They're a danger to society, and half the time it's they who upset the market by acting like lunatics. They get a lot of sentimental pity sometimes, those people; but after all, if they didn't try to cut in without capital, and play the game without knowing the rules, business would be much steadier and there would be fewer panics. They're the people who get frightened and run, not we. The fact is, they ought never to have been there. That's why I believe in big things myself.'

He paused, having apparently reached the end of his subject.

'Were you with the poor girl when she died?' asked the lady presently.

'No. She'd dined with a party and was in their box, and they were the last people who saw her. You read about the explosion. She bolted from the box in the dark, I was told, and as she couldn't be found afterwards they concluded she had rushed out and taken a cab home. It seemed natural, I suppose.'

'Who found her at last?'

'A man called Griggs—the author, you know. He carried her to the manager's room, still alive. They got a doctor, and as she wanted to see a woman, they sent for Cordova, the singer, from her dressing-room, and the girl died in her arms. They said it was heart failure, from shock.'

'It was very sad.'

'I'm sorry for poor Bamberger,' said Mr. Van Torp thoughtfully. 'She was his only child, and he doted on her. I never saw a man so cut up as he looked. I wanted to stay, but he said the mere sight of me drove him crazy, poor fellow, and as I had business over here and my passage was taken, I just sailed. Sometimes the kindest thing one can do is to get out. So I did. But I'm very sorry for him. I wish I could do anything to make it easier for him. It was nobody's fault, I suppose, though I do think the people she was with might have prevented her from rushing out in the dark.'

'They were frightened themselves. How could any one be blamed for her death?'

'Exactly. But if any one could be made responsible, I know Bamberger would do for him in some way. He's a resentful sort of man if any one does him an injury. Blood for blood is Bamberger's motto, every time. One thing I'm sure of. He'll run down whoever was responsible for that explosion, and he'll do for him, whoever he is, if it costs one million to get a conviction. I wouldn't like to be the fellow!'

'I can understand wishing to be revenged for the death of one's only child,' said the lady thoughtfully. 'Cannot you?'

The American turned his hard face to her.

'Yes,' he said, 'I can. It's only human, after all.'

She sighed and looked into the fire. She was married, but she was childless, and that was a constant regret to her. Mr. Van Torp knew it and understood.

'To change the subject,' he said cheerfully, 'I suppose you need money, don't you?'

'Oh yes! Indeed I do!'

Her momentary sadness had already disappeared, and there was almost a ripple in her tone again as she answered.

'How much?' asked the millionaire smiling.

She shook her head and smiled too; and as she met his eyes she settled herself and leaned far back in the shabby easy-chair. She was wonderfully graceful and good to look at in her easy attitude.

'I'm afraid to tell you how much!' She shook her head again, as she answered.

'Well,' said Mr. Van Torp in an encouraging tone, 'I've brought some cash in my pocket, and if it isn't enough I'll get you some more to-morrow. But I won't give you a cheque. It's too compromising. I thought of that before I left New York, so I brought some English notes from there.'

'How thoughtful you always are for me!'

'It's not much to do for a woman one likes. But I'm sorry if I've brought too little. Here it is, anyway.'

He produced a large and well-worn pocket-book, and took from it a small envelope, which he handed to her.

'Tell me how much more you'll need,' he said, 'and I'll give it to you to-morrow. I'll put the notes between the pages of a new book and leave it at your door. He wouldn't open a package that was addressed to you from a bookseller's, would he?'

'No,' answered the lady, her expression changing a little, 'I think he draws the line at the bookseller.'

'You see, this was meant for you,' said Mr. Van Torp. 'There are your initials on it.'

She glanced at the envelope, and saw that it was marked in pencil with the letters M.L. in one corner.

'Thank you,' she said, but she did not open it.

'You'd better count the notes,' suggested the millionaire. 'I'm open to making mistakes myself.'

The lady took from the envelope a thin flat package of new Bank of England notes, folded together in four. Without separating them she glanced carelessly at the first, which was for a hundred pounds, and then counted the others by the edges. She counted four after the first, and Mr. Van Torp watched her face with evident amusement.

'You need more than that, don't you?' he asked, when she had finished.

'A little more, perhaps,' she said quietly, though she could not quite conceal her disappointment, as she folded the notes and slipped them into the envelope again. 'But I shall try to make this last. Thank you very much.'

'I like you,' said Mr. Van Torp. 'You're the real thing. They'd call you a chief's daughter in the South Seas. But I'm not so mean as all that. I only thought you might need a little cash at once. That's all.'

A loud knocking at the outer door prevented the lady from answering.

She looked at Mr. Van Torp in surprise.

'What's that?' she asked, rather anxiously.

'I don't know,' he answered. 'He couldn't guess that you were here, could he?'

'Oh no! That's quite out of the question!'

'Then I'll open the door,' said the millionaire, and he left the sitting-room.

The lady had not risen, and she still leaned back in her seat. She idly tapped the knuckles of her gloved hand with the small envelope.

The knocking was repeated, she heard the outer door opened, and the sound of voices followed directly.

'Oh!' Mr. Van Torp exclaimed in a tone of contemptuous surprise, 'it's you, is it? Well, I'm busy just now. I can't see you till to-morrow.'

'My business will not keep till to-morrow,' answered an oily voice in a slightly foreign accent.

At the very first syllables the lady rose quickly to her feet, and resting one hand on the table she leant forward in the direction of the door, with an expression that was at once eager and anxious, and yet quite fearless.

'What you call your business is going to wait my convenience,' said Mr. Van Torp. 'You'll find me here to-morrow morning until eleven o'clock.'

From the sounds the lady judged that the American now attempted to shut the door in his visitor's face, but that he was hindered and that a scuffle followed.

'Hold him!' cried the oily voice in a tone of command. 'Bring him in! Lock the door!'

It was clear enough that the visitor had not come alone, and that Mr. Van Torp had been overpowered. The lady bit her salmon-coloured lip angrily and contemptuously.

A moment later a tall heavily-built man with thick fair hair, a long moustache, and shifty blue eyes, rushed into the room and did not stop till there was only the small table between him and the lady.

'I've caught you! What have you to say?' he asked.

'To you? Nothing!'

She deliberately turned her back on her husband, rested one elbow on the mantelpiece and set one foot upon the low fender, drawing up her velvet gown over her instep. But a moment later she heard other footsteps in the room, and turned her head to see Mr. Van Torp enter the room between two big men who were evidently ex-policemen. The millionaire, having failed to shut the door in the face of the three men, had been too wise to attempt any further resistance.

The fair man glanced down at the table and saw the envelope with his wife's initials lying beside the tea things. She had dropped it there when she had risen to her feet at the sound of his voice. He snatched it away as soon as he saw the pencilled letters on it, and in a moment he had taken out the notes and was looking over them.

'I should like you to remember this, please,' he said, addressing the two men who had accompanied him. 'This envelope is addressed to my wife, under her initials, in the handwriting of Mr. Van Torp. Am I right in taking it for your handwriting?' he inquired, in a disagreeably polite tone, and turning towards the millionaire.

'You are,' answered the American, in a perfectly colourless voice and without moving a muscle. 'That's my writing.'

'And this envelope,' continued the husband, holding up the notes before the men, 'contains notes to the amount of four thousand one hundred pounds.'

'Five hundred pounds, you mean,' said the lady coldly.

'See for yourself!' retorted the fair man, raising his eyebrows and holding out the notes.

'That's correct,' said Mr. Van Torp, smiling and looking at the lady. 'Four thousand one hundred. Only the first one was for a hundred, and the rest were thousands. I meant it for a little surprise, you see.'

'Oh, how kind! How dear and kind!' cried the lady gratefully, and with amazing disregard of her husband's presence.

The two ex-policemen had not expected anything so interesting as this, and their expressions were worthy of study. They had been engaged, through a private agency, to assist and support an injured husband, and afterwards to appear as witnesses of a vulgar clandestine meeting, as they supposed. It was not the first time they had been employed on such business, but they did not remember ever having had to deal with two persons who exhibited such hardened indifference; and though the incident of the notes was not new to them, they had never been in a case where the amount of cash received by the lady at one time was so very large.

'It is needless,' said the fair man, addressing them both, 'to ask what this money was for.'

'Yes,' said Mr. Van Torp coolly. 'You needn't bother. But I'll call your attention to the fact that the notes are not yours, and that I'd like to see them put back into that envelope and laid on that table before you go. You broke into my house by force anyhow. If you take valuables away with you, which you found here, it's burglary in England, whatever it may be in your country; and if you don't know it, these two professional gentlemen do. So you just do as I tell you, if you want to keep out of gaol.'

The fair man had shown a too evident intention of slipping the envelope into his own pocket, doubtless to be produced in evidence, but Mr. Van Torp's final argument seemed convincing.

'I have not the smallest intention of depriving my wife of the price of my honour, sir. Indeed, I am rather flattered to find that you both value it so highly.'

Mr. Van Torp's hard face grew harder, and a very singular light came into his eyes. He moved forwards till he was close to the fair man.

'None of that!' he said authoritatively. 'If you say another word against your wife in my hearing I'll make it the last you ever said to anybody. Now you'd better be gone before I telephone for the police. Do you understand?'

The two ex-policemen employed by a private agency thought the case was becoming more and more interesting; but at the same time they were made vaguely nervous by Mr. Van Torp's attitude.

'I think you are threatening me,' said the fair man, drawing back a step, and leaving the envelope on the table.

'No,' answered his adversary, 'I'm warning you off my premises, and if you don't go pretty soon I'll telephone for the police. Is that a threat?'

The last question was addressed to the two men.

'No, sir,' answered one of them.

'It would hardly be to your advantage to have more witnesses of my wife's presence here,' observed the fair man coldly, 'but as I intend to take her home we may as well go at once. Come, Maud! The carriage is waiting.'

The lady, whose name was now spoken for the first time since she had entered Mr. Van Torp's lodging, had not moved from the fireplace since she had taken up her position there. Women are as clever as Napoleon or Julius Caesar in selecting strong positions when there is to be an encounter, and a fireplace, with a solid mantelpiece to lean against, to strike, to cry upon or to cling to, is one of the strongest. The enemy is thus reduced to prowling about the room and handling knick-knacks while he talks, or smashing them if he is of a violent disposition.

The lady now leant back against the dingy marble shelf and laid one white-gloved arm along it, in an attitude that was positively regal. Her right hand might appropriately have been toying with the orb of empire on the mantelpiece, and her left, which hung down beside her, might have loosely held the sceptre. Mr. Van Torp, who often bought large pictures, was reminded of one recently offered to him in America, representing an empress. He would have bought the portrait if the dealer could have remembered which empress it represented, but the fact that he could not had seemed suspicious to Mr. Van Torp. It was clearly the man's business to know empresses by sight.

From her commanding position the Lady Maud refused her husband's invitation to go home with him.

'I shall certainly not go with you,' she said. 'Besides, I'm dining early at the Turkish Embassy and we are going to the play. You need not wait for me. I'll take care of myself this evening, thank you.'

'This is monstrous!' cried the fair man, and with a peculiarly un-English gesture he thrust his hand into his thick hair.

The foreigner in despair has always amused the genuine Anglo-Saxon. Lady Maud's lip did not curl contemptuously now, she did not raise her eyebrows, nor did her eyes flash with scorn. On the contrary, she smiled quite frankly, and the sweet ripple was in her voice, the ripple that drove some men almost crazy.

'You needn't make such a fuss,' she said. 'It's quite absurd, you know. Mr. Van Torp is an old friend of mine, and you have known him ever so long, and he is a man of business. You are, are you not?' she asked, looking to the American for assent.

'I'm generally thought to be that,' he answered.

'Very well. I came here, to Mr. Van Torp's rooms in the Temple, before going to dinner, because I wished to see him about a matter of business, in what is a place of business. It's all ridiculous nonsense to talk about having caught me—and worse. That money is for a charity, and I am going to take it before your eyes, and thank Mr. Van Torp for being so splendidly generous. Now go, and take those persons with you, and let me hear no more of this!'

Thereupon Lady Maud came forward from the mantelpiece and deliberately took from the table the envelope which contained four thousand one hundred pounds in new Bank of England notes; and she put it into the bosom of her gown, and smiled pleasantly at her husband.

Mr. Van Torp watched her with genuine admiration, and when she looked at him and nodded her thanks again, he unconsciously smiled too, and answered by a nod of approval.

The fair-haired foreign gentleman turned to his two ex-policemen with considerable dignity.

'You have heard and seen,' he said impressively. 'I shall expect you to remember all this when you are in the witness-box. Let us go.' He made a sweeping bow to his wife and Mr. Van Torp. 'I wish you an agreeable evening,' he said.

Thereupon he marched out of the room, followed by his men, who each made an awkward bow at nothing in particular before going out. Mr. Van Torp followed them at some distance towards the outer door, judging that as they had forced their way in they could probably find their way out. He did not even go to the outer threshold, for the last of the three shut the door behind him.

When the millionaire came back Lady Maud was seated in the easy-chair, leaning forward and looking thoughtfully into the fire. Assuredly no one would have suspected from her composed face that anything unusual had happened. She glanced at her friend when he came in, but did not speak, and he began to walk up and down on the other side of the table, with his hands behind him.

'You've got pretty good nerves,' he said presently.

'Yes,' answered Lady Maud, still watching the coals, 'they really are rather good.'

A long silence followed, during which she did not move and Mr. Van Torp steadily paced the floor.

'I didn't tell a fib, either,' she said at last. 'It's charity, in its way.'

'Certainly,' assented her friend. 'What isn't either purchase-money or interest, or taxes, or a bribe, or a loan, or a premium, or a present, or blackmail, must be charity, because it must be something, and it isn't anything else you can name.'

'A present may be a charity,' said Lady Maud, still thoughtful.

'Yes,' answered Mr. Van Torp. 'It may be, but it isn't always.'

He walked twice the length of the room before he spoke again.

'Do you think it's really to be war this time?' he asked, stopping beside the table. 'Because if it is, I'll see a lawyer before I go to Derbyshire.'

Lady Maud looked up with a bright smile. Clearly she had been thinking of something compared with which the divorce court was a delightful contrast.

'I don't know,' she answered. 'It must come sooner or later, because he wants to be free to marry that woman, and as he has not the courage to cut my throat, he must divorce me—if he can!'

'I've sometimes thought he might take the shorter way,' said Van Torp.

'He?' Lady Maud almost laughed, but her companion looked grave.

'There's a thing called homicidal mania,' he said. 'Didn't he shoot a boy in Russia a year ago?'

'A young man—one of the beaters. But that was an accident.'

'I'm not so sure. How about that poor dog at the Theobalds' last September?'

'He thought the creature was mad,' Lady Maud explained.

'He knows as well as you do that there's no rabies in the British Isles,' objected Mr. Van Torp. 'Count Leven never liked that dog for some reason, and he shot him the first time he got a chance. He's always killing things. Some day he'll kill you, I'm afraid.'

'I don't think so,' answered the lady carelessly. 'If he does, I hope he'll do it neatly! I should hate to be maimed or mangled.'

'Do you know it makes me uncomfortable to hear you talk like that? I wish you wouldn't! You can't deny that your husband's half a lunatic, anyway. He was behaving like one here only a quarter of an hour ago, and it's no use denying it.'

'But I'm not denying anything!'

'No, I know you're not,' said Mr. Van Torp. 'If you don't know how crazy he is, I don't suppose any one else does. But your nerves are better than mine, as I told you. The idea of killing anything makes me uncomfortable, and when it comes to thinking that he really might murder you some day—well, I can't stand it, that's all! If I didn't know that you lock your door at night I shouldn't sleep, sometimes. You do lock it, always, don't you?'

'Oh yes!'

'Be sure you do to-night. I wonder whether he is in earnest about the divorce this time, or whether the whole scene was just bluff, to get my money.'

'I don't know,' answered Lady Maud, rising. 'He needs money, I believe, but I'm not sure that he would try to get it just in that way.'

'Too bad? Even for him?'

'Oh dear, no! Too simple! He's a tortuous person.'

'He tried to pocket those notes with a good deal of directness!' observed Mr. Van Torp.

'Yes. That was an opportunity that turned up unexpectedly, but he didn't know it would. How could he? He didn't come here expecting to find thousands of pounds lying about on the table! It was easy enough to know that I was here, of course. I couldn't go out of my own house on foot, in a dinner-gown, and pick up a hansom, could I? I had one called and gave the address, and the footman remembered it and told my husband. There's nothing more foolish than making mysteries and giving the cabman first one address and then another. If Boris is really going to bring a suit, the mere fact that there was no concealment as to where I was going this evening would be strong evidence, wouldn't it? Evidence he cannot deny, too, since he must have learnt the address from the footman, who heard me give it! And people who make no secret of a meeting are not meeting clandestinely, are they?'

'You argue that pretty well,' said Mr. Van Torp, smiling.

'And besides,' rippled Lady Maud's sweet voice, as she shook out the folds of her black velvet, 'I don't care.'

Her friend held up the fur-lined cloak and put it over her shoulders. She fastened it at the neck and then turned to the fire for a moment before leaving.

'Rufus,' she said gravely, after a moment's pause, and looking down at the coals, 'you're an angel.'

'The others in the game don't think so,' answered Mr. Van Torp.

'No one was ever so good to a woman as you've been to me,' said Maud.

And all at once the joyful ring had died away from her voice and there was another tone in it that was sweet and low too, but sad and tender and grateful, all at once.

'There's nothing to thank me for,' answered Mr. Van Torp. 'I've often told you so. But I have a good deal of reason to be grateful to you for all you've given me.'

'Nonsense!' returned the lady, and the sadness was gone again, but not all the tenderness. 'I must be going,' she added a moment later, turning away from the fire.

'I'll take you to the Embassy in a hansom,' said the millionaire, slipping on his overcoat.

'No. You mustn't do that—we should be sure to meet some one at the door. Are you going anywhere in particular? I'll drop you wherever you like, and then go on. It will give us a few minutes more together.'

'Goodness knows we don't get too many!'

'No, indeed!'

So the two went down the dismal stairs of the house in Hare Court together.

CHAPTER VI

The position of a successful lyric primadonna with regard to other artists and the rest of the world is altogether exceptional, and is not easy to explain. Her value for purposes of advertisement apparently exceeds that of any other popular favourite, not to mention the majority of royal personages. A respectable publisher has been known to bring out a book in which he did not believe, solely because a leading lyric soprano promised him to say in an interview that it was the book of the year. Countless brands of cigars, cigarettes, wines and liquors, have been the fashion with the flash crowd that frequents public billiard-rooms and consumes unlimited tobacco and drink, merely because some famous 'Juliet' or 'Marguerite' has 'consented' to lend her name to the articles in question; and half the grog-shops on both sides of the Atlantic display to the admiring street the most alarming pink and white caricatures, or monstrously enlarged photographs, of the three or four celebrated lyric sopranos who happen to be before the public at any one time. In the popular mind those artists represent something which they themselves do not always understand. There is a legend about each; she is either an angel of purity and light, or a beautiful monster of iniquity; she has turned the heads of kings—'kings' in a vaguely royal plural—completely round on their shoulders, or she has built out of her earnings a hospital for crippled children; the watery-sentimental eye of the flash crowd in its cups sees in her a Phryne, a Mrs. Fry, or a Saint Cecilia. Goethe said that every man must be either the hammer or the anvil; the billiard-room public is sure that every primadonna is a siren or a martyred wife, or else a public benefactress, unless she is all three by turns, which is even more interesting.

In any case, the reporters are sure that every one wants to know just what she thinks about everything. In the United States, for instance, her opinion on political matters is often asked, and is advertised with 'scare-heads' that would stop a funeral or arrest the attention of a man on his way to the gallows.

Then, too, she has her 'following' of 'girls,' thousands of whom have her photograph, or her autograph, or both, and believe in her, and are ready to scratch out the eyes of any older person who suggests that she is not perfection in every way, or that to be a primadonna like her ought not to be every girl's highest ambition. They not only worship her, but many of them make real sacrifices to hear her sing; for most of them are anything but well off, and to hear an opera means living without little luxuries, and sometimes without necessaries, for days together. Their devotion to their idol is touching and true; and she knows it and is good-natured in the matter of autographs for them, and talks about 'my matinée girls' to the reporters, as if those eleven thousand virgins and more were all her younger sisters and nieces. An actress, even the most gifted, has no such 'following.' The greatest dramatic sopranos that ever sing Brunhilde and Kundry enjoy no such popularity. It belongs exclusively to the nightingale primadonnas, whose voices enchant the ear if they do not always stir the blood. It may be explicable, but no explanation is at all necessary, since the fact cannot be disputed.

To this amazing popularity Margaret Donne had now attained; and she was known to the matinée girls' respectful admiration as Madame Cordova, to the public generally and to her comrades as Cordova, to sentimental paragraph-writers as Fair Margaret, and to her friends as Miss Donne, or merely as Margaret. Indeed, from the name each person gave her in speaking of her, it was easy to know the class to which each belonged.

She had bought a house in London, because in her heart she still thought England the finest country in the world, and had never felt the least desire to live anywhere else. She had few relations left and none whom she saw; for her father, the Oxford scholar, had not had money, and they all looked with disapproval on the career she had chosen. Besides, she had been very little in England since her parents' death. Her mother's American friend, the excellent Mrs. Rushmore, who had taken her under her wing, was now in Versailles, where she had a house, and Margaret actually had the audacity to live alone, rather than burden herself with a tiresome companion.

Her courage in doing so was perhaps mistaken, considering what the world is and what it generally thinks of the musical and theatrical professions; and Mrs. Rushmore, who was quite powerless to influence Margaret's conduct, did not at all approve of it. The girl's will had always been strong, and her immense success had so little weakened her belief in herself, or softened her character, that she had grown almost too independent. The spirit of independence is not a fault in women, but it is a defect in the eyes of men. Darwin has proved that the dominant characteristic of male animals is vanity; and what is to become of that if women show that they can do without us? If the emancipation of woman had gone on as it began when we were boys, we should by this time be importing wives for our sons from Timbuctoo or the Friendly Islands. Happily, women are practical beings who rarely stray far from the narrow path along which usefulness and pleasure may still go hand in hand; for considering how much most women do that is useful, the amount of pleasure they get out of life is perfectly amazing; and when we try to keep up with them in the chase after amusement we are surprised at the number of useful things they accomplish without effort in twenty-four hours.

But, indeed, women are to us very like the moon, which has shown the earth only one side of herself since the beginning, though she has watched and studied our world from all its sides through uncounted ages. We men are alternately delighted, humiliated, and terrified when women anticipate our wishes, perceive our weaknesses, and detect our shortcomings, whether we be frisky young colts in the field or sober stagers plodding along between the matrimonial shafts in harness and blinkers. We pride ourselves on having the strength to smash the shafts, shake off the harness, and kick the cart to pieces if we choose, and there are men who can and do. But the man does not live who knows what the dickens women are up to when he is going quietly along the road, as a good horse should. Sometimes they are driving us, and then there is no mistake about it; and sometimes they are just sitting in the cart and dozing, and we can tell that they are behind us by their weight; but very often we are neither driven by them nor are we dragging them, and we really have not the faintest idea where they are, so that we are reduced to telling ourselves, with a little nervousness which we do not care to acknowledge, that it is noble and beautiful to trust what we love.

A part of the great feminine secret is the concealment of that independence about which there has been so much talk in our time. As for suffrage, wherever there is such a thing, the woman who does not vote always controls far more men's votes than the woman who goes to the polls, and has only her own vote to give.

Margaret, the primadonna, did not want to vote for or against anything; but she was a little too ready to assert that she could and would lead her own life as she pleased, without danger to her good name, because she had never done anything to be ashamed of. The natural consequence was that she was gradually losing something which is really much more worth having than commonplace, technical independence. Her friend Lushington realised the change as soon as she landed, and it hurt him to see it, because it seemed to him a great pity that what he had thought an ideal, and therefore a natural manifestation of art, should be losing the fine outlines that had made it perfect to his devoted gaze. But this was not all. His rather over-strung moral sense was offended as well as his artistic taste. He felt that Margaret was blunting the sensibilities of her feminine nature and wronging a part of herself, and that the delicate bloom of girlhood was opening to a blossom that was somewhat too evidently strong, a shade too vivid and more brilliant than beautiful.

There were times when she reminded him of his mother, and those were some of the most painful moments of his present life. It is true that compared with Madame Bonanni in her prime, as he remembered her, Margaret was as a lily of the valley to a giant dahlia; yet when he recalled the sweet and healthy English girl he had known and loved in Versailles three years ago, the vision was delicate and fairy-like beside the strong reality of the successful primadonna. She was so very sure of herself now, and so fully persuaded that she was not accountable to any one for her doings, her tastes, or the choice of her friends! If not actually like Madame Bonanni, she was undoubtedly beginning to resemble two or three of her famous rivals in the profession who were nearer to her own age. Her taste did not run in the direction of white fox cloaks, named diamonds, and imperial jade plates; she did not use a solid gold toothbrush with emeralds set in the handle, like Ismail Pacha; bridge did not amuse her at all, nor could she derive pleasure from playing at Monte Carlo; she did not even keep an eighty-horse-power motor-car worth five thousand pounds. Paul Griggs, who was old-fashioned, called motor-cars 'sudden-death carts,' and Margaret was inclined to agree with him. She cared for none of these things.

Nevertheless there was a quiet thoroughgoing luxury in her existence, an unseen private extravagance, such as Rufus Van Torp, the millionaire, had never dreamt of. She had first determined to be a singer in order to support herself, because she had been cheated of a fortune by old Alvah Moon; but before she had actually made her *début* a handsome sum had been recovered for her, and though she was not exactly what is now called rich, she was at least extremely well off, apart from her professional earnings, which were very large indeed. In the certainty that if her voice failed she would always have a more than sufficient income for the rest of her life, and considering that she was not under the obligation of supporting a number of poor relations, it was not surprising that she should spend a great deal of money on herself.

It is not every one who can be lavish without going a little beyond the finely-drawn boundary which divides luxury from extravagance; for useless profusion is by nature as contrary to what is aesthetic as fat in the wrong place, and is quite as sure to be seen. To spend well what rich people are justified in expending over and above an ample provision for the necessities and reasonable comforts of a large existence is an art in itself, and the modest muse of good taste loves not the rich man for his riches, nor the successful primadonna for the thousands she has a right to throw away if she likes.

Mr. Van Torp vaguely understood this, without at all guessing how the great artist spent her money. He had understood at least enough to hinder him from trying to dazzle her in the beginning of the New York season, when he had brought siege against her.

A week after her arrival in London, Margaret was alone at her piano and Lushington was announced. Unlike the majority of musicians in real fiction she had not been allowing her fingers to 'wander over the keys,' a relaxation that not seldom leads to outer darkness, where the consecutive fifth plays hide-and-seek with the falling sub-tonic to superinduce gnashing of teeth in them that hear. Margaret was learning her part in the *Elisir d'Amore*, and instead of using her voice she was whistling from the score and playing the accompaniment. The old opera was to be revived during the coming season with her and the great Pompeo Stromboli, and she was obliged to work hard to have it ready.

The music-room had a polished wooden floor, and the furniture consisted chiefly of a grand piano and a dozen chairs. The walls were tinted a pale green; there were no curtains at the windows, because they would have deadened sound, and a very small wood fire was burning in an almost miniature fireplace quite at the other end of the room. The sun had not quite set yet, and as the blinds were still open, a lurid glare came in from the western sky, over the houses on the opposite side of the wide square. There had been a heavy shower, but the streets were already drying. One shaded electric lamp stood on the desk of the piano, and the rest of the room was illuminated by the yellowish daylight.

Margaret was very much absorbed in her work, and did not hear the door open; but the servant came slowly towards her, purposely making his steps heard on the wooden floor in order to attract her attention. When she stopped playing and whistling, and looked round, the man said that Mr. Lushington was downstairs.

'Ask him to come up,' she answered, without hesitation.

She rose from the piano, went to the window and looked out at the smoky sunset.

Lushington entered the room in a few moments and saw only the outline of her graceful figure, as if she were cut out in black against the glare from the big window. She turned, and a little of the shaded light from the piano fell upon her face, just enough to show him her expression, and though her glad smile welcomed him, there was anxiety in her brown eyes. He came forward, fair and supernaturally neat, as ever, and much more self-possessed than in former days. It was not their first meeting since she had landed, for he had been to see her late in the afternoon on the day of her arrival, and she had expected him; but she had felt a sort of constraint in his manner then, which was new to her, and they had talked for half an hour about indifferent things. Moreover, he had refused a second cup of tea, which was a sure sign that something was wrong. So she had asked him to come again a week later, naming the day, and she had been secretly disappointed because he did not protest against being put off so long. She wondered what had happened, for his letters, his cable to her when she had left America, and the flowers he had managed to send on board the steamer, had made her believe that he had not changed since they had parted before Christmas.

As she was near the piano she sat down on the stool, while he took a small chair and established himself near the corner of the instrument, at the upper end of the keyboard. The shaded lamp cast a little light on both their faces, as the two looked at each other, and Margaret realised that she was not only very fond of him, but that his whole existence represented something she had lost and wished to get back, but feared that she could never have again. For many months she had not felt like her old self till a week ago, when he had come to see her after she had landed.

They had been in love with each other before she had begun her career, and she would have married him then, but a sort of quixotism, which was highly honourable if nothing else, had withheld him. He had felt that his mother's son had no right to marry Margaret Donne, though she had told him as plainly as a modest girl could that she was not of the same opinion. Then had come Logotheti's mad attempt to carry her off out of the theatre, after the dress rehearsal before her début, and Madame Bonanni and Lushington between them had spirited her away just in time. After that it had been impossible for him to keep up the pretence of avoiding her, and a sort of intimacy had continued, which neither of them quite admitted to be love, while neither would have called it mere friendship.

The most amazing part of the whole situation was that Margaret had continued to see Logotheti as if he had not actually tried to carry her off in his motor-car, very much against her will. And in spite of former jealousies and a serious quarrel Logotheti and Lushington spoke to each other when they met. Possibly Lushington consented to treat him civilly because the plot for carrying off Margaret had so completely failed that its author had got himself locked up on suspicion of being a fugitive criminal. Lushington, feeling that he had completely routed his rival on that occasion, could afford to be generous. Yet the man of letters, who was a born English gentleman on his father's side, and who was one altogether by his bringing up, was constantly surprised at himself for being willing to shake hands with a Greek financier who had tried to run away with an English girl; and possibly, in the complicated workings of his mind and conflicting sensibilities, half Anglo-Saxon and half Southern French, his present conduct was due to the fact that Margaret Donne had somehow ceased to be a 'nice English girl' when she joined the cosmopolitan legion that manoeuvres on the international stage of 'Grand Opera.' How could a 'nice English girl' remain herself if she associated daily with such people as

Pompeo Stromboli, Schreiermeyer, Herr Tiefenbach and Signorina Baci-Roventi, the Italian contralto who could pass for a man so well that she was said to have fought a real duel with sabres and wounded her adversary before he discovered that she was the very lady he had lately left for another—a regular Mademoiselle de Maupin! Had not Lushington once seen her kiss Margaret on both cheeks in a moment of enthusiastic admiration? He was not the average young man who falls in love with a singer, either; he knew the stage and its depths only too well, for he had his own mother's life always before him, a perpetual reproach.

Though Margaret had at first revolted inwardly against the details of her professional surroundings, she had grown used to them by sure and fatal degrees, and things that would once have disgusted her were indifferent to her now. Men who have been educated in conditions of ordinary refinement and who have volunteered in the ranks or gone to sea before the mast have experienced something very like what befell Margaret; but men are not delicately nurtured beings whose bloom is damaged by the rough air of reality, and the camp and the forecastle are not the stage. Perhaps nothing that is necessary shocks really sensible people; it is when disagreeable things are perfectly useless and quite avoidable—in theory—that they are most repugnant to men like Edmund Lushington. He had warned Margaret of what was in store for her, before she had taken the final step; but he had not warned himself that in spite of her bringing-up she might get used to it all and end by not resenting it any more than the rest of the professionals with whom she associated. It was this that chilled him.

'I hope I'm not interrupting your work,' he said as he sat down.

'My work?'

'I heard you studying when they let me in.'

'Oh!'

His voice sounded very indifferent, and a pause followed Margaret's mild ejaculation.

'It's rather a thankless opera for the soprano, I always think,' he observed. 'The tenor has it all his own way.'

'*The Elisir d'Amore?*'

'Yes.'

'I've not rehearsed it yet,' said Margaret rather drearily. 'I don't know.'

He evidently meant to talk of indifferent things again, as at their last meeting, and she felt that she was groping in the dark for something she had lost. There was no sympathy in his voice, no interest, and she was inclined to ask him plainly what was the matter; but her pride hindered her still, and she only looked at him with an expression of inquiry. He laid his hand on the corner of the piano, and his eyes rested on the shaded lamp as if it attracted him. Perhaps he wondered why he had nothing to say to her, and why she was unwilling to help the conversation a little, since her new part might be supposed to furnish matter for a few commonplace phrases. The smoky sunset was fading outside and the room was growing dark.

'When do the rehearsals begin?' he asked after a long interval, and as if he was quite indifferent to the answer.

'When Stromboli comes, I suppose.'

Margaret turned on the piano stool, so as to face the desk, and she quietly closed the open score and laid it on the little table on her other side, as if not caring to talk of it any more, but she did not turn to him again.

'You had a great success in New York,' he said, after some time.

To this she answered nothing, but she shrugged her shoulders a little, and though he was not looking directly at her he saw the movement, and was offended by it. Such a little shrug was scarcely a breach of manners, but it was on the verge of vulgarity in his eyes, because he was persuaded that she had begun to change for the worse. He had already told himself that her way of speaking was not what it had been last year, and he felt that if the change went on she would set his teeth on edge some day; and that he was growing more and more sensitive, while she was continually becoming less so.

Margaret could not have understood that, and would have been hurt if he had tried to explain it. She was disappointed, because his letters had made her think that she was going to find him just as she had left him, as indeed he had been till the moment when he saw her after her arrival; but then he had changed at once. He had been disappointed then, as she was now, and chilled, as she was now; he had felt that he was shrinking from her then, as she now shrank from him. He suffered a good deal in his quiet way, for he had never known any woman who had moved him as she once had; but she suffered too, and in a much more resentful way. Two years of maddening success had made her very sure that she had a prime right to anything she wanted—within reason! If she let him alone he would sit out his half-hour's visit, making an idle remark now and then, and he would go away; but she would not let him do that. It was too absurd that after a long and affectionate intimacy they should sit there in the soft light and exchange platitudes.

'Tom,' she said, suddenly resolving to break the ice, 'we have been much too good friends to behave in this way to each other. If something has come between us, I think you ought to tell me—don't you?'

'I wish I could,' Lushington answered, after a moment's hesitation.

'If you know, you can,' said Margaret, taking the upper hand and meaning to keep it.

'That does not quite follow.'

'Oh yes, it does,' retorted Margaret energetically. 'I'll tell you why. If it's anything on your side, it's not fair and honest to keep it from me after writing to me as you have written all winter. But if it's the other way, there's nothing you can possibly know about me which you cannot tell me, and if you think there is, then some one has been telling you what is not true.'

'It's nothing against you; I assure you it's not.'

'Then there is a woman in the case. Why should you not say so frankly? We are not bound to each other in any way, I'm sure. I believe I once asked you to marry me, and you refused!' She laughed rather sharply. 'That does not constitute an engagement!'

'You put the point rather brutally, I think,' said Lushington.

'Perhaps, but isn't it quite true? It was not said in so many words, but you knew I meant it, and but for a quixotic scruple of yours we should have been married. I remember asking you what we were making ourselves miserable about, since we both cared so much. It was at Versailles, the last time we walked together, and we had stopped, and I was digging little round holes in the road with my parasol. I'm not going to ask you again to marry me, so there is no reason in the world why you should behave differently to me if you have fallen in love with some one else.'

'I'm not in love with any one,' said Lushington sharply.

'Then something you have heard about me has changed you in spite of what you say, and I have a right to know what it is, because I've done nothing I'm ashamed of.'

'I've not heard a word against you,' he answered, almost angrily. 'Why do you imagine such things?'

'Because I'm honest enough to own that your friendship has meant a great deal to me, even at a distance; and as I see that it has broken its neck at some fence or other, I'm natural enough to ask what the jump was like!'

He would not answer. He only looked at her suddenly for an instant, with a slight pinching of the lids, and his blue eyes glittered a little; then he turned away with a displeased air.

'Am I just or not?' Margaret asked, almost sternly.

'Yes, you are just,' he said, for it was impossible not to reply.

'And do you think it is just to me to change your manner altogether, without giving me a reason? I don't!'

'You will force me to say something I would rather not say.'

'That is what I am trying to do,' Margaret retorted.

'Since you insist on knowing the truth,' answered Lushington, yielding to what was very like necessity, 'I think you are very much changed since I saw you last. You do not seem to me the same person.'

For a moment Margaret looked at him with something like wonder, and her lips parted, though she said nothing. Then they met again and shut very tight, while her brown eyes darkened till they looked almost black; she turned a shade paler, too, and there was something almost tragic in her face.

'I'm sorry,' Lushington said, watching her, 'but you made me tell you.'

'Yes,' she answered slowly. 'I made you tell me, and I'm glad I did. So I have changed as much as that, have I? In two years!'

She folded her hands on the little shelf of the empty music desk, bent far forwards and looked down between the polished wooden bars at the strings below, as if she were suddenly interested in the mechanism of the piano.

Lushington turned his eyes to the darkening windows, and both sat thus in silence for some time.

'Yes,' she repeated at last, 'I'm glad I made you tell me. It explains everything very well.'

Still Lushington said nothing, and she was still examining the strings. Her right hand stole to the keys, and she pressed down one note so gently that it did not strike; she watched the little hammer that rose till it touched the string and then fell back into its place.

'You said I should change—I remember your words.' Her voice was quiet and thoughtful, whatever she felt. 'I suppose there is something about me now that grates on your nerves.'

There was no resentment in her tone, nor the least intonation of sarcasm. But Lushington said nothing; he was thinking of the time when he had thought her an ideal of refined girlhood, and had believed in his heart that she could never stand the life of the stage, and would surely give it up in sheer disgust, no matter how successful she might be. Yet now, she did not even seem offended by what he had told her. So much the better, he thought; for he was far too truthful to take back one word in order to make peace, even if she burst into tears. Possibly, of the two, his reflections were sadder than hers just then, but she interrupted them with a question.

'Can you tell me of any one thing I do that jars on you?' she asked. 'Or is it what I say, or my way of speaking? I should like to know.'

'It's nothing, and it's everything,' answered Lushington, taking refuge in a commonplace phrase, 'and I suppose no one else would ever notice it. But I'm so awfully sensitive about certain things. You know why.'

She knew why; yet it was with a sort of wonder that she asked herself what there was in her tone or manner that could remind him of his mother; but though she had spoken quietly, and almost humbly, a cold and secret anger was slowly rising in her. The great artist, who held thousands spellbound and breathless, could not submit easily to losing in such a way the only friendship that had ever meant much to her. The man who had just told her that she had lost her charm for him meant that she was sinking to the level of her surroundings, and he was the only man she had ever believed that she loved. Two years ago, and even less, she would have been generously angry with him, and would have spoken out, and perhaps all would have been over; but those two years of life on the stage had given her the self-control of an actress when she chose to exercise it, and she had acquired an artificial command of her face and voice which had not belonged to her original frank and simple self. Perhaps Lushington knew that too, as a part of the change that offended his taste. At twenty-two, Margaret Donne would have coloured, and would have given him a piece of her young mind very plainly; Margarita da Cordova, aged twenty-four, turned a trifle paler, shut her lips, and was frigidly angry, as if some ignorant music-hall reporter had attacked her singing in print. She was convinced that Lushington was mistaken, and that he was merely yielding to that love of finding fault with what he liked which a familiar passage in Scripture attributes to the Divinity, but with which many of us are better acquainted in our friends; in her opinion, such fault-finding was personal criticism, and it irritated her vanity, over-fed with public adulation and the sincere praise of musical critics. 'If you don't like me as I am, there are so many people who do that you don't count!' That was the sub-conscious form of her mental retort, and it was in the manner of Cordova, and not of Margaret.

Once upon a time, when his exaggerated sense of honour was driving him away, she had said rather foolishly that if he left her she would not answer for herself. She had felt a little desperate, but he had told her quietly that he, who knew her, would answer for her, and her mood had changed, and she had been herself again. But it was different this time. He meant much more than he said; he meant that she had lowered herself, and she was sure that he would not 'answer' for her now. On the contrary, it was his intention to let her know that he no longer believed in her, and perhaps no longer respected or trusted her. Yet, little by little, during their last separation, his belief in her, and his respect for her, had grown in her estimation, because they alone still connected her with the maidenliness and feminine refinement in which she had grown up. Lushington had broken a link that had been strong.

She was at one of the cross-roads of her life; she was at a turning point in the labyrinth, after passing which it would be hard to come back and find the right way. Perhaps old Griggs could help her if it occurred to him; but that was unlikely, for he had reached the age when men who have seen much take people as they find them. Logotheti would certainly not help her, though she knew instinctively that she was still to him what she had always been, and that if he ever had the opportunity he sought, her chances of escape would be small indeed.

Therefore she felt more lonely after Lushington had spoken than she had ever felt since her parents had died, and much more desperate. But nothing in the world would have induced her to let him know it, and her anger against him rose slowly, and it was cold and enduring, as that sort of resentment is. She was so proud that it gave her the power to smile carelessly after a minute's silence, and she asked him some perfectly idle questions about the news of the day. He should not know that he had hurt her very much; he should not suspect for a moment that she wished him to go away.

She rose presently and turned up the lights, rang the bell, and when the window curtains were drawn, and tea was brought, she did everything she could to make Lushington feel at his ease; she did it out of sheer pride, for she did not meditate any vengeance, but was only angry, and wished to get rid of him without a scene.

At last he rose to go away, and when he held out his hand there was a dramatic moment.

'I hope you're not angry with me,' he said with a cheerful smile, for he was quite sure that she bore him no lasting grudge.

'I?'

She laughed so frankly and musically after pronouncing the syllable, that he took it for a disclaimer.

So he went away, shutting the door after him in a contented way, not sharply as if he were annoyed with her, nor very softly and considerately as if he were sorry for her, but with a moderate, businesslike snap of the latch as if everything were all right.

She went back to the piano when she was alone, and sat down on the music-stool, but her hands did not go to the keys till she was sure that Lushington was already far from the house.

A few chords, and then she suddenly began to sing with the full power of her voice, as if she were on the stage. She sang Rosina's song in the *Barbiere di Siviglia* as she had never sung it in her life, and for the first time the words pleased her.

'... una vipera sarò!'

What 'nice English girl' ever told herself or any one else that she would be a 'viper'?

CHAPTER VII

Two days later Margaret was somewhat surprised by an informal invitation to dine at the Turkish Embassy. The Ambassador had lately been transferred to London from Paris, where she had known him through Logotheti and had met him two or three times. The latter, as a Fanariote Greek, was a Turkish subject, and although he had once told Margaret that the Turks had murdered his father in some insurrection, and though he himself might have hesitated to spend much time in Constantinople, he nevertheless maintained friendly relations with the representatives of what was his country; and for obvious reasons, connected with Turkish finance, they treated him with marked consideration. On general principles and in theory Turks and Greeks hate each other; in practice they can live very amicably side by side. In the many cases in which Armenians have been attacked and killed by the Turks no Greek has ever been hurt except by accident; on the other hand, none has lifted a hand to defend an Armenian in distress, which sufficiently proves that the question of religion has not been concerned at all.

Margaret accepted the Ambassador's invitation, feeling tolerably sure of meeting Logotheti at the dinner. If there were any other women they would be of the meteoric sort, the fragments of former social planets that go on revolving in the old orbit, more or less divorced, bankrupt, or otherwise unsound, though still smart, the kind of women who are asked to fill a table on such occasions 'because they won't mind'—that is to say, they will not object to dining with a primadonna or an actress whose husband has become nebulous and whose reputation is mottled. The men, of whom there might be several, would be either very clever or overpoweringly noble, because all geniuses and all peers are supposed to like their birds of paradise a little high. I wonder why. I have met and talked with a good many men of genius, from Wagner and Liszt to Zola and some still living contemporaries, and, really, their general preference for highly correct social gatherings has struck me as phenomenal. There are even noblemen who seem to be quite respectable, and pretend that they would rather talk to an honest woman at a dinner party than drink bumpers of brut champagne out of Astarte's satin slipper.

Mustapha Pasha, the Turkish Ambassador, was a fair, pale man of fifty, who had spiritual features, quiet blue eyes, and a pleasant smile. His hands were delicately made and very white, but not effeminate. He had been educated partly in England, and spoke English without difficulty and almost without accent, as Logotheti did. He came forward to meet Margaret as she entered the room, and he greeted her warmly, thanking her for being so good as to come at short notice.

Logotheti was the next to take her hand, and she looked at him attentively when her eyes met his, wondering whether he, too, would think her changed. He himself was not, at all events. Mustapha Pasha, a born Musalman and a genuine Turk, never arrested attention in an English drawing-room by his appearance; but Constantino Logotheti, the Greek, was an Oriental in looks as well as in character. His beautiful eyes were almond-shaped, his lips were broad and rather flat, and the small black moustache grew upwards and away from them so as not to hide his mouth at all. He had an even olive complexion, and any judge of men would have seen at a glance that he was thoroughly sound and as strong as a professional athlete. His coat had a velvet collar; a single emerald stud, worth several thousand pounds, diffused a green refulgence round itself in the middle of his very shiny shirt front; his waistcoat was embroidered and adorned with diamond buttons, his trousers were tight, and his name, with those of three or four other European financiers, made it alternately possible or impossible for impecunious empires and kingdoms to raise money in England, France and Germany. In matters of business, in the East, the Jew fears the Greek, the Greek fears the Armenian, the Armenian fears the Persian, and the Persian fears only Allah. One reason why the Jews do not care to return to Palestine and Asia Minor is that they cannot get a living amongst Christians and Mohammedans, a plain fact which those eminent and charitable European Jews who are trying to draw their fellow-believers eastward would do well to consider. Even in Europe there are far more poor Jews than Christians realise; in Asia there are hardly any rich ones. The Venetians were too much for Shylock, and he lost his ducats and his daughter; amongst Christian Greeks, Christian Armenians, and Musalman Persians, from Constantinople to Tiflis, Teheran, Bagdad and Cairo, the poor man could not have saved sixpence a year.

This is not a mere digression, since it may serve to define Logotheti's position in the scale of the financial forces.

Margaret took his hand and looked at him just a little longer than she had looked at Mustapha Pasha. He never wrote to her, and never took the trouble to let her know where he was; but when they met his time was hers, and when he could be with her he seemed to have no other pre-occupation in life.

'I came over from Paris to-day,' he said. 'When may I come and see you?'

That was always the first question, for he never wasted time.

'To-morrow, if you like. Come late—about seven.'

The Ambassador was on her other side. A little knot of men and one lady were standing near the fire in an expectant sort of way, ready to be introduced to Margaret. She saw the bony head of Paul Griggs, and she smiled at him from a distance. He was talking to a very handsome and thoroughbred looking woman in plain black velvet, who had the most perfectly beautiful shoulders Margaret had ever seen.

Mustapha Pasha led the Primadonna to the group.

'Lady Maud,' he said to the beauty, 'this is my old friend Señorita da Cordova. Countess Leven,' he added, for Margaret's benefit.

She had not met him more than three times, but she did not resent being called his old friend. It was well meant, she thought.

Lady Maud held out her hand cordially.

'I've wanted to know you ever so long,' she said, in her sweet low voice.

'That's very kind of you,' Margaret answered.

It is not easy to find a proper reply to people who say they have long hoped to meet you, but Griggs came to the rescue, as he shook hands in his turn.

'That was not a mere phrase,' he said with a smile. 'It's quite true. Lady Maud wanted me to give her a letter to you a year ago.'

'Indeed I did,' asseverated the beauty, nodding, 'but Mr. Griggs said he didn't know you well enough!'

'You might have asked me,' observed Logotheti. 'I'm less cautious than Griggs.'

'You're too exotic,' retorted Lady Maud, with a ripple in her voice.

The adjective described the Greek so well that the others laughed.

'Exotic,' Margaret repeated the word thoughtfully.

'For that matter,' put in Mustapha Pasha with a smile, 'I can hardly be called a native!'

The Countess Leven looked at him critically.

'You could pass for one,' she said, 'but Monsieur Logotheti couldn't.' The other men, whom Margaret did not know, had been listening in silence, and maintained their expectant attitude. In the pause which followed Lady Maud's remark the Ambassador introduced them in foreign fashion: one was a middle-aged peer who wore gold-rimmed spectacles and looked like a student or a man of letters; another was the most successful young playwright of the younger generation, and he wore a very good coat and was altogether well turned out, for in his heart he prided himself on being the best groomed man in London; a third was a famous barrister who had a crisp and breezy way with him that made flat calms in conversation impossible. Lastly, a very disagreeable young man, who seemed a mere boy, was introduced to the Primadonna.

'Mr. Feist,' said the Ambassador, who never forgot names.

Margaret was aware of a person with an unhealthy complexion, thick hair of a dead-leaf brown colour, and staring blue eyes that made her think of glass marbles. The face had an unnaturally youthful look, and yet, at the same time, there was something profoundly vicious about it. Margaret wondered who in the world the young man might be and why he was at the Turkish Embassy, apparently invited there to meet her. She at once supposed that in spite of his appearance he must have some claim to celebrity.

'I'm a great admirer of yours, Señorita,' said Mr. Feist in a womanish voice and with a drawl. 'I was in the Metropolitan in New York when you sang in the dark and prevented a panic. I suppose that was about the finest thing any singer ever did.'

Margaret smiled pleasantly, though she felt the strongest repulsion for the man.

'I happened to be on the stage,' she said modestly. 'Any of the others would have done the same.'

'Well,' drawled Mr. Feist, 'may be. I doubt it.'

Dinner was announced.

'Will you keep house for me?' asked the Ambassador of Lady Maud.

'There's something rather appropriate about your playing Ambassadress here,' observed Logotheti.

Margaret heard but did not understand that her new acquaintance was a Russian subject. Mustapha Pasha held out his arm to take her in to dinner. The spectacled peer took in Lady Maud, and the men straggled in. At table Lady Maud sat opposite the Pasha, with the peer on her right and the barrister on her left. Margaret was on the right of the Ambassador, on whose other side Griggs was placed, and Logotheti was Margaret's other neighbour. Feist and the young playwright were together, between Griggs and the nobleman.

Margaret glanced round the table at the people and wondered about them. She had heard of the barrister and the novelist, and the peer's name had a familiar sound that suggested something unusual, though she could not quite remember what it was. It might be pictures, or the north pole, or the divorce court, or a new idiot asylum; it would never matter much. The new acquaintances on whom her attention fixed itself were Lady Maud, who attracted her strongly, and Mr. Feist, who repelled her. She wished she could speak Greek in order to ask Logotheti who the latter was and why he was present. To judge by appearances he was probably a rich young American who travelled and frequented theatres a good deal, and who wished to be able to say that he knew Cordova. He had perhaps arrived lately with a letter of introduction to the Ambassador, who had asked him to the first nondescript informal dinner he gave, because the man would not have fitted in anywhere else.

Logotheti began to talk at once, while Mustapha Pasha plunged into a political conversation with Griggs.

'I'm much more glad to see you than you can imagine,' the Greek said, not in an undertone, but just so softly that no one else could hear him.

'I'm not good at imagining,' answered Margaret. 'But I'm glad you are here. There are so many new faces.'

'Happily you are not shy. One of your most enviable qualities is your self-possession.'

'You're not lacking in that way either,' laughed Margaret. 'Unless you have changed very much.'

'Neither of us has changed much since last year. I only wish you would!'

Margaret turned her head to look at him.

'So you think I am not changed!' she said, with a little pleased surprise in her tone.

'Not a bit. If anything, you have grown younger in the last two years.'

'Does that mean more youthful? More frisky? I hope not!'

'No, not at all. What I see is the natural effect of vast success on a very, nice woman. Formerly, even after you had begun your career, you had some doubts as to the ultimate result. The future made you restless, and sometimes disturbed the peace of your face a little, when you thought about it too much. That's all gone now, and you are your real self, as nature meant you to be.'

'My real self? You mean, the professional singer!'

'No. A great artist, in the person of a thoroughly nice woman.'

Margaret had thought that blushing was a thing of the past with her, but a soft colour rose in her cheeks now, from sheer pleasure at what he had said.

'I hope you don't think it impertinent of me to tell you so,' said Logotheti with a slight intonation of anxiety.

'Impertinent!' cried Margaret. 'It's the nicest thing any one has said to me for months, and thank goodness I'm not above being pleased.'

Nor was Logotheti above using any art that could please her. His instinct about women, finding no scruples in the way, had led him into present favour by the shortest road. It is one thing to say brutally that all women like flattery; it is quite another to foresee just what form of flattery they will like. People who do not know professional artistic life from the inner side are much too ready to cry out that first-class professionals will swallow any amount of undiscriminating praise. The ability to judge their own work is one of the gifts which place them above the second class.

'I said what I thought,' observed Logotheti with a sudden air of conscientious reserve. 'For once in our acquaintance, I was not thinking of pleasing you. And then I was afraid that I had displeased you, as I so often have.'

The last words were spoken with a regret that was real.

'I have forgiven you,' said Margaret quietly; 'with conditions!' she added, as an afterthought, and smiling.

'Oh, I know—I'll never do it again.'

'That's what a runaway horse seems to say when he walks quietly home, with his head down and his ears limp, after nearly breaking one's neck!'

'I was a born runaway,' said Logotheti meekly, 'but you have cured me.'

In the pause that followed this speech, Mr. Feist leaned forward and spoke to Margaret across the table.

'I think we have a mutual friend, Madame,' he said.

'Indeed?' Margaret spoke coolly; she did not like to be called 'Madame' by people who spoke English.

'Mr. Van Torp,' explained the young man.

'Yes,' Margaret said, after a moment's hesitation, 'I know Mr. Van Torp; he came over on the same steamer.'

The others at the table were suddenly silent, and seemed to be listening. Lady Maud's clear eyes rested on Mr. Feist's face.

'He's quite a wonderful man, I think,' observed the latter.

'Yes,' assented the Primadonna indifferently.

'Don't you think he is a wonderful man?' insisted Mr. Feist, with his disagreeable drawl.

'I daresay he is,' Margaret answered, 'but I don't know him very well.'

'Really? That's funny!'

'Why?'

'Because I happen to know that he thinks everything of you, Madame Cordova. That's why I supposed, you were intimate friends.'

The others had listened hitherto in a sort of mournful silence, distinctly bored. Lady Maud's eyes now turned to Margaret, but the latter still seemed perfectly indifferent, though she was wishing that some one else would speak. Griggs turned to Mr. Feist, who was next to him.

'You mean that he is a wonderful man of business, perhaps,' he said.

'Well, we all know he's that, anyway,' returned his neighbour. 'He's not exactly a friend of mine, not exactly!' A meaning smile wrinkled the unhealthy face and suddenly made it look older. 'All the same, I think he's quite wonderful. He's not merely an able man, he's a man of powerful intellect.'

'A Nickel Napoleon,' suggested the barrister, who was bored to death by this time, and could not imagine why Lady Maud followed the conversation with so much interest.

'Your speaking of nickel,' said the peer, at her elbow, 'reminds me of that extraordinary new discovery—let me see—what is it?'

'America?' suggested the barrister viciously.

'No,' said his lordship, with perfect gravity, 'it's not that. Ah yes, I remember! It's a process for making nitric acid out of air.'

Lady Maud nodded and smiled, as if she knew all about it, but her eyes were again scrutinising Mr. Feist's face. Her neighbour, whose hobby was applied science, at once launched upon a long account of the invention. From time to time the beauty nodded and said that she quite understood, which was totally untrue, but well meant.

'That young man has the head of a criminal,' said the barrister on her other side, speaking very low.

She bent her head very slightly, to show that she had heard, and she continued to listen to the description of the new process. By this time every one was talking again. Mr. Feist was in conversation with Griggs, and showed his profile to the barrister, who quietly studied the retreating forehead and the ill-formed jaw, the latter plainly discernible to a practised eye, in spite of the round cheeks. The barrister was a little mad on the subject of degeneracy, and knew that an unnaturally boyish look in a grown man is one of the signs of it. In the course of a long experience at the bar he had appeared in defence of several 'high-class criminals.' By way of comparing Mr. Feist with a perfectly healthy specimen of humanity, he turned to look at Logotheti beside him. Margaret was talking with the Ambassador, and the Greek was just turning to talk to his neighbour, so that their eyes met, and each waited for the other to speak first.

'Are you a judge of faces?' asked the barrister after a moment.

'Men of business have to be, to some extent,' answered Logotheti.

'So do lawyers. What should you say was the matter with that one?'

It was impossible to doubt that he was speaking of the only abnormal head at the table, and Logotheti looked across the wide table at Mr. Feist for several seconds before he answered.

'Drink,' he said in an undertone, when he had finished his examination.

'Yes. Anything else?'

'May go mad any day, I should think,' observed Logotheti.

'Do you know anything about him?'

'Never saw him before.'

'And we shall probably never see him again,' said the Englishman. 'That's the worst of it. One sees such heads occasionally, but one very rarely hears what becomes of them.'

The Greek did not care a straw what became of Mr. Feist's head, for he was waiting to renew his conversation with Margaret.

Mustapha Pasha told her that she should go to Constantinople some day and sing to the Sultan, who would give her a pretty decoration in diamonds; and she laughed carelessly and answered that it might be very amusing.

'I shall be very happy to show you the way,' said the Pasha. 'Whenever you have a fancy for the trip, promise to let me know.'

Margaret had no doubt that he was quite in earnest, and would enjoy the holiday vastly. She was used to such kind offers and knew how to laugh at them, though she was very well aware that they were not made in jest.

'I have a pretty little villa on the Bosphorus,' said the Ambassador, 'If you should ever come to Constantinople it is at your disposal, with everything in it, as long as you care to use it.'

'It's too good of you!' she answered. 'But I have a small house of my own here which is very comfortable, and I like London.'

'I know,' answered the Pasha blandly; 'I only meant to suggest a little change.'

He smiled pleasantly, as if he had meant nothing, and there was a pause, of which Logotheti took advantage.

'You are admirable,' he said.

'I have had much more magnificent invitations,' she answered. 'You once wished to give me your yacht as a present if I would only make a trip to Crete—with a party of archaeologists! An archduke once proposed to take me for a drive in a cab!'

'If I remember,' said Logotheti, 'I offered you the owner with the yacht. But I fancy you thought me too "exotic," as Countess Leven calls me.'

'Oh, much!' Margaret laughed again, and then lowered her voice, 'by the bye, who is she?'

'Lady Maud? Didn't you know her? She is Lord Creedmore's daughter, one of seven or eight, I believe. She married a Russian in the diplomatic service, four years ago—Count Leven—but everybody here calls her Lady Maud. She hadn't a penny, for the Creedmores are poor. Leven was supposed to be rich, but there are all sorts of stories about him, and he's often hard up. As for her, she always wears that black velvet gown, and I've been told that she has no other. I fancy she gets a new one every year. But people say—'

Logotheti broke off suddenly.

'What do they say?' Margaret was interested.

'No, I shall not tell you, because I don't believe it.'

'If you say you don't believe the story, what harm can there be in telling it?'

'No harm, perhaps. But what is the use of repeating a bit of wicked gossip?'

Margaret's curiosity was roused about the beautiful Englishwoman.

'If you won't tell me, I may think it is something far worse!'

'I'm sure you could not imagine anything more unlikely!'

'Please tell me! Please! I know it's mere idle curiosity, but you've roused it, and I shall not sleep unless I know.'

'And that would be bad for your voice.'

'Of course! Please—'

Logotheti had not meant to yield, but he could not resist her winning tone.

'I'll tell you, but I don't believe a word of it, and I hope you will not either. The story is that her husband found her with Van Torp the other evening in rooms he keeps in the Temple, and there was an envelope on the table addressed to her in his handwriting, in which there were four thousand one hundred pounds in notes.'

Margaret looked thoughtfully at Lady Maud before she answered.

'She? With Mr. Van Torp, and taking money from him? Oh no! Not with that face!'

'Besides,' said Logotheti, 'why the odd hundred? The story gives too many details. People never know as much of the truth as that.'

'And if it is true,' returned Margaret, 'he will divorce her, and then we shall know.'

'For that matter,' said the Greek contemptuously, 'Leven would not be particular, provided he had his share of the profits.'

'Is it as bad as that? How disgusting! Poor woman!'

'Yes. I fancy she is to be pitied. In connection with Van Torp, may I ask an indiscreet question?'

'No question you can ask me about him can be indiscreet. What is it?'

'Is it true that he once asked you to marry him and you refused him?'

Margaret turned her pale face to Logotheti with a look of genuine surprise.

'Yes. It's true. But I never told any one. How in the world did you hear it?'

'And he quite lost his head, I heard, and behaved like a madman—'

'Who told you that?' asked Margaret, more and more astonished, and not at all pleased.

'He behaved so strangely that you ran into the next room and bolted the door, and waited till he went away—'

'Have you been paying a detective to watch me?'

There was anger in her eyes for a moment, but she saw at once that she was mistaken.

'No,' Logotheti answered with a smile, 'why should I? If a detective told me anything against you I should not believe it, and no one could tell me half the good I believe about you!'

'You're really awfully nice,' laughed Margaret, for she could not help being flattered. 'Forgive me, please!'

'I would rather that the Nike of Samothrace should think dreadful things of me than that she should not think of me at all!'

'Do I still remind you of her?' asked Margaret.

'Yes. I used to be quite satisfied with my Venus, but now I want the Victory from the Louvre. It's not a mere resemblance. She is you, and as she has no face. I see yours when I look at her. The other day I stood so long on the landing where she is, that a watchman took me for an anarchist waiting to deposit a bomb, and he called a policeman, who asked me my name and occupation. I was very near being arrested—on your account again! You are destined to turn the heads of men of business!'

At this point Margaret became aware that she and Logotheti were talking in undertones, while the conversation at the table had become general, and she reluctantly gave up the idea of again asking where he had got his information about her interview with Mr. Van Torp in New York. The dinner came to an end before long, and the men went out with the ladies, and began to smoke in the drawing-room, standing round the coffee.

Lady Maud put her arm through Margaret's.

'Cigarettes are bad for your throat, I'm sure,' she said, 'and I hate them.'

She led the Primadonna away through a curtained door to a small room furnished according to Eastern ideas of comfort, and she sat down on a low, hard divan, which was covered with a silk carpet. The walls were hung with Persian silks, and displayed three or four texts from the Koran, beautifully written in gold on a green ground. Two small inlaid tables stood near the divan, one at each end, and two deep English easy-chairs, covered with red leather, were placed symmetrically beside them. There was no other furniture, and there were no gimcracks about, such as Europeans think necessary in an 'oriental' room.

With her plain black velvet, Lady Maud looked handsomer than ever in the severely simple surroundings.

'Do you mind?' she asked, as Margaret sat down beside her. 'I'm afraid I carried you off rather unceremoniously!'

'No,' Margaret answered. 'I'm glad to be quiet, it's so long since I was at a dinner-party.'

'I've always hoped to meet you,' said Lady Maud, 'but you're quite different from what I expected. I did not know you were really so young—ever so much younger than I am.'

'Really?'

'Oh, yes! I'm seven-and-twenty, and I've been married four years.'

'I'm twenty-four,' said Margaret, 'and I'm not married yet.'

She was aware that the clear eyes were studying her face, but she did not resent their scrutiny. There was something about her companion that inspired her with trust at first sight, and she did not even remember the impossible story Logotheti had told her.

'I suppose you are tormented by all sorts of people who ask things, aren't you?'

Margaret wondered whether the beauty was going to ask her to sing for nothing at a charity concert.

'I get a great many begging letters, and some very amusing ones,' she answered cautiously. 'Young girls, of whom I never heard, write and ask me to give them pianos and the means of getting a musical education. I once took the trouble to have one of those requests examined. It came from a gang of thieves in Chicago.'

Lady Maud smiled, but did not seem surprised.

'Millionaires get lots of letters of that sort,' she said. 'Think of poor Mr. Van Torp!'

Margaret moved uneasily at the name, which seemed to pursue her since she had left New York; but her present companion was the first person who had applied to him the adjective 'poor.'

'Do you know him well?' she asked, by way of saying something.

Lady Maud was silent for a moment, and seemed to be considering the question.

'I had not meant to speak of him,' she answered presently. 'I like him, and from what you said at dinner I fancy that you don't, so we shall never agree about him.'

'Perhaps not,' said Margaret. 'But I really could not have answered that odious man's question in any other way, could I? I meant to be quite truthful. Though I have met Mr. Van Torp often since last Christmas, I cannot say that I know him very well, because I have not seen the best side of him.'

'Few people ever do, and you have put it as fairly as possible. When I first met him I thought he was a dreadful person, and now we're awfully good friends. But I did not mean to talk about him!'

'I wish you would,' protested Margaret. 'I should like to hear the other side of the case from some one who knows him well.'

'It would take all night to tell even what I know of his story,' said Lady Maud. 'And as you've never seen me before you probably would not believe me,' she added with philosophical calm. 'Why should you? The other side of the case, as I know it, is that he is kind to me, and good to people in trouble, and true to his friends.'

'You cannot say more than that of any man,' Margaret observed gravely.

'I could say much more, but I want to talk to you about other things.'

Margaret, who was attracted by her, and who was sure that the story Logotheti had told was a fabrication, as he said it was, wished that her new acquaintance would leave other matters alone and tell her what she knew about Van Torp.

'It all comes of my having mentioned him accidentally,' said Lady Maud. 'But I often do—probably because I think about him a good deal.'

Margaret thought her amazingly frank, but nothing suggested itself in the way of answer, so she remained silent.

'Did you know that your father and my father were friends at Oxford?' Lady Maud asked, after a little pause.

'Really?' Margaret was surprised.

'When they were undergrads. Your name is Donne, isn't it? Margaret Donne? My father was called Foxwell then. That's our name, you know. He didn't come into the title till his uncle died, a few years ago.'

'But I remember a Mr. Foxwell when I was a child,' said Margaret. 'He came to see us at Oxford sometimes. Do you mean to say that he was your father?'

'Yes. He is alive, you know—tremendously alive!—and he remembers you as a little girl, and wants me to bring you to see him. Do you mind very much? I told him I was to meet you this evening.'

'I should be very glad indeed,' said Margaret.

'He would come to see you,' said Lady Maud, rather apologetically, 'but he sprained his ankle the other day. He was chivvying a cat that was after the pheasants at Creedmore—he's absurdly young, you know—and he came down at some hurdles.'

'I'm so sorry! Of course I shall be delighted to go.'

'It's awfully good of you, and he'll be ever so pleased. May I come and fetch you? When? To-morrow afternoon about three? Are you quite sure you don't mind?'

Margaret was quite sure; for the prospect of seeing an old friend of her father's, and one whom she herself remembered well, was pleasant just then. She was groping for something she had lost, and the merest thread was worth following.

'If you like I'll sing for him,' she said.

'Oh, he simply hates music!' answered Lady Maud, with unconscious indifference to the magnificence of such an offer from the greatest lyric soprano alive.

Margaret laughed in spite of herself.

'Do you hate music too?' she asked.

'No, indeed! I could listen to you for ever. But my father is quite different. I believe he hears half a note higher with one ear than with the other. At all events the effect of music on him is dreadful. He behaves like a cat in a thunderstorm. If you want to please him, talk to him about old bindings. Next to shooting he likes bindings better than anything in the world—in fact he's a capital bookbinder himself.'

At this juncture Mustapha Pasha's pale and spiritual face appeared between the curtains of the small room, and he interrupted the conversation by a single word.

'Bridge?'

Lady Maud was on her feet in an instant.

'Rather!'

'Do you play?' asked the Ambassador, turning to Margaret, who rose more slowly.

'Very badly. I would rather not.'

The diplomatist looked disappointed, and she noticed his expression, and suspected that he would feel himself obliged to talk to her instead of playing.

'I'm very fond of looking on,' she added quickly, 'if you will let me sit beside you.'

They went back to the drawing-room, and presently the celebrated Señorita da Cordova, who was more accustomed to being the centre of interest than she realised, felt that she was nobody at all, as she sat at her host's elbow watching the game through a cloud of suffocating cigarette smoke. Even old Griggs, who detested cards, had sacrificed himself in order to make up the second table. As for Logotheti, he was too tactful to refuse a game in which every one knew him to be a past master, in order to sit out and talk to her the whole evening.

Margaret watched the players with some little interest at first. The disagreeable Mr. Feist lost and became even more disagreeable, and Margaret reflected that whatever he might be he was certainly not an adventurer, for she had seen a good many of the class. The Ambassador lost even more, but with the quiet indifference of a host who plays because his guests like that form of amusement. Lady Maud and the barrister were partners, and seemed to be winning a good deal; the peer whose hobby was applied science revoked and did dreadful things with his trumps, but nobody seemed to care in the least, except the barrister, who was no respecter of persons, and had fought his way to celebrity by terrorising juries and bullying the Bench.

At last Margaret let her head rest against the back of her comfortable chair, and when she closed her eyes because the cigarette smoke made them smart, she forgot to open them again, and went sound asleep; for she was a healthy young person, and had eaten a good dinner, and on evenings when she did not sing she was accustomed to go to bed at ten o'clock, if not earlier.

No one even noticed that she was sleeping, and the game went on till nearly midnight, when she was awakened by the sound of voices, and sprang to her feet with the impression of having done something terribly rude. Every one was standing, the smoke was as thick as ever, and it was tempered by a smell of Scotch whisky. The men looked more or less tired, but Lady Maud had not turned a hair.

The peer, holding a tall glass of weak whisky and soda in his hand, and blinking through his gold-rimmed spectacles, asked her if she were going anywhere else.

'There's nothing to go to yet,' she said rather regretfully.

'There are women's clubs,' suggested Logotheti.

'That's the objection to them,' answered the beauty with more sarcasm than grammatical sequence.

'Bridge till all hours, though,' observed the barrister.

'I'd give something to spend an evening at a smart women's club,' said the playwright in a musing tone. 'Is it true that the Crown Prince of Persia got into the one in Mayfair as a waiter?'

'They don't have waiters,' said Lady Maud. 'Nothing is ever true. I must be going home.'

Margaret was only too glad to go too. When they were downstairs she heard a footman ask Lady Maud if he should call a hansom for her. He evidently knew that she had no carriage.

'May I take you home?' Margaret asked.

'Oh, please do!' answered the beauty with alacrity. 'It's awfully good of you!'

It was raining as the two handsome women got into the singer's comfortable brougham.

'Isn't there room for me too?' asked Logotheti, putting his head in before the footman could shut the door.

'Don't be such a baby,' answered Lady Maud in a displeased tone.

The Greek drew back with a laugh and put up his umbrella; Lady Maud told the footman where to go, and the carriage drove away.

'You must have had a dull evening,' she said.

'I was sound asleep most of the time,' Margaret answered. 'I'm afraid the Ambassador thought me very rude.'

'Because you went to sleep? I don't believe he even noticed it. And if he did, why should you mind? Nobody cares what anybody does nowadays. We've simplified life since the days of our fathers. We think more of the big things than they did, and much less of the little ones.'

'All the same, I wish I had kept awake!'

'Nonsense!' retorted Lady Maud. 'What is the use of being famous if you cannot go to sleep when you are sleepy? This is a bad world as it is, but it would be intolerable if one had to keep up one's school-room manners all one's life, and sit up straight and spell properly, as if Society, with a big S, were a governess that could send us to bed without our supper if we didn't!'

Margaret laughed a little, but there was no ripple in Lady Maud's delicious voice as she made these singular statements. She was profoundly in earnest.

'The public is my schoolmistress,' said Margaret. 'I'm so used to being looked at and listened to on the stage that I feel as if people were always watching me and criticising me, even when I go out to dinner.'

'I've no right at all to give you my opinion, because I'm nobody in particular,' answered Lady Maud, 'and you are tremendously famous and all that! But you'll make yourself miserable for nothing if you get into the way of caring about anybody's opinion of you, except on the stage. And you'll end by making the other people uncomfortable too, because you'll make them think that you mean to teach them manners!'

'Heaven forbid!' Margaret laughed again.

The carriage stopped, and Lady Maud thanked her, bade her good-night, and got out.

'No,' she said, as the footman was going to ring the bell, 'I have a latch-key, thank you.'

It was a small house in Charles Street, Berkeley Square, and the windows were quite dark. There was not even a light in the hall when Margaret saw Lady Maud open the front door and disappear within.

Margaret went over the little incidents of the evening as she drove home alone, and felt better satisfied with herself than she had been since Lushington's visit, in spite of having deliberately gone to sleep in Mustapha Pasha's drawing-room. No one had made her feel that she was changed except for the better, and Lady Maud, who was most undoubtedly a smart woman of the world, had taken a sudden fancy to her. Margaret told herself that this would be impossible if she were ever so little vulgarised by her stage life, and in this reflection she consoled herself for what Lushington had said, and nursed her resentment against him.

The small weaknesses of celebrities are sometimes amazing. There was a moment that evening, as she stood before her huge looking-glass before undressing and scrutinised her face in it, when she would have given her fame and her fortune to be Lady Maud, who trusted to a passing hansom or an acquaintance's carriage for getting home from an Embassy, who let herself into a dark and cheerless little house with a latch-key, who was said to be married to a slippery foreigner, and about whom the gossips invented unedifying tales.

Margaret wondered whether Lady Maud would ever think of changing places with her, to be a goddess for a few hours every week, to have more money than she could spend on herself, and to be pursued with requests for autographs and grand pianos, not to mention invitations to supper from those supernal personages whose uneasy heads wear crowns or itch for them; and Señorita da Cordova told herself rather petulantly that Lady Maud would rather starve than be the most successful soprano that ever trilled on the high A till the house yelled with delight, and the royalties held up their stalking-glasses to watch the fluttering of her throat, if perchance they might see how the pretty noise was made.

But at this point Margaret Donne was a little ashamed of herself, and went to bed; and she dreamt that Edmund Lushington had suddenly taken to wearing a little moustache, very much turned up and flattened on his cheeks, and a single emerald for a stud, which cast a greenish refulgence round it upon a shirt-front that was hideously shiny; and the effect of these changes in his appearance was to make him perfectly odious.

CHAPTER VIII

Lord Creedmore had begun life as a poor barrister, with no particular prospects, had entered the House of Commons early, and had been a hard-working member of Parliament till he had inherited a title and a relatively exiguous fortune when he was over fifty by the unexpected death of his uncle and both the latter's sons within a year. He had married young; his wife was the daughter of a Yorkshire country gentleman, and had blessed him with ten children, who were all alive, and of whom Lady Maud was not the youngest. He was always obliged to make a little calculation to remember how old she was, and whether she was the eighth or the ninth. There were three sons and seven daughters. The sons were all in the army, and all stood between six and seven feet in their stockings; the daughters were all good-looking, but none was as handsome as Maud; they were all married, and all but she had children. Lady Creedmore had been a beauty too, but at the present time she was stout and gouty, had a bad temper, and alternately soothed and irritated her complaint and her disposition by following cures or committing imprudences. Her husband, who was now over sixty, had never been ill a day in his life; he was as lean and tough as a greyhound and as active as a schoolboy, a good rider, and a crack shot.

His connection with this tale, apart from the friendship which grew up between Margaret and Lady Maud, lies in the fact that his land in Derbyshire adjoined the estate which Mr. Van Torp had bought and re-named after himself. It was here that Lady Maud and the American magnate had first met, two years after her marriage, when she had come home on a long visit, very much disillusionised as to the supposed advantages of the marriage bond as compared with the freedom of a handsome English girl of three-and-twenty, who is liked in her set and has the run of a score of big country houses without any chaperonial encumbrance. For the chaperon is going down to the shadowy kingdom of the extinct, and is already reckoned with dodos, stagecoaches, muzzle loaders, crinolines, Southey's poems, the Thirty-nine Articles, Benjamin Franklin's reputation, the British workman, and the late Herbert Spencer's philosophy.

On the previous evening Lady Maud had not told Margaret that Lord Creedmore lived in Surrey, having let his town house since his youngest daughter had married. She now explained that it would be absurd to think of driving such a distance when one could go almost all the way by train. The singer was rather scared at the prospect of possibly missing trains, waiting in draughty stations, and getting wet by a shower; she was accustomed to think nothing of driving twenty miles in a closed carriage to avoid the slightest risk of a wetting.

But Lady Maud piloted her safely, and showed an intimate knowledge of the art of getting about by public conveyances which amazed her companion. She seemed to know by instinct the difference between one train and another, when all looked just alike, and when she had to ask a question of a guard or a porter her inquiry was met with business-like directness and brevity, and commanded the respect which all officials feel for people who do not speak to them without a really good reason—so different from their indulgent superiority when we enter into friendly conversation with them.

The journey ended in a walk of a quarter of a mile from the station to the gate of the small park in which the house stood. Lady Maud said she was sorry she had forgotten to telephone for a trap to be sent down, but added cheerfully that the walk would do Margaret good.

'You know your way wonderfully well,' Margaret said.

'Yes,' answered her companion carelessly. 'I don't think I could lose myself in London, from Limehouse to Wormwood Scrubs.'

She spoke quite naturally, as if it were not in the least surprising that a smart woman of the world should possess such knowledge.

'You must have a marvellous memory for places,' Margaret ventured to say.

'Why? Because I know my way about? I walk a great deal, that's all.'

Margaret wondered whether the Countess Leven habitually took her walks in the direction of Limehouse in the east or Shepherd's Bush in the west; and if so, why? As for the distance, the thoroughbred looked as if she could do twenty miles without turning a hair, and Margaret wished she would not walk quite so fast, for, like all great singers, she herself easily got out of breath if she was hurried; it was not the distance that surprised her, however, but the fact that Lady Maud should ever visit such regions.

They reached the house and found Lord Creedmore in the library, his lame foot on a stool and covered up with a chudder. His clear brown eyes examined Margaret's face attentively while he held her hand in his.

'So you are little Margery,' he said at last, with a very friendly smile. 'Do you remember me at all, my dear? I suppose I have changed almost more than you have.'

Margaret remembered him very well indeed as Mr. Foxwell, who used always to bring her certain particularly delicious chocolate wafers whenever he came to see her father in Oxford. She sat down beside him and looked at his face—clean-shaven, kindly, and energetic—the face of a clever lawyer and yet of a keen sportsman, a type you will hardly find out of England.

Lady Maud left the two alone after a few minutes, and Margaret found herself talking of her childhood and her old home, as if nothing very much worth mentioning had happened in her life during the last ten or a dozen years. While she answered her new friend's questions and asked others of him she unconsciously looked about the room. The writing-table was not far from her, and she saw on it two photographs in plain ebony frames; one was of her father, the other was a likeness of Lady Maud. Little by little she understood that her father had been Lord Creedmore's best friend from their schoolboy days till his death. Yet although they had constantly exchanged short visits, the one living in Oxford and the other chiefly in town, their wives had hardly known each other, and their children had never met.

'Take him all in all,' said the old gentleman gravely, 'Donne was the finest fellow I ever knew, and the only real friend I ever had.'

His eyes turned to the photograph on the table with a far-away manly regret that went to Margaret's heart. Her father had been a reticent man, and as there was no reason why he should have talked much about his absent friend Foxwell, it was not surprising that Margaret should never have known how close the tie was that bound them. But now, coming unawares upon the recollection of that friendship in the man who had survived, she felt herself drawn to him as if he were of her own blood, and she thought she understood why she had liked his daughter so much at first sight.

They talked for more than half an hour, and Margaret did not even notice that he had not once alluded to her profession, and that she had so far forgotten herself for the time as not to miss the usual platitudes about her marvellous voice and her astoundingly successful career.

'I hope you'll come and stop with us in Derbyshire in September,' he said at last. 'I'm quite ashamed to ask you there, for we are dreadfully dull people; but it would give us a great deal of pleasure.'

'You are very kind indeed,' Margaret said. 'I should be delighted to come.'

'Some of our neighbours might interest you,' said Lord Creedmore. 'There's Mr. Van Torp, for instance, the American millionaire. His land joins mine.'

'Really?'

Margaret wondered if she should ever again go anywhere without hearing of Mr. Van Torp.

'Yes. He bought Oxley Paddox some time ago and promptly re-christened it Torp Towers. But he's not a bad fellow. Maud likes him, though Lady Creedmore calls him names. He has such a nice little girl—at least, it's not exactly his child, I believe,' his lordship ran on rather hurriedly; 'but he's adopted her, I understand—at least, I fancy so. At all events she was born deaf, poor little thing; but he has had her taught to speak and to understand from the lips. Awfully pretty child! Maud delights in her. Nice governess, too—I forget her name; but she's a faithful sort of woman. It's a dreadfully hard position, don't you know, to be a governess if you're young and good-looking, and though Van Torp is rather a decent sort, I never feel quite sure—Maud likes him immensely, it's true, and that is a good sign; but Maud is utterly mad about a lot of things, and besides, she's singularly well able to take care of herself.'

'Yes,' said Margaret; but she thought of the story Logotheti had told her on the previous evening. 'I know Mr. Van Torp, and the little girl and Miss More,' she said after a moment. 'We came over in the same steamer.'

She thought it was only fair to say that she had met the people of whom he had been speaking. There was no reason why Lord Creedmore should be surprised by this, and he only nodded and smiled pleasantly.

'All the better. I shall set Maud on you to drag you down to Derbyshire in September,' he said. 'Women never have anything to do in September. Let me see—you're an actress, aren't you, my dear?'

Margaret laughed. It was positively delightful to feel that he had never heard of her theatrical career.

'No; I'm a singer,' she said. 'My stage name is Cordova.'

'Oh yes, yes,' answered Lord Creedmore, very vaguely. 'It's the same thing—you cannot possibly have anything to do in September, can you?'

'We shall see. I hope not, this year.'

'If it's not very indiscreet of me, as an old friend, you know, do you manage to make a living by the stage?'

'Oh—fair!' Margaret almost laughed again.

Lady Maud returned at this juncture, and Margaret rose to go, feeling that she had stayed long enough.

'Margery has half promised to come to us in September,' said Lord Creedmore to his daughter, 'You don't mind if I call you Margery, do you?' he asked, turning to Margaret. 'I cannot call you Miss Donne since you really remember the chocolate wafers! You shall have some as soon as I can go to see you!'

Margaret loved the name she had been called by as a child. Mrs. Rushmore had severely eschewed diminutives.

'Margery,' repeated Lady Maud thoughtfully. 'I like the name awfully well. Do you mind calling me Maud? We ought to have known each other when we were in pinafores!'

In this way it happened that Margaret found herself unexpectedly on something like intimate terms with her father's friend and the latter's favourite child less than twenty-four hours after meeting Lady Maud, and this was how she was asked to their place in the country for the month of September. But that seemed very far away.

Lady Maud took Margaret home, as she had brought her, without making her wait more than three minutes for a train, without exposing her to a draught, and without letting her get wet, all of which would seem easy enough to an old Londoner, but was marvellous in the eyes of the young Primadonna, and conveyed to her an idea of freedom that was quite new to her. She remembered that she used to be proud of her independence when she first went into Paris from Versailles alone for her singing lessons; but that trip, contrasted with the one from her own house to Lord Creedmore's on the Surrey side, was like going out for an hour's sail in a pleasure-boat on a summer's afternoon compared with working a sea-going vessel safely through an intricate and crowded channel at night.

Margaret noticed, too, that although Lady Maud was a very striking figure, she was treated with respect in places where the singer knew instinctively that if she herself had been alone she would have been afraid that men would speak to her. She knew very well how to treat them if they did, and was able to take care of herself if she chose to travel alone; but she ran the risk of being annoyed where the beautiful thoroughbred was in no danger at all. That was the difference.

Lady Maud left her at her own door and went off on foot, though the hansom that had brought them from the Baker Street Station was still lurking near.

Margaret had told Logotheti to come and see her late in the afternoon, and as she entered the hall she was surprised to hear voices upstairs. She asked the servant who was waiting.

With infinite difficulty in the matter of pronunciation the man informed her that the party consisted of Monsieur Logotheti, Herr Schreiermeyer, Signor Stromboli, the Signorina Baci-Roventi, and Fräulein Ottilie Braun. The four professionals had come at the very moment when Logotheti had gained admittance on the ground that he had an appointment, which was true, and they had refused to be sent away. In fact, unless he had called the police the poor footman could not have kept them out. The Signorina Baci-Roventi alone, black-browed, muscular, and five feet ten in her shoes, would have been almost a match for him alone; but she was backed by Signor Pompeo Stromboli, who weighed fifteen stone in his fur coat, was as broad as he was long, and had been seen to run off the stage with Madame Bonanni in his arms while he yelled a high G that could have been heard in Westminster if the doors had been open. Before the onslaught of such terrific foreigners a superior London footman could only protest with dignity and hold the door open for them to pass. Braver men than he had quailed before Schreiermeyer's stony eye, and gentle little Fräulein Ottilie slipped in like a swallow in the track of a storm.

Margaret felt suddenly inclined to shut herself up in her room and send word that she had a headache and could not see them. But Schreiermeyer was there. He would telephone for three doctors, and would refuse to leave the house till they signed an assurance that she was perfectly well and able to begin rehearsing the *Elisir d'Amore* the next morning. That was what Schreiermeyer would do, and when she next met him he would tell her that he would have 'no nonsense, no stupid stuff,' and that she had signed an engagement and must sing or pay.

She had never shammed an illness, either, and she did not mean to begin now. It was only that for two blessed hours and more, with her dead father's best friend and Maud, she had felt like her old self again, and had dreamt that she was with her own people. She had even disliked the prospect of seeing Logotheti after that, and she felt a much stronger repugnance for her theatrical comrades. She went to her own room before meeting them, and she sighed as she stood before the tall looking-glass for a moment after taking off her coat and hat. In pulling out the hat-pins her hair had almost come down, and Alphonsine proposed to do it over again, but Margaret was impatient.

'Give me something—a veil, or anything,' she said impatiently. 'They are waiting for me.'

The maid instantly produced from a near drawer a peach-coloured veil embroidered with green and gold. It was a rather vivid modern Turkish one given her by Logotheti, and she wrapped it quickly over her disordered hair, like a sort of turban, tucking one end in, and left the room almost without glancing at the glass again. She was discontented with herself now for having dreamt of ever again being anything but what she was—a professional singer.

The little party greeted her noisily as she entered the music-room. Her comrades had not seen her since she had left them in New York, and the consequence was that Signorina Baci-Roventi kissed her on both cheeks with dramatic force, and she kissed Fräulein Ottilie on both cheeks, and Pompeo Stromboli offered himself for a like favour and had to be fought off, while Schreiermeyer looked on gravely, very much as a keeper at the Zoo watches the gambols of the animals in his charge; but Logotheti shook hands very quietly, well perceiving that his chance of pleasing her just then lay in being profoundly respectful while the professionals were overpoweringly familiar. His almond-shaped eyes asked her how in the world she could stand it all, and she felt uncomfortable at the thought that she was used to it.

Besides, these good people really liked her. The only members of the profession who hated her were the other lyric sopranos. Schreiermeyer, rapacious and glittering, had a photograph of her hideously enamelled in colours inside the cover of his watch, and the facsimile of her autograph was engraved across the lid of his silver cigarette-case. Pompeo Stromboli carried some of her hair in a locket which he wore on his chain between two amulets against the Evil Eye. Fräulein Ottilie treasured a little water-colour sketch of her as Juliet on which Margaret had written a few friendly words, and the Baci-Roventi actually went to the length of asking her advice about the high notes the contralto has to sing in such operas as *Semiramide*. It would be hard to imagine a more sincere proof of affection and admiration than this.

Margaret knew that the greeting was genuine and that she ought to be pleased, but at the first moment the noise and the kissing and the rough promiscuity of it all disgusted her.

Then she saw that all had brought her little presents, which were arranged side by side on the piano, and she suddenly remembered that it was her birthday. They were small things without value, intended to make her laugh. Stromboli had sent to Italy for a Neapolitan clay figure of a shepherd, cleverly modelled and painted, and vaguely resembling himself—he had been a Calabrian goatherd. The contralto, who came from Bologna, the city of sausages, gave Margaret a tiny pig made of silver with holes in his back, in which were stuck a number of quill toothpicks.

'You will think of me when you use them at table,' she said, charmingly unconscious of English prejudices.

Schreiermeyer presented her with a bronze statuette of Shylock whetting his knife upon his thigh.

'It will encourage you to sign our next agreement,' he observed with stony calm. 'It is the symbol of business. We are all symbolic nowadays.'

Fräulein Ottilie Braun had wrought a remarkable little specimen of German sentiment. She had made a little blue pin-cushion and had embroidered some little flowers on it in brown silk. Margaret had no difficulty in looking pleased, but she also looked slightly puzzled.

'They are forget-me-nots,' said the Fräulein, 'but because my name is Braun I made them brown. You see? So you will remember your little Braun forget-me-not!'

Margaret laughed at the primitively simple little jest, but she was touched too, and somehow she felt that her eyes were not quite dry as she kissed the good little woman again. But Logotheti could not understand at all, and thought it all extremely silly. He did not like Margaret's improvised turban, either, though he recognised the veil as one he had given her. The headdress was not classic, and he did not think it becoming to the Victory of Samothrace.

He also had remembered her birthday and he had a small offering in his pocket, but he could not give it to her before the others. Schreiermeyer would probably insist on looking at it and would guess its value, whereas Logotheti was sure that Margaret would not. He would give it to her when they were alone, and would tell her that it was nothing but a seal for her writing-case, a common green stone of some kind with a little Greek head on it; and she would look at it and think it pretty, and take it, because it did not look very valuable to her unpractised eye. But the 'common green stone' was a great emerald, and the 'little Greek head' was an intaglio of Anacreon, cut some two thousand and odd hundred years ago by an art that is lost; and the setting had been made and chiselled for Maria de' Medici when she married Henry the Fourth of France. Logotheti liked to give Margaret things vastly more rare than she guessed them to be.

Margaret offered her visitors tea, and she and Logotheti took theirs while the others looked on or devoured the cake and bread and butter.

'Tea?' repeated Signor Stromboli. 'I am well. Why should I take tea? The tea is for to perspire when I have a cold.'

The Signorina Baci-Roventi laughed at him.

'Do you not know that the English drink tea before dinner to give themselves an appetite?' she asked. 'It is because they drink tea that they eat so much.'

'All the more,' answered Stromboli. 'Do you not see that I am fat? Why should I eat more? Am I to turn into a monument of Victor Emanuel?'

'You eat too much bread,' said Schreiermeyer in a resentful tone.

'It is my vice,' said the tenor, taking up four thin slices of bread and butter together and popping them all into his mouth without the least difficulty. 'When I see bread, I eat it. I eat all there is.'

'We see you do,' returned Schreiermeyer bitterly.

'I cannot help it. Why do they bring bread? They are in league to make me fat. The waiters know me. I go into the Carlton; the head-waiter whispers; a waiter brings a basket of bread; I eat it all. I go into Boisin's, or Henry's; the head-waiter whispers; it is a basket of bread; while I eat a few eggs, a chicken, a salad, a tart or two, some fruit, cheese, the bread is all gone. I am the tomb of all the bread in the world. So I get fat. There,' he concluded gravely, 'it is as I tell you. I have eaten all.'

And in fact, while talking, he had punctuated each sentence with a tiny slice or two of thin bread and butter, and everybody laughed, except Schreiermeyer, as the huge singer gravely held up the empty glass dish and showed it.

'What do you expect of me?' he asked. 'It is a vice, and I am not Saint Anthony, to resist temptation.'

'Perhaps,' suggested Fräulein Ottilie timidly, 'if you exercised a little strength of character—'

'Exercise?' roared Stromboli, not understanding her, for they spoke a jargon of Italian, German, and English. 'Exercise? The more I exercise, the more I eat! Ha, ha, ha! Exercise, indeed! You talk like crazy!'

'You will end on wheels,' said Schreiermeyer with cold contempt. 'You will stand on a little truck which will be moved about the stage from below. You will be lifted to Juliet's balcony by a hydraulic crane. But you shall pay for the machinery. Oh yes, oh yes! I will have it in the contract! You shall be weighed. So much flesh to move, so much money.'

'Shylock!' suggested Logotheti, glancing at the statuette and laughing.

'Yes, Shylock and his five hundred pounds of flesh,' answered Schreiermeyer, with a faint smile that disappeared again at once.

'But I meant character—' began Fräulein Ottilie, trying to go back and get in a word.

'Character!' cried the Baci-Roventi with a deep note that made the open piano vibrate. 'His stomach is his heart, and his character is his appetite!'

She bent her heavy brows and fixed her gleaming black eyes on him with a tragic expression.

'"Let them cant about decorum who have characters to lose,"' quoted Logotheti softly.

This delicate banter went on for twenty minutes, very much to Schreiermeyer's inward satisfaction, for it proved that at least four members of his company were on good terms with him and with each other; for when they had a grudge against him, real or imaginary, they became sullen and silent in his presence, and eyed him with the coldly ferocious expression of china dogs.

At last they all rose and went away in a body, leaving Margaret with Logotheti.

'I had quite forgotten that it was my birthday,' she said, when they were gone.

'I've brought you a little seal,' he answered, holding out the intaglio.

She took it and looked at it.

'How pretty!' she exclaimed. 'It's awfully kind of you to have remembered to-day, and I wanted a seal very much.'

'It's a silly little thing, just a head on some sort of green stone. But I tried it on sealing-wax, and the impression is not so bad. I shall be very happy if it's of any use, for I'm always puzzling my brain to find something you may like.'

'Thanks very much. It's the thought I care for.' She laid the seal on the table beside her empty cup. 'And now that we are alone,' she went on, 'please tell me.'

'What?'

'How you found out what you told me at dinner last night.'

She leant back in the chair, raising her arms and joining her hands above her head against the high top of the chair, and stretching herself a little. The attitude threw the curving lines of her figure into high relief, and was careless enough, but the tone in which she spoke was almost one of command, and there was a sort of expectant resentfulness in her eyes as they watched his face while she waited for his answer. She believed that he had paid to have her watched by some one who had bribed her servants.

'I did not find out anything,' he said quietly. 'I received an anonymous letter from New York giving me all the details of the scene. The letter was written with the evident intention of injuring Mr. Van Torp. Whoever wrote it must have heard what you said to each other, and perhaps he was watching you through the keyhole. It is barely possible that by some accident he overheard the scene through the local telephone, if there was one in the room. Should you care to see that part of the letter which concerns you? It is not very delicately worded!'

Margaret's expression had changed; she had dropped her hands and was leaning forward, listening with interest.

'No,' she said, 'I don't care to see the letter, but who in the world can have written it? You say it was meant to injure Mr. Van Torp—not me.'

'Yes. There is nothing against you in it. On the contrary, the writer calls attention to the fact that there never was a word breathed against your reputation, in order to prove what an utter brute Van Torp must be.'

'Tell me,' Margaret said, 'was that story about Lady Maud in the same letter?'

'Oh dear, no! That is supposed to have happened the other day, but I got the letter last winter.'

'When?'

'In January, I think.'

'He came to see me soon after New Year's Day,' said Margaret.' I wish I knew who told—I really don't believe it was my maid.'

'I took the letter to one of those men who tell character by handwriting,' answered Logotheti. 'I don't know whether you believe in that, but I do a little. I got rather a queer result, considering that I only showed half-a-dozen lines, which could not give any idea of the contents.'

'What did the man say?'

'He said the writer appeared to be on the verge of insanity, if not actually mad; that he was naturally of an accurate mind, with ordinary business capacities, such as a clerk might have, but that he had received a much better education than most clerks get, and must at one time have done intellectual work. His madness, the man said, would probably take some violent form.'

'There's nothing very definite about all that,' Margaret observed. 'Why in the world should the creature have written to you, of all people, to destroy Mr. Van Torp's character?'

'The interview with you was only an incident,' answered Logotheti. 'There were other things, all tending to show that he is not a safe person to deal with.'

'Why should you ever deal with him?'

Logotheti smiled.

'There are about a hundred and fifty men in different countries who are regarded as the organs of the world's financial body. The very big ones are the vital organs. Van Torp has grown so much of late that he is probably one of them. Some people are good enough to think that I'm another. The blood of the financial body—call it gold, or credit, or anything you like—circulates through all the organs, and if one of the great vital ones gets out of order the whole body is likely to suffer. Suppose that Van Torp wished to do something with the Nickel Trust in Paris, and that I had private information to the effect that he was not a man to be trusted, and that I believed this information, don't you see that I should naturally warn my friends against him, and that our joint weight would be an effective obstacle in his way?'

'Yes, I see that. But, dear me! do you mean to say that all financiers must be strictly virtuous, like little woolly white lambs?'

Margaret laughed carelessly. If Lushington had heard her, his teeth would have been set on edge, but Logotheti did not notice the shade of expression and tone.

'I repeat that the account of the interview with you was a mere incident, thrown in to show that Van Torp occasionally loses his head and behaves like a madman.'

'I don't want to see the letter,' said Margaret, 'but what sort of accusations did it contain? Were they all of the same kind?'

'No. There was one other thing—something about a little girl called Ida, who is supposed to be the daughter of that old Alvah Moon who robbed your mother. You can guess the sort of thing the letter said without my telling you.'

Margaret leaned forward and poked the small wood fire with a pair of unnecessarily elaborate gilt tongs, and she nodded, for she remembered how Lord Creedmore had mentioned the child that afternoon. He had hesitated a little, and had then gone on speaking rather hurriedly. She watched the sparks fly upward each time she touched the log, and she nodded slowly.

'What are you thinking of?' asked Logotheti.

But she did not answer for nearly half a minute. She was reflecting on a singular little fact which made itself clear to her just then. She was certainly not a child; she was not even a very young girl, at twenty-four; she had never been prudish, and she did not affect the pre-Serpentine innocence of Eve before the fall. Yet it was suddenly apparent to her that because she was a singer men treated her as if she were a married woman, and would have done so if she had been even five years younger. Talking to her as Margaret Donne, in Mrs. Rushmore's house, two years earlier, Logotheti would not have approached such a subject as little Ida Moon's possible relation to Mr. Van Torp, because the Greek had been partly brought up in England and had been taught what one might and might not say to a 'nice English girl.' Margaret now reflected that since the day she had set foot upon the stage of the Opera she had apparently ceased to be a 'nice English girl' in the eyes of men of the world. The profession of singing in public, then, presupposed that the singer was no longer the more or less imaginary young girl, the hothouse flower of the social garden, whose perfect bloom the merest breath of worldly knowledge must blight for ever. Margaret might smile at the myth, but she could not ignore the fact that she was already as much detached from it in men's eyes as if she had entered the married state. The mere fact of realising that the hothouse blossom was part of the social legend proved the change in herself.

'So that is the secret about the little girl,' she said at last. Then she started a little, as if she had made a discovery. 'Good heavens!' she exclaimed, poking the fire sharply. 'He cannot be as bad as that—even he!'

'What do you mean?' asked Logotheti, surprised.

'No—really—it's too awful,' Margaret said slowly, to herself. 'Besides,' she added, 'one has no right to believe an anonymous letter.'

'The writer was well informed about you, at least,' observed Logotheti. 'You say that the details are true.'

'Absolutely. That makes the other thing all the more dreadful.'

'It's not such a frightful crime, after all,' Logotheti answered with a little surprise. 'Long before he fell in love with you he may have liked some one else! Such things may happen in every man's life.'

'That one thing—yes, no doubt. But you either don't know, or you don't realise just what all the rest has been, up to the death of that poor girl in the theatre in New York.'

'He was engaged to her, was he not?'

'Yes.'

'I forget who she was.'

'His partner's daughter. She was called Ida Bamberger.'

'Ida? Like the little girl?'

'Yes. Bamberger divorced his wife, and she married Senator Moon. Don't you see?'

'And the girls were half-sisters—and—?' Logotheti stopped and stared.

'Yes.' Margaret nodded slowly again and poked the fire.

'Good heavens!' The Greek knew something of the world's wickedness, but his jaw dropped. 'Oedipus!' he ejaculated.

'It cannot be true,' Margaret said, quite in earnest. 'I detest him, but I cannot believe that of him.'

For in her mind all that she knew and that Griggs had told her, and that Logotheti did not know yet, rose up in orderly logic, and joined what was now in her mind, completing the whole hideous tale of wickedness that had ended in the death of Ida Bamberger, who had been murdered, perhaps, in desperation to avert a crime even more monstrous. The dying girl's faint voice came back to Margaret across the ocean.

'He did it—'

And there was the stain on Paul Griggs' hand; and there was little Ida's face on the steamer, when she had looked up and had seen Van Torp's lips moving, and had understood what he was saying to himself, and had dragged Margaret away in terror. And not least, there was the indescribable fear of him which Margaret felt when he was near her for a few minutes.

On the other side, what was there to be said for him? Miss More, quiet, good, conscientious Miss More, devoting her life to the child, said that he was one of the kindest men living. There was Lady Maud, with her clear eyes, her fearless ways, and her knowledge of the world and men, and she said that Van Torp was kind, and good to people in trouble and true to his friends. Lord Creedmore, the intimate friend of Margaret's father, a barrister half his life, and as keen as a hawk, said that Mr. Van Torp was a very decent sort of man, and he evidently allowed his daughter to like the American. It was true that a scandalous tale about Lady Maud and the millionaire was already going from mouth to mouth, but Margaret did not believe it. If she had known that the facts were accurately told, whatever their meaning might be, she would have taken them for further evidence against the accused. As for Miss More, she was guided by her duty to her employer, or her affection for little Ida, and she seemed to be of the charitable sort, who think no evil; but after what Lord Creedmore had said, Margaret had no doubt but that it was Mr. Van Torp who provided for the child, and if she was his daughter, the reason for Senator Moon's neglect of her was patent.

Then Margaret thought of Isidore Bamberger, the hard-working man of business who was Van Torp's right hand and figure-head, as Griggs had said, and who had divorced the beautiful, half-crazy mother of the two Idas because Van Torp had stolen her from him—Van Torp, his partner, and once his trusted friend. She remembered the other things Griggs had told her: how old Bamberger must surely have discovered that his daughter had been murdered, and that he meant to keep it a secret till he caught the murderer. Even now the detectives might be on the right scent, and if he whose child had been killed, and whose wife had been stolen from him by the man he had once trusted, learnt the whole truth at last, he would not be easily appeased.

'You have had some singular offers of marriage,' said Logotheti in a tone of reflection. 'You will probably marry a beggar some day—a nice beggar, who has ruined himself like a gentleman, but a beggar nevertheless!'

'I don't know,' Margaret said carelessly. 'Of one thing I am sure. I shall not marry Mr. Van Torp.'

Logotheti laughed softly.

'Remember the French proverb,' he said. '"Say not to the fountain, I will not drink of thy water."'

'Proverbs,' returned Margaret, 'are what Schreiermeyer calls stupid stuff. Fancy marrying that monster!'

'Yes,' assented Logotheti, 'fancy!'

CHAPTER IX

Three weeks later, when the days were lengthening quickly and London was beginning to show its better side to the cross-grained people who abuse its climate, the gas was lighted again in the dingy rooms in Hare Court. No one but the old woman who came to sweep had visited them since Mr. Van Torp had gone into the country in March, after Lady Maud had been to see him on the evening of his arrival.

As then, the fire was laid in the grate, but the man in black who sat in the shabby arm-chair had not put a match to the shavings, and the bright copper kettle on the movable hob shone coldly in the raw glare from the incandescent gaslight. The room was chilly, and the man had not taken off his black overcoat or his hat, which had a broad band on it. His black gloves lay on the table beside him. He wore patent leather boots with black cloth tops, and he turned in his toes as he sat. His aquiline features were naturally of the melancholic type, and as he stared at the fireplace his expression was profoundly sad. He did not move for a long time, but suddenly he trembled, as a man does who feels the warning chill in a malarious country when the sun goes down, and two large bright tears ran down his lean dark cheeks and were quickly lost in his grizzled beard. Either he did not feel them, or he would not take the trouble to dry them, for he sat quite still and kept his eyes on the grate.

Outside it was quite dark and the air was thick, so that the chimney-pots on the opposite roof were hardly visible against the gloomy sky. It was the time of year when spring seems very near in broad daylight, but as far away as in January when the sun goes down.

Mr. Isidore Bamberger was waiting for a visitor, as his partner Mr. Van Torp had waited in the same place a month earlier, but he made no preparations for a cheerful meeting, and the cheap japanned tea-caddy, with the brown teapot and the chipped cups and saucers, stood undisturbed in the old-fashioned cupboard in the corner, while the lonely man sat before the cold fireplace and let the tears trickle down his cheeks as they would.

At the double stroke of the spring door-bell, twice repeated, his expression changed as if he had been waked from a dream. He dried his cheeks roughly with the back of his hand, and his very heavy black eyebrows were drawn down and together, as if the tension of the man's whole nature had been relaxed and was now suddenly restored. The look of sadness hardened to an expression that was melancholy still, but grim and unforgiving, and the grizzled beard, clipped rather close at the sides, betrayed the angles of the strong jaw as he set his teeth and rose to let in his visitor. He was round-shouldered and slightly bow-legged when he stood up; he was heavily and clumsily built, but he was evidently strong.

He went out into the dark entry and opened the door, and a moment later he came back with Mr. Feist, the man with the unhealthy complexion whom Margaret had seen at the Turkish Embassy. Isidore Bamberger sat down in the easy-chair again without ceremony, leaving his guest to bring up a straight-backed chair for himself.

Mr. Feist was evidently in a very nervous condition. His hand shook perceptibly as he mopped his forehead after sitting down, and he moved his chair uneasily twice because the incandescent light irritated his eyes. He did not wait for Bamberger to question him, however.

'It's all right,' he said, 'but he doesn't care to take steps till after this season is over. He says the same thing will happen again to a dead certainty, and that the more evidence he has the surer he'll be of the decree. I think he's afraid Van Torp has some explanation up his sleeve that will swing things the other way.'

'Didn't he catch her here?' asked the elder man, evidently annoyed. 'Didn't he find the money on this table in an envelope addressed to her? Didn't he have two witnesses with him? Or is all that an invention?'

'It happened just so. But he's afraid there's some explanation—'

'Feist,' said Isidore Bamberger slowly, 'find out what explanation the man's afraid of, pretty quick, or I'll get somebody who will. It's my belief that he's just a common coward, who takes money from his wife and doesn't care how she gets it. I suppose she refused to pay one day, so he strengthened his position by catching her; but he doesn't want to divorce the goose that lays the golden egg as long as he's short of cash. That's about the measure of it, you may depend.'

'She may be a goose,' answered Feist, 'but she's a wild one, and she'll lead us a chase too. She's up to all sorts of games, I've ascertained. She goes out of the house at all hours and comes home when she's ready, and it isn't to meet your friend either, for he's not been in London again since he landed.'

'Then who else is it?' asked Bamberger.

Feist smiled in a sickly way.

'Don't know,' he said. 'Can't find out.'

'I don't like people who don't know and can't find out,' answered the other. 'I'm in a hurry, I tell you. I'm employing you, and paying you a good salary, and taking a great deal of trouble to have you pushed with letters of introduction where you can see her, and now you come here and tell me you don't know and you can't find out. It won't do, Feist. You're no better than you used to be when you were my secretary last year. You're a pretty bright young fellow when you don't drink, but when you do you're about as useful as a painted clock—and even a painted clock is right twice in twenty-four hours. It's more than you are. The only good thing about you is that you can hold your tongue, drunk or sober. I admit that.'

Having relieved himself of this plain opinion Isidore Bamberger waited to hear what Feist had to say, keeping his eyes fixed on the unhealthy face.

'I've not been drinking lately, anyhow,' he answered, 'and I'll tell you one thing, Mr. Bamberger, and that is, that I'm just as anxious as you can be to see this thing through, every bit.'

'Well, then, don't waste time! I don't care a cent about the divorce, except that it will bring the whole affair into publicity. As soon as all the papers are down on him, I'll start in on the real thing. I shall be ready by that time. I want public opinion on both sides of the ocean to run strong against him, as it ought to, and it's just that it should. If I don't manage that, he may get off in the end in spite of your evidence.'

'Look here, Mr. Bamberger,' said Feist, waking up, 'if you want my evidence, don't talk of dropping me as you did just now, or you won't get it, do you understand? You've paid me the compliment of telling me that I can hold my tongue. All right. But it won't suit you if I hold my tongue in the witness-box, will it? That's all, Mr. Bamberger. I've nothing more to say about that.'

There was a sudden vehemence in the young man's tone which portrayed that in spite of his broken nerves he could still be violent. But Isidore Bamberger was not the man to be brow-beaten by any one he employed. He almost smiled when Feist stopped speaking.

'That's all right,' he said half good-naturedly and half contemptuously. 'We understand each other. That's all right.'

'I hope it is,' Feist answered in a dogged way. 'I only wanted you to know.'

'Well, I do, since you've told me. But you needn't get excited like that. It's just as well you gave up studying medicine and took to business, Feist, for you haven't got what they call a pleasant bedside manner.'

Mr. Feist had once been a medical student, but had given up the profession on inheriting a sum of money with which he at once began to speculate. After various vicissitudes he had become Mr. Bamberger's private secretary, and had held that position some time in spite of his one failing, because he had certain qualities which made him invaluable to his employer until his nerves began to give away. One of those qualities was undoubtedly his power of holding his tongue even when under the influence of drink; another was his really extraordinary memory for details, and especially for letters he had written under dictation, and for conversations he had heard. He was skilful, too, in many ways when in full possession of his faculties; but though Isidore Bamberger used him, he despised him profoundly, as he despised every man who preferred present indulgence to future profit.

Feist lit a cigarette and blew a vast cloud of smoke round him, but made no answer to his employer's last observation.

'Now this is what I want you to do,' said the latter. 'Go to this Count Leven and tell him it's a cash transaction or nothing, and that he runs no risk. Find out what he'll really take, but don't come talking to me about five thousand pounds or anything of that kind, for that's ridiculous. Tell him that if proceedings are not begun by the first of May his wife won't get any more money from Van Torp, and he won't get any more from his wife. Use any other argument that strikes you. That's your business, because that's what I pay you for. What I want is the result, and that's justice and no more, and I don't care anything about the means. Find them and I'll pay. If you can't find them I'll pay somebody who can, and if nobody can I'll go to the end without. Do you understand?'

'Oh, I understand right enough,' answered Feist, with his bad smile.' If I can hit on the right scheme I won't ask you anything extra for it, Mr. Bamberger! By the bye, I wrote you I met Cordova, the Primadonna, at the Turkish Embassy, didn't I? She hates him as much as the other woman likes him, yet she and the other have struck up a friendship. I daresay I shall get something out of that too.'

'Why does Cordova hate him?' asked Bamberger.

'Don't quite know. Thought perhaps you might.'

'No.'

'He was attentive to her last winter,' Feist said. 'That's all I know for certain. He's a brutal sort of man, and maybe he offended her somehow.'

'Well,' returned Isidore Bamberger, 'maybe; but singers aren't often offended by men who have money. At least, I've always understood so, though I don't know much about that side of life myself.'

'It would be just one thing more to break his character if Cordova would say something against him,' suggested Feist. 'Her popularity is something tremendous, and people always believe a woman who says that a man has insulted her. In those things the bare word of a pretty lady who's no better than she should be is worth more than an honest man's character for thirty years.'

'That's so,' said Bamberger, looking at him attentively. 'That's quite true. Whatever you are, Feist, you're no fool. We may as well have the pretty lady's bare word, anyway.'

'If you approve, I'm nearly sure I can get it,' Feist answered. 'At least, I can get a statement which she won't deny if it's published in the right way. I can furnish the materials for an article on her that's sure to please her—born lady, never a word against her, highly connected, unassailable private life, such a contrast to several other celebrities on the stage, immensely charitable, half American, half English—every bit of that all helps, you see—and then an anecdote or two thrown in, and just the bare facts about her having had to escape in a hurry from a prominent millionaire in a New York hotel—fairly ran for her life and turned the key against him. Give his name if you like. If he brings action for libel, you can subpoena Cordova herself. She'll swear to it if it's true, and then you can unmask your big guns and let him have it hot.'

'No doubt, no doubt. But how do you propose to find out if it is true?'

'Well, I'll see; but it will answer almost as well if it's not true,' said Feist cynically. 'People always believe those things.'

'It's only a detail,' said Bamberger, 'but it's worth something, and if we can make this man Leven begin a suit against his wife, everything that's against Van Torp will be against her too. That's not justice, Feist, but it's fact. A woman gets considerably less pity for making mistakes with a blackguard than for liking an honest man too much, Feist.'

Mr. Bamberger, who had divorced his own wife, delivered these opinions thoughtfully, and, though she had made no defence, he might be supposed to know what he was talking about.

Presently he dismissed his visitor with final injunctions to lose no time, and to 'find out' if Lady Maud was interested in any one besides Van Torp, and if not, what was at the root of her eccentric hours.

Mr. Feist went away, apparently prepared to obey his employer with all the energy he possessed. He went down the dimly-lighted stairs quickly, but he glanced nervously upwards, as if he fancied that Isidore Bamberger might have silently opened the door again to look over the banister and watch him from above. In the dark entry below he paused a moment, and took a satisfactory pull at a stout flask before going out into the yellowish gloom that had settled on Hare Court.

When he was in the narrow alley he stopped again and laughed, without making any sound, so heartily that he had to stand still till the fit passed; and the expression of his unhealthy face just then would have disturbed even Mr. Bamberger, who knew him well.

But Mr. Bamberger was sitting in the easy-chair before the fireplace, and his eyes were fixed on the bright point at which the shiny copper kettle reflected the gaslight. His head had fallen slightly forward, so that his bearded chin was out of sight below the collar of his overcoat, leaving his eagle nose and piercing eyes above it. He was like a bird of prey looking down over the edge of its nest. He had not taken off his hat for Mr. Feist, and it was pushed back from his bony forehead now, giving his face a look that would have been half comic if it had not been almost terrifying: a tall hat set on a skull, a little back or on one side, produces just such an effect.

There was no moisture in the keen eyes now. In the bright spot on the copper kettle they saw the vision of the end towards which he was striving with all his strength, and all his heart, and all his wealth. It was a grim little picture, and the chief figure in it was a thick-set man who had a queer cap drawn down over his face and his hands tied; and the eyes that saw it were sure that under the cap there were the stony features of a man who had stolen his friend's wife and killed his friend's daughter, and was going to die for what he had done.

Then Isidore Bamberger's right hand disappeared inside the breast of his coat and closed lovingly upon a full pocket-book; but there was only a little money in it, only a few banknotes folded flat against a thick package of sheets of notepaper all covered with clear, close writing, some in ink and some in pencil; and if what was written there was all true, it was enough to hang Mr. Rufus Van Torp.

There were other matters, too, not written there, but carefully entered in the memory of the injured man. There was the story of his marriage with a beautiful, penniless girl, not of his own faith, whom he had taken in the face of strong opposition from his family. She had been an exquisite creature, fair and ethereal, as degenerates sometimes are; she had cynically married him for his money, deceiving him easily enough, for he was willing to be blinded; but differences had soon arisen between them, and had turned to open quarrelling, and Mr. Van Torp had taken it upon himself to defend her and to reconcile them, using the unlimited power his position gave him over his partner to force the latter to submit to his wife's temper and caprice, as the only alternative to ruin. Her friendship for Van Torp grew stronger, till they spent many hours of every day together, while her husband saw little of her, though he was never altogether estranged from her so long as they lived under one roof.

But the time came at last when Bamberger had power too, and Van Torp could no longer hold him in check with a threat that had become vain; for he was more than indispensable, he was a part of the Nickel Trust, he was the figure-head of the ship, and could not be discarded at will, to be replaced by another.

As soon as he was sure of this and felt free to act, Isidore Bamberger divorced his wife, in a State where slight grounds are sufficient. For the sake of the Nickel Trust Van Torp's name was not mentioned. Mrs. Bamberger made no defence, the affair was settled almost privately, and Bamberger was convinced that she would soon marry Van Torp. Instead, six weeks had not passed before she married Senator Moon, a man whom her husband had supposed she scarcely knew, and to Bamberger's amazement Van Torp's temper was not at all disturbed by the marriage. He acted as if he had expected it, and though he hardly ever saw her after that time, he exchanged letters with her during nearly two years.

Bamberger's little daughter Ida had never been happy with her beautiful mother, who had alternately spoilt her and vented her temper on her, according to the caprice of the moment. At the time of the divorce the child had been only ten years old; and as Bamberger was very kind to her and was of an even disposition, though never very cheerful, she had grown up to be extremely fond of him. She never guessed that he did not love her in return, for though he was cynical enough in matters of business, he was just according to his lights, and he would not let her know that everything about her recalled her mother, from her hair to her tone of voice, her growing caprices, and her silly fits of temper. He could not believe in the affection of a daughter who constantly reminded him of the hell in which he had lived for years. If what Van Torp told Lady Maud of his own pretended engagement to Ida was true, it was explicable only on that ground, so far as her father was concerned. Bamberger felt no affection for his daughter, and saw no reason why she should not be used as an instrument, with her own consent, for consolidating the position of the Nickel Trust.

As for the former Mrs. Bamberger, afterwards Mrs. Moon, she had gone to Europe in the autumn, not many months after her marriage, leaving the Senator in Washington, and had returned after nearly a year's absence, bringing her husband a fine little girl, whom she had christened Ida, like her first child, without consulting him. It soon became apparent that the baby was totally deaf; and not very long after this discovery, Mrs. Moon began to show signs of not being quite sane. Three years later she was altogether out of her mind, and as soon as this was clear the child was sent to the East to be taught. The rest has already been told. Bamberger, of course, had never seen little Ida, and had perhaps never heard of her existence, and Senator Moon did not see her again before he died.

Bamberger had not loved his own daughter in her life, but since her tragic death she had grown dear to him in memory, and he reproached himself unjustly with having been cold and unkind to her. Below the surface of his money-loving nature there was still the deep and unsatisfied sentiment to which his wife had first appealed, and by playing on which she had deceived him into marrying her. Her treatment of him had not killed it, and the memory of his fair young daughter now stirred it again. He accused himself of having misunderstood her. What had been unreal and superficial in her mother had perhaps been true and deep in her. He knew that she had loved him; he knew it now, and it was the recollection of that one being who had been devoted to him for himself, since he had been a grown man, that sometimes brought the tears from his eyes when he was alone. It would have been a comfort, now, to have loved her in return while she lived, and to have trusted in her love then, instead of having been tormented by the belief that she was as false as her mother had been.

But he had been disappointed of his heart's desire; for, strange as it may seem to those who have not known such men as Isidore Bamberger, his nature was profoundly domestic, and the ideal of his youth had been to grow old in his own home, with a loving wife at his side, surrounded by children and grandchildren who loved both himself and her. Next to that, he had desired wealth and the power money gives; but that had been first, until the hope of it was gone. Looking back now, he was sure that it had all been destroyed from root to branch, the hope and the possibility, and even the memory that might have still comforted him, by Rufus Van Torp, upon whom he prayed that he might live to be revenged. He sought no secret vengeance, either, no pitfall of ruin dug in the dark for the man's untimely destruction; all was to be in broad daylight, by the evidence of facts, under the verdict of justice, and at the hands of the law itself.

It had not been very hard to get what he needed, for his former secretary, Mr. Feist, had worked with as much industry and intelligence as if the case had been his own, and in spite of the vice that was killing him had shown a wonderful power of holding his tongue. It is quite certain that up to the day when Feist called on his employer in Hare Court, Mr. Van Torp believed himself perfectly safe.

CHAPTER X

A fortnight later Count Leven informed his wife that he was going home on a short leave, but that she might stay in London if she pleased. An aunt of his had died in Warsaw, he said, leaving him a small property, and in spite of the disturbed state of his own country it was necessary that he should go and take possession of the land without delay.

Lady Maud did not believe a word of what he said, until it became apparent that he had the cash necessary for his journey without borrowing of her, as he frequently tried to do, with varying success. She smiled calmly as she bade him good-bye and wished him a pleasant journey; he made a magnificent show of kissing her hand at parting, and waved his hat to the window when he was outside the house, before getting into the four-wheeler, on the roof of which his voluminous luggage made a rather unsafe pyramid. She was not at the window, and he knew it; but other people might be watching him from theirs, and the servant stood at the open door. It was always worth while, in Count Leven's opinion, to make an 'effect' if one got a chance.

Three days later Lady Maud received a document from the Russian Embassy informing her that her husband had brought an action to obtain a divorce from her in the Ecclesiastical Court of the Patriarch of Constantinople, on the ground of her undue intimacy with Rufus Van Torp of New York, as proved by the attested depositions of detectives. She was further informed that unless she appeared in person or by proxy before the Patriarch of Constantinople within one month of the date of the present notice, to defend herself against the charges made by her husband, judgment would go by default, and the divorce would be pronounced.

At first Lady Maud imagined this extraordinary document to be a stupid practical joke, invented by some half-fledged cousin to tease her. She had a good many cousins, among whom were several beardless undergraduates and callow subalterns in smart regiments, who would think it no end of fun to scare 'Cousin Maud.' There was no mistaking the official paper on which the document was written, and it bore the seal of the Chancery of the Russian Embassy; but in Lady Maud's opinion the mention of the Patriarch of Constantinople stamped it as an egregious hoax.

On reflection, however, she decided that it must have been perpetrated by some one in the Embassy for the express purpose of annoying her, since no outsider could have got at the seal, even if he could have obtained possession of the paper and envelope. As soon as this view presented itself, she determined to ascertain the truth directly, and to bring down the ambassadorial wrath on the offender.

Accordingly she took the paper to the Russian clerk who was in charge of the Chancery, and inquired who had dared to concoct such a paper and to send it to her.

To her stupefaction, the man smiled politely and informed her that the document was genuine. What had the Patriarch to do with it? That was very simple. Had she not been married to a Russian subject by the Greek rite in Paris? Certainly. Very well. All marriages of Russian subjects out of their own country took place under the authority of the Patriarch of Constantinople, and all suits for divorcing persons thus married came under his jurisdiction. That was all. It was such a simple matter that every Russian knew all about it. The clerk asked if he could be of service to her. He had been stationed in Constantinople, and knew just what to do; and, moreover, he had a friend at the Chancery there, who would take charge of the case if the Countess desired it.

Lady Maud thanked him coldly, replaced the document in its envelope, and left the Embassy with the intention of never setting foot in it again.

She understood why Leven had suddenly lost an aunt of whom she had never heard, and had got out of the way on pretence of an imaginary inheritance. The dates showed plainly that the move had been prepared before he left, and that he had started when the notice of the suit was about to be sent to her. The only explanation that occurred to her was that her husband had found some very rich woman who was willing to marry him if he could free himself; and this seemed likely enough.

She hesitated as to how she should act. Her first impulse was to go to her father, who was a lawyer and would give her good advice, but a moment's thought showed her that it would be a mistake to go to him. Being no longer immobilised by a sprained ankle, Lord Creedmore would probably leave England instantly in pursuit of Leven himself, and no one could tell what the consequences might be if he caught him; they would certainly be violent, and they might be disastrous.

Then Lady Maud thought of telegraphing to Mr. Van Torp to come to town to see her about an urgent matter; but she decided against that course too. Whatever her relations were with the American financier this was not the moment to call attention to them. She would write to him, and in order to see him conveniently she would suggest to her father to have a week-end house party in the country, and to ask his neighbour over from Oxley Paddox. Nobody but Mr. Van Torp and the post-office called the place Torp Towers.

She had taken a hansom to the Embassy, but she walked back to Charles Street because she was angry, and she considered nothing so good for a rage as a stiff walk. By the time she reached her own door she was as cool as ever, and her clear eyes looked upon the wicked world with their accustomed calm.

As she laid her hand on the door-bell, a smart brougham drove up quickly and stopped close to the pavement, and as she turned her head Margaret was letting herself out, before the footman could get round from the other side to open the door of the carriage.

'May I come in?' asked the singer anxiously, and Lady Maud saw that she seemed much disturbed, and had a newspaper in her hand. 'I'm so glad I just caught you,' Margaret added, as the door opened.

They went in together. The house was very small and narrow, and Lady Maud led the way into a little sitting-room on the right of the hall, and shut the door.

'Is it true?' Margaret asked as soon as they were alone.

'What?'

'About your divorce—'

Lady Maud smiled rather contemptuously.

'Is it already in the papers?' she asked, glancing at the one Margaret had brought. 'I only heard of it myself an hour ago!'

'Then it's really true! There's a horrid article about it—'

Margaret was evidently much more disturbed than her friend, who sat down in a careless attitude and smiled at her.

'It had to come some day. And besides,' added Lady Maud, 'I don't care!'

'There's something about me too,' answered Margaret, 'and I cannot help caring.'

'About you?'

'Me and Mr. Van Torp—the article is written by some one who hates him—that's clear!—and you know I don't like him; but that's no reason why I should be dragged in.'

She was rather incoherent, and Lady Maud took the paper from her hand quietly, and found the article at once. It was as 'horrid' as the Primadonna said it was. No names were given in full, but there could not be the slightest mistake about the persons referred to, who were all clearly labelled by bits of characteristic description. It was all in the ponderously airy form of one of those more or less true stories of which some modern weeklies seem to have an inexhaustible supply, but it was a particularly vicious specimen of its class so far as Mr. Van Torp was concerned. His life was torn up by the roots and mercilessly pulled to pieces, and he was shown to the public as a Leicester Square Lovelace or a Bowery Don Juan. His baleful career was traced from his supposed affair with Mrs. Isidore Bamberger and her divorce to the scene at Margaret's hotel in New York, and from that to the occasion of his being caught with Lady Maud in Hare Court by a justly angry husband; and there was, moreover, a pretty plain allusion to little Ida Moon.

Lady Maud read the article quickly, but without betraying any emotion. When she had finished she raised her eyebrows a very little, and gave the paper back to Margaret.

'It is rather nasty,' she observed quietly, as if she were speaking of the weather.

'It's utterly disgusting,' Margaret answered with emphasis. 'What shall you do?'

'I really don't know. Why should I do anything? Your position is different, for you can write to the papers and deny all that concerns you if you like—though I'm sure I don't know why you should care. It's not to your discredit.'

'I could not very well deny it,' said the Primadonna thoughtfully. Almost before the words had left her lips she was sorry she had spoken.

'Does it happen to be true?' asked Lady Maud, with an encouraging smile.

'Well, since you ask me—yes.' Margaret felt uncomfortable.

'Oh, I thought it might be,' answered Lady Maud. 'With all his good qualities he has a very rough side. The story about me is perfectly true too.'

Margaret was amazed at her friend's quiet cynicism.

'Not that about the—the envelope on the table—'

She stopped short.

'Oh yes! There were four thousand one hundred pounds in it. My husband counted the notes.'

The singer leaned back in her chair and stared in unconcealed surprise, wondering how in the world she could have been so completely mistaken in her judgment of a friend who had seemed to her the best type of an honest and fearless Englishwoman. Margaret Donne had not been brought up in the gay world; she had, however, seen some aspects of it since she had been a successful singer, and she did not exaggerate its virtues; but somehow Lady Maud had seemed to be above it, while living in it, and Margaret would have put her hand into the fire for the daughter of her father's old friend, who now acknowledged without a blush that she had taken four thousand pounds from Rufus Van Torp.

'I suppose it would go against me even in an English court,' said Lady Maud in a tone of reflection. 'It looks so badly to take money, you know, doesn't it? But if I must be divorced, it really strikes me as delightfully original to have it done by the Patriarch of Constantinople! Doesn't it, my dear?'

'It's not usual, certainly,' said Margaret gravely.

She was puzzled by the other's attitude, and somewhat horrified.

'I suppose you think I'm a very odd sort of person,' said Lady Maud, 'because I don't mind so much as most women might. You see, I never really cared for Leven, though if I had not thought I had a fancy for him I wouldn't have married him. My people were quite against it. The truth is, I couldn't have the husband I wanted, and as I did not mean to break my heart about it, I married, as so many girls do. That's my little story! It's not long, is it?'

She laughed, but she very rarely did that, even when she was amused, and now Margaret's quick ear detected here and there in the sweet ripple a note that did not ring quite like the rest. The intonation was not false or artificial, but only sad and regretful, as genuine laughter should not be. Margaret looked at her, still profoundly mystified, and still drawn to her by natural sympathy, though horrified almost to disgust at what seemed her brutal cynicism.

'May I ask one question? We've grown to be such good friends that perhaps you won't mind.'

Lady Maud nodded.

'Of course,' she said. 'Ask me anything you please. I'll answer if I can.'

'You said that you could not marry the man you liked. Was he—Mr. Van Torp?'

Lady Maud was not prepared for the question.

'Mr. Van Torp?' she repeated slowly. 'Oh dear no! Certainly not! What an extraordinary idea!' She gazed into Margaret's eyes with a look of inquiry, until the truth suddenly dawned upon her. 'Oh, I see!' she cried. 'How awfully funny!'

There was no minor note of sadness or regret in her rippling laughter now. It was so exquisitely true and musical that the great soprano listened to it with keen delight, and wondered whether she herself could produce a sound half so delicious.

'No, my dear,' said Lady Maud, as her mirth subsided. 'I never was in love with Mr. Van Torp. But it really is awfully funny that you should have thought so! No wonder you looked grave when I told you that I was really found in his rooms! We are the greatest friends, and no man was ever kinder to a woman than he has been to me for the last two years. But that's all. Did you really think the money was meant for me? That wasn't quite nice of you, was it?'

The bright smile was still on her face as she spoke the last words, for her nature was far too big to be really hurt; but the little rebuke went home sharply, and Margaret felt unreasonably ashamed of herself, considering that Lady Maud had not taken the slightest pains to explain the truth to her.

'I'm so sorry,' she said contritely. 'I'm dreadfully sorry. It was abominably stupid of me!'

'Oh no. It was quite natural. This is not a pretty world, and there's no reason why you should think me better than lots of other women. And besides, I don't care!'

'But surely you won't let your husband get a divorce for such a reason as that without making a defence?'

'Before the Patriarch of Constantinople?' Lady Maud evidently thought the idea very amusing. 'It sounds like a comic opera,' she added. 'Why should I defend myself? I shall be glad to be free; and as for the story, the people who like me will not believe any harm of me, and the people who don't like me may believe what they please. But I'm very glad you showed me that article, disgusting as it is.'

'I was beginning to be sorry I had brought it.'

'No. You did me a service, for I had no idea that any one was going to take advantage of my divorce to make a cowardly attack on my friend—I mean Mr. Van Torp. I shall certainly not make any defence before the Patriarch, but I shall make a statement which will go to the right people, saying that I met Mr. Van Torp in a lawyer's chambers in the Temple, that is, in a place of business, and about a matter of business, and that there was no secret about it, because my husband's servant called the cab that took me there, and gave the cabman the address. I often do go out without telling any one, and I let myself in with a latch-key when I come home, but on that particular occasion I did neither. Will you say that if you hear me talked about?'

'Of course I will.'

Nevertheless, Margaret thought that Lady Maud might have given her a little information about the 'matter of business' which had involved such a large sum of money, and had produced such important consequences.

CHAPTER XI

Mr. Van Torp was walking slowly down the Elm Walk in the park at Oxley Paddox. The ancient trees were not in full leaf yet, but there were myriads of tiny green feather points all over the rough brown branches and the smoother twigs, and their soft colour tinted the luminous spring air. High overhead all sorts and conditions of little birds were chirping and trilling and chattering together and by turns, and on the ground the sparrows were excessively busy and talkative, while the squirrels made wild dashes across the open, and stopped suddenly to sit bolt upright and look about them, and then dashed on again.

Little Ida walked beside the millionaire in silence, trustfully holding one of his hands, and as she watched the sparrows she tried to make out what sort of sound they could be making when they hopped forward and opened their bills so wide that she could distinctly see their little tongues. Mr. Van Torp's other hand held a newspaper, and he was reading the article about himself which Margaret had shown to Lady Maud. He did not take that particular paper, but a marked copy had been sent to him, and in due course had been ironed and laid on the breakfast-table with those that came regularly. The article was marked in red pencil.

He read it slowly with a perfectly blank expression, as if it concerned some one he did not know. Once only, when he came upon the allusion to the little girl, his eyes left the page and glanced quietly down at the large red felt hat with its knot of ribbands that moved along beside him, and hid all the child's face except the delicate chin and the corner of the pathetic little mouth. She did not know that he looked down at her, for she was intent on the sparrows, and he went back to the article and read to the end.

Then, in order to fold the paper, he gently let go of Ida's hand, and she looked up into his face. He did not speak, but his lips moved a little as he doubled the sheet to put it into his pocket; and instantly the child's expression changed, and she looked hurt and frightened, and stretched up her hand quickly to cover his mouth, as if to hide the words his lips were silently forming.

'Please, please!' she said, in her slightly monotonous voice. 'You promised me you wouldn't any more!'

'Quite right, my dear,' answered Mr. Van Torp, smiling, 'and I apologise. You must make me pay a forfeit every time I do it. What shall the forfeit be? Chocolates?'

She watched his lips, and understood as well as if she had heard.

'No,' she answered demurely. 'You mustn't laugh. When I've done anything wicked and am sorry, I say the little prayer Miss More taught me. Perhaps you'd better learn it too.'

'If you said it for me,' suggested Mr. Van Torp gravely, 'it would be more likely to work.'

'Oh no! That wouldn't do at all! You must say it for yourself. I'll teach it to you if you like. Shall I?'

'What must I say?' asked the financier.

'Well, it's made up for me, you see, and besides, I've shortened it a wee bit. What I say is: "Dear God, please forgive me this time, and make me never want to do it again. Amen." Can you remember that, do you think?'

'I think I could,' said Mr. Van Torp. 'Please forgive me and make me never do it again.'

'Never want to do it again,' corrected little Ida with emphasis. 'You must try not even to want to say dreadful things. And then you must say "Amen." That's important.'

'Amen,' repeated the millionaire.

At this juncture the discordant toot of an approaching motor-car was heard above the singing of the birds. Mr. Van Torp turned his head quickly in the direction of the sound, and at the same time instinctively led the little girl towards one side of the road. She apparently understood, for she asked no questions. There was a turn in the drive a couple of hundred yards away, where the Elm Walk ended, and an instant later an enormous white motor-car whizzed into sight, rushed furiously towards the two, and was brought to a standstill in an uncommonly short time, close beside them. An active man, in the usual driver's disguise of the modern motorist, jumped down, and at the same instant pushed his goggles up over the visor of his cap and loosened the collar of his wide coat, displaying the face of Constantino Logotheti.

'Oh, it's you, is it?' Mr. Van Torp asked the wholly superfluous question in a displeased tone. 'How did you get in? I've given particular orders to let in no automobiles.'

'I always get in everywhere,' answered Logotheti coolly. 'May I see you alone for a few minutes?'

'If it's business, you'd better see Mr. Bamberger,' said Van Torp. 'I came here for a rest. Mr. Bamberger has come over for a few days. You'll find him at his chambers in Hare Court.'

'No,' returned Logotheti, 'it's a private matter. I shall not keep you long.'

'Then run us up to the house in your new go-cart.'

Mr. Van Torp lifted little Ida into the motor as if she had been a rather fragile china doll instead of a girl nine years old and quite able to get up alone, and before she could sit down he was beside her. Logotheti jumped up beside the chauffeur and the machine ran up the drive at breakneck speed. Two minutes later they all got out more than a mile farther on, at the door of the big old house. Ida ran away to find Miss More; the two men entered together, and went into the study.

The room had been built in the time of Edward Sixth, had been decorated afresh under Charles the Second, the furniture was of the time of Queen Anne, and the carpet was a modern Turkish one, woven in colours as fresh as paint to fit the room, and as thick as a down quilt: it was the sort of carpet which has come into existence with the modern hotel.

'Well?' Mr. Van Torp uttered the monosyllable as he sat down in his own chair and pointed to a much less comfortable one, which Logotheti took.

'There's an article about you,' said the latter, producing a paper.

'I've read it,' answered Mr. Van Torp in a tone of stony indifference.

'I thought that was likely. Do you take the paper?'

'No. Do you?'

'No, it was sent to me,' Logotheti answered. 'Did you happen to glance at the address on the wrapper of the one that came to you?'

'My valet opens all the papers and irons them.'

Mr. Van Torp looked very bored as he said this, and he stared stonily at the pink and green waistcoat which his visitor's unfastened coat exposed to view. Hundreds of little gold beads were sewn upon it at the intersections of the pattern. It was a marvellous creation.

'I had seen the handwriting on the one addressed to me before,' Logotheti said.

'Oh, you had, had you?'

Mr. Van Torp asked the question in a dull tone without the slightest apparent interest in the answer.

'Yes,' Logotheti replied, not paying any attention to his host's indifference. 'I received an anonymous letter last winter, and the writing of the address was the same.'

'It was, was it?'

The millionaire's tone did not change in the least, and he continued to admire the waistcoat. His manner might have disconcerted a person of less assurance than the Greek, but in the matter of nerves the two financiers were well matched.

'Yes,' Logotheti answered, 'and the anonymous letter was about you, and contained some of the stories that are printed in this article.'

'Oh, it did, did it?'

'Yes. There was an account of your interview with the Primadonna at a hotel in New York. I remember that particularly well.'

'Oh, you do, do you?'

'Yes. The identity of the handwriting and the similarity of the wording make it look as if the article and the letter had been written by the same person.'

'Well, suppose they were—I don't see anything funny about that.'

Thereupon Mr. Van Torp turned at last from the contemplation of the waistcoat and looked out of the bay-window at the distant trees, as if he were excessively weary of Logotheti's talk.

'It occurred to me,' said the latter, 'that you might like to stop any further allusions to Miss Donne, and that if you happened to recognize the handwriting you might be able to do so effectually.'

'There's nothing against Madame Cordova in the article,' answered Mr. Van Torp, and his aggressive blue eyes turned sharply to his visitor's almond-shaped brown ones. 'You can't say there's a word against her.'

'There may be in the next one,' suggested Logotheti, meeting the look without emotion. 'When people send anonymous letters about broadcast to injure men like you and me, they are not likely to stick at such a matter as a woman's reputation.'

'Well—maybe not.' Mr. Van Torp turned his sharp eyes elsewhere. 'You seem to take quite an interest in Madame Cordova, Mr. Logotheti,' he observed, in an indifferent tone.

'I knew her before she went on the stage, and I think I may call myself a friend of hers. At all events, I wish to spare her any annoyance from the papers if I can, and if you have any regard for her you will help me, I'm sure.'

'I have the highest regard for Madame Cordova,' said Mr. Van Torp, and there was a perceptible change in his tone; 'but after this, I guess the best way I can show it is to keep out of her track. That's about all there is to do. You don't suppose I'm going to bring an action against that paper, do you?'

'Hardly!' Logotheti smiled.

'Well, then, what do you expect me to do, Mr. Logotheti?'

Again the eyes of the two men met.

'I'll tell you,' answered the Greek. 'The story about your visit to Miss Donne in New York is perfectly true.'

'You're pretty frank,' observed the American.

'Yes, I am. Very good. The man who wrote the letter and the article knows you, and that probably means that you have known him, though you may never have taken any notice of him. He hates you, for some reason, and means to injure you if he can. Just take the trouble to find out who he is and suppress him, will you? If you don't, he will throw more mud at honest women. He is probably some underling whose feelings you have hurt, or who has lost money by you, or both.'

'There's something in that,' answered Mr. Van Torp, showing a little more interest. 'Do you happen to have any of his writing about you? I'll look at it.'

Logotheti took a letter and a torn piece of brown paper from his pocket and handed both to his companion.

'Read the letter, if you like,' he said. 'The handwriting seems to be the same as that on the wrapper.'

Mr. Van Torp first compared the address, and then proceeded to read the anonymous letter. Logotheti watched his face quietly, but it did not change in the least. When he had finished, he folded the sheet, replaced it in the envelope, and returned it with the bit of paper.

'Much obliged,' he said, and he looked out of the window again and was silent.

Logotheti leaned back in his chair as he put the papers into his pocket again, and presently, as Mr. Van Torp did not seem inclined to say anything more, he rose to go. The American did not move, and still looked out of the window.

'You originally belonged to the East, Mr. Logotheti, didn't you?' he asked suddenly.

'Yes. I'm a Greek and a Turkish subject.'

'Do you happen to know the Patriarch of Constantinople?'

Logotheti stared in surprise, taken off his guard for once.

'Very well indeed,' he answered after an instant. 'He is my uncle.'

'Why, now, that's quite interesting!' observed Mr. Van Torp, rising deliberately and thrusting his hands into his pockets.

Logotheti, who knew nothing about the details of Lady Maud's pending divorce, could not imagine what the American was driving at, and waited for more. Mr. Van Torp began to walk up and down, with his rather clumsy gait, digging his heels into vivid depths of the new Smyrna carpet at every step.

'I wasn't going to tell you,' he said at last, 'but I may just as well. Most of the accusations in that letter are lies. I didn't blow up the subway. I know it was done on purpose, of course, but I had nothing to do with it, and any man who says I had, takes me for a fool, which you'll probably allow I'm not. You're a man of business, Mr. Logotheti. There had been a fall in Nickel, and for weeks before the explosion I'd been making a considerable personal sacrifice to steady things. Now you know as well as I do that all big accidents are bad for the market when it's shaky. Do you suppose I'd have deliberately produced one just then? Besides, I'm not a criminal. I didn't blow up the subway any more than I blew up the Maine to bring on the Cuban war! The man's a fool.'

'I quite agree with you,' said the Greek, listening with interest.

'Then there's another thing. That about poor Mrs. Moon, who's gone out of her mind. It's nonsense to say I was the reason of Bamberger's divorcing his wife. In the first place, there are the records of the divorce, and my name was never mentioned. I was her friend, that's all, and Bamberger resented it—he's a resentful sort of man anyway. He thought she'd marry me as soon as he got the divorce. Well, she didn't. She married old Alvah Moon, who was the only man she ever cared for. The Lord knows how it was, but that wicked old scarecrow made all the women love him, to his dying day. I had a high regard for Mrs. Bamberger, and I suppose she was right to marry him if she liked him. Well, she married him in too much of a hurry, and the child that was born abroad was Bamberger's and not his, and when he found it out he sent the girl East and would never see her again, and didn't leave her a cent when he died. That's the truth about that, Mr.

Logotheti. I tell you because you've got that letter in your pocket, and I'd rather have your good word than your bad word in business any day.'

'Thank you,' answered Logotheti. 'I'm glad to know the facts in the case, though I never could see what a man's private life can have to do with his reputation in the money market!'

'Well, it has, in some countries. Different kinds of cats have different kinds of ways. There's one thing more, but it's not in the letter, it's in the article. That's about Countess Leven, and it's the worst lie of the lot, for there's not a better woman than she is from here to China. I'm not at liberty to tell you anything of the matter she's interested in and on which she consults me. But her father is my next neighbour here, and I seem to be welcome at his house; he's a pretty sensible man, and that makes for her, it seems to me. As for that husband of hers, we've a good name in America for men like him. We'd call him a skunk over there. I suppose the English word is polecat, but it doesn't say as much. I don't think there's anything else I want to tell you.'

'You spoke of my uncle, the Patriarch,' observed Logotheti.

'Did I? Yes. Well, what sort of a gentleman is he, anyway?'

The question seemed rather vague to the Greek.

'How do you mean?' he inquired, buttoning his coat over the wonderful waistcoat.

'Is he a friendly kind of a person, I mean? Obliging, if you take him the right way? That's what I mean. Or does he get on his ear right away?'

'I should say,' answered Logotheti, without a smile, 'that he gets on his ear right away—if that means the opposite of being friendly and obliging. But I may be prejudiced, for he does not approve of me.'

'Why not, Mr. Logotheti?'

'My uncle says I'm a pagan, and worship idols.'

'Maybe he means the Golden Calf,' suggested Mr. Van Torp gravely.

Logotheti laughed.

'The other deity in business is the Brazen Serpent, I believe,' he retorted.

'The two would look pretty well out there on my lawn,' answered Mr. Van Torp, his hard face relaxing a little.

'To return to the point. Can I be of any use to you with the Patriarch? We are not on bad terms, though he does think me a heathen. Is there anything I can do?'

'Thank you, not at present. Much obliged. I only wanted to know.'

Logotheti's curiosity was destined to remain unsatisfied. He refused Mr. Van Torp's not very pressing invitation to stay to luncheon, given at the very moment when he was getting into his motor, and a few seconds later he was tearing down the avenue.

Mr. Van Torp stood on the steps till he was out of sight and then came down himself and strolled slowly away towards the trees again, his hands behind him and his eyes constantly bent upon the road, three paces ahead.

He was not always quite truthful. Scruples were not continually uppermost in his mind. For instance, what he had told Lady Maud about his engagement to poor Miss Bamberger did not quite agree with what he had said to Margaret on the steamer.

In certain markets in New York, three kinds of eggs are offered for sale, namely, Eggs, Fresh Eggs, and Strictly Fresh Eggs. I have seen the advertisement. Similarly in Mr. Van Torp's opinion there were three sorts of stories, to wit, Stories, True Stories, and Strictly True Stories. Clearly, each account of his engagement must have belonged to one of these classes, as well as the general statement he had made to Logotheti about the charges brought against him in the anonymous letter. The reason why he had made that statement was plain enough; he meant it to be repeated to Margaret because he really wished her to think well of him. Moreover, he had recognised the handwriting at once as that of Mr. Feist, Isidore Bamberger's former secretary, who knew a good many things and might turn out a dangerous enemy.

But Logotheti, who knew something of men, and had dealt with some very accomplished experts in fraud from New York and London to Constantinople, had his doubts about the truth of what he had heard, and understood at once why the usually reticent American had talked so much about himself. Van Torp, he was sure, was in love with the singer; that was his weak side, and in whatever affected her he might behave like a brute or a baby, but would certainly act with something like rudimentary simplicity in either case. In Logotheti's opinion Northern and English-speaking men might be as profound as Persians in matters of money, and sometimes were, but where women were concerned they were generally little better than sentimental children, unless they were mere animals. Not one in a thousand cared for the society of women, or even of one particular woman, for its own sake, for the companionship, and the exchange of ideas about things of which women know how to think. To the better sort, that is, to the sentimental ones, a woman always seemed what she was not, a goddess, a saint, or a sort of glorified sister; to the rest, she was an instrument of amusement and pleasure, more or less necessary and more or less purchasable. Perhaps an Englishman or an American, judging Greeks from what he could learn about them in ordinary intercourse, would get about as near the truth as Logotheti did. In his main conclusion the latter was probably right; Mr. Van Torp's affections might be of such exuberant nature as would admit of being divided between two or three objects at the same time, or they might not. But when he spoke of having the 'highest regard' for Madame Cordova, without denying the facts about the interview in which he had asked her to marry him and had lost his head because she refused, he was at least admitting that he was in love with her, or had been at that time.

Mr. Van Torp also confessed that he had entertained a 'high regard' for the beautiful Mrs. Bamberger, now unhappily insane. It was noticeable that he had not used the same expression in speaking of Lady Maud. Nevertheless, as in the Bamberger affair, he appeared as the chief cause of trouble between husband and wife. Logotheti was considered 'dangerous' even in Paris, and his experiences had not been dull; but, so far, he had found his way through life without inadvertently stepping upon any of those concealed traps through which the gay and unwary of both sexes are so often dropped into the divorce court, to the surprise of everybody. It seemed the more strange to him that Rufus Van Torp, only a few years his senior, should now find himself in that position for the second time. Yet Van Torp was not a ladies' man; he was hard-featured, rough of speech, and clumsy of figure, and it was impossible to believe that any woman could think him good-looking or be carried away by his talk. The case of Mrs. Bamberger could be explained; she might have had beauty, but she could have had little else that would have appealed to such a man as Logotheti. But there was Lady Maud, an acknowledged beauty in London, thoroughbred, aristocratic, not easily shocked perhaps, but easily disgusted, like most women of her class; and there was no doubt but that her husband had found her under extremely strange circumstances, in the act of receiving from Van Torp a large sum of money for which she altogether declined to account. Van Torp had not denied that story either, so it was probably true. Yet Logotheti, whom so many women thought irresistible, had felt instinctively that she was one of those who would smile serenely upon the most skilful and persistent besieger from the security of an impregnable fortress of virtue. Logotheti did not naturally feel unqualified respect for many women, but since he had known Lady Maud it had never occurred to him that any one could take the smallest liberty with her. On the other hand, though he was genuinely in love with Margaret and desired nothing so much as to marry her, he had never been in the least afraid of her, and he had deliberately attempted to carry her off against her will; and if she had looked upon his conduct then as anything more serious than a mad prank, she had certainly forgiven it very soon.

The only reason for his flying visit to Derbyshire had been his desire to keep Margaret's name out of an impending scandal in which he foresaw that Mr. Van Torp and Lady Maud were to be the central figures, and he believed that he had done something to bring about that result, if he had started the millionaire on the right scent. He judged Van Torp to be a good hater and a man of many resources, who would not now be satisfied till he had the anonymous writer of the letter and the article in his power. Logotheti had no means of guessing who the culprit was, and did not care to know.

He reached town late in the afternoon, having covered something like three hundred miles since early morning. About seven o'clock he stopped at Margaret's door, in the hope of finding her at home and of being asked to dine alone with her, but as he got out of his hansom and sent it away he heard the door shut and he found himself face to face with Paul Griggs.

'Miss Donne is out,' said the author, as they shook hands. 'She's been spending the day with the Creedmores, and when I rang she had just telephoned that she would not be back for dinner!'

'What a bore!' exclaimed Logotheti.

The two men walked slowly along the pavement together, and for some time neither spoke. Logotheti had nothing to do, or believed so because he was disappointed in not finding Margaret in. The elder man looked preoccupied, and the Greek was the first to speak.

'I suppose you've seen that shameful article about Van Torp,' he said.

'Yes. Somebody sent me a marked copy of the paper. Do you know whether
Miss Donne has seen it?'

'Yes. She got a marked copy too. So did I. What do you think of it?'

'Just what you do, I fancy. Have you any idea who wrote it?'

'Probably some underling in the Nickel Trust whom Van Torp has offended without knowing it, or who has lost money by him.'

Griggs glanced at his companion's face, for the hypothesis struck him as being tenable.

'Unless it is some enemy of Countess Leven's,' he suggested. 'Her husband is really going to divorce her, as the article says.'

'I suppose she will defend herself,' said Logotheti.

'If she has a chance.'

'What do you mean?'

'Do you happen to know what sort of man the present Patriarch of Constantinople is?'

Logotheti's jaw dropped, and he slackened his pace.

'What in the world—' he began, but did not finish the sentence. 'That's the second time to-day I've been asked about him.'

'That's very natural,' said Griggs calmly. 'You're one of the very few men in town who are likely to know him.'

'Of course I know him,' answered Logotheti, still mystified. 'He's my uncle.'

'Really? That's very lucky!'

'Look here, Griggs, is this some silly joke?'

'A joke? Certainly not. Lady Maud's husband can only get a divorce through the Patriarch because he married her out of Russia. You know about that law, don't you?'

Logotheti understood at last.

'No,' he said, 'I never heard of it. But if that is the case I may be able to do something—not that I'm considered orthodox at the Patriarchate! The old gentleman has been told that I'm trying to revive the worship of the Greek gods and have built a temple to Aphrodite Xenia in the Place de la Concorde!'

'You're quite capable of it,' observed Griggs.

'Oh, quite! Only, I've not done it yet. I'll see what I can do. Are you much interested in the matter?'

'Only on general principles, because I believe Lady Maud is perfectly straight, and it is a shame that such a creature as Leven should be allowed to divorce an honest Englishwoman. By the bye—speaking of her reminds me of that dinner at the Turkish Embassy—do you remember a disagreeable-looking man who sat next to me, one Feist, a countryman of mine?'

'Rather! I wondered how he came there.'

'He had a letter of introduction from the Turkish Minister in Washington. He is full of good letters of introduction.'

'I should think they would need to be good,' observed Logotheti. 'With that face of his he would need an introduction to a Port Said gambling-hell before they would let him in.'

'I agree with you. But he is well provided, as I say, and he goes everywhere. Some one has put him down at the Mutton Chop. You never go there, do you?'

'I'm not asked,' laughed Logotheti. 'And as for becoming a member, they say it's impossible.'

'It takes ten or fifteen years,' Griggs answered, 'and then you won't be elected unless every one likes you. But you may be put down as a visitor there just as at any other club. This fellow Feist, for instance—we had trouble with him last night—or rather this morning, for it was two o'clock. He has been dropping in often of late, towards midnight. At first he was more or less amusing with his stories, for he has a wonderful memory. You know the sort of funny man who rattles on as if he were wound up for the evening, and afterwards you cannot remember a word he has said. It's all very well for a while, but you soon get sick of it. Besides, this particular specimen drinks like a whale.'

'He looks as if he did.'

'Last night he had been talking a good deal, and most of the men who had been there had gone off. You know there's only one room at the Mutton Chop, with a long table, and if a man takes the floor there's no escape. I had come in about one o'clock to get something to eat, and Feist poured out a steady stream of stories as usual, though only one or two listened to him. Suddenly his eyes looked queer, and he stammered, and rolled off his chair, and lay in a heap, either dead drunk or in a fit, I don't know which.'

'And I suppose you carried him downstairs,' said Logotheti, for Griggs was known to be stronger than other men, though no longer young.

'I did,' Griggs answered. 'That's usually my share of the proceedings. The last person I carried—let me see—I think it must have been that poor girl who died at the Opera in New York. We had found Feist's address in the visitors' book, and we sent him home in a hansom. I wonder whether he got there!'

'I should think the member who put him down would be rather annoyed,' observed Logotheti.

'Yes. It's the first time anything of that sort ever happened at the Mutton Chop, and I fancy it will be the last. I don't think we shall see Mr. Feist again.'

'I took a particular dislike to his face,' Logotheti said. 'I remember thinking of him when I went home that night, and wondering who he was and what he was about.'

'At first I took him for a detective,' said Griggs. 'But detectives don't drink.'

'What made you think he might be one?'

'He has a very clever way of leading the conversation to a point and then asking an unexpected question.'

'Perhaps he is an amateur,' suggested Logotheti. 'He may be a spy. Is Feist an American name?'

'You will find all sorts of names in America. They prove nothing in the way of nationality, unless they are English, Dutch, or French, and even then they don't prove much. I'm an American myself, and I feel sure that Feist either is one or has spent many years in the country, in which case he is probably naturalised. As for his being a spy, I don't think I ever came across one in England.'

'They come here to rest in time of peace, or to escape hanging in other countries in time of war,' said the Greek. 'His being at the Turkish Embassy, of all places in the world, is rather in favour of the idea. Do you happen to remember the name of his hotel?'

'Are you going to call on him?' Griggs asked with a smile.

'Perhaps. He begins to interest me. Is it indiscreet to ask what sort of questions he put to you?'

'He's stopping at the Carlton—if the cabby took him there! We gave the man half-a-crown for the job, and took his number, so I suppose it was all right. As for the questions he asked me, that's another matter.'

Logotheti glanced quickly at his companion's rather grim face, and was silent for a few moments. He judged that Mr. Feist's inquiries must have concerned a woman, since Griggs was so reticent, and it required no great ingenuity to connect that probability with one or both of the ladies who had been at the dinner where Griggs and Feist had first met.

'I think I shall go and ask for Mr. Feist,' he said presently. 'I shall say that I heard he was ill and wanted to know if I could do anything for him.'

'I've no doubt he'll be much touched by your kindness!' said Griggs. 'But please don't mention the Mutton Chop Club, if you really see him.'

'Oh no! Besides, I shall let him do the talking.'

'Then take care that you don't let him talk you to death!'

Logotheti smiled as he hailed a passing hansom; he nodded to his companion, told the man to go to the Carlton, and drove away, leaving Griggs to continue his walk alone.

The elderly man of letters had not talked about Mr. Feist with any special intention, and was very far from thinking that what he had said would lead to any important result. He liked the Greek, because he liked most Orientals, under certain important reservations and at a certain distance, and he had lived amongst them long enough not to be surprised at anything they did. Logotheti had been disappointed in not finding the Primadonna at home, and he was not inclined to put up with the usual round of an evening in London during the early part of the season as a substitute for what he had lost. He was the more put out, because, when he had last seen Margaret, three or four days earlier, she had told him that if he came on that evening at about seven o'clock he would probably find her alone. Having nothing that looked at all amusing to occupy him, he was just in the mood to do anything unusual that presented itself.

Griggs guessed at most of these things, and as he walked along he vaguely pictured to himself the interview that was likely to take place.

CHAPTER XII

Opinion was strongly against Mr. Van Torp. A millionaire is almost as good a mark at which to throw mud as a woman of the world whose reputation has never before been attacked, and when the two can be pilloried together it is hardly to be expected that ordinary people should abstain from pelting them and calling them bad names.

Lady Maud, indeed, was protected to some extent by her father and brothers, and by many loyal friends. It is happily still doubtful how far one may go in printing lies about an honest woman without getting into trouble with the law, and when the lady's father is not only a peer, but has previously been a barrister of reputation and a popular and hard-working member of the House of Commons during a long time, it is generally safer to use guarded language; the advisability of moderation also increases directly as the number and size of the lady's brothers, and inversely as their patience. Therefore, on the whole, Lady Maud was much better treated by the society columns than Margaret at first expected.

On the other hand, they vented their spleen and sharpened their English on the American financier, who had no relations and scarcely any friends to stand by him, and was, moreover, in a foreign country, which always seems to be regarded as an aggravating circumstance when a man gets into any sort of trouble. Isidore Bamberger and Mr. Feist had roused and let loose upon him a whole pack of hungry reporters and paragraph writers on both sides of the Atlantic.

The papers did not at first print his name except in connection with the divorce of Lady Maud. But this was a landmark, the smallest reference to which made all other allusions to him quite clear. It was easy to speak of Mr. Van Torp as the central figure in a *cause célèbre*: newspapers love the French language the more as they understand it the less; just as the gentle amateur in literature tries to hide his cloven hoof under the thin elegance of italics.

Particular stress was laid upon the millionaire's dreadful hypocrisy. He taught in the Sunday Schools at Nickelville, the big village which had sprung up at his will and which was the headquarters of his sanctimonious wickedness. He was compared to Solomon, not for his wisdom, but on account of his domestic arrangements. He was indeed a father to his flock. It was a touching sight to see the little ones gathered round the knees of this great and good man, and to note how an unconscious and affectionate imitation reflected his face in theirs. It was true that there was another side to this truly patriarchal picture. In a city of the Far West, wrote an eloquent paragraph writer, a pale face, once divinely beautiful, was often seen at the barred window of a madhouse, and eyes that had once looked too tenderly into those of the Nickelville Solomon stared wildly at the palm-trees in the asylum grounds. This paragraph was rich in sentiment.

There were a good many mentions of the explosion in New York, too, and hints, dark, but uncommonly straight, that the great Sunday School teacher had been the author and stage-manager of an awful comedy designed expressly to injure a firm of contractors against whom he had a standing grudge. In proof of the assertion, the story went on to say that he had written four hours before the 'accident' happened to give warning of it to the young lady whom he was about to marry. She was a neurasthenic young lady, and in spite of the warning she died very suddenly at the theatre from shock immediately after the explosion, and his note was found on her dressing-table when she was brought home dead. Clearly, if the explosion had not been his work, and if he had been informed of it beforehand, he would have warned the police and the Department of Public Works at the same time. The young lady's untimely death had not prevented him from sailing for Europe three or four days later, and on the trip he had actually occupied alone the same 'thousand dollar suite' which he had previously engaged for himself and his bride. From this detail the public might form some idea of the Nickelville magnate's heartless character. In fact, if one-half of what was written, telegraphed, and printed about Rufus Van Torp on both sides of the Atlantic during the next fortnight was to be believed, he had no character at all.

To all this he answered nothing, and he did not take the trouble to allude to the matter in the few letters he wrote to his acquaintances. Day after day numbers of marked papers were carefully ironed and laid on the breakfast-table, after having been read and commented on in the servants' hall. The butler began to look askance at him, Mrs. Dubbs, the housekeeper, talked gloomily of giving warning, and the footmen gossiped with the stable hands; but the men all decided that it was not derogatory to their dignity to remain in the service of a master who was soon to be exhibited in the divorce court beside such a 'real lady' as Lord Creedmore's daughter; the housemaids agreed in this view, and the housekeeper consulted Miss More. For Mrs. Dubbs was an imposing person, morally and physically, and had a character to lose; and though the place was a very good one for her old age, because the master only spent six weeks or two months at Oxley Paddox each year, and never found fault, yet Mrs. Dubbs was not going to have her name associated with that of a gentleman who blew up underground works and took Solomon's view of the domestic affections. She came of very good people in the north; one of her brothers was a minister, and the other was an assistant steward on a large Scotch estate.

Miss More's quiet serenity was not at all disturbed by what was happening, for it could hardly be supposed that she was ignorant of the general attack on Mr. Van Torp, though he did not leave the papers lying about, where little Ida's quick eyes might fall on a marked passage. The housekeeper waited for an occasion when Mr. Van Torp had taken the child for a drive, as he often did, and Miss More was established in her favourite corner of the garden, just out of sight of the house. Mrs. Dubbs first exposed the situation, then expressed a strong opinion as to her own respectability, and finally asked Miss More's advice.

Miss More listened attentively, and waited till her large and sleek interlocutor had absolutely nothing more to say. Then she spoke.

'Mrs. Dubbs,' she said, 'do you consider me a respectable young woman?'

'Oh, Miss More!' cried the housekeeper. 'You! Indeed, I'd put my hand into the fire for you any day!'

'And I'm an American, and I've known Mr. Van Torp several years, though this is the first time you have seen me here. Do you think I would let the child stay an hour under his roof, or stay here myself, if I believed one word of all those wicked stories the papers are publishing? Look at me, please. Do you think I would?'

It was quite impossible to look at Miss More's quiet healthy face and clear eyes and to believe she would. There are some women of whom one is sure at a glance that they are perfectly trustworthy in every imaginable way, and above even the suspicion of countenancing any wrong.

'No,' answered Mrs. Dubbs, with honest conviction, 'I don't, indeed.'

'I think, then,' said Miss More, 'that if I feel I can stay here, you are safe in staying too. I do not believe any of these slanders, and I am quite sure that Mr. Van Torp is one of the kindest men in the world.'

'I feel as if you must be right, Miss More,' replied the housekeeper. 'But they do say dreadful things about him, indeed, and he doesn't deny a word of it, as he ought to, in my humble opinion, though it's not my business to judge, of course, but I'll say this, Miss More, and that is, that if the butler's character was publicly attacked in the papers, in the way Mr. Van Torp's is, and if I were Mr. Van Torp, which of course I'm not, I'd say "Crookes, you may be all right, but if you're going to be butler here any longer, it's your duty to defend yourself against these attacks upon you in the papers, Crookes, because as a Christian man you must not hide your light under a bushel, Crookes, but let it shine abroad." That's what I'd say, Miss More, and I should like to know if you don't think I should be right.'

'If the English and American press united to attack the butler's character,' answered Miss More without a smile, 'I think you would be quite right, Mrs. Dubbs. But as regards Mr. Van Torp's present position, I am sure he is the best judge of what he ought to do.'

These words of wisdom, and Miss More's truthful eyes, greatly reassured the housekeeper, who afterwards upbraided the servants for paying any attention to such wicked falsehoods; and Mr. Crookes, the butler, wrote to his aged mother, who was anxious about his situation, to say that Mr. Van Torp must be either a real gentleman or a very hardened criminal indeed, because it was only forgers and real gentlemen who could act so precious cool; but that, on the whole, he, Crookes, and the housekeeper, who was a highly respectable person and the sister of a minister, as he wished his mother to remember, had made up their minds that Mr. V.T. was A1, copper-bottomed—Mrs. Crookes was the widow of a seafaring man, and lived at Liverpool, and had heard Lloyd's rating quoted all her life—and that they, the writer and Mrs. Dubbs, meant to see him through his troubles, though he was a little trying at his meals, for he would have butter on the table at his dinner, and he wanted two and three courses served together, and drank milk at his luncheon, like no Christian gentleman did that Mr. Crookes had ever seen.

The financier might have been amused if he could have read this letter, which contained no allusion to the material attractions of Torp Towers as a situation; for like a good many American millionaires, Mr. Van Torp had a blind spot on his financial retina. He could deal daringly and surely with vast sums, or he could screw twice the normal quantity of work out of an underpaid clerk; but the household arithmetic that lies between the two was entirely beyond his comprehension. He 'didn't want to be bothered,' he said; he maintained that he 'could make more money in ten minutes than he could save in a year by checking the housekeeper's accounts'; he 'could live on coffee and pie,' but if he chose to hire the chef of the Cafe Anglais to cook for him at five thousand dollars a year he 'didn't want to know the price of a truffled pheasant or a chaudfroid of ortolans.' That was his way, and it was good enough for him. What was the use of having made money if you were to be bothered? And besides, he concluded, 'it was none of anybody's blank blank business what he did.'

Mr. Van Torp did not hesitate to borrow similes from another world when his rather limited command of refined language was unequal to the occasion.

But at the present juncture, though his face did not change, and though he slept as soundly and had as good an appetite as usual, no words with which he was acquainted could express his feelings at all. He had, indeed, consigned the writer of the first article to perdition with some satisfaction; but after his interview with Logotheti, when he had understood that a general attack upon him had begun, he gathered his strength in silence and studied the position with all the concentration of earnest thought which his exceptional nature could command.

He had recognised Feist's handwriting, and he remembered the man as his partner's former secretary. Feist might have written the letter to Logotheti and the first article, but Van Torp did not believe him capable of raising a general hue and cry on both sides of the Atlantic. It undoubtedly happened sometimes that when a fire had been smouldering long unseen a single spark sufficed to start the blaze, but Mr. Van Torp was too well informed as to public opinion about him to have been in ignorance of any general feeling against him, if it had existed; and the present attack was of too personal a nature to have been devised by financial rivals. Besides, the Nickel Trust had recently absorbed all its competitors to such an extent that it had no rivals at all, and the dangers that threatened it lay on the one hand in the growing strength of the Labour Party in its great movement against capital, and on the other in its position with regard to recent American legislation about Trusts. From the beginning Mr. Van Torp had been certain that the campaign of defamation had not been begun by the Unions, and by its nature it could have no connection with the legal aspect of his position. It was therefore clear that war had been declared upon him by one or more individuals on purely personal grounds, and that Mr. Feist was but the chief instrument in the hands of an unknown enemy.

But at first sight it did not look as if his assailant were Isidore Bamberger. The violent attack on him might not affect the credit of the Nickel Trust, but it was certainly not likely to improve it and Mr. Van Torp believed that if his partner had a grudge against him, any attempt at revenge would be made in a shape that would not affect the Trust's finances. Bamberger was a resentful sort of man, but on the other hand he was a man of business, and his fortune depended on that of his great partner.

Mr. Van Torp walked every morning in the park, thinking over these things, and little Ida tripped along beside him watching the squirrels and the birds, and not saying much; but now and then, when she felt the gentle pressure of his hand on hers, which usually meant that he was going to speak to her, she looked up to watch his lips, and they did not move; only his eyes met hers, and the faint smile that came into his face then was not at all like the one which most people saw there. So she smiled back, happily, and looked at the squirrels again, sure that a rabbit would soon make a dash over the open and cross the road, and hoping for the rare delight of seeing a hare. And the tame red and fallow deer looked at her suspiciously from a distance, as if she might turn into a motor-car. In those morning walks she did not again see his lips forming words that frightened her, and she began to be quite sure that he had stopped swearing to himself because she had spoken to him so seriously.

Once he looked at her so long and with so much earnestness that she asked him what he was thinking of, and he gently pushed back the broad-brimmed hat she wore, so as to see her forehead and beautiful golden hair.

'You are growing very like your mother,' he said, after a little while.

They had stopped in the broad drive, and little Ida gazed gravely up at him for a moment. Then she put up her arms.

'I think I want to give you a kiss, Mr. Van Torp,' she said with the utmost gravity. 'You're so good to me.'

Mr. Van Torp stooped, and she put her arms round his short neck and kissed the hard, flat cheek once, and he kissed hers rather awkwardly.

'Thank you, my dear,' he said, in an odd voice, as he straightened himself.

He took her hand again to walk on, and the great iron mouth was drawn a little to one side, and it looked as if the lips might have trembled if they had not been so tightly shut. Perhaps Mr. Van Torp had never kissed a child before.

She was very happy and contented, for she had spent most of her life in a New England village alone with Miss More, and the great English country-house was full of wonder and mystery for her, and the park was certainly the Earthly Paradise. She had hardly ever been with other children and was rather afraid of them, because they did not always understand what she said, as most grown people did; so she was not at all lonely now. On the contrary, she felt that her small existence was ever so much fuller than before, since she now loved two people instead of only one, and the two people seemed to agree so well together. In America she had only seen Mr. Van Torp at intervals, when he had appeared at the cottage near Boston, the bearer of toys and chocolates and other good things, and she had not been told till after she had landed in Liverpool that she was to be taken to stop with him in the country while he remained in England. Till then he had always called her 'Miss Ida,' in an absurdly formal way, but ever since she had arrived at Oxley Paddox he had dropped the 'Miss,' and had never failed to spend two or three hours alone with her every day. Though his manner had not changed much, and he treated her with a sort of queer formality, much as he would have behaved if she had been twenty years old instead of nine, she had been growing more and more sure that he loved her and would give her anything in the world she asked for, though there was really nothing she wanted; and in return she grew gratefully fond of him by quick degrees, till her affection expressed itself in her solemn proposal to 'give him a kiss.'

Not long after that Mr. Van Torp found amongst his letters one from Lady Maud, of which the envelope was stamped with the address of her father's country place, 'Craythew.' He read the contents carefully, and made a note in his pocket-book before tearing the sheet and the envelope into a number of small bits.

There was nothing very compromising in the note, but Mr. Van Torp certainly did not know that his butler regularly offered first and second prizes in the servants' hall, every Saturday night, for the 'best-put-together letters' of the week—to those of his satellites, in other words, who had been most successful in piecing together scraps from the master's wastepaper basket. In houses where the post-bag has a patent lock, of which the master keeps the key, this diversion has been found a good substitute for the more thrilling entertainment of steaming the letters and reading them before taking them upstairs. If Mrs. Dubbs was aware of Mr. Crookes' weekly distribution of rewards she took no notice of it; but as she rarely condescended to visit the lower regions, and only occasionally asked Mr. Crookes to dine in her own sitting-room, she may be allowed the benefit of the doubt; and, besides, she was a very superior person.

On the day after he had received Lady Maud's note, Mr. Van Torp rode out by himself. No one, judging from his looks, would have taken him for a good rider. He rode seldom, too, never talked of horses, and was never seen at a race. When he rode he did not even take the trouble to put on gaiters, and, after he had bought Oxley Paddox, the first time that his horse was brought to the door, by a groom who had never seen him, the latter could have sworn that the millionaire had never been on a horse before and was foolishly determined to break his neck. On that occasion Mr. Van Torp came down the steps, with a big cigar in his mouth, in his ordinary clothes, without so much as a pair of straps to keep his trousers down, or a bit of a stick in his hand. The animal was a rather ill-tempered black that had arrived from Yorkshire two days previously in charge of a boy who gave him a bad character. As Mr. Van Torp descended the steps with his clumsy gait, the horse laid his ears well back for a moment and looked as if he meant to kick anything within reach. Mr. Van Torp looked at him in a dull way, puffed his cigar, and made one remark in the form of a query.

'He ain't a lamb, is he?'

'No, sir,' answered the groom with sympathetic alacrity, 'and if I was you, sir, I wouldn't—'

But the groom's good advice was checked by an unexpected phenomenon. Mr. Van Torp was suddenly up, and the black was plunging wildly as was only to be expected; what was more extraordinary was that Mr. Van Torp's expression showed no change whatever, the very big cigar was stuck in his mouth at precisely the same angle as before, and he appeared to be glued to the saddle. He sat perfectly erect, with his legs perpendicularly straight, and his hands low and quiet.

The next moment the black bolted down the drive, but Mr. Van Torp did not seem the least disturbed, and the astonished groom, his mouth wide open and his arms hanging down, saw that the rider gave the beast his head for a couple of hundred yards, and then actually stopped him short, bringing him almost to the ground on his haunches.

'My Gawd, 'e's a cowboy!' exclaimed the groom, who was a Cockney, and had seen a Wild West show and recognised the real thing. 'And me thinkin' 'e was goin' to break his precious neck and wastin' my bloomin' sympathy on 'im!'

Since that first day Mr. Van Torp had not ridden more than a score of times in two years. He preferred driving, because it was less trouble, and partly because he could take little Ida with him. It was therefore always a noticeable event in the monotonous existence at Torp Towers when he ordered a horse to be saddled, as he did on the day after he had got Lady Maud's note from Craythew.

He rode across the hilly country at a leisurely pace, first by lanes and afterwards over a broad moor, till he entered a small beech wood by a bridle-path not wide enough for two to ride together, and lined with rhododendrons, lilacs, and laburnum. A quarter of a mile from the entrance a pretty glade widened to an open lawn, in the middle of which stood a ruin, consisting of the choir and chancel arch of a chapel. Mr. Van Torp drew rein before it, threw his right leg over the pommel before him, and remained sitting sideways on the saddle, for the very good reason that he did not see anything to sit on if he got down, and that it was of no use to waste energy in standing. His horse might have resented such behaviour on the part of any one else, but accepted the western rider's eccentricities quite calmly and proceeded to crop the damp young grass at his feet.

Mr. Van Torp had come to meet Lady Maud. The place was lonely and conveniently situated, being about half-way between Oxley Paddox and Craythew, on Mr. Van Torp's land, which was so thoroughly protected against trespassers and reporters by wire fences and special watchmen that there was little danger of any one getting within the guarded boundary. On the side towards Craythew there was a gate with a patent lock, to which Lady Maud had a key.

Mr. Van Torp was at the meeting-place at least a quarter of an hour before the appointed time. His horse only moved a short step every now and then, eating his way slowly across the grass, and his rider sat sideways, resting his elbows on his knees and staring at nothing particular, with that perfectly wooden expression of his which indicated profound thought.

But his senses were acutely awake, and he caught the distant sound of hoofs on the soft woodland path just a second before his horse lifted his head and pricked his ears. Mr. Van Torp did not slip to the ground, however, and he hardly changed his position. Half a dozen young pheasants hurled themselves noisily out of the wood on the other side of the ruin, and scattered again as they saw him, to perch on the higher boughs of the trees not far off instead of settling on the sward. A moment later Lady Maud appeared, on a lanky and elderly thoroughbred that had been her own long before her marriage. Her old-fashioned habit was evidently of the same period too; it had been made before the modern age of skirted coats, and fitted her figure in a way that would have excited open disapproval and secret admiration in Rotten Row. But she never rode in town, so that it did not matter; and, besides, Lady Maud did not care.

Mr. Van Torp raised his hat in a very un-English way, and at the same time, apparently out of respect for his friend, he went so far as to change his seat a little by laying his right knee over the pommel and sticking his left foot into the stirrup, so that he sat like a woman. Lady Maud drew up on his off side and they shook hands.

'You look rather comfortable,' she said, and the happy ripple was in her voice.

'Why, yes. There's nothing else to sit on, and the grass is wet. Do you want to get off?'

'I thought we might make some tea presently,' answered Lady Maud. 'I've brought my basket.'

'Now I call that quite sweet!' Mr. Van Torp seemed very much pleased, and he looked down at the shabby little brown basket hanging at her saddle.

He slipped to the ground, and she did the same before he could go round to help her. The old thoroughbred nosed her hand as if expecting something good, and she produced a lump of sugar from the tea-basket and gave it to him.

Mr. Van Torp pulled a big carrot from the pocket of his tweed jacket and let his horse bite it off by inches. Then he took the basket from Lady Maud and the two went towards the ruin.

'We can sit on the Earl,' said Lady Maud, advancing towards a low tomb on which was sculptured a recumbent figure in armour. 'The horses won't run away from such nice grass.'

So the two installed themselves on each side of the stone knight's armed feet, which helped to support the tea-basket, and Lady Maud took out her spirit-lamp and a saucepan that just held two cups, and a tin bottle full of water, and all the other things, arranging them neatly in order.

'How practical women are!' exclaimed Mr. Van Torp, looking on. 'Now I would never have thought of that.'

But he was really wondering whether she expected him to speak first of the grave matters that brought them together in that lonely place.

'I've got some bread and butter,' she said, opening a small sandwich-box, 'and there is a lemon instead of cream.'

'Your arrangements beat Hare Court hollow,' observed the millionaire. 'Do you remember the cracked cups and the weevilly biscuits?'

'Yes, and how sorry you were when you had burnt the little beasts! Now light the spirit-lamp, please, and then we can talk.'

Everything being arranged to her satisfaction, Lady Maud looked up at her companion.

'Are you going to do anything about it?' she asked.

'Will it do any good if I do? That's the question.'

'Good? What is good in that sense?' She looked at him a moment, but as he did not answer she went on. 'I cannot bear to see you abused in print like this, day after day, when I know the truth, or most of it.'

'It doesn't matter about me. I'm used to it. What does your father say?'

'He says that when a man is attacked as you are, it's his duty to defend himself.'

'Oh, he does, does he?'

Lady Maud smiled, but shook her head in a reproachful way.

'You promised me that you would never give me your business answer, you know!'

'I'm sorry,' said Mr. Van Torp, in a tone of contrition. 'Well, you see, I forgot you weren't a man. I won't do it again. So your father thinks I'd better come out flat-footed with a statement to the press. Now, I'll tell you. I'd do so, if I didn't feel sure that all this circus about me isn't the real thing yet. It's been got up with an object, and until I can make out what's coming I think I'd best keep still. Whoever's at the root of this is counting on my losing my temper and hitting out, and saying things, and then the real attack will come from an unexpected quarter. Do you see that? Under the circumstances, almost any man in my position would get interviewed and talk back, wouldn't he?'

'I fancy so,' answered Lady Maud.

'Exactly. If I did that, I might be raising against another man's straight flush, don't you see? A good way in a fight is never to do what everybody else would do. But I've got a scheme for getting behind the other man, whoever he is, and I've almost concluded to try it.'

'Will you tell me what it is?'

'Don't I always tell you most things?'

Lady Maud smiled at the reservation implied in 'most.'

'After all you have done for me, I should have no right to complain if you never told me anything,' she answered. 'Do as you think best. You know that I trust you.'

'That's right, and I appreciate it,' answered the millionaire. 'In the first place, you're not going to be divorced. I suppose that's settled.'

Lady Maud opened her clear eyes in surprise.

'You didn't know that, did you?' asked Mr. Van Torp, enjoying her astonishment.

'Certainly not, and I can hardly believe it,' she answered.

'Look here, Maud,' said her companion, bending his heavy brows in a way very unusual with him, 'do you seriously think I'd let you be divorced on my account? That I'd allow any human being to play tricks with your good name by coupling it with mine in any sort of way? If I were the kind of man about whom you had a right to think that, I wouldn't deserve your friendship.'

It was not often that Rufus Van Torp allowed his face to show feeling, but the look she saw in his rough-hewn features for a moment almost frightened her. There was something Titanic in it.

'No, Rufus—no!' she cried, earnestly. 'You know how I have believed in you and trusted you! It's only that I don't see how—'

'That's a detail,' answered the American. 'The "how" don't matter when a man's in earnest.' The look was gone again, for her words had appeased him instantly. 'Well,' he went on, in his ordinary tone, 'you can take it for granted that the divorce will come to nothing. There'll be a clear statement in all the best papers next week, saying that your husband's suit for a divorce has been dismissed with costs because there is not the slightest evidence of any kind against you. It will be stated that you came to my partner's chambers in Hare Court on a matter of pure business, to receive certain money, which was due to you from me in the way of business, for which you gave me the usual business acknowledgment. So that's that! I had a wire yesterday to say it's as good as settled. The water's boiling.'

The steam was lifting the lid of the small saucepan, which stood securely on the spirit-lamp between the marble knight's greaved shins. But Lady Maud took no notice of it.

'It's like you,' said she. 'I cannot find anything else to say!'

'It doesn't matter about saying anything,' returned Mr. Van Torp. 'The water's boiling.'

'Will you blow out the lamp?' As she spoke she dropped a battered silver tea-ball into the water, and moved it about by its little chain.

Mr. Van Torp took off his hat, and bent down sideways till his flat cheek rested on the knight's stone shin, and he blew out the flame with one well-aimed puff. Lady Maud did not look at the top of his head, nor steal a furtive glance at the strong muscles and sinews of his solid neck. She did nothing of the kind. She bobbed the tea-ball up and down in the saucepan by its chain, and watched how the hot water turned brown.

'But I did not give you a "business acknowledgment," as you call it,' she said thoughtfully. 'It's not quite truthful to say I did, you know.'

'Does that bother you? All right.'

He produced his well-worn pocket-book, found a scrap of white paper amongst the contents, and laid it on the leather. Then he took his pencil and wrote a few words.

'Received of R. Van Torp £4100 to balance of account.'

He held out the pencil, and laid the pocket-book on his palm for her to write. She read the words with out moving.

'"To balance of account"—what does that mean?'

'It means that it's a business transaction. At the time you couldn't make any further claim against me. That's all it means.'

He put the pencil to the paper again, and wrote the date of the meeting in Hare Court.

'There! If you sign your name to that, it just means that you had no further claim against me on that day. You hadn't, anyway, so you may just as well sign!'

He held out the paper, and Lady Maud took it with a smile and wrote her signature.

'Thank you,' said Mr. Van Torp. 'Now you're quite comfortable, I suppose, for you can't deny that you have given me the usual business acknowledgment. The other part of it is that I don't care to keep that kind of receipt long, so I just strike a match and burn it.' He did so, and watched the flimsy scrap turn black on the stone knight's knee, till the gentle breeze blew the ashes away. 'So there!' he concluded. 'If you were called upon to swear in evidence that you signed a proper receipt for the money, you couldn't deny it, could you? A receipt's good if given at any time after the money has been paid. What's the matter? Why do you look as if you doubted it? What is truth, anyhow? It's the agreement of the facts with the statement of them, isn't it? Well, I don't see but the statement coincides with the facts all right now.'

While he had been talking Lady Maud had poured out the tea, and had cut some thin slices from the lemon, glancing at him incredulously now and then, but smiling in spite of herself.

'That's all sophistry,' she said, as she handed him his cup.

'Thanks,' he answered, taking it from her. 'Look here! Can you deny that you have given me a formal dated receipt for four thousand one hundred pounds?'

'No—'

'Well, then, what can't be denied is the truth; and if I choose to publish the truth about you, I don't suppose you can find fault with it.'

'No, but—'

'Excuse me for interrupting, but there is no "but." What's good in law is good enough for me, and the Attorney-General and all his angels couldn't get behind that receipt now, if they tried till they were black in the face.'

Mr. Van Torp's similes were not always elegant.

'Tip-top tea,' he remarked, as Lady Maud did not attempt to say anything more. 'That was a bright idea of yours, bringing the lemon, too.'

He took several small sips in quick succession, evidently appreciating the quality of the tea as a connoisseur.

'I don't know how you have managed to do it,' said Lady Maud at last. 'As you say, the "how" does not matter very much. Perhaps it's just as well that I should not know how you got at the Patriarch. I couldn't be more grateful if I knew the whole story.'

'There's no particular story about it. When I found he was the man to be seen, I sent a man to see him. That's all.'

'It sounds very simple,' said Lady Maud, whose acquaintance with American slang was limited, even after she had known Mr. Van Torp intimately for two years. 'You were going to tell me more. You said you had a plan for catching the real person who is responsible for this attack on you.'

'Well, I have a sort of an idea, but I'm not quite sure how the land lays. By the bye,' he said quickly, correcting himself, 'isn't that one of the things I say wrong? You told me I ought to say how the land "lies," didn't you? I always forget.'

Lady Maud laughed as she looked at him, for she was quite sure that he had only taken up his own mistake in order to turn the subject from the plan of which he did not mean to speak.

'You know that I'm not in the least curious,' she said, 'so don't waste any cleverness in putting me off! I only wish to know whether I can help you to carry out your plan. I had an idea too. I thought of getting my father to have a week-end party at Craythew, to which you would be asked, by way of showing people that he knows all about our friendship, and approves of it in spite of what my husband has been trying to do. Would that suit you? Would it help you or not?'

'It might come in nicely after the news about the divorce appears,' answered Mr. Van Torp approvingly. 'It would be just the same if I went over to dinner every day, and didn't sleep in the house, wouldn't it?'

'I'm not sure,' Lady Maud said. 'I don't think it would, quite. It might seem odd that you should dine with us every day, whereas if you stop with us people cannot but see that my father wants you.'

'How about Lady Creedmore?'

'My mother is on the continent. Why in the world do you not want to come?'

'Oh, I don't know,' answered Mr. Van Torp vaguely. 'Just like that, I suppose. I was thinking. But it'll be all right, and I'll come any way, and please tell your father that I highly appreciate the kind invitation. When is it to be?'

'Come on Thursday next week and stay till Tuesday. Then you will be there when the first people come and till the last have left. That will look even better.'

'Maybe they'll say you take boarders,' observed Mr. Van Torp facetiously. 'That other piece belongs to you.'

While talking they had finished their tea, and only one slice of bread and butter was left in the sandwich-box.

'No,' answered Lady Maud, 'it's yours. I took the first.'

'Let's go shares,' suggested the millionaire.

'There's no knife.'

'Break it.'

Lady Maud doubled the slice with conscientious accuracy, gently pulled the pieces apart at the crease, and held out one half to her companion. He took it as naturally as if they had been children, and they ate their respective shares in silence. As a matter of fact Mr. Van Torp had been unconsciously and instinctively more interested in the accuracy of the division than in the very beautiful white fingers that performed it.

'Who are the other people going to be?' he asked when he had finished eating, and Lady Maud was beginning to put the tea-things back into the basket.

'That depends on whom we can get. Everybody is awfully busy just now, you know. The usual sort of set, I suppose. You know the kind of people who come to us—you've met lots of them. I thought of asking Miss Donne if she is free. You know her, don't you?'

'Why, yes, I do. You've read those articles about our interview in New York, I suppose.'

Lady Maud, who had been extremely occupied with her own affairs of late, had almost forgotten the story, and was now afraid that she had made a mistake, but she caught at the most evident means of setting it right.

'Yes, of course. All the better, if you are seen stopping in the same house. People will see that it's all right.'

'Well, maybe they would. I'd rather, if it'll do her any good. But perhaps she doesn't want to meet me. She wasn't over-anxious to talk to me on the steamer, I noticed, and I didn't bother her much. She's a lovely woman!'

Lady Maud looked at him, and her beautiful mouth twitched as if she wanted to laugh.

'Miss Donne doesn't think you're a "lovely" man at all,' she said.

'No,' answered Mr. Van Torp, in a tone of child-like and almost sheepish regret, 'she doesn't, and I suppose she's right. I didn't know how to take her, or she wouldn't have been so angry.'

'When? Did you really ask her to marry you?' Lady Maud was smiling now.

'Why, yes, I did. Why shouldn't I? I guess it wasn't very well done, though, and I was a fool to try and take her hand after she'd said no.'

'Oh, you tried to take her hand?'

'Yes, and the next thing I knew she'd rushed out of the room and bolted the door, as if I was a dangerous lunatic and she'd just found it out. That's what happened—just that. It wasn't my fault if I was in earnest, I suppose.'

'And just after that you were engaged to poor Miss Bamberger,' said Lady Maud in a tone of reflection.

'Yes,' answered Mr. Van Torp slowly. 'Nothing mattered much just then, and the engagement was the business side. I told you about all that in Hare Court.'

'You're a singular mixture of several people all in one! I shall never quite understand you.'

'Maybe not. But if you don't, nobody else is likely to, and I mean to be frank to you every time. I suppose you think I'm heartless. Perhaps I am. I don't know. You have to know about the business side sometimes; I wish you didn't, for it's not the side of myself I like best.'

The aggressive blue eyes softened a little as he spoke, and there was a touch of deep regret in his harsh voice.

'No,' answered Lady Maud, 'I don't like it either. But you are not heartless. Don't say that of yourself, please—please don't! You cannot fancy how it would hurt me to think that your helping me was only a rich man's caprice, that because a few thousand pounds are nothing to you it amused you to throw the money away on me and my ideas, and that you would just as soon put it on a horse, or play with it at Monte Carlo!'

'Well, you needn't worry,' observed Mr. Van Torp, smiling in a reassuring way. 'I'm not given to throwing away money. In fact, the other people think I'm too much inclined to take it. And why shouldn't I? People who don't know how to take care of money shouldn't have it. They do harm with it. It is right to take it from them since they can't keep it and haven't the sense to spend it properly. However, that's the business side of me, and we won't talk about it, unless you like.'

'I don't "like"!' Lady Maud smiled too.

'Precisely. You're not the business side, and you can have anything you like to ask for. Anything I've got, I mean.'

The beautiful hands were packing the tea-things.

'Anything in reason,' suggested Lady Maud, looking into the shabby basket.

'I'm not talking about reason,' answered Mr. Van Torp, gouging his waistcoat pockets with his thick thumbs, and looking at the top of her old grey felt hat as she bent her head. 'I don't suppose I've done much good in my life, but maybe you'll do some for me, because you understand those things and I don't. Anyhow, you mean to, and I want you to, and that constitutes intention in both parties, which is the main thing in law. If it happens to give you pleasure, so much the better. That's why I say you can have anything you like. It's an unlimited order.'

'Thank you,' said Lady Maud, still busy with the things. 'I know you are in earnest, and if I needed more money I would ask for it. But I want to make sure that it is really the right way—so many people would not think it was, you know, and only time can prove that I'm not mistaken. There!' She had finished packing the basket, and she fastened the lid regretfully. 'I'm afraid we must be going. It was awfully good of you to come!'

'Wasn't it? I'll be just as good again the day after to-morrow, if you'll ask me!'

'Will you?' rippled the sweet voice pleasantly. 'Then come at the same time, unless it rains really hard. I'm not afraid of a shower, you know, and the arch makes a very fair shelter here. I never catch cold, either.'

She rose, taking up the basket in one hand and shaking down the folds of her old habit with the other.

'All the same, I'd bring a jacket next time if I were you,' said her companion, exactly as her mother might have made the suggestion, and scarcely bestowing a glance on her almost too visibly perfect figure.

The old thoroughbred raised his head as they crossed the sward, and made two or three steps towards her of his own accord. Her foot rested a moment on Mr. Van Torp's solid hand, and she was in the saddle. The black was at first less disposed to be docile, but soon yielded at the sight of another carrot. Mr. Van Torp did not take the trouble to put his foot into the stirrup, but vaulted from the ground with no apparent effort. Lady Maud smiled approvingly, but not as a woman who loves a man and feels pride in him when he does anything very difficult. It merely pleased and amused her to see with what ease and indifference the rather heavily-built American did a thing which many a good English rider, gentleman or groom, would have found it hard to do at all. But Mr. Van Torp had ridden and driven cattle in California for his living before he had been twenty.

He wheeled and came to her side, and held out his hand.

'Day after to-morrow, at the same time,' he said as she took it. 'Good-bye!'

'Good-bye, and don't forget Thursday!'

They parted and rode away in opposite directions, and neither turned, even once, to look back at the other.

CHAPTER XIII

The *Elisir d'Amore* was received with enthusiasm, but the tenor had it all his own way, as Lushington had foretold, and when Pompeo Stromboli sang 'Una furtiva lacrima' the incomparable Cordova was for once eclipsed in the eyes of a hitherto faithful public. Covent Garden surrendered unconditionally. Metaphorically speaking, it rolled over on its back, with its four paws in the air, like a small dog that has got the worst of a fight and throws himself on the bigger dog's mercy.

Margaret was applauded, but as a matter of course. There was no electric thrill in the clapping of hands; she got the formal applause which is regularly given to the sovereign, but not the enthusiasm which is bestowed spontaneously on the conqueror. When she buttered her face and got the paint off, she was a little pale, and her eyes were not kind. It was the first time that she had not carried everything before her since she had begun her astonishing career, and in her first disappointment she had not philosophy enough to console herself with the consideration that it would have been infinitely worse to be thrown into the shade by another lyric soprano, instead of by the most popular lyric tenor on the stage. She was also uncomfortably aware that Lushington had predicted what had happened, and she was informed that he had not even taken the trouble to come to the first performance of the opera. Logotheti, who knew everything about his old rival, had told her that Lushington was in Paris that week, and was going on to see his mother in Provence.

The Primadonna was put out with herself and with everybody, after the manner of great artists when a performance has not gone exactly as they had hoped. The critics said the next morning that the Señorita da Cordova had been in good voice and had sung with excellent taste and judgment, but that was all: as if any decent soprano might not do as well! They wrote as if she might have been expected to show neither judgment nor taste, and as if she were threatened with a cold. Then they went on to praise Pompeo Stromboli with the very words they usually applied to her. His voice was full, rich, tender, vibrating, flexible, soft, powerful, stirring, natural, cultivated, superb, phenomenal, and perfectly fresh. The critics had a severe attack of 'adjectivitis.'

Paul Griggs had first applied the name to that inflammation of language to which many young writers are subject when cutting their literary milk-teeth, and from which musical critics are never quite immune. Margaret could no longer help reading what was written about her; that was one of the signs of the change that had come over her, and she disliked it, and sometimes despised herself for it, though she was quite unable to resist the impulse. The appetite for flattery which comes of living on it may be innocent, but it is never harmless. Dante consigned the flatterers to Inferno, and more particularly to a very nasty place there: it is true that there were no musical critics in his day; but he does not say much about the flattered, perhaps because they suffer enough when they find out the truth, or lose the gift for which they have been over-praised.

The Primadonna was in a detestably uncomfortable state of mind on the day after the performance of the revived opera. Her dual nature was hopelessly mixed; Cordova was in a rage with Stromboli, Schreiermeyer, Baci-Roventi, and the whole company, not to mention Signor Bambinelli the conductor, the whole orchestra, and the dead composer of the *Elisir d'Amore*; but Margaret Donne was ashamed of herself for caring, and for being spoilt, and for bearing poor Lushington a grudge because he had foretold a result that was only to be expected with such a tenor as Stromboli; she despised herself for wickedly wishing that the latter had cracked on the final high note and had made himself ridiculous. But he had not cracked at all; in imagination she could hear the note still, tremendous, round, and persistently drawn out, as if it came out of a tenor trombone and had all the world's lungs behind it.

In her mortification Cordova was ready to give up lyric opera and study Wagner, in order to annihilate Pompeo Stromboli, who did not even venture *Lohengrin*. Schreiermeyer had unkindly told him that if he arrayed his figure in polished armour he would look like a silver teapot; and Stromboli was very sensitive to ridicule. Even if he had possessed a dramatic voice, he could never have bounded about the stage in pink tights and the exiguous skin of an unknown wild animal as Siegfried, and in the flower scene of *Parsifal* he would have looked like Falstaff in *The Merry Wives of Windsor*. But Cordova could have made herself into a stately Brunhilde, a wild and lovely Kundry, or a fair and fateful Isolde, with the very least amount of artificial aid that theatrical illusion admits.

Margaret Donne, disgusted with Cordova, said that her voice was about as well adapted for one of those parts as a sick girl's might be for giving orders at sea in a storm. Cordova could not deny this, and fell back upon the idea of having an opera written for her, expressly to show off her voice, with a *crescendo* trill in every scene and a high D at the end; and Margaret Donne, who loved music for its own sake, was more disgusted than ever, and took up a book in order to get rid of her professional self, and tried so hard to read that she almost gave herself a headache.

Pompeo Stromboli was really the most sweet-tempered creature in the world, and called during the afternoon with the idea of apologising for having eclipsed her, but was told that she was resting and would see no one. Fräulein Ottilie Braun also came, and Margaret would probably have seen her, but had not given any special orders, so the kindly little person trotted off, and Margaret knew nothing of her coming; and the day wore on quickly; and when she wanted to go out, it at once began to rain furiously; and, at last, in sheer impatience at everything, she telephoned to Logotheti, asking him to come and dine alone with her if he felt that he could put up with her temper, which, she explained, was atrocious. She heard the Greek laugh gaily at the other end of the wire.

'Will you come?' she asked, impatient that anybody should be in a good humour when she was not.

'I'll come now, if you'll let me,' he answered readily.

'No. Come to dinner at half-past eight.' She waited a moment and then went on. 'I've sent down word that I'm not at home for any one, and I don't like to make you the only exception.'

'Oh, I see,' answered Logotheti's voice. 'But I've always wanted to be the only exception. I say, does half-past eight mean a quarter past nine?'

'No. It means a quarter past eight, if you like. Good-bye!'

She cut off the communication abruptly, being a little afraid that if she let him go on chattering any longer she might yield and allow him to come at once. In her solitude she was intensely bored by her own bad temper, and was nearer to making him the 'only exception' than she had often been of late. She said to herself that he always amused her, but in her heart she was conscious that he was the only man in the world who knew how to flatter her back into a good temper, and would take the trouble to do so. It was better than nothing to look forward to a pleasant evening, and she went back to her novel and her cup of tea already half reconciled with life.

It rained almost without stopping. At times it poured, which really does not happen often in much-abused London; but even heavy rain is not so depressing in spring as it is in winter, and when the Primadonna raised her eyes from her book and looked out of the big window, she was not thinking of the dreariness outside but of what she should wear in the evening. To tell the truth, she did not often trouble herself much about that matter when she was not going to sing, and all singers and actresses who habitually play 'costume parts' are conscious of looking upon stage-dressing and ordinary dressing from totally different points of view. By far the larger number of them have their stage clothes made by a theatrical tailor, and only an occasional eccentric celebrity goes to Worth or Doucet to be dressed for a 'Juliet,' a 'Tosca,' or a 'Doña Sol.'

Margaret looked at the rain and decided that Logotheti should not find her in a tea-gown, not because it would look too intimate, but because tea-gowns suggest weariness, the state of being misunderstood, and a craving for sympathy. A woman who is going to surrender to fate puts on a tea-gown, but a well-fitting body indicates strength of character and virtuous firmness.

I remember a smart elderly Frenchwoman who always bestowed unusual care on every detail of her dress, visible and invisible, before going to church. Her niece was in the room one Sunday while she was dressing for church, and asked why she took so much trouble.

'My dear,' was the answer, 'Satan is everywhere, and one can never know what may happen.'

Margaret was very fond of warm greys, and fawn tints, and dove colour, and she had lately got a very pretty dress that was exactly to her taste, and was made of a newly invented thin material of pure silk, which had no sheen and cast no reflections of light, and was slightly elastic, so that it fitted as no ordinary silk or velvet ever could. Alphonsine called the gown a 'legend,' but a celebrated painter who had lately seen it said it was an 'Indian twilight,' which might mean anything, as Paul Griggs explained, because there is no twilight to speak of in India. The dress-maker who had made it called the colour 'fawn's stomach,' which was less poetical, and the fabric, 'veil of nun in love,' which showed little respect for monastic institutions. As for the way in which the dress was made, it is folly to rush into competition with tailors and dress-makers, who know what they are talking about, and are able to say things which nobody can understand.

The plain fact is that the Primadonna began to dress early, out of sheer boredom, had her thick brown hair done in the most becoming way in spite of its natural waves, which happened to be unfashionable just then, and she put on the new gown with all the care and consideration which so noble a creation deserved.

'Madame is adorable,' observed Alphonsine. 'Madame is a dream. Madame has only to lift her little finger, and kings will fall into ecstasy before her.'

'That would be very amusing,' said Margaret, looking at herself in the glass, and less angry with the world than she had been. 'I have never seen a king in ecstasy.'

'The fault is Madame's,' returned Alphonsine, possibly with truth.

When Margaret went into the drawing-room Logotheti was already there, and she felt a thrill of pleasure when his expression changed at sight of her. It is not easy to affect the pleased surprise which the sudden appearance of something beautiful brings into the face of a man who is not expecting anything unusual.

'Oh, I say!' exclaimed the Greek. 'Let me look at you!'

And instead of coming forward to take her hand, he stepped back in order not to lose anything of the wonderful effect by being too near. Margaret stood still and smiled in the peculiar way which is a woman's equivalent for a cat's purring. Then, to Logotheti's still greater delight, she slowly turned herself round, to be admired, like a statue on a pivoted pedestal, quite regardless of a secret consciousness that Margaret Donne would not have done such a thing for him, and probably not for any other man.

'You're really too utterly stunning!' he cried.

In moments of enthusiasm he sometimes out-Englished Englishmen.

'I'm glad you like it,' Margaret said. 'This is the first time I've worn it.'

'If you put it on for me, thank you! If not, thank you for putting it on! I'm not asking, either. I should think you would wear it if you were alone for the mere pleasure of feeling like a goddess.'

'You're very nice!'

She was satisfied, and for a moment she forgot Pompeo Stromboli, the *Elisir d'Amore*, the public, and the critics. It was particularly 'nice' of him, too, not to insist upon being told that she had put on the new creation solely for his benefit. Next to not assuming rashly that a woman means anything of the sort expressly for him, it is wise of a man to know when she really does, without being told. At least, so Margaret thought just then; but it is true that she wanted him to amuse her and was willing to be pleased.

She executed the graceful swaying movement which only a well-made woman can make just before sitting down for the first time in a perfectly new gown. It is a slightly serpentine motion; and as there is nothing to show that Eve did not meet the Serpent again after she had taken to clothes, she may have learnt the trick from him. There is certainly something diabolical about it when it is well done.

Logotheti's almond-shaped eyes watched her quietly, and he stood motionless till she was established on her chair. Then he seated himself at a little distance.

'I hope I was not rude,' he said, in artful apology, 'but it's not often that one's breath is taken away by what one sees. Horrid weather all day, wasn't it? Have you been out at all?'

'No. I've been moping. I told you that I was in a bad humour, but I don't want to talk about it now that I feel better. What have you been doing? Tell me all sorts of amusing things, where you have been, whom you have seen, and what people said to you.'

'That might be rather dull,' observed the Greek.

'I don't believe it. You are always in the thick of everything that's happening.'

'We have agreed to-day to lend Russia some more money. But that doesn't interest you, does it? There's to be a European conference about the Malay pirates, but there's nothing very funny in that. It would be more amusing to hear the pirates' view of Europeans. Let me see. Some one has discovered a conspiracy in Italy against Austria, and there is another in Austria against the Italians. They are the same old plots that were discovered six months ago, but people had forgotten about them, so they are as good as new. Then there is the sad case of that Greek.'

'What Greek? I've not heard about that. What has happened to him?'

'Oh, nothing much. It's only a love-story—the same old thing.'

'Tell me.'

'Not now, for we shall have to go to dinner just when I get to the most thrilling part of it, I'm sure.' Logotheti laughed. 'And besides,' he added, 'the man isn't dead yet, though he's not expected to live. I'll tell you about your friend Mr. Feist instead. He has been very ill too.'

'I would much rather know about the Greek love-story,' Margaret objected. 'I never heard of Mr. Feist.'

She had quite forgotten the man's existence, but Logotheti recalled to her memory the circumstances under which they had met, and Feist's unhealthy face with its absurdly youthful look, and what he had said about having been at the Opera in New York on the night of the explosion.

'Why do you tell me all this?' Margaret asked. 'He was a disgusting-looking man, and I never wish to see him again. Tell me about the Greek. When we go to dinner you can finish the story in French. We spoke French the first time we met, at Madame Bonanni's. Do you remember?'

'Yes, of course I do. But I was telling you about Mr. Feist—'

'Dinner is ready,' Margaret said, rising as the servant opened the door.

To her surprise the man came forward. He said that just as he was going to announce dinner Countess Leven had telephoned that she was dining out, and would afterwards stop on her way to the play in the hope of seeing Margaret for a moment. She had seemed to be in a hurry, and had closed the communication before the butler could answer. And dinner was served, he added.

Margaret nodded carelessly, and the two went into the dining-room. Lady Maud could not possibly come before half-past nine, and there was plenty of time to decide whether she should be admitted or not.

'Mr. Feist has been very ill,' Logotheti said as they sat down to table under the pleasant light, 'and I have been taking care of him, after a fashion.'

Margaret raised her eyebrows a little, for she was beginning to be annoyed at his persistency, and was not much pleased at the prospect of Lady Maud's visit.

'How very odd!' she said, rather coldly. 'I cannot imagine anything more disagreeable.'

'It has been very unpleasant,' Logotheti answered, 'but he seemed to have no particular friends here, and he was all alone at an hotel, and really very ill. So I volunteered.'

'I've no objection to being moderately sorry for a young man who falls ill at an hotel and has no friends,' Margaret said, 'but are you going in for nursing? Is that your latest hobby? It's a long way from art, and even from finance!'

'Isn't it?'

'Yes. I'm beginning to be curious!'

'I thought you would be before long,' Logotheti answered coolly, but suddenly speaking French. 'One of the most delightful things in life is to have one's curiosity roused and then satisfied by very slow degrees!'

'Not too slow, please. The interest might not last to the end.'

'Oh yes, it will, for Mr. Feist plays a part in your life.'

'About as distant as Voltaire's Chinese Mandarin, I fancy,' Margaret suggested.

'Nearer than that, though I did not guess it when I went to see him. In the first place, it was owing to you that I went to see him the first time.'

'Nonsense!'

'Not at all. Everything that happens to me is connected with you in some way. I came to see you late in the afternoon, on one of your off-days not long ago, hoping that you would ask me to dine, but you were across the river at Lord Creedmore's. I met old Griggs at your door, and as we walked away he told me that Mr. Feist had fallen down in a fit at a club, the night before, and had been sent home in a cab to the Carlton. As I had nothing to do, worth doing, I went to see him. If you had been at home, I should never have gone. That is what I mean when I say that you were the cause of my going to see him.'

'In the same way, if you had been killed by a motor-car as you went away from my door, I should have been the cause of your death!'

'You will be in any case,' laughed Logotheti, 'but that's a detail! I found Mr. Feist in a very bad way.'

'What was the matter with him?' asked Margaret.

'He was committing suicide,' answered the Greek with the utmost calm. 'If I were in Constantinople I should tell you that this turbot is extremely good, but as we are in London I suppose it would be very bad manners to say so, wouldn't it? So I am thinking it.'

'Take the fish for granted, and tell me more about Mr. Feist!'

'I found him standing before the glass with a razor in his hand and quite near his throat. When he saw me he tried to laugh and said he was just going to shave; I asked him if he generally shaved without soap and water, and he burst into tears.'

'That's rather dreadful,' observed Margaret. 'What did you do?'

'I saved his life, but I don't think he's very grateful yet. Perhaps he may be by and by. When he stopped sobbing he tried to kill me for hindering his destruction, but I had got the razor in my pocket, and his revolver missed fire. That was lucky, for he managed to stick the muzzle against my chest and pull the trigger just as I got him down. I wished I had brought old Griggs with me, for they say he can bend a good horse-shoe double, even now, and the fellow had the strength of a lunatic in him. It was rather lively for a few seconds, and then he broke down again, and was as limp as a rag, and trembled with fright, as if he saw queer things in the room.'

'You sent for a doctor then?'

'My own, and we took care of him together that night. You may laugh at the idea of my having a doctor, as I never was ill in my life. I have him to dine with me now and then, because he is such good company, and is the best judge of a statue or a picture I know. The habit of taking the human body to pieces teaches you a great deal about the shape of it, you see. In the morning we moved Mr. Feist from the hotel to a small private hospital where cases of that sort are treated. Of course he was perfectly helpless, so we packed his belongings and papers.'

'It was really very kind of you to act the Good Samaritan to a stranger,' Margaret said, but her tone showed that she was disappointed at the tame ending of the story.

'No,' Logotheti answered. 'I was never consciously kind, as you call it. It's not a Greek characteristic to love one's neighbour as one's self. Teutons, Anglo-Saxons, Latins, and, most of all, Asiatics, are charitable, but the old Greeks were not. I don't believe you'll find an instance of a charitable act in all Greek history, drama, and biography! If you did find one I should only say that the exception proves the rule. Charity was left out of us at the beginning, and we never could understand it, except as a foreign sentiment imported with Christianity from Asia. We have had every other virtue, including hospitality. In the *Iliad* a man declines to kill his enemy on the ground that their people had dined together, which is going rather far, but it is not recorded that any ancient Greek, even Socrates himself, ever felt pity or did an act of spontaneous kindness! I don't believe any one has said that, but it's perfectly true.'

'Then why did you take all that trouble for Mr. Feist?'

'I don't know. People who always know why they do things are great bores. It was probably a caprice that took me to see him, and then it did not occur to me to let him cut his throat, so I took away his razor; and, finally, I telephoned for my doctor, because my misspent life has brought me into contact with Western civilisation. But when we began to pack Mr. Feist's papers I became interested in him.'

'Do you mean to say that you read his letters?' Margaret inquired.

'Why not? If I had let him kill himself, somebody would have read them, as he had not taken the trouble to destroy them!'

'That's a singular point of view.'

'So was Mr. Feist's, as it turned out. I found enough to convince me that he is the writer of all those articles about Van Torp, including the ones in which you are mentioned. The odd thing about it is that I found a very friendly invitation from Van Torp himself, begging Mr. Feist to go down to Derbyshire and stop a week with him.'

Margaret leaned back in her chair and looked at her guest in quiet surprise.

'What does that mean?' she asked. 'Is it possible that Mr. Van Torp has got up this campaign against himself in order to play some trick on the Stock Exchange?'

Logotheti smiled and shook his head.

'That's not the way such things are usually managed,' he answered. 'A hundred years ago a publisher paid a critic to attack a book in order to make it succeed, but in finance abuse doesn't contribute to our success, which is always a question of credit. All these scurrilous articles have set the public very much against Van Torp, from Paris to San Francisco, and this man Feist is responsible for them. He is either insane, or he has some grudge against Van Torp, or else he has been somebody's instrument, which looks the most probable.'

'What did you find amongst his papers?' Margaret asked, quite forgetting her vicarious scruples about reading a sick man's letters.

'A complete set of the articles that have appeared, all neatly filed, and a great many notes for more, besides a lot of stuff written in cypher. It must be a diary, for the days are written out in full and give the days of the week.'

'I wonder whether there was anything about the explosion,' said Margaret thoughtfully. 'He said he was there, did he not?'

'Yes. Do you remember the day?'

'It was a Wednesday, I'm sure, and it was after the middle of March. My maid can tell us, for she writes down the date and the opera in a little book each time I sing. It's sometimes very convenient. But it's too late now, of course, and, besides, you could not have read the cypher.'

'That's an easy matter,' Logotheti answered. 'All cyphers can be read by experts, if there is no hurry, except the mechanical ones that are written through holes in a square plate which you turn round till the sheet is full. Hardly any one uses those now, because when the square is raised the letters don't form words, and the cable companies will only transmit real words in some known language, or groups of figures. The diary is written hastily, too, not at all as if it were copied from the sheet on which the perforated plate would have had to be used, and besides, the plate itself would be amongst his things, for he could not read his own notes without it.'

'All that doesn't help us, as you have not the diary, but I should really be curious to know what he had to say about the accident, since some of the articles hint that Mr. Van Torp made it happen.'

'My doctor and I took the liberty of confiscating the papers, and we set a very good man to work on the cypher at once. So your curiosity shall be satisfied. I said it should, didn't I? And you are not so dreadfully bored after all, are you? Do say that I'm very nice!'

'I won't!' Margaret answered with a little laugh. 'I'll only admit that I'm not bored! But wasn't it rather a high-handed proceeding to carry off Mr. Feist like that, and to seize his papers?'

'Do you call it high-handed to keep a man from cutting his throat?'

'But the letters——?'

'I really don't know. I had not time to ask a lawyer's opinion, and so I had to be satisfied with my doctor's.'

'Are you going to tell Mr. Van Torp what you've done?'

'I don't know. Why should I? You may if you like.'

Logotheti was eating a very large and excellent truffle, and after each short sentence he cut off a tiny slice and put it into his mouth. The Primadonna had already finished hers, and watched him thoughtfully.

'I'm not likely to see him,' she said. 'At least, I hope not!'

'My interest in Mr. Feist,' answered Logotheti, 'begins and ends with what concerns you. Beyond that I don't care a straw what happens to Mr. Van Torp, or to any one else. To all intents and purposes I have got the author of the stories locked up, for a man who has consented to undergo treatment for dipsomania in a private hospital, by the advice of his friends and under the care of a doctor with a great reputation, is as really in prison as if he were in gaol. Legally, he can get out, but in real fact nobody will lift a hand to release him, because he is shut up for his own good and for the good of the public, just as much as if he were a criminal. Feist may have friends or relations in America, and they may come and claim him; but as there seems to be nobody in London who cares what becomes of him, it pleases me to keep him in confinement, because I mean to prevent any further mention of your name in connection with the Van Torp scandals.'

His eyes rested on Margaret as he spoke, and lingered afterwards, with a look that did not escape her. She had seen him swayed by passion, more than once, and almost mad for her, and she had been frightened though she had dominated him. What she saw in his face now was not that; it was more like affection, faithful and lasting, and it touched her English nature much more than any show of passion could.

'Thank you,' she said quietly.

They did not talk much more while they finished the short dinner, but when they were going back to the drawing-room Margaret took his arm, in foreign fashion, which she had never done before when they were alone. Then he stood before the mantelpiece and watched her in silence as she moved about the room; for she was one of those women who always find half a dozen little things to do as soon as they get back from dinner, and go from place to place, moving a reading lamp half an inch farther from the edge of a table, shutting a book that has been left open on another, tearing up a letter that lies on the writing-desk, and slightly changing the angle at which a chair stands. It is an odd little mania, and the more people there are in the room the less the mistress of the house yields to it, and the more uncomfortable she feels at being hindered from 'tidying up the room,' as she probably calls it.

Logotheti watched Margaret with keen pleasure, as every step and little movement showed her figure in a slightly different attitude and light, indiscreetly moulded in the perfection of her matchless gown. In less than two minutes she had finished her trip round the room and was standing beside him, her elbows resting on the mantelpiece, while she moved a beautiful Tanagra a little to one side and then to the other, trying for the twentieth time how it looked the best.

'There is no denying it,' Logotheti said at last, with profound conviction. 'I do not care a straw what becomes of any living creature but you.'

She did not turn her head, and her fingers still touched the Tanagra, but he saw the rare blush spread up the cheek that was turned to him; and because she stopped moving the statuette about, and looked at it intently, he guessed that she was not colouring from annoyance at what he had said. She blushed so very seldom now, that it might mean much more than in the old days at Versailles.

'I did not think it would last so long,' she said gently, after a little while.

'What faith can one expect of a Greek!'

He laughed, too wise in woman's ways to be serious too long just then. But she shook her head and turned to him with the smile he loved.

'I thought it was something different,' she said. 'I was mistaken. I believed you had only lost your head for a while, and would soon run after some one else. That's all.'

'And the loss is permanent. That's all!' He laughed again as he repeated her words. 'You thought it was "something different"—do you know that you are two people in one?'

She looked a little surprised.

'Indeed I do!' she answered rather sadly. 'Have you found it out?'

'Yes. You are Margaret Donne and you are Cordova. I admire Cordova immensely, I am extremely fond of Margaret, and I'm in love with both. Oh yes! I'm quite frank about it, and it's very unlucky, for whichever one of your two selves I meet I'm just as much in love as ever! Absurd, isn't it?'

'It's flattering, at all events.'

'If you ever took it into your handsome head to marry me—please, I'm only saying "if"—the absurdity would be rather reassuring, wouldn't it? When a man is in love with two women at the same time, it really is a little unlikely that he should fall in love with a third!'

'Mr. Griggs says that marriage is a drama which only succeeds if people preserve the unities!'

'Griggs is always trying to coax the Djin back into the bottle, like the fisherman in the *Arabian Nights*,' answered Logotheti. 'He has read Kant till he believes that the greatest things in the world can be squeezed into a formula of ten words, or nailed up amongst the Categories like a dead owl over a stable door. My intelligence, such as it is, abhors definitions!'

'So do I. I never understand them.'

'Besides, you can only define what you know from past experience and can reflect upon coolly, and that is not my position, nor yours either.'

Margaret nodded, but said nothing and sat down.

'Do you want to smoke?' she asked. 'You may, if you like. I don't mind a cigarette.'

'No, thank you.'

'But I assure you I don't mind it in the least. It never hurts my throat.'

'Thanks, but I really don't want to.'

'I'm sure you do. Please—'

'Why do you insist? You know I never smoke when you are in the room.'

'I don't like to be the object of little sacrifices that make people uncomfortable.'

'I'm not uncomfortable, but if you have any big sacrifice to suggest, I promise to offer it at once.'

'Unconditionally?' Margaret smiled. 'Anything I ask?'

'Yes. Do you want my statue?'

'The Aphrodite? Would you give her to me?'

'Yes. May I telegraph to have her packed and brought here from Paris?'

He was already at the writing-table looking for a telegraph form. Margaret watched his face, for she knew that he valued the wonderful statue far beyond all his treasures, both for its own sake and because he had nearly lost his life in carrying it off from Samos, as has been told elsewhere.

As Margaret said nothing, he began to write the message. She really had not had any idea of testing his willingness to part with the thing he valued most, at her slightest word, and was taken by surprise; but it was impossible not to be pleased when she saw that he was in earnest. In her present mood, too, it restored her sense of power, which had been rudely shaken by the attitude of the public on the previous evening.

It took some minutes to compose the message.

'It's only to save time by having the box ready,' he said, as he rose with the bit of paper in his hand. 'Of course I shall see the statue packed myself and come over with it.'

She saw his face clearly in the light as he came towards her, and there was no mistaking the unaffected satisfaction it expressed. He held out the telegram for her to read, but she would not take it, and she looked up quietly and earnestly as he stood beside her.

'Do you remember Delorges?' she asked. 'How the lady tossed her glove amongst the lions and bade him fetch it, if he loved her, and how he went in and got it—and then threw it in her face? I feel like her.'

Logotheti looked at her blankly.

'Do you mean to say you won't take the statue?' he asked in a disappointed tone.

'No, indeed! I was taken by surprise when you went to the writing-table.'

'You did not believe I was in earnest? Don't you see that I'm disappointed now?' His voice changed a little. 'Don't you understand that if the world were mine I should want to give it all to you?'

'And don't you understand that the wish may be quite as much to me as the deed? That sounds commonplace, I know. I would say it better if I could.'

She folded her hands on her knee, and looked at them thoughtfully while he sat down beside her.

'You say it well enough,' he answered after a little pause. 'The trouble lies there. The wish is all you will ever take. I have submitted to that; but if you ever change your mind, please remember that I have not changed mine. For two years I've done everything I can to make you marry me whether you would or not, and you've forgiven me for trying to carry you off against your will, and for several other things, but you are no nearer to caring for me ever so little than you were the first day we met. You "like" me! That's the worst of it!'

'I'm not so sure of that,' Margaret answered, raising her eyes for a moment and then looking at her hands again.

He turned his head slowly, but there was a startled look in his eyes.

'Do you feel as if you could hate me a little, for a change?' he asked.

'No.'

'There's only one other thing,' he said in a low voice.

'Perhaps,' Margaret answered, in an even lower tone than his. 'I'm not quite sure to-day.'

Logotheti had known her long, and he now resisted the strong impulse to reach out and take the hand she would surely have let him hold in his for a moment. She was not disappointed because he neither spoke nor moved, nor took any sudden advantage of her rather timid admission, for his silence made her trust him more than any passionate speech or impulsive action could have done.

'I daresay I am wrong to tell you even that much,' she went on presently, 'but I do so want to play fair. I've always despised women who cannot make up their minds whether they care for a man or not. But you have found out my secret; I am two people in one, and there are days when each makes the other dreadfully uncomfortable! You understand.'

'And it's the Cordova that neither likes me nor hates me just at this moment,' suggested Logotheti. 'Margaret Donne sometimes hates me and sometimes likes me, and on some days she can be quite indifferent too! Is that it?'

'Yes. That's it.'

'The only question is, which of you is to be mistress of the house,' said Logotheti, smiling, 'and whether it is to be always the same one, or if there is to be a perpetual hide-and-seek between them!'

'Box and Cox,' suggested Margaret, glad of the chance to say something frivolous just then.

'I should say Hera and Aphrodite,' answered the Greek, 'if it did not look like comparing myself to Adonis!'

'It sounds better than Box and Cox, but I have forgotten my mythology.'

'Hera and Aphrodite agreed that each should keep Adonis one-third of the year, and that he should have the odd four months to himself. Now that you are the Cordova, if you could come to some such understanding about me with Miss Donne, it would be very satisfactory. But I am afraid Margaret does not want even a third of me!'

Logotheti felt that it was rather ponderous fun, but he was in such an anxious state that his usually ready wit did not serve him very well. For the first time since he had known her, Margaret had confessed that she might possibly fall in love with him; and after what had passed between them in former days, he knew that the smallest mistake on his part would now be fatal to the realisation of such a possibility. He was not afraid of being dull, or of boring her, but he was afraid of wakening against him the wary watchfulness of that side of her nature which he called Margaret Donne, as distinguished from Cordova, of the 'English-girl' side, of the potential old maid that is dormant in every young northern woman until the day she marries, and wakes to torment her like a biblical devil if she does not. There is no miser like a reformed spendthrift, and no ascetic will go to such extremes of self-mortification as a converted libertine; in the same way, there are no such portentously virginal old maids as those who might have been the most womanly wives; the opposite is certainly true also, for the variety 'Hemiparthenos,' studied after nature by Marcel Prévost, generally makes an utter failure of matrimony, and becomes, in fact, little better than a half-wife.

Logotheti took it as a good sign that Margaret laughed at what he said. He was in the rather absurd position of wishing to leave her while she was in her present humour, lest anything should disturb it and destroy his advantage; yet, after what had just passed, it was next to impossible not to talk of her, or of himself. He had exceptionally good nerves, he was generally cool to a fault, and he had the daring that makes great financiers. But what looked like the most important crisis of his life had presented itself unexpectedly within a few minutes; a success which he reckoned far beyond all other successes was almost within his grasp, and he felt that he was unprepared. For the first time he did not know what to say to a woman.

Happily for him, Margaret helped him unexpectedly.

'I shall have to see Lady Maud,' she said, 'and you must either go when she comes or leave with her. I'm sorry, but you understand, don't you?'

'Of course. I'll go a moment after she comes. When am I to see you again? To-morrow? You are not to sing again this week, are you?'

'No,' the Primadonna answered vaguely, 'I believe not.'

She was thinking of something else. She was wondering whether Logotheti would wish her to give up the stage, if by any possibility she ever married him, and her thoughts led her on quickly to the consideration of what that would mean, and to asking herself what sort of sacrifice it would really mean to her. For the recollection of the *Elisir d'Amore* awoke and began to rankle again just then.

Logotheti did not press her for an answer, but watched her cautiously while her eyes were turned away from him. At that moment he felt like a tamer who had just succeeded in making a tiger give its paw for the first time, and has not the smallest idea whether the creature will do it again or bite off his head.

She, on her side, being at the moment altogether the artist, was thinking that it would be pleasant to enjoy a few more triumphs, to make the tour of Europe with a company of her own—which is always the primadonna's dream as it is the actress's—and to leave the stage at twenty-five in a blaze of glory, rather than to risk one more performance of the opera she now hated. She knew quite well that it was not at all an impossibility. To please her, and with the expectation of marrying her in six months, Logotheti would cheerfully pay the large forfeit that would be due to Schreiermeyer if she broke her London engagement at the height of the season, and the Greek financier would produce all the ready money necessary for getting together an opera company. The rest would be child's play, she was sure, and she would make a triumphant progress through the capitals of Europe which should be remembered for half a century. After that, said the Primadonna to herself, she would repay her friend all the money he had lent her, and would then decide at her leisure whether she would marry him or not. For one moment her cynicism would have surprised even Schreiermeyer; the next, the Primadonna herself was ashamed of it, quite independently of what her better self might have thought.

Besides, it was certainly not for his money that her old inclination for Logotheti had begun to grow again. She could say so, truly enough, and when she felt sure of it she turned her eyes to see his face.

She did not admire him for his looks, either. So far as appearance was concerned, she preferred Lushington, with his smooth hair and fair complexion. Logotheti was a handsome and showy Oriental, that was all, and she knew instinctively that the type must be common in the East. What attracted her was probably his daring masculineness, which contrasted so strongly with Lushington's quiet and rather bashful manliness. The Englishman would die for a cause and make no noise about it, which would be heroic; but the Greek would run away with a woman he loved, at the risk of breaking his neck, which was romantic in the extreme. It is not easy to be a romantic character in the eyes of a lady who lives on the stage, and by it, and constantly gives utterance to the most dramatic sentiments at a pitch an octave higher than any one else; but Logotheti had succeeded. There never was a woman yet to whom that sort of thing has not appealed once; for one moment she has felt everything whirling with her as if the centre of gravity had gone mad, and the Ten Commandments might drop out of the solid family Bible and get lost. That recollection is probably the only secret of a virtuously colourless existence, but she hides it, like a treasure or a crime, until she is an old and widowed woman; and one day, at last, she tells her grown-up granddaughter, with a far-away smile, that there was once a man whose eyes and voice stirred her strongly, and for whom she might have quite lost her head. But she never saw him again, and that is the end of the little story; and the tall girl in her first season thinks it rather dull.

But it was not likely that the chronicle of Cordova's youth should come to such an abrupt conclusion. The man who moved her now had been near her too often, the sound of his voice was too easily recalled, and, since his rival's defection, he was too necessary to her; and, besides, he was as obstinate as Christopher Columbus.

'Let me see,' she said thoughtfully. 'There's a rehearsal to-morrow morning. That means a late luncheon. Come at two o'clock, and if it's fine we can go for a little walk. Will you?'

'Of course. Thank you.'

He had hardly spoken the words when a servant opened the door and Lady Maud came in. She had not dropped the opera cloak she wore over her black velvet gown; she was rather pale, and the look in her eyes told that something was wrong, but her serenity did not seem otherwise affected. She kissed Margaret and gave her hand to Logotheti.

'We dined early to go to the play,' she said, 'and as there's a curtain-raiser, I thought I might as well take a hansom and join them later.'

She seated herself beside Margaret on one of those little sofas that are measured to hold two women when the fashions are moderate, and are wide enough for a woman and one man, whatever happens. Indeed they must be, since otherwise no one would tolerate them in a drawing-room. When two women instal themselves in one, and a man is present, it means that he is to go away, because they are either going to make confidences or are going to fight.

Logotheti thought it would be simpler and more tactful to go at once, since Lady Maud was in a hurry, having stopped on her way to the play, presumably in the hope of seeing Margaret alone. To his surprise she asked him to stay; but as he thought she might be doing this out of mere civility he said he had an engagement.

'Will it keep for ten minutes?' asked Lady Maud gravely.

'Engagements of that sort are very convenient. They will keep any length of time.'

Logotheti sat down again, smiling, but he wondered what Lady Maud was going to say, and why she wished him to remain.

'It will save a note,' she said, by way of explanation. 'My father and I want you to come to Craythew for the week-end after this,' she continued, turning to Margaret. 'We are asking several people, so it won't be too awfully dull, I hope. Will you come?'

'With pleasure,' answered the singer.

'And you too?' Lady Maud looked at Logotheti.

'Delighted—most kind of you,' he replied, somewhat surprised by the invitation, for he had never met Lord and Lady Creedmore. 'May I take you down in my motor?' he spoke to Margaret. 'I think I can do it under four hours. I'm my own chauffeur, you know.'

'Yes, I know,' Margaret answered with a rather malicious smile. 'No, thank you!'

'Does he often kill?' inquired Lady Maud coolly.

'I should be more afraid of a runaway,' Margaret said.

'Get that new German brake,' suggested Lady Maud, not understanding at all. 'It's quite the best I've seen. Come on Friday, if you can. You don't mind meeting Mr. Van Torp, do you? He is our neighbour, you remember.'

The question was addressed to Margaret, who made a slight movement and unconsciously glanced at Logotheti before she answered.

'Not at all,' she said.

'There's a reason for asking him when there are other people. I'm not divorced after all—you had not heard? It will be in the *Times* to-morrow morning. The Patriarch of Constantinople turns out to be a very sensible sort of person.'

'He's my uncle,' observed Logotheti.

'Is he? But that wouldn't account for it, would it? He refused to believe what my husband called the evidence, and dismissed the suit. As the trouble was all about Mr. Van Torp my father wants people to see him at Craythew.

That's the story in a nutshell, and if any of you like me you'll be nice to him.'

She leaned back in her corner of the little sofa and looked first at one and then at the other in an inquiring way, but as if she were fairly sure of the answer.

'Every one likes you,' said Logotheti quietly, 'and every one will be nice to him.'

'Of course,' chimed in Margaret.

She could say nothing else, though her intense dislike of the American millionaire almost destroyed the anticipated pleasure of her visit to Derbyshire.

'I thought it just as well to explain,' said Lady Maud.

She was still pale, and in spite of her perfect outward coolness and self-reliance her eyes would have betrayed her anxiety if she had not managed them with the unconscious skill of a woman of the world who has something very important to hide. Logotheti broke the short silence that followed her last speech.

'I think you ought to know something I have been telling Miss Donne,' he said simply. 'I've found the man who wrote all those articles, and I've locked him up.'

Lady Maud leaned forward so suddenly that her loosened opera-cloak slipped down behind her, leaving her neck and shoulders bare. Her eyes were wide open in her surprise, the pupils very dark.

'Where?' she asked breathlessly. 'Where is he? In prison?'

'In a more convenient and accessible place,' answered the Greek.

He had known Lady Maud some time, but he had never seen her in the least disturbed, or surprised, or otherwise moved by anything. It was true that he had only met her in society.

He told the story of Mr. Feist, as Margaret had heard it during dinner, and Lady Maud did not move, even to lean back in her seat again, till he had finished. She scarcely seemed to breathe, and Logotheti felt her steady gaze on him, and would have sworn that through all those minutes she did not even wink. When he ceased speaking she drew a long breath and sank back to her former attitude; but he saw that her white neck heaved suddenly again and again, and her delicate nostrils quivered once or twice. For a little while there was silence in the room. Then Lady Maud rose to go.

'I must be going too,' said Logotheti.

Margaret was a little sorry that she had given him such precise instructions, but did not contradict herself by asking him to stay longer. She promised Lady Maud again to be at Craythew on Friday of the next week if possible, and certainly on Saturday, and Lady Maud and Logotheti went out together.

'Get in with me,' she said quietly, as he helped her into her hansom.

He obeyed, and as he sat down she told the cabman to take her to the Haymarket Theatre. Logotheti expected her to speak, for he was quite sure that she had not taken him with her without a purpose; the more so, as she had not even asked him where he was going.

Three or four minutes passed before he heard her voice asking him a question, very low, as if she feared to be overheard.

'Is there any way of making that man tell the truth against his will? You have lived in the East, and you must know about such things.'

Logotheti turned his almond-shaped eyes slowly towards her, but he could not see her face well, for it was not very light in the broad West End street. She was white; that was all he could make out. But he understood what she meant.

'There is a way,' he answered slowly and almost sternly. 'Why do you ask?'

'Mr. Van Torp is going to be accused of murder. That man knows who did it. Will you help me?'

It seemed an age before the answer to her whispered question came.

'Yes.'

CHAPTER XIV

When Logotheti and his doctor had taken Mr. Feist away from the hotel, to the no small satisfaction of the management, they had left precise instructions for forwarding the young man's letters and for informing his friends, if any appeared, as to his whereabouts. But Logotheti had not given his own name.

Sir Jasper Threlfall had chosen for their patient a private establishment in Ealing, owned and managed by a friend of his, a place for the treatment of morphia mania, opium-eating, and alcoholism.

To all intents and purposes, as Logotheti had told Margaret, Charles Feist might as well have been in gaol. Every one knows how indispensable it is that persons who consent to be cured of drinking or taking opium, or whom it is attempted to cure, should be absolutely isolated, if only to prevent weak and pitying friends from yielding to their heart-rending entreaties for the favourite drug and bringing them 'just a little'; for their eloquence is often extraordinary, and their ingenuity in obtaining what they want is amazing.

So Mr. Feist was shut up in a pleasant room provided with double doors and two strongly barred windows that overlooked a pretty garden, beyond which there was a high brick wall half covered by a bright creeper, then just beginning to flower. The walls, the doors, the ceiling, and the floor were sound-proof, and the garden could not in any way be reached without passing through the house.

As only male patients were received, the nurses and attendants were all men; for the treatment needed more firmness and sometimes strength than gentleness. It was uncompromising, as English methods often are. Except where life was actually in danger, there was no drink and no opium for anybody; when absolutely necessary the resident doctor gave the patient hypodermics or something which he called by an unpronounceable name, lest the sufferer should afterwards try to buy it; he smilingly described it as a new vegetable poison, and in fact it was nothing but dionine, a preparation of opium that differs but little from ordinary morphia.

Now Sir Jasper Threlfall was a very great doctor indeed, and his name commanded respect in London at large and inspired awe in the hospitals. Even the profession admitted reluctantly that he did not kill more patients than he cured, which is something for one fashionable doctor to say of another; for the regular answer to any inquiry about a rival practitioner is a smile—'a smile more dreadful than his own dreadful frown'—an indescribable smile, a meaning smile, a smile that is a libel in itself.

It had been an act of humanity to take the young man into medical custody, as it were, and it had been more or less necessary for the safety of the public, for Logotheti and the doctor had found him in a really dangerous state, as was amply proved by his attempting to cut his own throat and then to shoot Logotheti himself. Sir Jasper said he had nothing especial the matter with him except drink, that when his nerves had recovered their normal tone his real character would appear, so that it would then be possible to judge more or less whether he had will enough to control himself in future. Logotheti agreed, but it occurred to him that one need not be knighted, and write a dozen or more mysterious capital letters after one's name, and live in Harley Street, in order to reach such a simple conclusion; and as Logotheti was a millionaire, and liked his doctor for his own sake rather than for his skill, he told him this, and they both laughed heartily. Almost all doctors, except those in French plays, have some sense of humour.

On the third day Isidore Bamberger came to the door of the private hospital and asked to see Mr. Feist. Not having heard from him, he had been to the hotel and had there obtained the address. The doorkeeper was a quiet man who had lost a leg in South Africa, after having been otherwise severely wounded five times in previous engagements. Mr. Bamberger, he said, could not see his friend yet. A part of the cure consisted in complete isolation from friends during the first stages of the treatment. Sir Jasper Threlfall had been to see Mr. Feist that morning. He had been twice already. Dr. Bream, the resident physician, gave the doorkeeper a bulletin every morning at ten for the benefit of each patient's friend; the notes were written on a card which the man held in his hand.

At the great man's name, Mr. Bamberger became thoughtful. A smart brougham drove up just then and a tall woman, who wore a thick veil, got out and entered the vestibule where Bamberger was standing by the open door. The doorkeeper evidently knew her, for he glanced at his notes and spoke without being questioned.

'The young gentleman is doing well this week, my lady,' he said. 'Sleeps from three to four hours at a time. Is less excited. Appetite improving.'

'Can I see him?' asked a sad and gentle voice through the veil.

'Not yet, my lady.'

She sighed as she turned to go out, and Mr. Bamberger thought it was one of the saddest sighs he had ever heard. He was rather a soft-hearted man.

'Is it her son?' he asked, in a respectful sort of way.

'Yes, sir.'

'Drink?' inquired Mr. Bamberger in the same tone.

'Not allowed to give any information except to family or friends, sir,' answered the man. 'Rule of the house, sir. Very strict.'

'Quite right, of course. Excuse me for asking. But I must see Mr. Feist, unless he's out of his mind. It's very important.'

'Dr. Bream sees visitors himself from ten to twelve, sir, after he's been his rounds to the patients' rooms. You'll have to get permission from him.'

'But it's like a prison!' exclaimed Mr. Bamberger.

'Yes, sir,' answered the old soldier imperturbably. 'It's just like a prison. It's meant to be.'

It was evidently impossible to get anything more out of the man, who did not pay the slightest attention to the cheerful little noise Mr. Bamberger made by jingling sovereigns in his waistcoat pocket; there was nothing to do but to go away, and Mr. Bamberger went out very much annoyed and perplexed.

He knew Van Torp well, or believed that he did, and it was like the man whose genius had created the Nickel Trust to have boldly sequestrated his enemy's chief instrument, and in such a clever way as to make it probable that Mr. Feist might be kept in confinement as long as his captor chose. Doubtless such a high-handed act would ultimately go against the latter when on his trial, but in the meantime the chief witness was locked up and could not get out. Sir Jasper Threlfall would state that his patient was in such a state of health, owing to the abuse of alcohol, that it was not safe to set him at liberty, and that in his present condition his mind was so unsettled by drink that he could not be regarded as a sane witness; and if Sir Jasper Threlfall said that, it would not be easy to get Charles Feist out of Dr. Bream's establishment in less than three months.

Mr. Bamberger was obliged to admit that his partner, chief, and enemy had stolen a clever march on him. Being of a practical turn of mind, however, and not hampered by much faith in mankind, even in the most eminent, who write the mysterious capital letters after their names, he wondered to what extent Van Torp owned Sir Jasper, and he went to see him on pretence of asking advice about his liver.

The great man gave him two guineas' worth of thumping, auscultating, and poking in the ribs, and told him rather disagreeably that he was as healthy as a young crocodile, and had a somewhat similar constitution. A partner of

Mr. Van Torp, the American financier? Indeed! Sir Jasper had heard the name but had never seen the millionaire, and asked politely whether he sometimes came to England. It is not untruthful to ask a question to which one knows the answer. Mr. Bamberger himself, for instance, who knew that he was perfectly well, was just going to put down two guineas for having been told so, in answer to a question.

'I believe you are treating Mr. Feist,' he said, going more directly to the point.

'Mr. Feist?' repeated the great authority vaguely.

'Yes. Mr. Charles Feist. He's at Dr. Bream's private hospital in West Kensington.'

'Ah, yes,' said Sir Jasper. 'Dr. Bream is treating him. He's not a patient of mine.'

'I thought I'd ask you what his chances are,' observed Isidore Bamberger, fixing his sharp eyes on the famous doctor's face. 'He used to be my private secretary.'

He might just as well have examined the back of the doctor's head.

'He's not a patient of mine,' Sir Jasper said. 'I'm only one of the visiting doctors at Dr. Bream's establishment. I don't go there unless he sends for me, and I keep no notes of his cases. You will have to ask him. If I am not mistaken his hours are from ten to twelve. And now'—Sir Jasper rose—'as I can only congratulate you on your splendid health—no, I really cannot prescribe anything—literally nothing—'

Isidore Bamberger had left three patients in the waiting-room and was obliged to go away, as his 'splendid health' did not afford him the slightest pretext for asking more questions. He deposited his two guineas on the mantelpiece neatly wrapped in a bit of note-paper, while Sir Jasper examined the handle of the door with a stony gaze, and he said 'good morning' as he went out.

'Good morning,' answered Sir Jasper, and as Mr. Bamberger crossed the threshold the single clanging stroke of the doctor's bell was heard, summoning the next patient.

The American man of business was puzzled, for he was a good judge of humanity, and was sure that when the Englishman said that he had never seen Van Torp he was telling the literal truth. Mr. Bamberger was convinced that there had been some agreement between them to make it impossible for any one to see Feist. He knew the latter well, however, and had great confidence in his remarkable power of holding his tongue, even when under the influence of drink.

When Tiberius had to choose between two men equally well fitted for a post of importance, he had them both to supper, and chose the one who was least affected by wine, not at all for the sake of seeing the match, but on the excellent principle that in an age when heavy drinking was the rule the man who could swallow the largest quantity without becoming talkative was the one to be best trusted with a secret; and the fact that Tiberius himself had the strongest head in the Empire made him a good judge.

Bamberger, on the same principle, believed that Charles Feist would hold his tongue, and he also felt tolerably sure that the former secretary had no compromising papers in his possession, for his memory had always been extraordinary. Feist had formerly been able to carry in his mind a number of letters which Bamberger 'talked off' to him consecutively without even using shorthand, and could type them afterwards with unfailing accuracy. It was therefore scarcely likely that he kept notes of the articles he wrote about Van Torp.

But his employer did not know that Feist's memory was failing from drink, and that he no longer trusted his marvellous faculty. Van Torp had sequestrated him and shut him up, Bamberger believed; but neither Van Torp nor any one else would get anything out of him.

And if any one made him talk, what great harm would be done, after all? It was not to be supposed that such a man as Isidore Bamberger had trusted only to his own keenness in collecting evidence, or to a few pencilled notes as a substitute for the principal witness himself, when an accident might happen at any moment to a man who led such a life. The case for the prosecution had been quietly prepared during several months past, and the evidence that was to send Rufus Van Torp to execution, or to an asylum for the Criminal Insane for life, was in the safe of Isidore Bamberger's lawyer in New York, unless, at that very moment, it was already in the hands of the Public Prosecutor. A couple of cables would do the rest at any time, and in a few hours. In murder cases, the extradition treaty works as smoothly as the telegraph itself. The American authorities would apply to the English Home Secretary, the order would go to Scotland Yard, and Van Torp would be arrested immediately and taken home by the first steamer, to be tried in New York.

Six months earlier he might have pleaded insanity with a possible chance, but in the present state of feeling the plea would hardly be admitted. A man who has been held up to public execration in the press for weeks, and whom no one attempts to defend, is in a bad case if a well-grounded accusation of murder is brought against him at such a moment; and Isidore

Bamberger firmly believed in the truth of the charge and in the validity of the evidence.

He consoled himself with these considerations, and with the reflection that Feist was actually safer where he was, and less liable to accident than if he were at large. Mr. Bamberger walked slowly down Harley Street to Cavendish Square, with his head low between his shoulders, his hat far back on his head, his eyes on the pavement, and the shiny toes of his patent leather boots turned well out. His bowed legs were encased in loose black trousers, and had as many angles as the forepaws of a Dachshund or a Dandie Dinmont. The peculiarities of his ungainly gait and figure were even more apparent than usual, and as he walked he swung his long arms, that ended in large black gloves which looked as if they were stuffed with sawdust.

Yet there was something in his face that set him far beyond and above ridicule, and the passers-by saw it and wondered gravely who and what this man in black might be, and what great misfortune and still greater passion had moulded the tragic mark upon his features; and none of those who looked at him glanced at his heavy, ill-made figure, or noticed his clumsy walk, or realised that he was most evidently a typical German Jew, who perhaps kept an antiquity shop in Wardour Street, and had put on his best coat to call on a rich collector in the West End.

Those who saw him only saw his face and went on, feeling that they had passed near something greater and sadder and stronger than anything in their own lives could ever be.

But he went on his way, unconscious of the men and women he met, and not thinking where he went, crossing Oxford Street and then turning down Regent Street and following it to Piccadilly and the Haymarket. Just before he reached the theatre, he slackened his pace and looked about him, as if he were waking up; and there, in the cross street, just behind the theatre, he saw a telegraph office.

He entered, pushed his hat still a little farther back, and wrote a cable message. It was as short as it could be, for it consisted of one word only besides the address, and that one word had only two letters:

'Go.'

That was all, and there was nothing mysterious about the syllable, for almost any one would understand that it was used as in starting a footrace, and meant, 'Begin operations at once!' It was the word agreed upon between Isidore Bamberger and his lawyer. The latter had been allowed all the latitude required in such a case, for he had instructions to lay the evidence before the District Attorney-General without delay, if anything happened to make immediate action seem advisable. In any event, he was to do so on receiving the message which had now been sent.

The evidence consisted, in the first place, of certain irrefutable proofs that Miss Bamberger had not died from shock, but had been killed by a thin and extremely sharp instrument with which she had been stabbed in the back. Isidore Bamberger's own doctor had satisfied himself of this, and had signed his statement under oath, and Bamberger had instantly thought of a certain thin steel letter-opener which Van Torp always had in his pocket.

Next came the affidavit of Paul Griggs. The witness knew the Opera House well. Had been in the stalls on the night in question. Had not moved from his seat till the performance was over, and had been one of the last to get out into the corridor. There was a small door in the corridor on the south side which was generally shut. It opened upon a passage communicating with the part of the building that is let for business offices. Witness's attention had been attracted by part of a red silk dress which lay on the floor outside the door, the latter being ajar. Suspecting an accident, witness opened door, found Miss Bamberger, and carried her to manager's room not far off. On reaching home had found stains of blood on his hands. Had said nothing of this, because he had seen notice of the lady's death from shock in next morning's paper. Was nevertheless convinced that blood must have been on her dress.

The murder was therefore proved. But the victim had not been robbed of her jewellery, which demonstrated that, if the crime had not been committed by a lunatic, the motive for it must have been personal.

With regard to identity of the murderer, Charles Feist deposed that on the night in question he had entered the Opera late, having only an admission to the standing room, that he was close to one of the doors when the explosion took place and had been one of the first to leave the house. The emergency lights in the corridors were on a separate circuit, but had been also momentarily extinguished. They were up again before those in the house. The crowd had at once become jammed in the doorways, so that people got out much more slowly than might have been expected. Many actually fell in the exits and were trampled on. Then Madame Cordova had begun to sing in the dark, and the panic had ceased in a few seconds. The witness did not think that more than three hundred people altogether had got out through the several doors. He himself had at once made for the main entrance. A few persons rushed past him in the dark, descending the stairs from the boxes. One or two fell on the steps. Just as the emergency lights went up again, witness saw a young lady in a red silk dress fall, but did not see her face distinctly; he was certain that she had a short string of pearls round her throat. They gleamed in the light as she fell. She was instantly lifted to her feet by Mr. Rufus Van Torp, who must have been following her closely. She seemed to have hurt herself a little, and he almost carried her down the corridor in the direction of the carriage lobby on the Thirty-Eighth Street side. The two then disappeared through a door. The witness would swear to the door, and he described its position accurately. It seemed to have been left ajar, but there was no light on the other side of it. The witness did not know where the door led to. He had often wondered. It was not for the use of the public. He frequently went to the Opera and was perfectly familiar with the corridors. It was behind this door that Paul Griggs had found Miss Bamberger. Questioned as to a possible motive for the murder, the witness stated that Rufus Van Torp was known to have shown homicidal tendencies, though otherwise perfectly sane. In his early youth he had lived four years on a cattle-ranch as a cow-puncher, and had undoubtedly killed two men during that time. Witness had been private secretary to his partner, Mr. Isidore Bamberger, and while so employed Mr. Van Torp had fired a revolver at him in his private office in a fit of passion about a message witness was sent to deliver. Two clerks in a neighbouring room had heard the shot. Believing Mr. Van Torp to be mad, witness had said nothing at the time, but had left Mr. Bamberger soon afterwards. It was always said that, several years ago, on board of his steam yacht, Mr. Van Torp had once violently pulled a friend who was on board out of his berth at two in the morning, and had dragged him on deck, saying that he must throw him overboard and drown him, as the only way of saving his soul. The watch on deck had had great difficulty in overpowering Mr. Van Torp, who was very strong. With regard to the late Miss Bamberger the witness thought that Mr. Van Torp had killed her to get rid of her, because she was in possession of facts that would ruin him if they were known and because she had threatened to reveal them to her father. If she had done so, Van Torp would have been completely in his partner's power. Mr. Bamberger could have made a beggar of him as the only alternative to penal servitude. Questioned as to the nature of this information, witness said that it concerned the explosion, which had been planned by Van Torp for his own purposes. Either in a moment of expansion, under the influence of the drug he was in the habit of taking, or else in real anxiety for her safety, he had told Miss Bamberger that the explosion would take place, warning her to remain in her home, which was situated on the Riverside Drive, very far from the scene of the disaster. She had undoubtedly been so horrified that she had thereupon insisted upon dissolving her engagement to marry him, and had threatened to inform her father of the horrible plot. She had never really wished to marry Van Torp, but had accepted him in deference to her father's wishes. He was known to be devoting himself at that very time to a well-known primadonna engaged at the Metropolitan Opera, and Miss Bamberger probably had some suspicion of this. Witness said the motive seemed sufficient, considering that the accused had already twice taken human life. His choice lay between killing her and falling into the power of his partner. He had injured Mr. Bamberger, as was well known, and Mr. Bamberger was a resentful man.

The latter part of Charles Feist's deposition was certainly more in the nature of an argument than of evidence pure and simple, and it might not be admitted in court; but Isidore Bamberger had instructed his lawyer, and the Public Prosecutor would say it all, and more also, and much better; and public opinion was roused all over the United States against the Nickel Tyrant, as Van Torp was now called.

In support of the main point there was a short note to Miss Bamberger in Van Torp's handwriting, which had afterwards been found on her dressing-table. It must have arrived before she had gone out to dinner. It contained a final and urgent entreaty that she would not go to the Opera, nor leave the house that evening, and was signed with Van Torp's initials only, but no one who knew his handwriting would be likely to doubt that the note was genuine.

There were some other scattered pieces of evidence which fitted the rest very well. Mr. Van Torp had not been seen at his own house, nor in any club, nor down town, after he had gone out on Wednesday afternoon, until the following Friday, when he had returned to make his final arrangements for sailing the next morning. Bamberger had employed a first-rate detective, but only one, to find out all that could be discovered about Van Torp's movements. The millionaire had been at the house on Riverside Drive early in the afternoon to see Miss Bamberger, as he had told Margaret on board the steamer, but Bamberger had not seen his daughter after that till she was brought home dead, for he had been detained by an important meeting at which he presided, and knowing that she was dining out to go to the theatre he had telephoned that he would dine at his club. He himself had tried to telephone to Van Torp later in the evening but had not been able to find him, and had not seen him till Friday.

This was the substance of the evidence which Bamberger's lawyer and the detective would lay before the District Attorney-General on receiving the cable.

CHAPTER XV

When Lady Maud stopped at Margaret's house on her way to the theatre she had been dining at Princes' with a small party of people, amongst whom Paul Griggs had found himself, and as there was no formality to hinder her from choosing her own place she had sat down next to him. The table was large and round, the sixty or seventy other diners in the room made a certain amount of noise, so that it was easy to talk in undertones while the conversation of the others was general.

The veteran man of letters was an old acquaintance of Lady Maud's; and as she made no secret of her friendship with Rufus Van Torp, it was not surprising that Griggs should warn her of the latter's danger. As he had expected when he left New York, he had received a visit from a 'high-class' detective, who came to find out what he knew about Miss Bamberger's death. This is a bad world, as we all know, and it is made so by a good many varieties of bad people. As Mr. Van Torp had said to Logotheti, 'different kinds of cats have different kinds of ways,' and the various classes of criminals are pursued by various classes of detectives. Many are ex-policemen, and make up the pack that hunts the well-dressed lady shoplifter, the gentle pickpocket, the agile burglar, the Paris Apache, and the common murderer of the Bill Sykes type; they are good dogs in their way, if you do not press them, though they are rather apt to give tongue. But when they are not ex-policemen, they are always ex-something else, since there is no college for detectives, and it is not probable that any young man ever deliberately began life with the intention of becoming one. Edgar Poe invented the amateur detective, and modern writers have developed him till he is a familiar and always striking figure in fiction and on the stage. Whether he really exists or not does not matter. I have heard a great living painter ask the question: What has art to do with truth? But as a matter of fact Paul Griggs, who had seen a vast deal, had never met an amateur detective; and my own impression is that if one existed he would instantly turn himself into a professional because it would be so very profitable.

The one who called on Griggs in his lodgings wrote 'barrister-at-law' after his name, and had the right to do so. He had languished in chambers, briefless and half starving, either because he had no talent for the bar, or because he had failed to marry a solicitor's daughter. He himself was inclined to attribute his want of success to the latter cause. But he had not wasted his time, though he was more than metaphorically threadbare, and his waist would have made a sensation at a staymaker's. He had watched and pondered on many curious cases for years; and one day, when a 'high-class' criminal had baffled the police and had well-nigh confounded the Attorney-General and proved himself a saint, the starving barrister had gone quietly to work in his own way, had discovered the truth, had taken his information to the prosecution, had been the means of sending the high-class one to penal servitude, and had covered himself with glory; since when he had grown sleek and well-liking, if not rich, as a professional detective.

Griggs had been perfectly frank, and had told without hesitation all he could remember of the circumstances. In answer to further questions he said he knew Mr. Van Torp tolerably well, and had not seen him in the Opera House on the evening of the murder. He did not know whether the financier's character was violent. If it was, he had never seen any notable manifestation of temper. Did he know that Mr. Van Torp had once lived on a ranch, and had killed two men in a shooting affray? Yes, he had heard so, but the shooting might have been in self-defence. Did he know anything about the blowing up of the works of which Van Torp had been accused in the papers? Nothing more than the public knew. Or anything about the circumstances of Van Torp's engagement to Miss Bamberger? Nothing whatever. Would he read the statement and sign his name to it? He would, and he did.

Griggs thought the young man acted more like an ordinary lawyer than a detective, and said so with a smile.

'Oh no,' was the quiet answer. 'In my business it's quite as important to recognise honesty as it is to detect fraud. That's all.'

For his own part the man of letters did not care a straw whether Van Torp had committed the murder or not, but he thought it very unlikely. On general principles, he thought the law usually found out the truth in the end, and he was ready to do what he could to help it. He held his tongue, and told no one about the detective's visit, because he had no intimate friend in England; partly, too, because he wished to keep his name out of what was now called 'the Van Torp scandal.'

He would never have alluded to the matter if he had not accidentally found himself next to Lady Maud at dinner. She had always liked him and trusted him, and he liked her and her father. On that evening she spoke of Van Torp within the first ten minutes, and expressed her honest indignation at the general attack made on 'the kindest man that ever lived.' Then Griggs felt that she had a sort of right to know what was being done to bring against her friend an accusation of murder, for he believed Van Torp innocent, and was sure that Lady Maud would warn him; but it was for her sake only that Griggs spoke, because he pitied her.

She took it more calmly than he had expected, but she grew a little paler, and that look came into her eyes which Margaret and Logotheti saw there an hour afterwards; and presently she asked Griggs if he too would join the week-end party at Craythew, telling him that Van Torp would be there. Griggs accepted, after a moment's hesitation.

She was not quite sure why she had so frankly appealed to Logotheti for help when they left Margaret's house together, but she was not disappointed in his answer. He was 'exotic,' as she had said of him; he was hopelessly in love with Cordova, who disliked Van Torp, and he could not be expected to take much trouble for any other woman; she had not the very slightest claim on him. Yet she had asked him to help her in a way which might be anything but lawful, even supposing that it did not involve positive cruelty.

For she had not been married to Leven four years without learning something of Asiatic practices, and she knew that there were more means of making a man tell a secret than by persuasion or wily cross-examination. It was all very well to keep within the bounds of the law and civilisation, but where the whole existence of her best friend was at stake, Lady Maud was much too simple, primitive, and feminine to be hampered by any such artificial considerations, and she turned naturally to a man who did not seem to be a slave to them either. She had not quite dared to hope that he would help her, and his readiness to do so was something of a surprise; but she would have been astonished if he had been in the least shocked at the implied suggestion of deliberately torturing Charles Feist till he revealed the truth about the murder. She only felt a little uncomfortable when she reflected that Feist might not know it after all, whereas she had boldly told Logotheti that he did.

If the Greek had hesitated for a few seconds before giving his answer, it was not that he was doubtful of his own willingness to do what she wished, but because he questioned his power to do it. The request itself appealed to the Oriental's love of excitement and to his taste for the uncommon in life. If he had not sometimes found occasions for satisfying both, he could not have lived in Paris and London at all, but would have gone back to Constantinople, which is the last refuge of romance in Europe, the last hiding-place of mediaeval adventure, the last city of which a new Decameron of tales could still be told, and might still be true.

Lady Maud had good nerves, and she watched the play with her friends and talked between the acts, very much as if nothing had happened, except that she was pale and there was that look in her eyes; but only Paul Griggs noticed it, because he had a way of watching the small changes of expression that may mean tragedy, but more often signify indigestion, or too much strong tea, or a dun's letter, or a tight shoe, or a bad hand at bridge, or the presence of a bore in the room, or the flat failure of expected pleasure, or sauce spilt on a new gown by a rival's butler, or being left out of something small and smart, or any of those minor aches that are the inheritance of the social flesh, and drive women perfectly mad while they last.

But Griggs knew that none of these troubles afflicted Lady Maud, and when he spoke to her now and then, between the acts, she felt his sympathy for her in every word and inflection.

She was glad when the evening was over and she was at home in her dressing-room, and there was no more effort to be made till the next day. But even alone, she did not behave or look very differently; she twisted up her thick brown hair herself, as methodically as ever, and laid out the black velvet gown on the lounge after shaking it out, so that it should be creased as little as possible; but when she was ready to go to bed she put on a dressing-gown and sat down at her table to write to Rufus Van Torp.

The letter was begun and she had written half a dozen lines when she laid down the pen, to unlock a small drawer from which she took an old blue envelope that had never been sealed, though it was a good deal the worse for wear. There was a photograph in it, which she laid before her on the letter; and she looked down at it steadily, resting her elbows on the table and her forehead and temples in her hands.

It was a snapshot photograph of a young officer in khaki and puttees, not very well taken, and badly mounted on a bit of white pasteboard that might have been cut from a bandbox with a penknife; but it was all she had, and there could never be another.

She looked at it a long time.

'You understand, dear,' she said at last, very low; 'you understand.'

She put it away again and locked the drawer before she went on with her letter to Van Torp. It was easy enough to tell him what she had learned about Feist from Logotheti; it was even possible that he had found it out for himself, and had not taken the trouble to inform her of the fact. Apart from the approval that friendship inspires, she had always admired the cool discernment of events which he showed when great things were at stake. But it was one thing, she now told him, to be indifferent to the stupid attacks of the press, it would be quite another to allow himself to be accused of murder; the time had come when he must act, and without delay; there was a limit beyond which indifference became culpable apathy; it was clear enough now, she said, that all these attacks on him had been made to ruin him in the estimation of the public on both sides of the

Atlantic before striking the first blow, as he himself had guessed; Griggs was surely not an alarmist, and Griggs said confidently that Van Torp's enemies meant business; without doubt, a mass of evidence had been carefully got together during the past three months, and it was pretty sure that an attempt would be made before long to arrest him; would he do nothing to make such an outrage impossible? She had not forgotten, she could never forget, what she owed him, but on his side he owed something to her, and to the great friendship that bound them to each other. Who was this man Feist, and who was behind him? She did not know why she was so sure that he knew the truth, supposing that there had really been a murder, but her instinct told her so.

Lady Maud was not gifted with much power of writing, for she was not clever at books, or with pen and ink, but she wrote her letter with deep conviction and striking clearness. The only point of any importance which she did not mention was that Logotheti had promised to help her, and she did not write of that because she was not really sure that he could do anything, though she was convinced that he would try. She was very anxious. She was horrified when she thought of what might happen if nothing were done. She entreated Van Torp to answer that he would take steps to defend himself; and that, if possible, he would come to town so that they might consult together.

She finished her letter and went to bed; but her good nerves failed her for once, and it was a long time before she could get to sleep. It was absurd, of course, but she remembered every case she had ever heard of in which innocent men had been convicted of crimes they had not committed and had suffered for them; and in a hideous instant, between waking and dozing, she saw Rufus Van Torp hanged before her eyes.

The impression was so awful that she started from her pillow with a cry and turned up the electric lamp. It was not till the light flooded the room that the image quite faded away and she could let her head rest on the pillow again, and even then her heart was beating violently, as it had only beaten once in her life before that night.

CHAPTER XVI

Sir Jasper Threlfall did not know how long it would be before Mr. Feist could safely be discharged from the establishment in which Logotheti had so kindly placed him. Dr. Bream said 'it was as bad a case of chronic alcoholism as he often saw.' What has grammar to do with the treatment of the nerves? Mr. Feist said he did not want to be cured of chronic alcoholism, and demanded that he should be let out at once. Dr. Bream answered that it was against his principles to discharge a patient half cured. Mr. Feist retorted that it was a violation of personal liberty to cure a man against his will. The physician smiled kindly at a view he heard expressed every day, and which the law shared, though it might not be very ready to support it. Physically, Mr. Feist was afraid of Dr. Bream, who had played football for Guy's Hospital and had the complexion of a healthy baby and a quiet eye. So the patient changed his tone, and whined for something to calm his agitated nerves. One teaspoonful of whisky was all he begged for, and he promised not to ask for it to-morrow if he might have it to-day. The doctor was obdurate about spirits, but felt his pulse, examined the pupils of his eyes, and promised him a calming hypodermic in an hour. It was too soon after breakfast, he said. Mr. Feist only once attempted to use violence, and then two large men came into the room, as quiet and healthy as the doctor himself, and gently but firmly put him to bed, tucking him up in such an extraordinary way that he found it quite impossible to move or to get his hands out; and Dr. Bream, smiling with exasperating calm, stuck a needle into his shoulder, after which he presently fell asleep.

He had been drinking hard for years, so that it was a very bad case; and besides, he seemed to have something on his mind, which made it worse.

Logotheti came to see him now, and took a vast deal of trouble to be agreeable. At his first visit Feist flew into a rage and accused the Greek of having kidnapped him and shut him up in a prison, where he was treated like a lunatic; but to this Logotheti was quite indifferent; he only shook his head rather sadly, and offered Feist a very excellent cigarette, such as it was quite impossible to buy, even in London. After a little hesitation the patient took it, and the effect was very soothing to his temper. Indeed it was wonderful, for in less than two minutes his features relaxed, his eyes became quiet, and he actually apologised for having spoken so rudely. Logotheti had been kindness itself, he said, had saved his life at the very moment when he was going to cut his throat, and had been in all respects the good Samaritan. The cigarette was perfectly delicious. It was about the best smoke he had enjoyed since he had left the States, he said. He wished

Logotheti to please to understand that he wanted to settle up for all expenses as soon as possible, and to pay his weekly bills at Dr. Bream's. There had been twenty or thirty pounds in notes in his pocket-book, and a letter of credit, but all his things had been taken away from him. He concluded it was all right, but it seemed rather strenuous to take his papers too. Perhaps Mr. Logotheti, who was so kind, would make sure that they were in a safe place, and tell the doctor to let him see any other friends who called. Then he asked for another of those wonderful cigarettes, but Logotheti was awfully sorry—there had only been two, and he had just smoked the other himself. He showed his empty case.

'By the way,' he said, 'if the doctor should happen to come in and notice the smell of the smoke, don't tell him that you had one of mine. My tobacco is rather strong, and he might think it would do you harm, you know. I see that you have some light ones there, on the table. Just let him think that you smoked one of them. I promise to bring some more to-morrow, and we'll have a couple together.'

That was what Logotheti said, and it comforted Mr. Feist, who recognised the opium at once; all that afternoon and through all the next morning he told himself that he was to have another of those cigarettes, and perhaps two, at three o'clock in the afternoon, when Logotheti had said that he would come again.

Before leaving his own rooms on the following day, the Greek put four cigarettes into his case, for he had not forgotten his promise; he took two from a box that lay on the table, and placed them so that they would be nearest to his own hand when he offered his case, but he took the other two from a drawer which was always locked, and of which the key was at one end of his superornate watch-chain, and he placed them on the other side of the case, conveniently for a friend to take. All four cigarettes looked exactly alike.

If any one had pointed out to him that an Englishman would not think it fair play to drug a man deliberately, Logotheti would have smiled and would have replied by asking whether it was fair play to accuse an innocent man of murder, a retort which would only become unanswerable if it could be proved that Van Torp was suspected unjustly. But to this objection, again, the Greek would have replied that he had been brought up in Constantinople, where they did things in that way; and that, except for the trifling obstacle of the law, there was no particular reason for not strangling Mr. Feist with the English equivalent for a bowstring, since he had printed a disagreeable story about Miss Donne, and was, besides, a very offensive sort of person in appearance and manner. There had always been a certain directness about Logotheti's view of man's rights.

He went to see Mr. Feist every day at three o'clock, in the most kind way possible, made himself as agreeable as he could, and gave him cigarettes with a good deal of opium in them. He also presented Feist with a pretty little asbestos lamp which was constructed to purify the air, and had a really wonderful capacity for absorbing the rather peculiar odour of the cigarettes. Dr. Bream always made his round in the morning, and the men nurses he employed to take care of his patients either did not notice anything unusual, or supposed that Logotheti smoked some 'outlandish Turkish stuff,' and, because he was a privileged person, they said nothing about it. As he had brought the patient to the establishment to be cured, it was really not to be supposed that he would supply him with forbidden narcotics.

Now, to a man who is poisoned with drink and is suddenly deprived of it, opium is from the beginning as delightful as it is nauseous to most healthy people when they first taste it; and during the next four or five days, while Feist appeared to be improving faster than might have been expected, he was in reality acquiring such a craving for his daily dose of smoke that it would soon be acute suffering to be deprived of it; and this was what Logotheti wished. He would have supplied him with brandy if he had not been sure that the contraband would be discovered and stopped by the doctor; but opium, in the hands of one who knows exactly how it is used, is very much harder to detect, unless the doctor sees the smoker when he is under the influence of the drug, while the pupils of the eye are unnaturally contracted and the face is relaxed in that expression of beatitude which only the great narcotics can produce—the state which Baudelaire called the Artificial Paradise.

During these daily visits Logotheti became very confidential; that is to say, he exercised all his ingenuity in the attempt to make Feist talk about himself. But he was not very successful. Broken as the man was, his characteristic reticence was scarcely at all relaxed, and it was quite impossible to get beyond the barrier. One day Logotheti gave him a cigarette more than usual, as an experiment, but he went to sleep almost immediately, sitting up in his chair. The opium, as a moderate substitute for liquor, temporarily restored the habitual tone of his system and revived his natural self-control, and Logotheti soon gave up the idea of extracting any secret from him in a moment of garrulous expansion.

There was the other way, which was now prepared, and the Greek had learned enough about his victim to justify him in using it. The cypher expert, who had been at work on Feist's diary, had now completed his key and brought Logotheti the translation. He was a rather shabby little man, a penman employed to do occasional odd jobs about the Foreign Office, such as engrossing documents and the like, by which he earned from eighteenpence to half-a-crown an hour, according to the style of penmanship required, and he was well known in the criminal courts as an expert on handwriting in forgery cases.

He brought his work to Logotheti, who at once asked for the long entry concerning the night of the explosion. The expert turned to it and read it aloud. It was a statement of the circumstances to which Feist was prepared to swear, and which have been summed up in a previous chapter. Van Torp was not mentioned by name in the diary, but was referred to as 'he'; the other entries in the journal, however, fully proved that Van Torp was meant, even if Logotheti had felt any doubt of it.

The expert informed him, however, that the entry was not the original one, which had apparently been much shorter, and had been obliterated in the ordinary way with a solution of chloride of lime. Here and there very pale traces of the previous writing were faintly visible, but there was not enough to give the sense of what was gone. This proved that the ink had not been long dry when it had been removed, as the expert explained. It was very hard to destroy old writing so completely that neither heat nor chemicals would bring it out again. Therefore Feist must have decided to change the entry soon after he had made it, and probably on the next day. The expert had not found any other page which had been similarly treated. The shabby little man looked at Logotheti, and Logotheti looked at him, and both nodded; and the Greek paid him generously for his work.

It was clear that Feist had meant to aid his own memory, and had rather clumsily tampered with his diary in order to make it agree with the evidence he intended to give, rather than meaning to produce the notes in court. What Logotheti meant to find out was what the man himself really knew and what he had first written down; that, and some other things. In conversation, Logotheti had asked him to describe the panic at the theatre, and Cordova's singing in the dark, but Feist's answers had been anything but interesting.

'You can't remember much about that kind of thing,' he had said in his drawling way, 'because there isn't much to remember. There was a crash and the lights went out, and people fought their way to the doors in the dark till there was a general squash; then Madame Cordova began to sing, and that kind of calmed things down till the lights went up again. That's about all I remember.'

His recollections did not at all agree with what he had entered in his diary; but though Logotheti tried a second time two days later, Feist repeated the same story with absolute verbal accuracy. The Greek asked him if he had known 'that poor Miss Bamberger who died of shock.' Feist blew out a cloud of drugged tobacco smoke before he answered, with one of his disagreeable smiles, that he had known her pretty well, for he had been her father's private secretary. He explained that he had given up the place because he had come into some money. Mr. Bamberger was 'a very pleasant gentleman,' Feist declared, and poor Miss Bamberger had been a 'superb dresser and a first-class conversationalist, and was a severe loss to her friends and admirers.' Though Logotheti, who was only a Greek, did not understand every word of this panegyric, he perceived that it was intended for the highest praise. He said he should like to know Mr. Bamberger, and was sorry that he had not known Miss Bamberger, who had been engaged to marry Mr. Van Torp, as every one had heard.

He thought he saw a difference in Feist's expression, but was not sure of it. The pale, unhealthy, and yet absurdly youthful face was not naturally mobile, and the almost colourless eyes always had rather a fixed and staring look. Logotheti was aware of a new meaning in them rather than of a distinct change. He accordingly went on to say that he had heard poor Miss Bamberger spoken of as heartless, and he brought out the word so unexpectedly that Feist looked sharply at him.

'Well,' he said, 'some people certainly thought so. I daresay she was. It don't matter much, now she's dead, anyway.'

'She paid for it, poor girl,' answered Logotheti very deliberately. 'They say she was murdered.'

The change in Feist's face was now unmistakable. There was a drawing down of the corners of the mouth, and a lowering of the lids that meant something, and the unhealthy complexion took a greyish shade. Logotheti was too wise to watch his intended victim, and leaned back in a careless attitude, gazing out of the window at the bright creeper on the opposite wall.

'I've heard it suggested,' said Mr. Feist rather thickly, out of a perfect storm of drugged smoke.

It came out of his ugly nostrils, it blew out of his mouth, it seemed to issue even from his ears and eyes.

'I suppose we shall never know the truth,' said Logotheti in an idle tone, and not seeming to look at his companion. 'Mr. Griggs—do you remember Mr. Griggs, the author, at the Turkish Embassy, where we first met? Tall old fellow, sad-looking, bony, hard; you remember him, don't you?'

'Why, yes,' drawled Feist, emitting more smoke, 'I know him quite well.'

'He found blood on his hands after he had carried her. Had you not heard that? I wondered whether you saw her that evening. Did you?'

'I saw her from a distance in the box with her friends,' answered Feist steadily.

'Did you see her afterwards?'

The direct question came suddenly, and the strained look in Feist's face became more intense. Logotheti fancied he understood very well what was passing in the young man's mind; he intended to swear in court that he had seen Van Torp drag the girl to the place where her body was afterwards found, and if he now denied this, the Greek, who was probably Van Torp's friend, might appear as a witness and narrate the present conversation; and though this would not necessarily invalidate the evidence, it might weaken it in the opinion of the jury. Feist had of course suspected that Logotheti had some object in forcing him to undergo a cure, and this suspicion had been confirmed by the opium cigarettes, which he would have refused after the first time if he had possessed the strength of mind to do so.

While Logotheti watched him, three small drops of perspiration appeared high up on his forehead, just where the parting of his thin light hair began; for he felt that he must make up his mind what to say, and several seconds had already elapsed since the question.

'As a matter of fact,' he said at last, with an evident effort, 'I did catch sight of Miss Bamberger later.'

He had been aware of the moisture on his forehead, and had hoped that Logotheti would not notice it, but the drops now gathered and rolled down, so that he was obliged to take out his handkerchief.

'It's getting quite hot,' he said, by way of explanation.

'Yes,' answered Logotheti, humouring him, 'the room is warm. You must have been one of the last people who saw Miss Bamberger alive,' he added. 'Was she trying to get out?'

'I suppose so.'

Logotheti pretended to laugh a little.

'You must have been quite sure when you saw her,' he said.

Feist was in a very overwrought condition by this time, and Logotheti reflected that if his nerve did not improve he would make a bad impression on a jury.

'Now I'll tell you the truth,' he said rather desperately.

'By all means!' And Logotheti prepared to hear and remember accurately the falsehood which would probably follow immediately on such a statement.

But he was disappointed.

'The truth is,' said Feist, 'I don't care much to talk about this affair at present. I can't explain now, but you'll understand one of these days, and you'll say I was right.'

'Oh, I see!'

Logotheti smiled and held out his case, for Feist had finished the first cigarette. He refused another, however, to the other's surprise.

'Thanks,' he said, 'but I guess I won't smoke any more of those. I believe they get on to my nerves.'

'Do you really not wish me to bring you any more of them?' asked Logotheti, affecting a sort of surprised concern. 'Do you think they hurt you?'

'I do. That's exactly what I mean. I'm much obliged, all the same, but I'm going to give them up, just like that.'

'Very well,' Logotheti answered. 'I promise not to bring any more. I think you are very wise to make the resolution, if you really think they hurt you—though I don't see why they should.'

Like most weak people who make good resolutions, Mr. Feist did not realise what he was doing. He understood horribly well, forty-eight hours later, when he was dragging himself at his tormentor's feet, entreating the charity of half a cigarette, of one teaspoonful of liquor, of anything, though it were deadly poison, that could rest his agonised nerves for a single hour, for ten minutes, for an instant, offering his life and soul for it, parching for it, burning, sweating, trembling, vibrating with horror, and sick with fear for the want of it.

For Logotheti was an Oriental and had lived in Constantinople; and he knew what opium does, and what a man will do to get it, and that neither passion of love, nor bond of affection, nor fear of man or God, nor of death and damnation, will stand against that awful craving when the poison is within reach.

CHAPTER XVII

The society papers printed a paragraph which said that Lord Creedmore and Countess Leven were going to have a week-end party at Craythew, and the list of guests included the names of Mr. Van Torp and Señorita da Cordova, 'Monsieur Konstantinos Logotheti' and Mr. Paul Griggs, after those of a number of overpoweringly smart people.

Lady Maud's brothers saw the paragraph, and the one who was in the Grenadier Guards asked the one who was in the Blues if 'the Governor was going in for zoology or lion-taming in his old age'; but the brother in the Blues said it was 'Maud who liked freaks of nature, and Greeks, and things, because they were so amusing to photograph.'

At all events, Lady Maud had studiously left out her brothers and sisters in making up the Craythew party, a larger one than had been assembled there for many years; it was so large indeed that the 'freaks' would not have been prominent figures at all, even if they had been such unusual persons as the young man in the Blues imagined them.

For though Lord Creedmore was not a rich peer, Craythew was a fine old place, and could put up at least thirty guests without crowding them and without causing that most uncomfortable condition of things in which people run over each other from morning to night during week-end parties in the season, when there is no hunting or shooting to keep the men out all day. The house itself was two or three times as big as Mr. Van Torp's at Oxley Paddox. It had its hall, its long drawing-room for dancing, its library, its breakfast-room and its morning-room, its billiard-room, sitting-room, and smoking-room, like many another big English country house; but it had also a picture gallery, the library was an historical collection that filled three good-sized rooms, and it was completed by one which had always been called the study, beyond which there were two little dwelling-rooms, at the end of the wing, where the librarian had lived when there had been one. For the old lord had been a bachelor and a book lover, but the present master of the house, who was tremendously energetic and practical, took care of the books himself. Now and then, when the house was almost full, a guest was lodged in the former librarian's small apartment, and on the present occasion Paul Griggs was to be put there, on the ground that he was a man of letters and must be glad to be near books, and also because he could not be supposed to be afraid of Lady Letitia Foxwell's ghost, which was believed to have spent the nights in the library for the last hundred and fifty years, more or less, ever since the unhappy young girl had hanged herself there in the time of George the Second, on the eve of her wedding day.

The ancient house stood more than a mile from the high road, near the further end of such a park as is rarely to be seen, even in beautiful Derbyshire, for the Foxwells had always loved their trees, as good Englishmen should, and had taken care of them. There were ancient oaks there, descended by less than four tree-generations from Druid times; all down the long drive the great elms threw their boughs skywards; there the solemn beeches grew, the gentler ash, and the lime; there the yews spread out their branches, and here and there the cedar of Lebanon, patriarch of all trees that bear cones, reared his royal crown above the rest; in and out, too, amongst the great boulders that strewed the park, the sharp-leaved holly stood out boldly, and the exquisite white thorn, all in flower, shot up to three and four times a man's height; below, the heather grew close and green to blossom in the summer-time; and in the deeper, lonelier places the blackthorn and hoe ran wild, and the dog-rose in wild confusion; the alder and the gorse too, the honeysuckle and ivy, climbed up over rocks and stems; you might see a laurel now and then, and bilberry bushes by thousands, and bracken everywhere in an endless profusion of rich, dark-green lace.

Squirrels there were, dashing across the open glades and running up the smooth beeches and chestnut trees, as quick as light, and rabbits, dodging in and out amongst the ferns, and just showing the snow-white patch under their little tails as they disappeared, and now and again the lordly deer stepping daintily and leisurely through the deep fern; all these lived in the wonderful depths of Craythew Park, and of birds there was no end. There were game birds and song birds, from the handsome pheasants to the modest little partridges, the royalists and the puritans of the woods, from the love-lorn wood-pigeon, cooing in the tall firs, to the thrush and the blackbird, making long hops as they quartered the ground for grubs; and the robin, the linnet, and little Jenny Wren all lived there in riotous plenty of worms and snails; and nearer to the great house the starlings and jackdaws shot down in a great hurry from the holes in old trees where they had their nests, and many of them came rushing from their headquarters in the ruined tower by the stream to waddle about the open lawns in their ungainly fashion, vain because they were not like swallows, but could really walk when they chose, though they did it rather badly. And where the woods ended they were lined with rhododendrons, and lilacs, and laburnum. There are even bigger parks in England than Craythew, but there is none more beautiful, none richer in all sweet and good things that live, none more musical with song of birds, not one that more deeply breathes the world's oldest poetry.

Lady Maud went out on foot that afternoon and met Van Torp in the drive, half a mile from the house. He came in his motor car with Miss More and Ida, who was to go back after tea. It was by no means the first time that they had been at Craythew; the little girl loved nature, and understood by intuition much that would have escaped a normal child. It was her greatest delight to come over in the motor and spend two or three hours in the park, and when none of the family were in the country she was always free to come and go, with Miss More, as she pleased.

Lady Maud kissed her kindly and shook hands with her teacher before the car went on to leave Mr. Van Torp's things at the house. Then the two walked slowly along the road, and neither spoke for some time, nor looked at the other, but both kept their eyes on the ground before them, as if expecting something.

Mr. Van Torp's hands were in his pockets, his soft straw hat was pushed rather far back on his sandy head, and as he walked he breathed an American tune between his teeth, raising one side of his upper lip to let the faint sound pass freely without turning itself into a real whistle. It is rather a Yankee trick, and is particularly offensive to some people, but Lady Maud did not mind it at all, though she heard it distinctly. It always meant that Mr. Van Torp was in deep thought, and she guessed that, just then, he was thinking more about her than of himself. In his pocket he held in his right hand a small envelope which he meant to bring out presently and give to her, where nobody would be likely to see them.

Presently, when the motor had turned to the left, far up the long drive, he raised his eyes and looked about him. He had the sight of a man who has lived in the wilderness, and not only sees, but knows how to see, which is a very different thing. Having satisfied himself, he withdrew the envelope and held it out to his companion.

'I thought you might just as well have some more money,' he said, 'so I brought you some. I may want to sail any minute. I don't know. Yes, you'd better take it.'

Lady Maud had looked up quickly and had hesitated to receive the envelope, but when he finished speaking she took it quickly and slipped it into the opening of her long glove, pushing it down till it lay in the palm of her hand. She fastened the buttons before she spoke.

'How thoughtful you always are for me!'

She unconsciously used the very words with which she had thanked him in Hare Court the last time he had given her money. The tone told him how deeply grateful she was.

'Well,' he said in answer, 'as far as that goes, it's for you yourself, as much as if I didn't know where it went; and if I'm obliged to sail suddenly I don't want you to be out of your reckoning.'

'You're much too good, Rufus. Do you really mean that you may have to go back at once, to defend yourself?'

'No, not exactly that. But business is business, and somebody responsible has got to be there, since poor old Bamberger has gone crazy and come abroad to stay—apparently.'

'Crazy?'

'Well, he behaves like it, anyway. I'm beginning to be sorry for that man. I'm in earnest. You mayn't believe it, but I really am. Kind of unnatural, isn't it, for me to be sorry for people?'

He looked steadily at Lady Maud for a moment, then smiled faintly, looked away, and began to blow his little tune through his teeth again.

'You were sorry for little Ida,' suggested Lady Maud.

'That's different. I——I liked her mother a good deal, and when the child was turned adrift I sort of looked after her. Anybody'd do that, I expect.'

'And you're sorry for me, in a way,' said Lady Maud.

'You're different, too. You're my friend. I suppose you're about the only one I've got, too. We can't complain of being crowded out of doors by our friends, either of us, can we? Besides, I shouldn't put it in that way, or call it being sorry, exactly. It's another kind of feeling I have. I'd like to undo your life and make it over again for you, the right way, so that you'd be happy. I can do a great deal, but all the cursed nickel in the world won't bring back the—' he checked himself suddenly, shutting his hard lips with an audible clack, and looking down. 'I beg your pardon, my dear,' he said in a low voice, a moment later.

For he had been very near to speaking of the dead, and he felt instinctively that the rough speech, however kindly meant, would have pained her, and perhaps had already hurt her a little. But as she looked down, too, her hand gently touched the sleeve of his coat to tell him that there was nothing to forgive.

'He knows,' she said, more softly than sadly. 'Where he is, they know about us—when we try to do right.'

'And you haven't only tried,' Van Torp answered quietly, 'you've done it.'

'Have I?' It sounded as if she asked the question of herself, or of some one to whom she appealed in her heart. 'I often wonder,' she added thoughtfully.

'You needn't worry,' said her companion, more cheerily than he had yet spoken. 'Do you want to know why I think you needn't fuss about your conscience and your soul, and things?'

He smiled now, and so did she, but more at the words he used than at the question itself.

'Yes,' she said. 'I should like to know why.'

'It's a pretty good sign for a lady's soul when a lot of poor creatures bless her every minute of their lives for fishing them out of the mud and landing them in a decent life. Come, isn't it now? You know it is. That's all. No further argument's necessary. The jury is satisfied and the verdict is that you needn't fuss. So that's that, and let's talk about something else.'

'I'm not so sure,' Lady Maud answered. 'Is it right to bribe people to do right? Sometimes it has seemed very like that!'

'I don't set up to be an expert in morality,' retorted Van Torp, 'but if money, properly used, can prevent murder, I guess that's better than letting the murder be committed. You must allow that. The same way with other crimes, isn't it? And so on, down to mere misdemeanours, till you come to ordinary morality. Now what have you got to say? If it isn't much better for the people themselves to lead decent lives just for money's sake, it's certainly much better for everybody else that they should. That appears to me to be unanswerable. You didn't start in with the idea of making those poor things just like you, I suppose. You can't train a cart-horse to win the Derby. Yet all their nonsense about equality rests on the theory that you can. You can't make a good judge out of a criminal, no matter how the criminal repents of his crimes. He's not been born the intellectual equal of the man who's born to judge him. His mind is biassed. Perhaps he's a degenerate—everything one isn't oneself is called degenerate nowadays. It helps things, I suppose. And you can't expect to collect a lot of poor wretches together and manufacture first-class Magdalens out of ninety-nine per cent of them, because you're the one that needs no repentance, can you? I forget whether the Bible says it was ninety-nine who did or ninety-nine who didn't, but you'll understand my drift, I daresay. It's logic, if it isn't Scripture. All right. As long as you can stop the evil, without doing wrong yourself, you're bringing about a good result. So don't fuss. See?'

'Yes, I see!' Lady Maud smiled. 'But it's your money that does it!'

'That's nothing,' Van Torp said, as if he disliked the subject.

He changed it effectually by speaking of his own present intentions and explaining to his friend what he meant to do.

His point of view seemed to be that Bamberger was quite mad since his daughter's death, and had built up a sensational but clumsy case, with the help of the man Feist, whose evidence, as a confirmed dipsomaniac, would be all but worthless. It was possible, Van Torp said, that Miss Bamberger had been killed; in fact, Griggs' evidence alone would almost prove it. But the chances were a thousand to one that she had been killed by a maniac. Such murders were not so uncommon as Lady Maud might think. The police in all countries know how many cases occur which can be explained only on that theory, and how diabolically ingenious madmen are in covering their tracks.

Lady Maud believed all he told her, and had perfect faith in his innocence, but she knew instinctively that he was not telling her all; and the certainty that he was keeping back something made her nervous.

In due time the other guests came; each in turn met Mr. Van Torp soon after arriving, if not at the moment when they entered the house; and they shook hands with him, and almost all knew why he was there, but those who did not were soon told by the others.

The fact of having been asked to a country house for the express purpose of being shown by ocular demonstration that something is 'all right' which has been very generally said or thought to be all wrong, does not generally contribute to the light-heartedness of such parties. Moreover, the very young element was hardly represented, and there was a dearth of those sprightly boys and girls who think it the acme of delicate wit to shut up an aunt in the ice-box and throw the billiard-table out of the window. Neither Lady Maud nor her father liked what Mr. Van Torp called a 'circus'; and besides, the modern youths and maids who delight in practical jokes were not the people whose good opinion about the millionaire it was desired to obtain, or to strengthen, as the case might be. The guests, far from being what Lady Maud's brothers called a menagerie, were for the most part of the graver sort whose approval weighs in proportion as they are themselves social heavyweights. There was the Leader of the House, there were a couple of members of the Cabinet, there was the Master of the Foxhounds, there was the bishop of the diocese, and there was one of the big Derbyshire landowners; there was an ex-governor-general of something, an ex-ambassador to the United States, and a famous general; there was a Hebrew financier of London, and Logotheti, the Greek financier from Paris, who were regarded as colleagues of Van Torp, the American financier; there was the scientific peer who had dined at the Turkish Embassy with Lady Maud, there was the peer whose horse had just won the

Derby, and there was the peer who knew German and was looked upon as the coming man in the Upper House. Many had their wives with them, and some had lost their wives or could not bring them; but very few were looking for a wife, and there were no young women looking for husbands, since the Señorita da Cordova was apparently not to be reckoned with those.

Now at this stage of my story it would be unpardonable to keep my readers in suspense, if I may suppose that any of them have a little curiosity left. Therefore I shall not narrate in detail what happened on Friday, Saturday, and Sunday, seeing that it was just what might have been expected to happen at a week-end party during the season when there is nothing in the world to do but to play golf, tennis, or croquet, or to ride or drive all day, and to work hard at bridge all the evening; for that is what it has come to.

Everything went very well till Sunday night, and most of the people formed a much better opinion of Mr. Van Torp than those who had lately read about him in the newspapers might have thought possible. The Cabinet Ministers talked politics with him and found him sound—for an American; the M.F.H. saw him ride, and felt for him exactly the sympathy which a Don Cossack, a cowboy, and a Bedouin might feel for each other if they met on horseback, and which needs no expression in words; and the three distinguished peers liked him at once, because he was not at all impressed by their social greatness, but was very much interested in what they had to say respectively about science, horse-breeding, and Herr Bebel. The great London financier, and he, and Monsieur Logotheti exchanged casual remarks which all the men who were interested in politics referred to mysterious loans that must affect the armaments of the combined powers and the peace of Europe.

Mr. Van Torp kept away from the Primadonna, and she watched him curiously, a good deal surprised to see that most of the others liked him better than she had expected. She was rather agreeably disappointed, too, at the reception she herself met with Lord Creedmore spoke of her only as 'Miss Donne, the daughter of his oldest friend,' and every one treated her accordingly. No one even mentioned her profession, and possibly some of the guests did not quite realise that she was the famous Cordova. Lady Maud never suggested that she should sing, and Lord Creedmore detested music. The old piano in the long drawing-room was hardly ever opened. It had been placed there in Victorian days when 'a little music' was the rule, and since the happy abolition of that form of terror it had been left where it stood, and was tuned once a year, in case anybody should want a dance when there were young people in the house.

A girl might as well master the Assyrian language in order to compose hymns to Tiglath-Pileser as learn to play the piano nowadays, but bridge is played at children's parties; let us not speak ill of the Bridge that has carried us over.

Margaret was not out of her element; on the contrary, she at first had the sensation of finding herself amongst rather grave and not uncongenial English people, not so very different from those with whom she had spent her early girlhood at Oxford. It was not strange to her, but it was no longer familiar, and she missed the surroundings to which she had grown accustomed. Hitherto, when she had been asked to join such parties, there had been at least a few of those persons who are supposed to delight especially in the society of sopranos, actresses, and lionesses generally; but none of them were at Craythew. She was suddenly transported back into regions where nobody seemed to care a straw whether she could sing or not, where nobody flattered her, and no one suggested that it would be amusing and instructive to make a trip to Spain together, or that a charming little kiosk at Therapia was at her disposal whenever she chose to visit the Bosphorus.

There was only Logotheti to remind her of her everyday life, for Griggs did not do so at all; he belonged much more to the 'atmosphere,' and though she knew that he had loved in his youth a woman who had a beautiful voice, he understood nothing of music and never talked about it. As for Lady Maud, Margaret saw much less of her than she had expected; the hostess was manifestly preoccupied, and was, moreover, obliged to give more of her time to her guests than would have been necessary if they had been of the younger generation or if the season had been winter.

Margaret noticed in herself a new phase of change with regard to Logotheti, and she did not like it at all: he had become necessary to her, and yet she was secretly a little ashamed of him. In that temple of respectability where she found herself, in such 'a cloister of social pillars' as Logotheti called the party, he was a discordant figure. She was haunted by a painful doubt that if he had not been a very important financier some of those quiet middle-aged Englishmen might have thought him a 'bounder,' because of his ruby pin, his summer-lightning waistcoats, and his almond-shaped eyes. It was very unpleasant to be so strongly drawn to a man whom such people probably thought a trifle 'off.'

It irritated her to be obliged to admit that the London financier, who was a professed and professing Hebrew, was in appearance an English gentleman, whereas Konstantinos Logotheti, with a pedigree of Christian and not unpersecuted Fanariote ancestors, that went back to Byzantine times without the least suspicion of any Semitic marriage, might have been taken for a Jew in Lombard Street, and certainly would have been thought one in Berlin. A man whose eyes suggested dark almonds need not cover himself with jewellery and adorn himself in naming colours, Margaret thought; and she resented his way of dressing, much more than ever before. Lady Maud had called him exotic, and Margaret could not forget that. By 'exotic' she was sure that her friend meant something like vulgar, though Lady Maud said she liked him.

But the events that happened at Craythew on Sunday evening threw such insignificant details as these into the shade, and brought out the true character of the chief actors, amongst whom Margaret very unexpectedly found herself.

It was late in the afternoon after a really cloudless June day, and she had been for a long ramble in the park with Lord Creedmore, who had talked to her about her father and the old Oxford days, till all her present life seemed to be a mere dream; and she could not realise, as she went up to her room, that she was to go back to London on the morrow, to the theatre, to rehearsals, to Pompeo Stromboli, Schreiermeyer, and the public.

She met Logotheti in the gallery that ran round two sides of the hall, and they both stopped and leaned over the balustrade to talk a little.

'It has been very pleasant,' she said thoughtfully. 'I'm sorry it's over so soon.'

'Whenever you are inclined to lead this sort of life,' Logotheti answered with a laugh, 'you need only drop me a line. You shall have a beautiful old house and a big park and a perfect colonnade of respectabilities—and I'll promise not to be a bore.'

Margaret looked at him earnestly for some seconds, and then asked a very unexpected and frivolous question, because she simply could not help it.

'Where did you get that tie?'

The question was strongly emphasised, for it meant much more to her just then than he could possibly have guessed; perhaps it meant something which was affecting her whole life. He laughed carelessly.

'It's better to dress like Solomon in all his glory than to be taken for a Levantine gambler,' he answered. 'In the days when I was simple-minded, a foreigner in a fur coat and an eyeglass once stopped me in the Boulevard des Italiens and asked if I could give him the address of any house where a roulette-table was kept! After that I took to jewels and dress!'

Margaret wondered why she could not help liking him; and by sheer force of habit she thought that he would make a very good-looking stage Romeo.

While she was thinking of that and smiling in spite of his tie, the old clock in the hall below chimed the hour, and it was a quarter to seven; and at the same moment three men were getting out of a train that had stopped at the Craythew station, three miles from Lord Creedmore's gate.

CHAPTER XVIII

The daylight dinner was over, and the large party was more or less scattered about the drawing-room and the adjoining picture-gallery in groups of three and four, mostly standing while they drank their coffee, and continued or finished the talk begun at table.

By force of habit Margaret had stopped beside the closed piano, and had seated herself on the old-fashioned stool to have her coffee. Lady Maud stood beside her, leaning against the corner of the instrument, her cup in her hand, and the two young women exchanged rather idle observations about the lovely day that was over, and the perfect weather. Both were preoccupied and they did not look at each other; Margaret's eyes watched Logotheti, who was half-way down the long room, before a portrait by Sir Peter Lely, of which he was apparently pointing out the beauties to the elderly wife of the scientific peer. Lady Maud was looking out at the light in the sunset sky above the trees beyond the flower-beds and the great lawn, for the piano stood near an open window. From time to time she turned her head quickly and glanced towards Van Torp, who was talking with her father at some distance; then she looked out of the window again.

It was a warm evening; in the dusk of the big rooms the hum of voices was low and pleasant, broken only now and then by Van Torp's more strident tone. Outside it was still light, and the starlings and blackbirds and thrushes were finishing their supper, picking up the unwary worms and the tardy little snails, and making a good deal of sweet noise about it.

Margaret set down her cup on the lid of the piano, and at the slight sound Lady Maud turned towards her, so that their eyes met. Each noticed the other's expression.

'What is it?' asked Lady Maud, with a little smile of friendly concern. 'Is anything wrong?'

'No—that is—' Margaret smiled too, as she hesitated—'I was going to ask you the same question,' she added quickly.

'It's nothing more than usual,' returned her friend. 'I think it has gone very well, don't you, these three days? He has made a good impression on everybody—don't you think so?'

'Oh yes!' Margaret answered readily. 'Excellent! Could not be better! I confess to being surprised, just a little—I mean,' she corrected herself hastily, 'after all the talk there has been, it might not have turned out so easy.'

'Don't you feel a little less prejudiced against him yourself?' asked Lady Maud.

'Prejudiced!' Margaret repeated the word thoughtfully. 'Yes, I suppose I'm prejudiced against him. That's the only word. Perhaps it's hateful of me, but I cannot help it—and I wish you wouldn't make me own it to you, for it's humiliating! I'd like him, if I could, for your sake. But you must take the wish for the deed.'

'That's better than nothing!' Lady Maud seemed to be trying to laugh a little, but it was with an effort and there was no ripple in her voice. 'You have something on your mind, too,' she went on, to change the subject. 'Is anything troubling you?'

'Only the same old question. It's not worth mentioning!'

'To marry, or not to marry?'

'Yes. I suppose I shall take the leap some day, and probably in the dark, and then I shall be sorry for it. Most of you have!'

She looked up at Lady Maud with a rather uncertain, flickering smile, as if she wished her mind to be made up for her, and her hands lay weakly in her lap, the palms almost upwards.

'Oh, don't ask me!' cried her friend, answering the look rather than the words, and speaking with something approaching to vehemence.

'Do you wish you had waited for the other one till now?' asked Margaret softly, but she did not know that he had been killed in South Africa; she had never seen the shabby little photograph.

'Yes—for ever!'

That was all Lady Maud said, and the two words were not uttered dramatically either, though gravely and without the least doubt.

The butler and two men appeared, to collect the coffee cups; the former had a small salver in his hand and came directly to Lady Maud. He brought a telegram for her.

'You don't mind, do you?' she asked Margaret mechanically, as she opened it.

'Of course,' answered the other in the same tone, and she looked through the open window while her friend read the message.

It was from the Embassy in London, and it informed her in the briefest terms that Count Leven had been killed in St. Petersburg on the previous day, in the street, by a bomb intended for a high official. Lady Maud made no sound, but folded the telegram into a small square and turned her back to the room for a moment in order to slip it unnoticed into the body of her black velvet gown. As she recovered her former attitude she was surprised to see that the butler was still standing two steps from her where he had stopped after he had taken the cups from the piano and set them on the small salver on which he had brought the message. He evidently wanted to say something to her alone.

Lady Maud moved away from the piano, and he followed her a little beyond the window, till she stopped and turned to hear what he had to say.

'There are three persons asking for Mr. Van Torp, my lady,' he said in a very low tone, and she noticed the disturbed look in his face. 'They've got a motor-car waiting in the avenue.'

'What sort of people are they?' she asked quietly; but she felt that she was pale.

'To tell the truth, my lady,' the butler spoke in a whisper, bending his head, 'I think they are from Scotland Yard.'

Lady Maud knew it already; she had almost guessed it when she had glanced at his face before he spoke at all.

'Show them into the old study,' she said, 'and ask them to wait a moment.'

The butler went away with his two coffee cups, and scarcely any one had noticed that Lady Maud had exchanged a few words with him by the window. She turned back to the piano, where Margaret was still sitting on the stool with her hands in her lap, looking at Logotheti in the distance and wondering whether she meant to marry him or not.

'No bad news, I hope?' asked the singer, looking up as her friend came to her side.

'Not very good,' Lady Maud answered, leaning her elbow on the piano. 'Should you mind singing something to keep the party together while I talk to some tiresome men who are in the old study? On these June evenings people have a way of wandering out into the garden after dinner. I should like to keep every one in the house for a quarter of an hour, and if you will only sing for them they won't stir. Will you?'

Margaret looked at her curiously.

'I think I understand,' Margaret said. 'The people in the study are asking for Mr. Van Torp.'

Lady Maud nodded, not surprised that Logotheti should have told the Primadonna something about what he had been doing.

'Then you believe he is innocent,' she said confidently. 'Even though you don't like him, you'll help me, won't you?'

'I'll do anything you ask me. But I should think—'

'No,' Lady Maud interrupted. 'He must not be arrested at all. I know that he would rather face the detectives than run away, even for a few hours, till the truth is known. But I won't let him. It would be published all over the world to-morrow morning that he had been arrested for murder in my father's house, and it would never be forgotten against him, though he might be proved innocent ten times over. That's what I want to prevent. Will you help me?'

As she spoke the last words she raised the front lid of the piano, and Margaret turned on her seat towards the instrument to open the keyboard, nodding her assent.

'Just play a little, till I am out of the room, and then sing,' said Lady Maud.

The great artist's fingers felt the keys as her friend turned away. Anything theatrical was natural to her now, and she began to play very softly, watching the moving figure in black velvet as she would have watched a fellow singer on the stage while waiting to go on.

Lady Maud did not speak to Van Torp first, but to Griggs, and then to Logotheti, and the two men slipped away together and disappeared. Then she came back to Van Torp, smiling pleasantly. He was still talking with Lord Creedmore, but the latter, at a word from his daughter, went off to the elderly peeress whom Logotheti had abruptly left alone before the portrait.

Margaret did not hear what Lady Maud said to the American, but it was evidently not yet a warning, for her smile did not falter, and he looked pleased as he came back with her, and they passed near the piano to go out through the open window upon the broad flagged terrace that separated the house from the flower-beds.

The Primadonna played a little louder now, so that every one heard the chords, even in the picture-gallery, and a good many men were rather bored at the prospect of music.

Then the Señorita da Cordova raised her head and looked over the grand piano, and her lips parted, and boredom vanished very suddenly; for even those who did not take much pleasure in the music were amazed by the mere sound of her voice and by its incredible flexibility.

She meant to astonish her hearers and keep them quiet, and she knew what to sing to gain her end, and how to sing it. Those who have not forgotten the story of her beginnings will remember that she was a thorough musician as well as a great singer, and was one of those very few primadonnas who are able to accompany themselves from memory without a false note through any great piece they know, from *Lucia* to *Parsifal*.

She began with the waltz song in the first act of *Romeo and Juliet*. It was the piece that had revealed her talent to Madame Bonanni, who had accidentally overheard her singing to herself, and it suited her purpose admirably. Such fireworks could not fail to astound, even if they did not please, and half the full volume of her voice was more than enough for the long drawing-room, into which the whole party gathered almost as soon as she began to sing. Such trifles as having just dined, or having just waked up in the morning, have little influence on the few great natural voices of the world, which begin with twice the power and beauty that the 'built-up' ones acquire in years of study. Ordinary people go to a concert, to the opera, to a circus, to university sports, and hear and see things that interest or charm, or sometimes surprise them; but they are very much amazed if they ever happen to find out in private life what a really great professional of any sort can do at a pinch, if put to it by any strong motive. If it had been necessary, Margaret could have sung to the party in the drawing-room at Craythew for an hour at a stretch with no more rest than her accompaniments afforded.

Her hearers were the more delighted because it was so spontaneous, and there was not the least affectation about it. During these days no one had even suggested that she should make music, or be anything except the 'daughter of Lord Creedmore's old friend.' But now, apparently, she had sat down to the piano to give them all a concert, for the sheer pleasure of singing, and they were not only pleased with her, but with themselves; for the public, and especially audiences, are more easily flattered by a great artist who chooses to treat his hearers as worthy of his best, than the artist himself is by the applause he hears for the thousandth time.

So the Señorita da Cordova held the party at Craythew spellbound while other things were happening very near them which would have interested them much more than her trills, and her 'mordentini,' and her soaring runs, and the high staccato notes that rang down from the ceiling as if some astounding and invisible instrument were up there, supported by an unseen force.

Meanwhile Paul Griggs and Logotheti had stopped a moment in the first of the rooms that contained the library, on their way to the old study beyond.

It was almost dark amongst the huge oak bookcases, and both men stopped at the same moment by a common instinct, to agree quickly upon some plan of action. They had led adventurous lives, and were not likely to stick at trifles, if they believed themselves to be in the right; but if they had left the drawing-room with the distinct expectation of anything like a fight, they would certainly not have stopped to waste their time in talking.

The Greek spoke first.

'Perhaps you had better let me do the talking,' he said.

'By all means,' answered Griggs. 'I am not good at that. I'll keep quiet, unless we have to handle them.'

'All right, and if you have any trouble I'll join in and help you. Just set your back against the door if they try to get out while I am speaking.'

'Yes.'

That was all, and they went on in the gathering gloom, through the three rooms of the library, to the door of the old study, from which a short winding staircase led up to the two small rooms which Griggs was occupying.

Three quiet men in dark clothes were standing together in the twilight, in the bay window at the other side of the room, and they moved and turned their heads quickly as the door opened. Logotheti went up to them, while Griggs remained near the door, looking on.

'What can I do for you?' inquired the Greek, with much urbanity.

'We wished to speak with Mr. Van Torp, who is stopping here,' answered the one of the three men who stood farthest forward.

'Oh yes, yes!' said Logotheti at once, as if assenting. 'Certainly! Lady Maud Leven, Lord Creedmore's daughter—Lady Creedmore is away, you know—has asked us to inquire just what you want of Mr. Van Torp.'

'It's a personal matter,' replied the spokesman. 'I will explain it to him, if you will kindly ask him to come here a moment.'

Logotheti smiled pleasantly.

'Quite so,' he said. 'You are, no doubt, reporters, and wish to interview him. As a personal friend of his, and between you and me, I don't think he'll see you. You had better write and ask for an appointment. Don't you think so, Griggs?'

The author's large, grave features relaxed in a smile of amusement as he nodded his approval of the plan.

'We do not represent the press,' answered the man.

'Ah! Indeed? How very odd! But of course—' Logotheti pretended to understand suddenly—'how stupid of me! No doubt you are from the bank. Am I not right?'

'No. You are mistaken. We are not from Threadneedle Street.'

'Well, then, unless you will enlighten me, I really cannot imagine who you are or where you come from!'

'We wish to speak in private with Mr. Van Torp.'

'In private, too?' Logotheti shook his head, and turned to Griggs. 'Really, this looks rather suspicious; don't you think so?'

Griggs said nothing, but the smile became a broad grin.

The spokesman, on his side, turned to his two companions and whispered, evidently consulting them as to the course he should pursue.

'Especially after the warning Lord Creedmore has received,' said Logotheti to Griggs in a very audible tone, as if explaining his last speech.

The man turned to him again and spoke in a gravely determined tone—

'I must really insist upon seeing Mr. Van Torp immediately,' he said.

'Yes, yes, I quite understand you,' answered Logotheti, looking at him with a rather pitying smile, and then turning to Griggs again, as if for advice.

The elder man was much amused by the ease with which the Greek had so far put off the unwelcome visitors and gained time; but he saw that the scene must soon come to a crisis, and prepared for action, keeping his eye on the three, in case they should make a dash at the door that communicated with the rest of the house.

During the two or three seconds that followed, Logotheti reviewed the situation. It would be an easy matter to trick the three men into the short winding staircase that led up to the rooms Griggs occupied, and if the upper and lower doors were locked and barricaded, the prisoners could not forcibly get out. But it was certain that the leader of the party had a warrant about him, and this must be taken from him before locking him up, and without any acknowledgment of its validity; for even the lawless Greek was aware that it was not good to interfere with officers of the law in the execution of their duty. If there had been more time he might have devised some better means of attaining his end than occurred to him just then.

'They must be the lunatics,' he said to Griggs, with the utmost calm.

The spokesman started and stared, and his jaw dropped. For a moment he could not speak.

'You know Lord Creedmore was warned this morning that a number had escaped from the county asylum,' continued Logotheti, still speaking to Griggs, and pretending to lower his voice.

'Lunatics?' roared the man when he got his breath, exasperated out of his civil manner. 'Lunatics, sir? We are from Scotland Yard, sir, I'd have you know!'

'Yes, yes,' answered the Greek, 'we quite understand. Humour them, my dear chap,' he added in an undertone that was meant to be heard. 'Yes,' he continued in a cajoling tone, 'I guessed at once that you were from police headquarters. If you'll kindly show me your warrant—'

He stopped politely, and nudged Griggs with his elbow, so that the detectives should be sure to see the movement. The chief saw the awkwardness of his own position, measured the bony veteran and the athletic foreigner with his eye, and judged that if the two were convinced that they were dealing with madmen they would make a pretty good fight.

'Excuse me,' the officer said, speaking calmly, 'but you are under a gross misapprehension about us. This paper will remove it at once, I trust, and you will not hinder us in the performance of an unpleasant duty.'

He produced an official envelope, handed it to Logotheti, and waited for the result.

It was unexpected when it came. Logotheti took the paper, and as it was now almost dark he looked about for the key of the electric light. Griggs was now close to him by the door through which they had entered, and behind which the knob was placed.

'If I can get them upstairs, lock and barricade the lower door,' whispered the Greek as he turned up the light.

He took the paper under a bracket light on the other side of the room, beside the door of the winding stair, and began to read.

His face was a study, and Griggs watched it, wondering what was coming. As Logotheti read and reread the few short sentences, he was apparently seized by a fit of mirth which he struggled in vain to repress, and which soon broke out into uncontrollable laughter.

'The cleverest trick you ever saw!' he managed to get out between his paroxysms.

It was so well done that the detective was seriously embarrassed; but after a moment's hesitation he judged that he ought to get his warrant back at all hazards, and he moved towards Logotheti with a menacing expression.

But the Greek, pretending to be afraid that the supposed lunatic was going to attack him, uttered an admirable yell of fear, opened the door close at his hand, rushed through, slammed it behind him, and fled up the dark stairs.

The detective lost no time, and followed in hot pursuit, his two companions tearing up after him into the darkness. Then Griggs quietly turned the key in the lock, for he was sure that Logotheti had reached the top in time to fasten the upper door, and must be already barricading it. Griggs proceeded to do the same, quietly and systematically, and the great strength he had not yet lost served him well, for the furniture in the room was heavy. In a couple of minutes it would have needed sledge-hammers and crowbars to break out by the lower entrance, even if the lock had not been a solid one.

Griggs then turned out the lights, and went quietly back through the library to the other part of the house to find Lady Maud.

Logotheti, having meanwhile made the upper door perfectly secure, descended by the open staircase to the hall, and sent the first footman he met to call the butler, with whom he said he wished to speak. The butler came at once.

'Lady Maud asked me to see those three men,' said Logotheti in a low tone. 'Mr. Griggs and I are convinced that they are lunatics escaped from the asylum, and we have locked them up securely in the staircase beyond the study.'

'Yes, sir,' said the butler, as if Logotheti had been explaining how he wished his shoe-leather to be treated.

'I think you had better telephone for the doctor, and explain everything to him over the wire without speaking to Lord Creedmore just yet.'

'Yes, sir.'

'How long will it take the doctor to get here?'

'Perhaps an hour, sir, if he's at home. Couldn't say precisely, sir.'

'Very good. There is no hurry; and of course her ladyship will be particularly anxious that none of her friends should guess what has happened; you see there would be a general panic if it were known that there are escaped lunatics in the house.'

'Yes, sir.'

'Perhaps you had better take a couple of men you can trust, and pile up some more furniture against the doors, above and below. One cannot be too much on the safe side in such cases.'

'Yes, sir. I'll do it at once, sir.'

Logotheti strolled back towards the gallery in a very unconcerned way. As for the warrant, he had burnt it in the empty fireplace in Griggs' room after making all secure, and had dusted down the black ashes so carefully that they had quite disappeared under the grate. After all, as the doctor would arrive in the firm expectation of finding three escaped madmen under lock and key, the Scotland Yard men might have some difficulty in proving themselves sane until they could communicate with their headquarters, and by that time Mr. Van Torp could be far on his way if he chose.

When Logotheti reached the door of the drawing-room, Margaret was finishing Rosina's Cavatina from the *Barbiere di Siviglia* in a perfect storm of fireworks, having transposed the whole piece two notes higher to suit her own voice, for it was originally written for a mezzo-soprano.

Lady Maud and Van Torp had gone out upon the terrace unnoticed a moment before Margaret had begun to sing. The evening was still and cloudless, and presently the purple twilight would pale under the summer moon, and the garden and the lawns would be once more as bright as day. The friends walked quickly, for Lady Maud set the pace and led Van Torp toward the trees, where the stables stood, quite hidden from the house. As soon as she reached the shade she stood still and spoke in a low voice.

'You have waited too long,' she said. 'Three men have come to arrest you, and their motor is over there in the avenue.'

'Where are they?' inquired the American, evidently not at all disturbed. 'I'll see them at once, please.'

'And give yourself up?'

'I don't care.'

'Here?'

'Why not? Do you suppose I am going to run away? A man who gets out in a hurry doesn't usually look innocent, does he?'

Lady Maud asserted herself.

'You must think of me and of my father,' she said in a tone of authority Van Torp had never heard from her. 'I know you're as innocent as I am, but after all that has been said and written about you, and about you and me together, it's quite impossible that you should let yourself be arrested in our house, in the midst of a party that has been asked here expressly to be convinced that my father approves of you. Do you see that?'

'Well—' Mr. Van Torp hesitated, with his thumbs in his waistcoat pockets.

Across the lawn, from the open window, Margaret's voice rang out like a score of nightingales in unison.

'There's no time to discuss it,' Lady Maud said. 'I asked her to sing, so as to keep the people together. Before she has finished, you must be out of reach.'

Mr. Van Torp smiled. 'You're remarkably positive about it,' he said.

'You must get to town before the Scotland Yard people, and I don't know how much start they will give you. It depends on how long Mr. Griggs and Logotheti can keep them in the old study. It will be neck and neck, I fancy. I'll go with you to the stables. You must ride to your own place as hard as you can, and go up to London in your car to-night. The roads are pretty clear on Sundays, and there's moonlight, so you will have no trouble. It will be easy to say here that you have been called away suddenly. Come, you must go!'

Lady Maud moved towards the stables, and Van Torp was obliged to follow her. Far away Margaret was singing the last bars of the waltz song.

'I must say,' observed Mr. Van Torp thoughtfully, as they walked on, 'for a lady who's generally what I call quite feminine, you make a man sit up pretty quick.'

'It's not exactly the time to choose for loafing,' answered Lady Maud. 'By the bye,' she added, 'you may as well know. Poor Leven is dead. I had a telegram a few minutes ago. He was killed yesterday by a bomb meant for somebody else.'

Van Torp stood still, and Lady Maud stopped with evident reluctance.

'And there are people who don't believe in Providence,' he said slowly. 'Well, I congratulate you anyway.'

'Hush, the poor man is dead. We needn't talk about him. Come, there's no time to lose!' She moved impatiently.

'So you're a widow!' Van Torp seemed to be making the remark to himself without expecting any answer, but it at once suggested a question. 'And now what do you propose to do?' he inquired. 'But I expect you'll be a nun, or something. I'd like you to arrange so that I can see you sometimes, will you?'

'I'm not going to disappear yet,' Lady Maud answered gravely.

They reached the stables, which occupied three sides of a square yard. At that hour the two grooms and the stable-boy were at their supper, and the coachman had gone home to his cottage. A big brown retriever on a chain was sitting bolt upright beside his kennel, and began to thump the flagstones with his tail as soon as he recognised Lady Maud. From within a fox-terrier barked two or three times. Lady Maud opened a door, and he sprang out at her yapping, but was quiet as soon as he knew her.

'You'd better take the Lancashire Lass,' she said to Van Torp. 'You're heavier than my father, but it's not far to ride, and she's a clever creature.'

She had turned up the electric light while speaking, for it was dark inside the stable; she got a bridle, went into the box herself, and slipped it over the mare's pretty head. Van Torp saw that it was useless to offer help.

'Don't bother about a saddle,' he said; 'it's a waste of time.'

He touched the mare's face and lips with his hand, and she understood him, and let him lead her out. He vaulted upon her back, and Lady Maud walked beside him till they were outside the yard.

'If you had a high hat it would look like the circus,' she said, glancing at his evening dress. 'Now get away! I'll be in town on Tuesday; let me know what happens. Good-bye! Be sure to let me know.'

'Yes. Don't worry. I'm only going because you insist, anyhow. Good-bye. God bless you!'

He waved his hand, the mare sprang forward, and in a few seconds he was out of sight amongst the trees. Lady Maud listened to the regular sound of the galloping hoofs on the turf, and at the same time from very far off she heard Margaret's high trills and quick staccato notes. At that moment the moon was rising through the late twilight, and a nightingale high overhead, no doubt judging her little self to be quite as great a musician as the famous Cordova, suddenly began a very wonderful piece of her own, just half a tone higher than Margaret's, which might have distressed a sensitive musician, but did not jar in the least on Lady Maud's ear.

Now that she had sent Van Torp on his way, she would gladly have walked alone in the park for half an hour to collect her thoughts; but people who live in the world are rarely allowed any pleasant leisure when they need it, and many of the most dramatic things in real life happen when we are in such a hurry that we do not half understand them. So the moment that should have been the happiest of all goes dashing by when we are hastening to catch a train; so the instant of triumph after years of labour or weeks of struggling is upon us when we are perhaps positively obliged to write three important notes in twenty minutes; and sometimes, too, and mercifully, the pain of parting is numbed just as the knife strikes the nerve, by the howling confusion of a railway station that forces us to take care of ourselves and our belongings; and when the first instant of joy, or victory, or acute suffering is gone in a flash, memory never quite brings back all the happiness nor all the pain.

Lady Maud could not have stayed away many minutes longer. She went back at once, entered by the garden window just as Margaret was finishing Rosina's song, and remained standing behind her till she had sung the last note. English people rarely applaud conventional drawing-room music, but this had been something more, and the Craythew guests clapped their hands loudly, and even the elderly wife of the scientific peer emitted distinctly audible sounds of satisfaction. Lady Maud bent her handsome head and kissed the singer affectionately, whispering words of heartfelt thanks.

CHAPTER XIX

Through the mistaken efforts of Isidore Bamberger, justice had got herself into difficulties, and it was as well for her reputation, which is not good nowadays, that the public never heard what happened on that night at Craythew, how the three best men who had been available at headquarters were discomfited in their well-meant attempt to arrest an innocent man, and how they spent two miserable hours together locked up in a dark winding staircase. For it chanced, as it will chance to the end of time, that the doctor was out when the butler telephoned to him; it happened, too, that he was far from home, engaged in ushering a young gentleman of prosperous parentage into this world, an action of which the kindness might be questioned, considering that the poor little soul presumably came straight from paradise, with an indifferent chance of ever getting there again. So the doctor could not come.

The three men were let out in due time, however, and as no trace of a warrant could be discovered at that hour, Logotheti and Griggs being already sound asleep, and as Lord Creedmore, in his dressing-gown and slippers, gave them a written statement to the effect that Mr. Van Torp was no longer at Craythew, they had no choice but to return to town, rather the worse for wear. What they said to each other by the way may safely be left to the inexhaustible imagination of a gentle and sympathising reader.

Their suppressed rage, their deep mortification, and their profound disgust were swept away in their overwhelming amazement, however, when they found that Mr. Rufus Van Torp, whom they had sought in Derbyshire, was in Scotland Yard before them, closeted with their Chief and explaining what an odd mistake the justice of two nations had committed in suspecting him to have been at the Metropolitan Opera-House in New York at the time of the explosion, since he had spent that very evening in Washington, in the private study of the Secretary of the Treasury, who wanted his confidential opinion on a question connected with Trusts before he went abroad. Mr. Van Torp stuck his thumbs into his waistcoat pockets and blandly insisted that the cables should be kept red-hot—at international expense—till the member of the Cabinet in Washington should answer corroborating the statement. Four o'clock in the morning in London was only eleven o'clock of the previous evening, Mr. Van Torp explained, and it was extremely unlikely that the Secretary of the Treasury should be in bed so early. If he was, he was certainly not asleep; and with the facilities at the disposal of governments there was no reason why the answer should not come back in forty minutes.

It was impossible to resist such simple logic. The lines were cleared for urgent official business between London and Washington, and in less than an hour the answer came back, to the effect that Mr. Rufus Van Torp's statement was correct in every detail; and without any interval another official message arrived, revoking the request for his extradition, which 'had been made under a most unfortunate misapprehension, due to the fact that Mr. Van Torp's visit to the Secretary of the Treasury had been regarded as confidential by the latter.'

Scotland Yard expressed its regret, and Mr. Van Torp smiled and begged to be allowed, before leaving, to 'shake hands' with the three men who had been put to so much inconvenience on his account. This democratic proposal was promptly authorised, to the no small satisfaction and profit of the three haggard officials. So Mr. Van Torp went away, and in a few minutes he was sound asleep in the corner of his big motor-car on his way back to Derbyshire.

Lady Maud found Margaret and Logotheti walking slowly together under the trees about eleven o'clock on the following morning. Some of the people were already gone, and most of the others were to leave in the course of the day. Lady Maud had just said good-bye to a party of ten who were going off together, and she had not had a chance to speak to Margaret, who had come down late, after her manner. Most great singers are portentous sleepers. As for Logotheti, he always had coffee in his room wherever he was, he never appeared at breakfast, and he got rid of his important correspondence for the day before coming down.

'I've had a letter from Threlfall,' he said as Lady Maud came up. 'I was just telling Miss Donne about it. Feist died in Dr. Bream's Home yesterday afternoon.'

'Rather unfortunate at this juncture, isn't it?' observed Margaret.

But Lady Maud looked shocked and glanced at Logotheti as if asking a question.

'No,' said the Greek, answering her thought. 'I did not kill him, poor devil! He did it himself, out of fright, I think. So that side of the affair ends. He had some sealed glass capsules of hydrocyanide of potassium in little brass tubes, sewn up in the lining of a waistcoat, and he took one, and must have died instantly. I believe the stuff turns into prussic acid, or something of that sort, when you swallow it—Griggs will know.'

'How dreadful!' exclaimed Lady Maud. 'I'm sure you drove him to it!'

'I'll bear the responsibility of having rid the world of him, if I did. But my share consisted in having given him opium and then stopped it suddenly, till he surrendered and told the truth—or a large part of it—what I have told you already. He would not own that he killed Miss Bamberger himself with the rusty little knife that had a few red silk threads sticking to the handle. He must have put it back into his case of instruments as it was, and he never had the courage to look at it again. He had studied medicine, I believe. But he confessed everything else, how he had been madly in love with the poor girl when he was her father's secretary, and how she treated him like a servant and made her father turn him out, and how he hated Van Torp furiously for being engaged to marry her. He hated the Nickel Trust, too, because he had thought the shares were going down and had risked the little he had as margin on a drop, and had lost it all by the unexpected rise. He drank harder after that, till he was getting silly from it, when the girl's death gave him his chance against Van Torp, and he manufactured the evidence in the diary he kept, and went to Bamberger with it and made the poor man believe whatever he invented. He told me all that, with a lot of details, but I could not make him admit that he had killed the girl himself, so I gave him his opium and he went to sleep. That's my story. Or rather, it's his, as I got it from him last Thursday. I supposed there was plenty of time, but Mr. Bamberger seems to have been in a hurry after we had got Feist into the Home.'

'Had you told Mr. Van Torp all this?' asked Lady Maud anxiously.

'No,' Logotheti answered. 'I was keeping the information ready in case it should be needed.'

A familiar voice spoke behind them.

'Well, it's all right as it is. Much obliged, all the same.'

All three turned suddenly and saw that Mr. Van Torp had crept up while they were talking, and the expression of his tremendous mouth showed that he had meant to surprise them, and was pleased with his success in doing so.

'Really!' exclaimed Lady Maud.

'Goodness gracious!' cried the Primadonna.

'By the Dog of Egypt!' laughed Logotheti.

'Don't know the breed,' answered Van Torp, not understanding, but cheerfully playful. 'Was it a trick dog?'

'I thought you were in London,' Margaret said.

'I was. Between one and four this morning, I should say. It's all right.' He nodded to Lady Maud as he spoke the last words, but he did not seem inclined to say more.

'Is it a secret?' she asked.

'I never have secrets,' answered the millionaire. 'Secrets are everything that must be found out and put in the paper right away, ain't they? But I had no trouble at all, only the bother of waiting till the office got an answer from the other side. I happened to remember where I'd spent the evening of the explosion, that's all, and they cabled sharp and found my statement correct.'

'Why did you never tell me?' asked Lady Maud reproachfully. 'You knew how anxious I was!'

'Well,' replied Mr. Van Torp, dwelling long on the syllable, 'I did tell you it was all right anyhow, whatever they did, and I thought maybe you'd accept the statement. The man I spent that evening with is a public man, and he mightn't exactly think our interview was anybody else's business, might he?'

'And you say you never keep a secret!'

The delicious ripple was in Lady Maud's sweet voice as she spoke. Perhaps it came a little in spite of herself, and she would certainly have controlled her tone if she had thought of Leven just then. But she was a very natural creature, after all, and she could not and would not pretend to be sorry that he was dead, though the manner of his end had seemed horrible to her when she had been able to think over the news, after Van Torp had got safely away. So far there had only been three big things in her life: her love for a man who was dead, her tremendous determination to do some real good for his memory's sake, and her deep gratitude to Van Torp, who had made that good possible, and who, strangely enough, seemed to her the only living person who really understood her and liked her for her own sake, without the least idea of making love. And she saw in him what few suspected, except little Ida and Miss More—the real humanity and faithful kindness that dwelt in the terribly hard and coarse-grained fighting financier. Lady Maud had her faults, no doubt, but she was too big, morally, to be disturbed by what seemed to Margaret Donne an intolerable vulgarity of manner and speech.

As for Margaret, she now felt that painful little remorse that hurts us when we realise that we have suspected an innocent person of something dreadful, even though we may have contributed to the ultimate triumph of the truth. Van Torp unconsciously deposited a coal of fire on her head.

'I'd just like to say how much I appreciate your kindness in singing last night, Madame da Cordova,' he said. 'From what you knew and told me on the steamer, you might have had a reasonable doubt, and I couldn't very well explain it away before. I wish you'd some day tell me what I can do for you. I'm grateful, honestly.'

Margaret saw that he was much in earnest, and as she felt that she had done him great injustice, she held out her hand with a frank smile.

'I'm glad I was able to be of use,' she said. 'Come and see me in town.'

'Really? You won't throw me out if I do?'

Margaret laughed.

'No, I won't throw you out!'

'Then I'll come some day. Thank you.'

Van Torp had long given up all hope that she would ever marry him, but it was something to be on good terms with her again, and for the sake of that alone he would have risked a good deal.

The four paired off, and Lady Maud walked in front with Van Torp, while Margaret and Logotheti followed more slowly; so the couples did not long keep near one another, and in less than five minutes they lost each other altogether among the trees.

Margaret had noticed something very unusual in the Greek's appearance when they had met half an hour earlier, and she had been amazed when she realised that he wore no jewellery, no ruby, no emeralds, no diamonds, no elaborate chain, and that his tie was neither green, yellow, sky-blue, nor scarlet, but of a soft dove grey which she liked very much. The change was so surprising that she had been on the point of asking him whether anything dreadful had happened; but just then Lady Maud had come up with them.

They walked a little way now, and when the others were out of sight Margaret sat down on one of the many boulders that strewed the park. Her companion stood before her, and while he lit a cigarette she surveyed him deliberately from head to foot. Her fresh lips twitched as they did when she was near laughing, and she looked up and met his eyes.

'What in the world has happened to you since yesterday?' she asked in a tone of lazy amusement. 'You look almost like a human being!'

'Do I?' he asked, between two small puffs of smoke, and he laughed a little.

'Yes. Are you in mourning for your lost illusions?'

'No. I'm trying "to create and foster agreeable illusions" in you. That's the object of all art, you know.'

'Oh! It's for me, then? Really?'

'Yes. Everything is. I thought I had explained that the other night!' His tone was perfectly unconcerned, and he smiled carelessly as he spoke.

'I wonder what would happen if I took you at your word,' said Margaret, more thoughtfully than she had spoken yet.

'I don't know. You might not regret it. You might even be happy!'

There was a little silence, and Margaret looked down.

'I'm not exactly miserable as it is,' she said at last. 'Are you?'

'Oh no!' answered Logotheti. 'I should bore you if I were!'

'Awfully!' She laughed rather abruptly. 'Should you want me to leave the stage?' she asked after a moment.

'You forget that I like the Cordova just as much as I like Margaret Donne.'

'Are you quite sure?'

'Absolutely!'

'Let's try it!'

Milton Keynes UK
Ingram Content Group UK Ltd.
UKHW010653270624
444769UK00017B/237